THIS SPLENDID EARTH

V. J. Banis

NEW ENGLISH LIBRARY/TIMES MIRROR

To Sam

First published in the USA in 1978 by St Martin's Press, Inc.
First published in Great Britain in 1978 by New English Library

© 1978 by V. J. Banis

First NEL Paperback Edition September 1979

NEL Books are published by
New English Library Limited from
Barnard's Inn, Holborn,
London EC1N 2JR.
Made and printed in Great Britain by
Hunt Barnard Printing Ltd.,
Aylesbury, Bucks.

45004287 1

To

Mum

From

Jackie

Happy

Birthday

XXX

And Noah began to be a husbandman,
and he planted a vineyard;
And he drank of the wine, and was
drunken . . .

THE BOOKS OF GENESIS

PART I

The
VINES

1

Afterward, Anne would remember the night with burning clarity – every touch, every gesture, every word.

'Anne.'

'Emile, darling!'

She had come down from the terrace, past the pool where the shadow of the moon lay among the lily pads, down the wide stairs with their stone balustrades, through the perfumed darkness of the flower gardens, running on silent, slippered feet to the summerhouse where he waited, the young man in the guardsman's uniform. He saw her and opened his arms and she came into them, clinging hotly to him.

After a moment he kissed her and her heart seemed to sing; in the distance a nightingale heard the song and picked it up: 'I am yours, beloved, I am yours!' he trilled in ecstatic abandonment.

'I was afraid you weren't coming.'

'Mama came to my room to talk to me. I had to get ready for bed or she would have become suspicious, and then when she was gone, I had to dress all over again.'

Wasted effort, he thought, smiling into the darkness; aloud, he said, 'Did she want to talk about your baron again?'

'Not my baron, never,' she said hotly. 'They can talk forever, I will never marry him.'

He kissed her throat. His hands found the buttons of her dress and in a moment he had freed her breasts from their confines. She had dressed in a hurry; there was nothing beneath the dress to hinder his explorations, nothing but silken young flesh. He cupped one breast in his hand and kissed it, feeling her shiver at his touch.

'They say he's very wealthy,' he murmured, only to occupy her mind with conversation; in fact he did not care if she married her baron or not. What he wanted from her he intended to get long before then.

'He's old, nearly as old – oh! – ' His lips had found the

delicate tip of flesh and she started involuntarily at the un-familiar sensation. ' . . . Nearly as old as my father. And he's a bourgeois, even Mama calls him "that merchant".'

'Old men make few demands, they say.'

'I don't care, I don't want to marry him, I want to marry you – oh! Emile, I . . . '

'Don't be frightened, my sweet.'

'I – I'm not. I love you, oh Emile, I love you so.'

'Beloved.'

The silk of her skirts made soft, rustling sounds. The moon-light gave her bared flesh a silver luster.

'So beautiful,' he murmured.

'Emile – ah! Emile, you will marry me, won't you?'

' . . . So very precious . . . '

The moon had glided into a trap, a web of tangled clouds, and now it was caught. For a moment it struggled; then it was drawn into a giant dragon's mouth and was gone. The darkness was complete.

There was silence for a time and then a faint, muffled cry. The nightingale held his breath for a moment but there was nothing more to hear and at last, bored with the song he had been singing, he took wing and flew off into the night.

It seemed an eternity later that she crept back into her room. The fire on the hearth had burned to ashes and the candles burned low in their own drippings. Her maids, Jeanette and Bertha, had fallen asleep waiting for her, Bertha curled up in a chair and Jeanette seated primly on the sofa, her mouth hang-ing comically open. The de Grenville women always had two personal maids to attend them; when she was married, Anne would have three.

At the furtive click of the door, Jeanette woke and sprang to attention, giving the other girl's slippered foot a swift kick. Bertha murmured and stretched, waking more slowly; when she opened her eyes and saw her mistress, however, she too scrambled to her feet.

Jeanette could not help smiling at her mistress's radiance; there was only one thing, in her mind, that could give a girl that kind of glow.

'Mademoiselle,' she said, smiling and revealing a missing tooth that marred her otherwise pretty features.

'Oh, Jeanette,' Anne cried, hugging her maid ecstatically. 'Jeanette, he loves me, he's going to marry me.'

Over her shoulder, the two maids exchanged knowing glances. They had followed this little romance from its beginnings, when their mistress had first met the handsome guardsman at a ball; each secret letter, each moonlit tryst. A young lady might be able to keep that sort of affair from her parents, but she could hardly fool her personal maids.

But as to promises of love and marriage, well, they both knew about such moonlight promises. Aristocratic young ladies led sheltered lives; they did not understand the ways of young men; but a servant girl in the Paris of 1830 learned such lessons early. There would be no marriage to this guardsman, both of the maids would have sworn to that; but then, why spoil their lady's happiness? Just now she was walking in a dream; there would be time enough and plenty for rude awakenings.

'Help me out of this dress,' Anne was saying, tugging at the shoulders of her gown. 'It will be dawn soon – oh, Jeanette, I may never sleep again.'

Jeanette smiled again and helped her mistress with the dress; it was of silk, a shimmering sea green that emphasized Anne's green eyes and the shining copper of her hair. The gown was new, saved by Anne for just this night. It was designed to cling to her young body and reveal its every line and curve.

And like as not he never even noticed the dress, Jeanette thought.

'Oh, it's torn here, see,' Jeanette said, discovering the tear at the gown's waist. She thought of the passion with which the young man must have ripped the dress from her mistress's body. It gave her a little pang of envy.

Well, perhaps one night . . . once when she had accompanied her mistress to one of her meetings with the guardsman, Jeanette had caught an unmistakable look from him; it would be pleasant if . . . but she hoped he did not tear her dress; she had few enough to spare. Still, it might be worth it, remembering the look of him.

Anne dismissed the tear with a little toss of her head. 'It doesn't matter,' she cried, wriggling as the gown was tugged over her head. 'Jeanette, you may have the gown.'

'But Mademoiselle, it is new – and it cost a fortune. Just this morning your papa was complaining of the dressmaker's bills.'

'Oh, what do I care for that? I only wanted the dress for tonight, for him, and now I could never wear it again – take it, perhaps it will bring you luck, too.'

'Thank you, Mademoiselle.' Jeanette hugged the gown to

herself, rubbing the fine cloth against her cheek. What luck! In this dress, the men would mistake her for a fine lady. Perhaps she would even meet her own guardsman.

In the mirror Anne saw Bertha's quick pout of resentment. 'And Bertha,' she said, 'you may have a bonnet – that new one with the plumes that you admire so.'

'Mademoiselle, you are too generous . . . ' Bertha's eyes gleamed greedily.

'Nonsense, go and get it now. I want you to have it, truly. I want everyone to be as happy as I am this night.'

'Shall we help you to bed?'

'No, no, I'll manage myself. Go to bed yourselves – and thank you, both.

The maids left, murmuring good nights and hugging their new treasures. When they had gone, Anne threw back her head and laughed from sheer delight. She twirled about, hugging herself, and catching sight of herself in the long mirror on the wall, she laughed again. What wicked madness to be dancing naked about her room in the hours just before dawn!

She paused and went to stand before the mirror, examining herself. Yes, there was a bruise there at the base of her throat and, heavens, another one on her breast; she must remember to wear a dress with a high bodice tomorrow. She smiled as she discovered yet another bruise on her thigh, but no one would be likely to discover that one.

She stretched lazily, extending her arms over her head, and appraised her reflection, trying to see herself as Emile would see her. That she was lovely she knew; she had heard it often enough since her infancy. Her hair was a striking red-gold mane that framed her face and set off the vivid green of her eyes and the creamy luster of her skin. She had a small chin with just the suggestion of a dimple, and a pert, uptilted nose; but it was her mouth that made her beautiful – perfectly shaped, full-lipped; Emile had told her it was the mouth of a courtesan, designed to drive men mad, and certainly it had seemed to drive him to a mad passion.

And naked she was even more lovely than clothed; her waist was tiny, her breasts straight and firm, and they stood out from her chest as though carved from marble. It was, in fact, a body designed and planned for love. In the fading light of the candles, her flesh had a silvery gold quality; the only color was the rosy pink of her nipples and the darkness where her thighs met.

A candle sputtered and went out, interrupting her reverie. She looked and saw that the windows were growing light with the approaching dawn. She went to them and tugged the thick brocade draperies shut over them.

At last she slipped between the silken sheets of her bed, drawing the curtains closed about it to isolate her further from the day that was at hand. She wanted to hold it at bay, to make this night last as long as possible, perhaps forever.

She had never slept naked before, but she felt disinclined to summon her maids back to help her into a nightgown. Tonight, at any rate, she wanted to be free, to revel in the new awareness of physical sensation that Emile had awakened in her.

She wriggled her toes, savoring the tender ache that lingered in her loins, and fell asleep almost at once.

2

Emile was whistling when he arrived back at the little apartment he kept in the rue Notre Dame de Lorette. He had planned on bringing Anne back here tonight, but there had been the delay, and then after all it had not been necessary. As for the little champagne supper he had prepared, it would be just the thing to celebrate the evening's accomplishment.

On the other hand, it seemed a shame to waste a good champagne and an excellent pâté on oneself alone. He paused with one foot on the stairs; there was a maid he knew who worked in a house not far from the de Grenvilles' mansion. She slept by the kitchen; perhaps he could – but no. He smiled to himself and shook his head. It was nearly dawn, and anyway, to follow Anne de Grenville with a scullery maid, even one as pretty as Lizette, was like following a particularly good supper with a cheap sailor's rum.

No, he would savor the pâté alone, along with his memories of the time spent in the little summerhouse. And tomorrow, perhaps, he would arrange to see his little Lizette.

He reached the top of the stairs, strolled toward his door and again came to a stop.

That light under the door – surely he had not left the

candles burning when he had gone out earlier. But then who . . . ?

One hand on the hilt of his sword, he advanced quietly to the door. He tried it. It was unlocked. He knew he had locked it earlier when he went out. He hesitated, considering the possibilities. Paris was a dangerous city just now. There was talk of another popular uprising, and hardly a day went by without some clash between police and citizens.

On the other hand, suppose it was a woman inside. He kept this little apartment especially for amorous trysts, and once or twice ardent ladies had surprised him with unplanned visits. Some of the ladies were of the aristocratic class; not a few of them had husbands. The gendarmerie could prove an embarrassment.

He gave the door an inward push and as it swung open stepped lightly into the room, his hand ready on his sword.

It was not a woman but a man, a stranger to him, who sat at the little table by the open window. He was helping himself to the pâté that had been set out earlier, and the opened champagne bottle close at his hand looked half-empty.

'Monsieur . . . ' Emile was at a loss. If the man had risen, had shown a weapon, any of the things one would normally expect, it would be simple to deal with the situation. He had only to finish drawing his sword, already halfway out of its scabbard, and run him through; no one would bother him over the killing of an intruder.

But this man – he still wore a heavy black cloak and a tall hat, as if he had merely been passing by and had stepped in for a moment to refresh himself – only glanced up at him in an off-handed way and continued eating.

'Come in, come in,' he said, gesturing with a crust of bread. 'And close the door, please.'

Instinctively Emile did as he was bade. He advanced into the room, keeping his hand on the hilt of his weapon.

'How did you get in here?' he demanded. 'The concierge . . . '

'Is asleep by now, dreaming of the purchases he will make tomorrow with his newfound wealth.'

'The swine!'

'Do not be too angry with him, Monsieur; he did not value your trust cheaply.'

'Who are you? What the devil are you doing here, eating my food, drinking my wine – that supper cost a pretty penny, you know.'

The stranger unconcernedly took another sip of champagne. He had finished the pâté, and now he wiped his mouth neatly with the napkin.

'I am the Baron de Brussac,' he said finally. He turned in the chair so that he was facing Emile, although he did not stand up.

For a moment it meant nothing to Emile. Then comprehension began to dawn.

'Ah, yes, now I see,' he said. He smiled and, going to the table, poured himself a glass of champagne. 'You are the gentleman who would like to marry Anne de Grenville, am I correct?'

'I am the man she will marry.'

Emile sipped the wine and studied the man guardedly. What had he come here for? Surely he did not mean to fight a duel; that was so old-fashioned, and anyway, it was against the law now. But no, there was nothing belligerent about the man's manner; he looked quite at his ease, confident – a stranger coming into the room just now would have assumed it was the baron's apartment and that he, Emile, was the guest. It was intriguing.

'What can I do for you, Monsieur?'

'I've come to discuss the young comtesse. As you can perhaps guess, my agents have already told me a great deal about you and about your relationship with her.'

'My relationship with the comtesse, as you call it, is entirely innocent.'

'A young lady of her years and estate does not spend an "innocent" night until nearly dawn in a darkened summerhouse with a young man of, shall we say, your charm and reputation.'

Emile choked on the champagne.

'As you see,' the baron added, 'my agents are very thorough.'

'This is infamous – you come here to slander the reputation of an innocent girl . . . '

'Do not excite yourself unduly. I do not intend to inform the girl's father of her liaison with you.' He paused, then added, 'At least, I am confident that will not be necessary. He is a man of violent temper, they say. And of some influence in the city.'

For a moment the two men studied one another. Emile found himself a little frightened by the determination he saw in the other man's eyes. It was implacable; it was merciless.

He pulled out the chair at the opposite side of the table and sat heavily in it.

'What do you want?' he asked.

'As I've told you, my agents are thorough.' The baron refilled his glass. He lifted the bottle across the table in a questioning manner and, at Emile's nod, filled Emile's glass again, too. 'They've told me quite a lot about you. I feel that I know you quite well, although we have not met before now.'

Emile made no reply; he was beginning to be intrigued again. He had never met anyone quite like this before. When the man said, quite simply, that he was going to marry Anne de Grenville, one was almost tempted to believe him.

'They have informed me, my agents, that you are in love.'

Emile cocked an eyebrow, amused; perhaps the man's agents were less thorough than he believed.

'They tell me, in fact, that there are two great loves in your life – two *grandes amours* – and neither one of them is actually Anne de Grenville.'

The baron looked across the table, and for the first time in the interview, he smiled. It was unexpected and it caught Emile off guard; it gave him the odd sensation that the man had read his thoughts.

'One of them,' the baron went on without waiting for an answer, 'is women.'

It was Emile's turn to smile. 'I see that you used the plural,' he said.

'*Indiscriminately* was the word that was used, if my memory serves me.'

'I protest. Not quite that – but plentifully, I will admit.'

'The man who will eat anything rarely goes hungry,' the baron said; he did not wait for Emile to object but went on. 'But even this is not the great, the overwhelming passion of your life.'

'Which is?' Emile was beginning to enjoy himself after all. He had decided there was no danger here for him, and it looked as if there might even be some profit in this situation.

The baron answered in one word: 'Money.'

Emile chuckled and nodded. 'Your agents are thorough, as you say. But what is all this leading up to?'

'It's all very simple, isn't it? I plan to marry the young countess, but she will hardly consider such a marriage so long as she entertains the hope of marrying you – I might say the futile hope, as we both know. And you do not love Anne de Grenville. You love first, money, and second, women. I had in mind giving you enough of the first to insure your continued – and generous – pursuit of the second.'

Emile looked down into the wine in his glass and drummed his fingers thoughtfully on the tabletop. It was a cheap table, scarred and stained. 'And how much of the first did you have in mind?' he asked.

The baron mentioned a figure. It was so staggering that Emile could not even pretend indifference. 'But surely . . . Monsieur is joking.'

The baron reached under the table and brought out a case; it had been hidden before by the drape of his cloak. He opened it away from Emile so that Emile could not see inside and brought out a stack of bills. He put them on the table. He brought out another stack from the case and put it beside the first, then another, and still another. Emile's eyes grew wider with each addition, and a cold sweat broke out on his forehead.

The baron closed the case and returned it to the floor. For a long moment there was silence in the room. Emile ran his tongue over his lips; his mouth felt dry. He wondered if the case was now empty or if there were more stacks of bills in it.

'After all,' the baron went on suavely, as if there had been no pause, 'you have expensive tastes. That pâté was excellent, by the way, but I'm afraid the wine was a disappointment.'

'It was highly recommended to me. And expensive, as you say.'

'It was not worth whatever you paid. I suggest you find another wine merchant; this one is robbing you.'

The small talk had relieved some of the tension in the room. Emile cleared his throat and said, 'You are very generous. I would be foolish not to accept your offer. You may be assured, I will be no obstacle to your marriage.'

He got up and came around the table, extending his hand. 'You have my word on it, as a gentleman and a man of honor.'

The baron ignored the offered hand. 'I myself am not a gentleman,' he said. 'And I fear neither one of us is quite a man of honor. But I think in this instance we may agree that a bargain has been struck to everyone's satisfaction.'

'Except perhaps the lady's.' Emile could not resist the gibe; he had been offended at the refusal to shake his hand.

The baron rose and then, as if it were an afterthought, said, 'There is one more thing that I could do for you.'

'And that is?'

'I was to dine tomorrow night with the Marquise de Marcheval. Do you know her?'

'I know of her. They say she's the richest woman in Paris.'

'And the loneliest. Since her father died there has been no man in her life to – to guide her. Perhaps you would like to go in my place tomorrow? I would send a letter, of course.'

'They say she's very ugly.' He did not say it with disinterest, however. He was no fool; even the stack of money still standing on the table would not last forever. Paris could be very expensive for a man of his tastes. Already he was thinking ahead – a better apartment, a horse he had heard was for sale, his own carriage . . .

'Ah, well, in the dark . . . ' The baron shrugged. 'One could always count francs.'

The two men smiled at one another. 'You're too generous, Monsieur,' Emile said. 'They say Madame la Marquise sets a splendid table.'

'Yes, you see, I have an agent in her house, too, so I already know the menu for tomorrow night. And at any rate, I also know what Madame is hungry for.' He let his eyes go up and down the length of the guardsman's body; it was young, hard, lean, designed for a lonely woman's erotic fantasies. He had no doubt how tomorrow night would end.

Emile said casually, 'I have no plans for tomorrow evening. If you're sure it will be all right –'

'I have the letter here; it explains simply that I am unable to be with her and that you have come in my place. I had added that you are eager to do everything within your power to make her evening a pleasant one.' The baron withdrew an envelope from his pocket. 'You may deliver it for me when you go. Eight o'clock – you know the house?'

Emile nodded, grinning. 'You were very sure of yourself, Monsieur.'

'Yes.' The baron handed him the letter and started for the door.

'But why?' Emile asked. 'Why this in addition to the money? I had already accepted your proposal. You needn't have feared; I would have honored our agreement.'

'But of course. It would have been tragically foolish for you to do otherwise.'

'Then . . . ?'

'A woman might pine forever for a man who has simply disappeared from her life – especially a man she fancied herself in love with. But for a man who has jilted her for another woman, never. Especially for an ugly woman.'

He nodded and said, 'Good night,' and let himself out. For a moment Emile stared after him in a sort of fascinated admiration. Then he remembered the money and, going back to the table, gave a delighted chuckle when he saw it again. He began to count it, not because he distrusted the baron but simply for the pleasure of feeling so many notes in his hands at once.

He thought of the coming night. The Marquise de Marcheval. By God, was it possible?

But of course it was. He was good looking, women had always thrown themselves at him, and when he chose to direct his attention toward a particular woman, well, not one in a hundred could resist him.

As to her ugly face, what did that matter – he had made love to countless women, both ugly and pretty. The baron was right – in the dark there was no difference.

The baron's coach was waiting. He paused at the curb and glanced at the windows above. He could just see the shadow of the guardsman, no doubt counting his money.

De Brussac sighed. He had known, of course, exactly how the interview would come out; by the time he had come for this meeting, he had known the young man better than his family and friends knew him.

And yet, although he had gotten his way, as he had expected, he could not quite get a faintly bitter taste out of his mouth. He had long since learned that if you wanted to strike a bargain with a man, you were wise to come down to his level; but sometimes the descent was distasteful.

Men were greedy, and they were lascivious. It was not his fault they were that way, but he knew they were, and he had often used it to his purpose. When you offered a man the things that he thought he desired most, the outcome was predictable.

But still there remained within him one tiny portion of consciousness that hoped, as it had hoped tonight, that he might be proven wrong.

Ah, well. He was accustomed to the sins of others, as he was to the sins within his own breast. They were different sins, for the most part, but they were of the same family, and they greeted one another darkly in passing.

The footman had come to open the door for him. The Baron de Brussac sighed again and entered his coach, and a moment later it pulled away, the horse's hooves clip-clopping over the cobblestones along the empty street.

Seated within the darkened coach, the baron contemplated the girl for whose life he had been bargaining. That he would soon be married to her he did not for a moment doubt. It would be his second marriage, although he had lived nearly twenty years now without a wife. His life, so orderly, so carefully planned until now, was about to start on a new course, and while he had waited tonight for the young guardsman to return home, he had been looking back over the life he had led until now, and forward to what his life would be henceforth.

He was forty-one, so much of his life was over. He thought of the people he had loved, of the places he had been. He thought of the old passions, the dreams, the longings and the agonies. How important they had seemed once, and what did they matter now?

He remembered a girl he had loved, who had not loved him back. Then he had thought of taking his life; now he could smile bitterly and think of the many others who had parted their thighs for him – and of them all, those who had and those who had not, what had they added to, or taken away from, his life?

Did nothing matter then, was life but a path from birth to death, nothing in itself but only that which came between the two? He had traveled to the far borders of his mind, to the distant reaches of consciousness, for something that mattered, for that something which might give significance to what was otherwise only a passage of time, but he had returned from his journeys empty-handed.

Why, then, was he going to marry this girl whom he did not love, for whom he did not even feel any real tenderness? Perhaps he had not loved his first wife either, but he had felt affectionate and protective toward her.

He had an idea, though, that if there were any meaning, any significance at all to life, it was in the order of things, in the patterns they formed; and although he could not perceive the pattern of his life, let alone grasp its significance, he had made it a point always to impose order and a kind of symmetry upon it.

For some time it had seemed to him that his life was incomplete, lacking. A year ago a friend had made the chance comment, 'What you lack is a wife.'

At the time he had scoffed, but later he came to the conclusion that this was indeed the flaw in the pattern of his life, and so he had set out to find himself a wife – not just a wife, but the right wife. If there were other reasons for seeking one – longings, desires, needs – they remained unrecognized by him.

He had seen Anne de Grenville at a ball and had said to himself at once, 'She is the one.' She was beautiful and young, possessed of the social graces of her class, and she had a title and position which could not fail to be beneficial to him. If there were other reasons, instincts even, that drew him to her, they did not occur to him. From that first moment of meeting, he had known that he would marry her. That the outcome might have been any different had never so much as crossed his mind.

But of course he had no delusions regarding her. Because he was not in love, he had no need to romanticize her, to make her seem better than she was. He had known from the first, as her family still did not, of her affair with the guardsman. It had not mattered in the least to him. So long as a wife was faithful after the wedding, he did not much care what she had done before; to his way of thinking virginity was an overrated commodity.

The stillness of the night was broken by the sound of voices. Someone shouted, and a pistol was fired.

The baron leaned from the window. There was a sound of running feet, and two young men, little more than boys, darted from a side street in front of the coach.

From behind them someone shouted, 'Stop, in the name of the king!'

'François,' the baron called, rapping on the side of the coach with his walking stick, 'turn here, quickly.'

The driver chuckled softly and did as he was bade, smartly wheeling the coach into the narrow side street and blocking the path of the two guardsmen who had been pursuing the fleeing youngsters.

There was a moment of confusion; horses whinnied and guardsmen cursed, and at length the coach was backed out of the way, but by this time the two young men had disappeared into the surrounding alleys.

An angry captain of the guards appeared at the door of the coach; even in the dim light his face was livid, and when he spoke, his breathlessness robbed his words of much of their effect.

'Monsieur,' he said, pausing to gulp air, 'you are under arrest. I must ask you to step down.'

'Indeed?' The baron did not stir from his seat. 'And what is the charge?'

'It is a crime to interfere with the king's justice. Futhermore, there is a curfew in effect within the city.'

'Ah yes, the curfew. I was discussing it just this evening over cards with my friend, General Lemoyne – do you know the general?' He arched an eyebrow in the direction of the officer.

The young captain seemed to grow still shorter of breath; General Lemoyne was in command of all the King's Guards within the confines of the city. Although the baron was acquainted with him, he had hardly been playing cards with him – the two men, in fact, were bitter enemies – but the captain was not likely to know that.

The ruse worked; the officer seemed at a loss to know what to do now, and at length the baron came to his aid.

'It is late,' he said. 'It would be unfortunate to disturb the general at this hour. However, if you wish . . . ' He shrugged as if to say it was of no consequence to him one way or the other.

'That will not be necessary, Monsieur.' The captain stepped back from the coach and clicked his heels smartly. 'But you would do well to remember the curfew in the future. There are hoodlums about – the streets are not entirely safe.'

'I'm grateful, of course, for your protection. I shall be certain to tell the general what a fine job his men are doing.'

The officer hesitated, not quite sure how to end the incident gracefully. At last he snapped his fingers in the direction of the driver and said sharply, 'Drive on.'

François cracked his whip and the coach began to move again. The baron leaned back into the seat. He thought of the two young men he had saved from arrest, and wondered what crime they had committed that they should be pursued by the guards. Perhaps they had stolen a loaf of bread to feed their families, or perhaps they were guilty of nothing more than violating the curfew. But of course, for all he knew they might have been murderers.

Of one thing he was certain, however – whatever their crime, however great or small, they would have been shown no mercy at the hands of the guardsmen. The city would deal with its own; if they were guilty they would find justice in due time; if they were innocent it was as well for them that they did not fall into the hands of the king or his officers.

The coach rolled to a stop; the footman leapt down to open the gates. They were at home, and it was dawn. For the moment the baron forgot about thieves and kings, countesses and lovers. He thought of nothing but the comfortable bed waiting for him, and for once he was grateful that it would be empty.

3

'I simply cannot understand this. I cannot think what has come over you.'

Madame la Comtesse looked upon her daughter with a kind of bewildered exasperation, as if to ask, Who is this impossible creature who complicates my life this way?

Anne said, for perhaps the hundredth time, 'Mama, I do not love him, this merchant baron of yours.'

'Love?' The older comtesse flung her hands into the air. 'What has that to do with it? If girls never married except for love, half the women of France would be in nunneries. Who do you think would love Cook, or Madame Grisolde, your dressmaker? No, no, my dear, you shall have to give me a better argument than that.'

'All right, I will. He's old, he's ugly, he's a bore, he's middle-class . . .'

'He's exceedingly rich.'

It was Anne's turn to throw her hands in the air in an imitation of her mother's gesture. 'Oh, his wealth, his wealth, his wealth, I'm sick of hearing about his wealth. What do I care if he owns half of France?'

'Two-thirds of it, more likely, and half the New World, too, from what I hear. And you had better start caring if you know what's good for you.'

The comtesse came to the dressing-table and shook her daughter's shoulders gently.

'Don't be a goose. You know what it's been like for us. At one time the de Grenvilles may have had all the money they wanted or needed, but that was before the Revolution. And what the mobs didn't steal, that old fool Louis gave away after he got the throne back. How do you think the middle classes got so much wealth – they stole it from us. When I was a girl, there wasn't any such thing as a middle class – not that I ever heard of – and the world was a better place, too.'

'Mama, it doesn't seem to me that we're especially poor.' Anne was quite fond of both her parents, especially her papa, but she did not take her mother's protestations of poverty seriously. After all, there was always enough money for whatever she wanted.

'Well, we are; we are barely managing to keep up appearances, if you only knew the half of it. And if we are to survive at all, we must get back some of what was stolen from us. I tell you, if we don't get Monsieur de Brussac's money, and get it soon, we shall lose this house, the chateau – everything. You'll find yourself living in a hovel; that's where your foolishness will bring you.'

'I wouldn't care, if I were with someone I loved,' Anne said to herself in the mirror.

Her mother gave a sigh and looked heavenward.

'You wouldn't care? And what about me, your mother – you think it's all right for me to be thrown into the streets? After all your father and I have done for you, this is how you repay us, ungrateful child?'

Anne made no reply to this much-repeated criticism. She had only been half-listening to her mother's complaints; her thoughts were back in the summerhouse, with Emile – his voice sweet in her ear, his hands, his body upon her body.

It had been a month since that night. A month! It seemed forever. She was half-sick with waiting and worrying. If only he would write and tell her when to meet him again.

For the hundredth time she wondered if something had happened to him. Perhaps he was sick. Perhaps, after all, she should go to him, although he had told her firmly never to do that.

How she longed for him!

Her mother, tiring of their argument, drew her shoulders back in a haughty manner and strode to the door. She was a handsome woman, elegantly dressed despite her protestations of poverty. She wore a loose gown of pale pink with little silver bows, and at her throat she wore a splendid pink diamond adorned with pearls. In her exquisitely tinted hair were more bows, pink and silver to match her dress.

Anne, in contrast, wore a long satin robe over a nightgown of precious lace. She looked ready to retire for the night, which in fact she was. A table was laid for supper in one corner of the room, with roses and lighted candles, and the bed was already turned down.

'Very well,' her mother said. 'If that's the way you feel, you shall remain in your room until you have come to your senses. And you will not attend tonight's ball.'

She paused at the door, hoping for an about-face on her daughter's part; it would save so much bother. She dreaded having to go to her husband and confess that she had been unable to change Anne's mind. She knew that he would some-how blame her for the failure. But what could she do? The threat of the ball had been the greatest inducement she could think of, and Anne hardly seemed to mind at all.

She added on a hopeful note, 'They say it's to be the event of the season.'

Anne, who found the marquise's balls invariably dull and had not planned on attending this one, ignored the bait and con-tinued to brush her gleaming hair.

'What's more,' her mother added slyly, 'they say Madame la Marquise means to announce her engagement tonight.'

'Louise?' Anne was too surprised to pretend indifference. 'Who on earth would want to marry Louise? She's so ugly.'

'Ugly and rich, just like Baron de Brussac. And they say her money has brought her a very handsome young guardsman. Of course, she's marrying beneath her station, but what can she do? Her family *would* have an ugly child. And, I might add, if she can marry a guardsman, there's no reason why you shouldn't marry a baron.'

The hand with the gilt hairbrush had paused mid-stroke.

'What guardsman?' Anne asked softly.

'What do you mean?'

'The guardsman, the one Louise is going to marry, who is he?'

'Why, he's nobody, of course. Related to the Duc de Fon-taine, they say, but only a cousin and not in line for the title at all. Henri, I believe his name is, or, no, Emile something-or-other. Or was it – but what does it matter? It's no one we know, at any rate. It's dreadful, really, when you think about it; it could never have happened in the old days. I blame Napoleon, you know, putting commoners on thrones, peasants marrying aristocrats – they got rid of him, but they can't turn back the clock. Where will it all lead?'

The comtesse paused for a moment to look at the back of her daughter's head.

'Anne, dear, I do wish you would reconsider this nonsense. Your father's going to be just furious when I tell him. And you will miss the ball. You ought to think about that, at least. Won't you let me just tell him . . .'

'I don't care to go to the ball tonight, Mama,' Anne said. She was grateful that her back was turned and her mother could not see her face. It had gone white while her mother talked. It was a mistake, of course, a mere coincidence; there must be hundreds – no, thousands – of guardsmen named Emile; and anyone could say he was a cousin to the duc whether he was or not; and yet she sat frozen with fear, not daring to turn around lest her mother read everything written upon her face.

After another moment her mother sighed again and said, 'Very well, if that is how you feel, but I must say I think you are being exceedingly foolish.'

She went out. The door had no more than closed when Anne leapt to her feet and ran across the room to give the bell cord by the door a violent tug that threatened to pull it loose from its moorings. After a few seconds she yanked it once again.

Jeanette came in a moment later, out of breath from running up the stairs to answer the urgent summons. She found Anne seated at her writing-table, hastily scrawling some words upon a piece of paper.

'Jeanette,' she said without pausing in her writing, 'I want you to deliver a letter for me. Take it to 136, rue Notre Dame de Lorette, on the first story above the ground floor. You are to tell the gentleman that your instructions are to wait for an answer.'

Jeanette bobbed a curtsy and said, 'Oui, Mademoiselle.' The address was not new to her; she had heard it before, although not from her mistress. Lizette, a girl she knew who worked as a servant in a house nearby, had told her of the little apartment this particular guardsman kept for his trysts, which were frequent. She knew that Lizette had been there within the last month; she knew, too, that her mistress had not heard from the guardsman during that time. Of course, she would not have dared to mention any of this to her mistress, who was foolish enough to think the guardsman's heart was hers alone.

Anne signed the note and, sealing it, wrote Emile's name on the outside and handed it to the maid. Jeanette smiled a conspiratorial smile and curtsied again.

'I shall go at once, Mademoiselle.'

'And Jeanette – ' The maid paused at the door. 'I wouldn't want anyone to know of this, you understand.'

'I understand, Mademoiselle.'

'And . . . ' Again Jeanette paused on her way out. 'Don't forget to get an answer.'

Jeanette nodded and hurried away before her mistress could think of any further instructions.

She was back within the hour, looking pale and frightened. She slipped into the room, still wearing her cloak, and stood pressed against the carved wood of the door.

Anne had spent the interval pacing anxiously to and fro. She had felt as if icy fingers were clutching at her heart; now, at the sight of Jeanette's frightened expression, the fingers seemed to give her heart a painful wrench.

'What is it? Have you brought me an answer?'

'No, Mademoiselle.' Jeanette spoke in such a tiny voice that it was all but lost in the spacious room.

'No answer? But I specifically told you . . . '

'The gentleman is gone.'

It was as though Anne had been struck a blow. She swayed on her feet and had to put out a hand to steady herself.

'What do you mean, gone?'

'He's gone – he's given up the room – the concierge says . . . ' She stumbled over the words and could go no further.

Anne sprang toward her like an enraged lioness and, seizing her by the shoulders, shook her with such violence that Jeanette's hair came loose and fell about her face.

'What did he say, you little fool, tell me, tell me or I'll . . . '

'The concierge says the gentleman is to be married; he's to announce his engagement tonight.'

Tears, both of sympathy and fright, were streaming down Jeanette's cheeks. She had never seen her mistress like this before. That normally gentle creature looked like a madwoman now, with that wild light in her eyes and the way she had shaken her.

'Tonight – his engagement?'

'To la Marquise . . . '

'Ah . . . ' Anne gasped and released her so suddenly that Jeanette staggered backward and nearly fell over a chair.

'Mademoiselle . . . '

'Get out.' Anne spoke in a whisper that sent a fresh spasm of fear through the maid. Still, although she backed toward the door, Jeanette did not immediately run away. She felt as if her own heart were broken and wished she knew how to comfort her mistress.

'If you would like . . . ' she started to say.

'Get out!' It was a shriek this time, and it sent the maid scurrying like a whipped dog. But before she reached the door, another sound stopped her.

'Jeanette.' It was a tiny voice this time, not angry, but full of all the anguish that comes with an aching heart. And it was a plea for comfort.

'Mademoiselle.'

Jeanette came back to her and Anne went into her arms as if they were sisters. The servant's scrawny arms held the delicate, shuddering body of her aristocratic mistress; Anne's sobs were muffled against the coarse fabric of her apron. Jeanette made little cooing sounds and patted the trembling shoulders.

'There, there, poor lamb,' she murmured.

At length, when the sobs had become litttle snuffling sounds, Jeanette asked, 'Shall I fetch you something? There's some brandy in the kitchen.'

Anne withdrew from the maid's embrace and daubed at her eyes with a handkerchief. 'No, I'll be all right,' she said.

Now that the fit of crying was past, both women felt embarrassed by the lack of restraint they had shown. Jeanette shifted her weight from one foot to the other. She did not know whether to wait to be dismissed again or leave of her own volition. She was horrified at her boldness and yet glad at the same time that she had been able to offer some comfort.

'You may go now,' Anne said at last. 'And thank you.'

Jeanette dropped a quick curtsy and hurried away. She paused on the back stairs to wipe the tears from her own face and to rearrange her hair. It would not do to have the old comtesse see her like this and question her.

When Jeanette had gone, Anne continued to stand where she was, shoulders bent, breasts heaving with the force of her emotion. The first horrible anguish had passed and in its wake, like the debris left on the beach by the receding tide, was anger.

What a fool she had been! She saw it all now with painful clarity. He had given her the cheap ring she wore on a chain, concealed in the bodice of her dress, and he had told her again and yet again how he loved her.

Lies! He had never loved her; even while he had whispered those words to her, he had been planning his engagement to Louise Marcheval. She had defied her parents, even her dear papa, refused a marriage that would bring her a fortune, and had given him the most precious gift a woman had to give; and he had gone from her arms to prepare for his wedding to that cow. Louise? She didn't need a man so much as a milkmaid.

Perhaps if she could see him – if she went to the ball tonight – if his engagement were to be announced, surely he would be there. She would go to her mother and seek a truce, tell her – tell her anything. What did that matter in comparison to this?

She almost went to the door, but at the last moment something held her back – pride, wounded vanity, the dignity that had been bred into her class through generations.

If he had died, if he had been separated from her by some unalterable circumstance, if he had been around the world from her, she could have borne that, but to know that he was here, a carriage ride away – that was unendurable. He had thrown her over for another woman, another woman who was her inferior in every respect except one – she was rich.

She would never go to him, never see him again, never. As quickly as it had first bloomed, all the love in her heart withered and died and bloomed again as hatred. In all her pampered, petted life, she had never been rebuffed or refused anything that she had wanted, until now. And now this man, this monster – it was more than she could bear!

A sudden fury seized her. She picked up a gold and tortoise-shell box from a table and, smashing it against the inlaid mantel, she threw the pieces into the fire. She had intended it as a gift for her lover; she had meant to give it to him the next time they were together.

She tore from her throat the slender gold chain with its cheap ring and flung them to the floor, crushing them with her foot.

She took his letters from their hiding place behind a drawer and threw them, too, into the fire, and dashed everything about with a poker until there was only a shapeless debris.

Then she flung herself on the sofa and lay there with white

face and tearless eyes, staring at the fire until the whole room seemed to be bathed with blood-red flames.

Her father sent for her in the morning, saying that he wished to see her in his study. She had not slept but had spent the entire night in front of the fire, reliving in painful detail every hour, every moment that she had spent with her guardsman. She had stripped her soul naked and flailed herself mercilessly with the once-tender words and phrases that he had used to seduce her.

Now she felt drained and strangely light-headed. She was pale and drawn-looking, but her eyes were dry and her chin when she came into the study was tilted proudly upward. Perhaps for the first time she looked every inch the aristocrat that she was. The fine steel of which she was shaped had been tempered by the fire.

Her father and mother both were there. He wore the stodgy look that he always assumed when he was about to put his foot down. Her mother looked as though she had been crying, and Anne assumed with no particular gratitude that her mother had been trying to defend her against her father's anger.

'I am afraid, Anne, that we shall have to have a very serious discussion,' he began, speaking gravely with his hands folded behind his back. 'Your mother tells me . . . '

'Papa, there is something I must say before you begin,' she interrupted him. 'I . . . ' For a moment her voice faltered, but she swallowed and said quickly, 'You may tell your baron he has bought his bride.'

Her father had been annoyed by the interruption, but his annoyance quickly became relief and then pleasure as he realized the significance of her words. Mama clapped her hands together before her vast bosom as if she were applauding a clever piece of business in a play.

'Do you mean to say . . . ?'

'Yes, Papa,' she again interrupted him. She was impatient to have it said, as if once it had been put into words, it would be accomplished and there would be no turning back. 'I will marry Jean de Brussac.'

4

'They are ready, Monsieur.'

'Thank you, I shall be down shortly.'

The servant bowed and went out, leaving Baron Jean de Brussac once more alone. The baron had been standing at the window, looking down upon the courtyard of his townhouse. At the moment it was a scene of bedlam. The courtyard was filled with carriages and livery; servants, his own and those of his guests, bustled importantly to and fro, and beyond the massive iron gates a crowd of the curious and the envious had gathered to watch the happenings within. In Paris a wedding, especially an expensive wedding, could always be counted on to attract a crowd.

Nevertheless, the baron studied the crowd with a critical eye. He wanted nothing to interfere with his wedding, and there had been rumors throughout the day of popular uprisings. Although 'The Great Revolution' had come to a conclusion with the defeat of Napoleon at Waterloo, the people of France, especially of radical Paris, had not forgotten the lessons they had learned there; especially that they were not at all powerless, even at the hands of the most powerful despot. The people now in power were fools, in the baron's opinion, to think that in defeating Napoleon and restoring the monarchy, they had turned the clock back and made everything as it was before.

Right now Paris was smoldering with resentment of the king's five July Ordinances, issued a few days ago, that had severely limited the power of the press and changed the electoral system. There were those who said that with these ordinances the French people finally lost everything they had gained in the Revolution.

A short time before he had talked to two important ministers of the government who were among the wedding guests, and they had assured him the rumors were exaggerated and that there was no danger.

'*Après tout*,' one of them had said, 'it is an entirely different situation from what we had in '89.'

Jean, however, was not so sure; moreover, he had noted that the minister was more concerned than he cared to admit. The man was old enough to have lived through the Revolution, and no doubt he knew firsthand what a monster the Parisian mob could be when roused.

Jean had been born in the Revolution, in the very throes of the uprising, in fact. His pregnant mother had been in the crowds at the storming of the Bastille, and it may have been the excitement that brought on her labor. Little Jean had been born in a gutter on a side street.

'An auspicious beginning,' he was accustomed to saying; he was fond of the story and told it often, to the horror of his more aristocratic friends.

'From the gutter in which I lay, I soaked up all the hardness of the street. The streets of Paris are hard and the people who live in them harder. They are shrewd and tough, and now they have learned that they are stronger than those who rule them.

'And all of this, you see, I learned before I was an hour old.'

His friends laughed, but they knew there was truth in what he said. Jean de Brussac was a merchant like his father before him. His father had joined the Revolution a penniless peasant; he had emerged from it a wealthy merchant. But when it came to the ability to see an opportunity and seize it, and hold tenaciously to it in the face of any challenge, the father was nothing compared to the son.

Jean was known as honest as well as shrewd, a man whose word in a transaction was better than any contract, but he was not a man to try to fool or cheat.

He began tying the laces of his shirt. It did not occur to him to call his valet; he was accustomed to managing for himself. For a man of his wealth, his staff was regarded as meager. Even more peculiar, as his aristocratic friends saw it, was that they were all free men, paid employees; there were no serfs on his estates, no indentured peasants on his staff.

'You get better work and more loyalty from a fair deal than you do with Articles of Indenture,' was his explanation, and while many of them privately scoffed at his revolutionary ideas, none could deny that the baron's staff was the equal of any in the city in both performance and loyalty. Many a nobleman had tried privately to bribe away de Brussac's majordomo or his justly admired chef, only to have the most splendid offers mysteriously but firmly turned down.

Jean decided that the crowd outside looked harmless enough,

a throng of Parisians participating vicariously in the splendor of the occasion.

'Hey, Mireau,' a voice carried up to him from below, 'who's getting married?'

'A countess is marrying a baron.' Old habits die hard; even with the great Revolution some forty years behind them, the Parisians had not forgotten their snobbery. They had overthrown and slaughtered their aristocracy, and still they inherently disapproved of anyone overstepping class divisions.

'The beauty and the beast,' someone else yelled.

There were shouts and whoops of laughter, and several more ribald comments were volleyed back and forth.

Jean de Brussac turned from the window, unperturbed by the remarks he had overheard, and donned his coat. He knew that he was no beauty. Whatever attraction he exercised for women, and experience had long since shown that some attraction existed, it was not physical beauty. He suspected it was the mystique of power, of strength that transcended mere physical strength. He was a man of will, of drive; it was written in the squared bulk of his thick, sturdy frame, in the craggy, unrefined lines of his face. He was inclined to think that success in a venture was a simple proposition of deciding what you wanted, and then getting it.

After all, he had gotten his wedding. Of course, it was his good fortune, not entirely unexpected, that the Marquise de Marcheval had fallen quite in love with the young guardsman he had sent her and had publicly announced her engagement to him after only a few days – and of course as many nights. They had been married only a few weeks before.

There was a noise in the corridor. They were waiting for him with increasing impatience. His majordomo, Philippe, tapped at the door and entered at his command.

'Monsieur? Everything is ready.'

'Yes, I'm coming,' Jean said. He started toward the door, then hesitated.

'Philippe, what do you think of those crowds?'

'They look innocent enough, Monsieur.'

'Have there been any more rumors among the servants?' Ministers could talk and ponder, but if there were to be uprisings, it was the servants who would know.

'They say there's a mob gathering near the Sorbonne,' Philippe replied.

Jean went to an ormolu desk alongside the windows and

brought a pistol from a drawer. He checked it, then thrust it into his belt beneath his waistcoat, where it could not be seen.

'Have the grooms armed,' he said. 'And Philippe, tell the servants that if there are any among them whose sympathies are with the rebels, they are free to go without recrimination.'

He was reasonably sure of the loyalty of his servants; still, it was better to take no chances. If it should be necessary to defend themselves against an unruly mob, he would prefer to have no one inside whose sympathies were with those outside.

'Very good, sir,' Philippe said, bowing from the waist.

Jean paused for a moment before the mirror to straighten his cravat and to adjust his waistcoat. His craggy face glowered back at him. His attire was that of an elegant French aristocrat: fine lace cravat, embroidered coat and breeches, even jeweled buckles on his shoes; yet had he but changed his elegant clothes for a horned cap and an animal cape, he would have passed for one of the conquerors of old.

He left the room and went down to the wedding. It was time to claim his bride.

5

'It will be over soon.'

Anne repeated the words silently, but they brought her little comfort. She felt faint in the airless room. The ceremony, of which she was scarcely aware, was taking place in the tiny chapel of the baron's townhouse. Most of the guests had been obliged to stand outside in the main corridor, but even the favored group who had been allowed into the chapel constituted a crowd in that limited space.

The heat was made even more oppressive by the weight of her gown of rich ivory brocade embroidered with threads of silver and tiny diamonds. She wore a matching train, trimmed in ermine, as was the hem of her gown, and a veil of priceless lace that had been worn at their weddings by three generations of de Grenville women before her. At her throat was her husband's wedding gift, an awesome choker of perfectly matched diamonds, and in their center an emerald the size of a pigeon's egg that matched exactly the color of her eyes and was said to have belonged to Madame Du Barry herself.

Yet for all the richness of the occasion, there was no splendor in her heart.

How had she come to this? She listened to the words of the priest and dreamed of being rescued from the ridiculous situation in which she found herself. She imagined Emile, come to his senses at last and realizing how desperately he loved and needed her, striding down the aisle in the middle of the ceremony to claim her as his own. That Emile was already married himself did not discourage her dream.

All the while, though, one part of her mind, the reasoning, sensible part, told her it was only a dream. Emile would not come. She had deliberately invited Louise, thinking that he would come with his wife; but Louise had had a previous engagement.

Anne had even gone to the little apartment on the rue Notre Dame de Lorette to see for herself that he was really gone; but even as she went, prepared to humble herself, to fling herself at his feet if she must, she had known he would not be there; and secretly hidden from her aching heart was a sense of thankfulness that he was not, that she might be spared that final shame.

She heard the baron's voice, a stranger's voice, pledging his love for her in the words of the ceremony. But this was not love, this was a business agreement; it was a mockery of what she had known with Emile. Whatever that had cost her in shame and pain, that was love!

The priest surreptitiously wiped the sweat from his brow and continued in his monotonous voice.

It was late July, one of those weighted, damp days that sometimes descended upon Paris in the summer. The guests were perspiring and red-faced. Only the baron seemed cool and composed; his face was expressionless as he listened to the words of the priest.

He frightened her in a way she did not understand; she found that she did not like looking at him directly. He seemed always at ease and yet there was an aura of tension about him, of something barely contained, so that when he moved or spoke, she sometimes expected the air to crackle about him. When he stood talking to other men, he looked solid and immovable, and the first time she danced with him she was surprised to discover that he did so with elegance and lightness of foot.

Yet for all that he puzzled and frightened her, she had more than once had an odd feeling that if only she were not marrying him, it might be possible for them to be friends. During the months of their engagement, he had surprised her with his kindness and restraint; it was almost as if he knew the secret grief that she carried in her heart.

His gentleness and tact with her were all the more surprising in that she knew he was a man of fierce determination and strong, even violent, temper. Once or twice, when she was not nursing her heartache, she had observed her fiancé's actions, and she had overheard others talking about him; she knew that few cared to stand in his way when he had made up his mind to something. Once, his conversation with her had touched upon his enemies.

'You mean you have enemies?' she had asked, surprised; she had always lived in a world in which, so far as she knew, everyone adored her.

'The only man who has no enemies is the man who has nothing else,' he had replied.

'But aren't you afraid of them?'

He had smiled in that puzzling way he had and said, 'Not at all. I make it my business to see that they remain afraid of me.'

Now he reached for her hand, slipping the ring upon her finger.

More words. They droned about her head like bothersome flies. He moved; for a moment she thought that he had fallen; perhaps after all he had felt the heat, too.

Then she realized he was kneeling, and she hastily knelt beside him, embarrassed by her near *faux pas.*

'And now, my children,' the priest intoned, 'leave this holy place in the unity of God's blessing and the sanctity of your married state; love one another and obey God's laws. I will pray for you both.'

It was over; she was married. The moment had come and gone, and no tall, handsome figure in guardsman's uniform had come striding down the aisle to claim her. She had been claimed by the ominous stranger beside her, who took her arm possessively to lead her from the chapel.

Possessive; yes, he was already possessive of her, although she had never before formed the thought in that exact word. She remembered a reception they had attended just a few days before; a foppish Italian nobleman had accidentally jostled her, and the baron had theatened to run the man through on the spot. The Italian had fled, virtually in tears.

Well, he would find that he did not own her, marriage or no marriage.

'Are you warm, my dear?' His voice was solicitous in her ear. She must have shuddered involuntarily.

'I feel faint,' she murmured; it was true, although she walked beside him with an imperiousness to match his own, a smile affixed to her lips, her back straight, head high. They talked in undertones that would not reach the ears of those lining the corridor.

'You will have time to rest before the ball begins, if you wish,' he said. He stopped abruptly, his grip on her arm bringing her to a neat halt as well.

'I will kiss you now,' he said.

She had a moment of panic; he had not heretofore done more than kiss her hand politely. For a fraction of a second, she had the look of a hunted deer. Her nose was shiny with perspiration, and he saw the quick, sudden flare of her nostrils as if she sniffed the air for the scent of danger.

He kissed her. She held her breath until it was finished. He was surprisingly gentle, mercifully brief, as if he knew how she felt and was obliging her.

The onlookers murmured their aproval and someone, a masculine voice, laughed a little drunkenly; could it be . . . but it was a young man she did not know, a student. She wondered if he had actually been invited or if he had only slipped in when no one was looking to watch the show and have some free food. He looked drunk and his eyes had a mischievous glow as they watched her.

Beneath her feet the Carrara marble of the floor had been polished until it was as slick as glass. Candles blazed in the *torcheres* that lined the hall and the bronze and gold chandeliers that hung from the ceiling. A sumptuous buffet had been laid out in two of the adjoining rooms, and a stage had been constructed at one end of the hall for the orchestra that would play later.

It was a splendid scene, and she wished it were any other occasion.

'My darling child,' her mama cried, hurrying through the crowd to embrace her. Mama had been crying loudly during the ceremony; her eyes were still red and her face flushed, but she looked delighted.

As well she might, Anne thought petulantly. Only a short time before the ceremony the baron had fixed an impressive amount of money upon her parents. She supposed that in truth she had become his bride in that moment when the money had been paid; the wedding service had only been a formality.

There were other embraces, kisses, well wishes. It would probably have gone on for hours, but she was suddenly aware that her new husband had been piloting her politely but skillfully toward the stairs. Suddenly she was out of the throng, and she realized with an almost resentful gratitude how adroitly he had hurried her through the smothering crowd, sparing her as much discomfort as possible.

Holding to her mama's arm, she hurried up the stairs. Her head was throbbing violently, and she thought she would scream if one more person wished her happiness.

Happiness? She would never know happiness again!

6

'Oh, dear, they've started the dancing without us. I'm sure that must be unlucky, not to mention what people are probably saying.' Mama's fan fluttered nervously in her hand.

'Let them say what they wish. It wasn't necessary for you to stay with me, you know.'

'Oh, but I was afraid – you looked so pale . . . ' The comtesse hesitated, her eyes studying her daughter's profile. 'Anne . . . '

'It's all right, Mama.'

' . . . He's a very gentle man, so thoughtful; and you'll never want for anything. He'll see that you have everything you ever want.'

She stopped as Anne turned to look at her. 'Everything, Mama?' For a moment she thought she saw on her mother's face – what? Guilt? Shame? Anne felt a pang of remorse for hurting her, but she quickly thrust it aside. From now on she intended to be as cold and heartless to everyone as everyone had been to her.

'Well . . . ' Her mother looked away and fluttered her fan again. Below, the music and the shuffle and thump of the dancers came to a brief pause. 'Shall we go down?'

The wedding ball was well underway. It was evening and the

french windows had been opened to the night, allowing the breezes to come in and giving the throng that lingered outside the gates a better view of the festivities. Light spilled from every window, and the air inside was thick with the mingled scents of perfume, sweaty bodies and candle smoke.

Anne paused on the stairs and smiled bitterly down upon the shifting mass of people. It was a brilliant assemblage. She counted half a dozen counts, several marquises, a duchess, even one pretender to the throne, and more government figures than she cared to count. The light from the flaming chandeliers reflected and gleamed upon a fortune in jewels, medals, braid, and gold.

The violins began to scrape and saw again, and the scene became an iridescent kaleidoscope of movement, fabulous gowns and the black of men's coats, with here and there flashes of scarlet and blue as men in uniform shoved their way through the throng.

She knew, of course, why the baron had insisted upon having the wedding here rather than in her home, as was the custom, or the church. It was the only way that some of these people would ever have set foot in his house. The old aristocracy, many of whom had openly snubbed him before, had come for her sake. Not, she suspected, that he really cared about rubbing elbows with them, only in proving that he could do so if he chose.

The music rose and fell. She did not mind if she had spoiled the ball by letting it start without the bride. She would have stayed in the bedroom all evening if she had not gotten restless; and the music *had* sounded tempting.

Papa was by the open windows, listening with apparent fascination to an old hag of a woman. He was leaning forward, absorbed in her words as if she were the most charming woman on earth. But of course Papa would have looked the same if she were a monumental bore, which was more likely the truth.

She did not see her new husband. She hoped he was not waiting to dance with her. She had agreed to marry him, but she had not agreed to cater to his whims and desires – any of them.

She stared down again, Mama at her side craning to see everything happening below; and again Anne paused. That uniform, coming in at the door, surely it was not – her breath caught in her throat and she lifted a trembling hand to her breast.

'What is it?' Mama asked.

It was not Emile, only someone who looked much like him. The handsome soldier, a stranger to her, paused below, looking up. He saw her and she saw the quick, appraising look he gave her.

'Nothing,' she said. She gave her head a haughty toss and tilted her chin upward, but her legs were weak as she descended the stairs, and her eyes glinted with tears.

'Oh, look,' Mama whispered, forgetting everything else in the glamour of the occasion. 'There's the Duchesse de Camford, and she's wearing an old dress, I'd swear before a tribunal I've seen that outfit before. And that Mademoiselle Riviere, they say her salon is terribly *ancien régime*.'

Why hadn't he come? Even if he was married to Louise, surely he must have known she was only marrying this fool of a merchant out of spite. Hadn't he married Louise for her money? What other reason could there have been? Oh, Emile! Even now her heart – and her body – ached for him.

'Mademoiselle?'

It was the handsome soldier, who had waited for her to descend the stairs. Anne had intended to sweep by him without a glance, but now she paused, ignoring Mama's frosty look.

'Sir . . . ' Mama began, but Anne interrupted her.

'Yes?' she said.

'The music, it is very inviting. Shall we?'

His eyes seemed to be laughing and he had a little mustache that curled at the ends, giving his face a devilish look.

My, but he was handsome though. Despite her unhappiness she felt that little thrill of excitement that always accompanied a flirtation.

She arranged her mouth in a very pretty pout. 'Monsieur, I should love to dance, but I must find my husband. This is my wedding ball, as you can see.'

He threw a hand to his breast as if he had been surprised by the statement, although the wedding gown she was wearing must have made it obvious all along. His look was so pained that she could not help a little laugh.

'How wonderful for you,' he said. 'And how tragic for me.'

He brought his heels together audibly and, taking her hand in his, bent neatly to kiss it. His tousled hair gleamed like polished ebony in the candlelight; she longed to run her fingers through it.

'There you are, my dear.'

She started guiltily. It was her husband, and she had been

completely unaware of his approach. Now she suddenly found him standing at her elbow, his dark, watchful eyes studying the young soldier.

Mama looked frightened. 'We were just coming down,' she said quickly, 'when this young man spoke to us.'

Anne snatched her hand back rather too quickly and pretended that she did not see the glint of amusement in the soldier's eyes.

'Our guests have been asking for you,' Jean said. 'And of course I have missed you, too. Shall we dance?'

He took her arm, his grip gentle yet insistent, and led her to the dance floor. They were playing a Polish mazurka.

'I don't know this very well,' she said.

'That all right; I do.'

He held her firmly by the hand, his head lifted, one foot poised behind the other. She was aware that others had paused to watch them, and she waited uneasily for him to begin.

He suddenly glanced sideways at her and gave a tap of his foot. He sprang from the floor and whirled about, taking her with him. He seemed to fly across the floor, one foot forward, dashing at a line of guests as if he would run right into them. Then, suddenly, he stopped short, paused, clicked his heels, spun about, clicked his heels again, spun again.

She seemed to know instinctively what he was going to do and followed his lead with ease. She was amazed again that this man who seemed so stolid and graceless should dance with such ease, such elegance. It was as if the music and the magic of dancing feet transformed him for a space of time and he was no longer ugly or old. There was the rippling sensuality of a gamboling colt in the easy swing of his hips and thighs.

He spun her around, first on one arm, then the other. He fell to his knee, whirling her about him, and then once more he was up and dashing across the room at a dizzying speed.

It ended at last. He clicked his heels again, bowing to her, and she remembered to make a curtsy. She was so exhilarated that she almost forgot she disliked him.

'Where did you learn to do that?' Their guests were applauding, beaming approval at them.

'I have interests in Poland,' he said. 'A prostitute taught it to me. She said she learned it from a prince.'

It seemed to her that he was mocking her, reminding her of the difference in their stations. Her face burning crimson, she turned away from him and went to speak to some friends.

7

It was not likely that Anne would remain morose for very long. She was young and high-spirited, used to laughing a great deal and enjoying life. Moreover, it was a warm summer night and a ball was in progress; this was the native land, in a manner of speaking, of her soul, and she trod it with the expertise of one born to the realm.

She danced with her papa and after him with a gentleman as old as him who regarded her with the frankest lust in his eyes.

And she danced with the soldier who had kissed her hand.

His name was Guy and he came from Provence. When he smiled, he smiled with the languor and indolence of the hot southern coast, as Italian as it was French. He told her she was as beautiful as the banks of flowers that bloomed above the sea there. She laughed delightedly and sipped the champagne he brought her when the dance was ended.

Already she was enjoying the party more; after all, what had changed? She was married, that was all. And she was rich. She did not have much grasp of money matters and so had only the vaguest idea of how rich she was, but she was sure her new husband's wealth was vast.

If she wanted, she could have balls such as this every week – even every day. Of course, they would not be wedding balls, but this was Paris; one needed no excuse to throw a party.

With her husband's wealth and her own beauty and charm, she would become the most famous hostess in Paris. Perhaps she would have a salon, like Mademoiselle Riviere. People – men – would vie with one another for invitations, and she would lead them in glittering conversation; she did not know exactly what was talked about at such salons, but she had never been at a loss for words. She would have the most famous, the most interesting people – and, of course, the handsomest men.

She suddenly imagined Emile standing at the door of her house (they would need something grander than this townhouse, something more suited to the entertainments she had in mind), pleading for entrance. At last she would let him come in.

He would be without Louise, of course. Should she let him dance with her or not? Perhaps she would let him suffer while she flirted with all the handsome men flocking around her, courting her favor.

Her husband was conspicuously absent from these fancies.

She sipped more champagne. She danced with the minister of fine arts. She danced with a young man who said he had been to America.

And she danced with the young soldier again.

The third time she danced with him, he held her very close and whispered in her ear, 'Aren't you warm from all this dancing?'

'A little.'

'Let's go outside for a breath of air.'

'I . . .'

'No one will notice. Look, here we are.'

She saw that while they danced he had steered her deftly to the doors that opened onto the terrace at the side of the house, away from the gawking crowd in front. Now, taking her hesitation for assent, he led her out onto the darkened terrace.

She would have objected, but the fresh air did feel so good. She had not realized how warm and flushed she was from the champagne, the dancing. She felt giddy and breathless. Was this what it felt like to be tipsy?

'Why are you so sad?' he asked.

'Does it show?'

'Yes – to me, at least.'

She did not answer. She had stopped in the rectangle of light that fell through the open door, but he led her toward the deeper shadows under the chestnut tree.

'I was thinking of running away,' she said. Actually she had not thought of it at all until the words had seemed to slip from her lips, but now she considered the possibility. What would they say if she just kept on her way, out the postern gate, through the darkened streets to – to where?

'Perhaps your marriage will not be so bad,' he said.

'Perhaps, perhaps. I'm sick of perhaps,' she said. 'If only one could know – ' She was talking nonsense and knew it; she couldn't think why her head was so muddled.

'That's always the question, isn't it – whether to trade a known present, however unpleasant, for an unknown future.'

But for her it was too late, the trade had already been made; the future was unknown and the past was lost to her.

'Anne,' he murmured. They had reached the deep shadows under the tree, and he turned her toward him. She had a sense of déjà vu, of having been here before. The warm, scented darkness; the handsome young man. He stood half in shadow, half in moonlight, so that she could see the shiny buttons of his uniform but not his face. He was so tall, so broad-shouldered . . . she hadn't meant to kiss him.

'Emile . . . '

If he noticed that she called him by another's name, or cared, he gave no sign. He gathered her into his arms, his lips fastening hungrily upon her trembling ones.

But he wasn't Emile and this wasn't the same; this was foolish at best. She put her hands flat against his chest, meaning to end the kiss, to insist that they return to the ball inside. In a flash of insight rare for her, she saw how badly she was behaving and was ashamed of her actions.

She felt the young soldier suddenly stiffen. He took a step back from her, so abruptly that she swayed off balance and had to put her hand on his arm.

'Please,' she said, before she realized that he was not looking at her at all, but beyond her. His face was pale, the laughter gone from his eyes.

'Yes, please indeed, Monsieur.'

It was her husband's voice, icy cold. She turned to find he had followed them onto the terrace. He regarded them both with a look of barely contained fury.

'Monsieur le Baron . . . ' The guardsman attempted to speak but Jean ignored him and, turning his back, went to the door opening onto the ball. Anne felt a strange surprise to see that it was still going on exactly as it had been.

'Philippe!' Jean barked his majordomo's name. Several of the guests looked curiously in his direction, but he ignored them.

'Philippe!'

The majordomo appeared, hurrying through the crowd.

'Have the carriage brought around at once,' Jean ordered.

The servant looked confused.

'At once,' Jean repeated. He turned back to his wife and the soldier.

'As for you,' he addressed Guy, 'you will leave my house immediately, before I have you whipped like a dog and thrown into the streets.'

The guardsman was twenty years younger and nearly a head

taller; ordinarily the young man would have challenged such a remark, but something about the look in the other man's eyes and the tone of his voice gave him pause.

He clicked his heels smartly and bowed. 'Monsieur, my apologies,' he said. He strode briskly away, disappearing inside without so much as a backward glance at Anne. She might have been, she thought, some *fille de joie* that he had picked up off the streets.

She was left alone in the moonlight with her enraged husband. Shock and fear had cleared her head of any befuddlement, and she stared wide-eyed back at him as he turned his attention to her.

'My dear,' he said, speaking with frigid contempt, 'did you really think I would allow you to give someone else what I paid so dearly for?'

She managed the courage to say, 'How dare you!' but he was not interested in her remarks or her indignation. He seized her wrist in a grip so harsh it sent a jolt of pain up her arm.

'Come with me,' he said.

'Let go of me, I won't.'

But she did because she had no choice. He fairly dragged her back into the ball and through it, past the startled faces of their wedding guests. He looked neither right nor left, nor did he so much as pause, even when her mother came running up white-faced.

'What's wrong?' Mama cried, but they rushed right on by her.

'Where are you taking me?' Anne demanded; he made no answer.

A lackey rushed to open the front door, and for a moment Anne thought he meant to have her whipped and thrown into the street as he had threatened to do with the soldier.

The carriage came clattering into the courtyard, the driver hastily trying to button his coat as he came. It stopped, and before the footman could hurry down to open the door, Jean had dragged her to it and, throwing the door open, shoved her forcibly inside.

He's mad, she thought, terrified. She looked desperately at the crowd that had followed them to the door, but although they all watched in astonishment, no one moved to intervene. This was her husband, after all, dragging her about like a piece of baggage. Husbands did what they would with their wives; it was the order of things. And it sometimes made for delicious gossip.

Jean spoke to the driver – she was in too much of a state to even try to hear what he said – and then he, too, climbed into the carriage, slamming the door, and a moment later it lumbered off, clattering across the stones of the courtyard. The gates were opened; the crowd outside parted before them. The wedding guests gaped after them, some of them bewildered, others plainly amused. *Tiens*, they would not soon forget this wedding ball.

For Anne it was too much to bear – the humiliation, being dragged away in the middle of the ball and carried off to God alone knew where, still dressed in her wedding gown. She began to cry, sobbing noisily into her hands. Once he moved on the seat beside her, and she threw herself into the far corner of the carriage.

'Don't touch me,' she cried, but apparently he had no interest in touching her; he was only making himself more comfortable.

She became increasingly angry as they went along. She was cool without a wrap of any kind. She had no idea how long they would be out because she had no idea where they were going and disdained to ask. They drove through the darkened streets of Paris, only occasionally passing another carriage or some foot traffic. She could hear shouts in the distance from time to time. Once she thought she saw a pale glow in the sky and wondered if it could already be dawn, but she dismissed the idea at once; she knew it could be no more than midnight.

The coach came to a halt. Glancing out, she saw some soldiers on horseback talking to the driver. Her husband got out of the carriage and went forward to talk to them himself. She leaned as far out the window as she dared, trying to get the gist of their conversation.

' . . . Another uprising,' she heard, and, 'They've barricaded the streets . . . burning . . . fighting going on . . . '

One word, snatched from all the others, made her shudder and draw fearfully back into the carriage; she heard one of the soldiers say, 'Revolution.'

Another revolution! It struck terror into her aristocratic heart. It had been forty years since the Great Revolution, but no one of her class had ever forgotten what happened. She had not been born then, of course, but she knew the stories. Her own grandfather on her mother's side had taken that horrible ride to the guillotine, and one of her aunts had been slain by the mobs. Surely not even her madman of a husband would risk remaining out on a night such as this one.

The soldiers rode away. Looking out, she saw her husband talking earnestly to the driver. She heard him say, 'We'll take the rue Bercy,' as he turned and strode back to the carriage.

'Are we going home?' she asked when the carriage started up again. They were the first words she had spoken to him since ordering him not to touch her.

He did not answer, but when he turned to look at her, she cringed inwardly. The answer was written plain on his face. He hated her. He would not care if they were killed by the Parisian mobs.

'In the name of God,' she cried, 'if you will not think of me, think of yourself, what good – '

She stopped short in mid-sentence. The carriage had been speeding along, but now as they rounded a corner it halted again. They had only to glance from the window to see why.

The street ahead was barricaded with wood, furniture, even an overturned buggy. Standing on either side of the barricade were peasants armed with guns, pitchforks, axes, even rocks. A block or so beyond them a house was afire, its flames providing an eerie light that silhouetted the peasants and sent their shadows dancing crazily along the street.

Shouts went up as the men at the barricade saw the carriage. She heard someone shout, 'You there, driver, bring the coach up here where we can have a look.'

Her husband leaned out the window and called to the driver, 'Turn around.'

The carriage began to turn, the driver urging the horses forward, back, forward again, trying to work the vehicle around in the narrow space. The horses whinnied nervously, scenting the danger.

The men at the barricade shouted again when they saw what was happening, and several began to run toward the carriage. Anne's window was turned toward them now and she watched in fascinated terror as they came closer, closer – she could see the sweat gleaming on their faces and she fancied she saw the maniacal light in their eyes.

One of the men raised a gun. 'Stop or we'll shoot,' he yelled.

The carriage was around. The driver cracked the whip and the horses leapt forward, sending the carriage rocking and swaying wildly.

'Get back, you fool,' her husband said, yanking her roughly out of the way of the window.

A gun fired. Something struck the rear of the coach. Anne sat huddled in terror as they clattered pell-mell through the now-haunted streets. The coach tilted crazily back and forth, knocking her first this way and then that.

What if they overturned? What if those men caught them? She had horrible visions of herself dragged screaming through the streets, led to a waiting guillotine. She began to cry again.

'Oh, Mama, where is Mama?' she sobbed hysterically.

The carriage skittered around yet another corner and again came to an abrupt stop. Two men blocked the way, one with a pitchfork in his hands, the other with a musket. The street was little more than an alley, too narrow for them to go around the men or to attempt to turn again.

They were trapped!

Anne whimpered helplessly into her hands, unable to prevent herself from watching wide-eyed as the two men approached. The one with the pitchfork remained in the center of the road in front of the horses, blocking the way. The other, with the musket, came to the carriage. He said something to the driver, then, barely pausing, came back to where they sat. His face suddenly appeared in the window. She saw that he was looking directly at her, his eyes feverish with excitement, his lips curved in an ugly snarl of a smile. He laughed, and it made her want to scream with terror.

She did not see the pistol appear in her husband's hands, nor where it came from. He suddenly lifted it to the window and fired point-blank into the grinning face.

The face seemed to explode from within. Drops of blood and pieces of something else she did not want to name spattered inside the carriage, staining the leather upholstery and the white skirt of her wedding gown.

She slumped back into the corner with a sigh and fainted dead away.

8

It was cold and dark in the carriage when she awoke. She looked and saw that her husband was asleep in the opposite corner. He had taken off his coat and wrapped it around her while she slept. She thrust it from her, resenting the act of consideration, but in a moment she snatched it back, glad for the warmth.

She leaned forward gingerly. Her head throbbed and she was thirsty. It was dark outside the carriage window. For a moment she could see nothing; then she had a glimpse of what appeared to be a farmhouse alongside the road. A moment later they drove past a thick stand of trees.

Why, they were outside Paris, in the country. But where on earth could he be taking her? They were supposed to go to Venice on their honeymoon, but surely he was not setting out for Venice like this, with no clothes and no servants.

Her eyes dropped downward and she saw the stains across the front of her gown. At once the entire nightmare came back to her – the men blocking the streets, the race through the darkness, that leering face at the window, and finally . . . her husband had killed a man, shot him point-blank. He had dragged her away from her own wedding ball, before the astonished eyes of their guests and over her own protests, and he was taking her – where?

Lord of heaven, how had she gotten into this? He had seemed such a harmless person – old and all that perhaps, but not mad or dangerous. And now here she was, wherever she was, and heaven only knew where or when it would end.

She began to cry, but her head was throbbing and the crying only made it worse. She closed her eyes and in a little while fell asleep again, rocked by the coach's gentle swaying motion.

When she opened her eyes again, it was growing light outside the window. Morning was approaching. She had glimpses of more trees lining the road.

The wealth and glamour of her life in Paris did not extend

to the little towns and villages that dotted the countryside. The servants of the de Grenvilles were well fed and well cared for, but their treatment was much the same as would have been given pedigreed animals. Despite the Great Revolution, despite all that Napoleon had done for the common man, the lot of most peasants was no better than it had been during the Dark Ages. They lived lives of sullen desperation; underfed, frightened, uneducated.

The carriage sped past a little cluster of windowless hovels. A group of half-naked children ran after the coach begging for alms. Anne tried not to mind the sight; she knew how common it was, even within the city of Paris, and her mother had always told her one must close one's eyes to such sights, but for some reason she could not look upon such pitiful creatures without feeling a discomfort that was oddly akin to shame.

France was a rich country, yet all but a handful of her people remained poor. The peasants farmed as they had hundreds of years before, men pulling the plows and women sowing and reaping by hand or with the help of primitive tools. There was no proper drainage and no form of waste disposal, the result being that plagues periodically ravaged the country. And whenever, by some freak of nature, the peasants were able to produce more than their barest subsistence, it was at once snatched up by their aristocratic masters for taxes or by corrupt officials of the government.

Anne felt rather than saw her husband stir on the seat beside her. She could not bear the thought of quarreling with him just now, or even facing him, so she closed her eyes again, pretending to be asleep. Still she was curious and watched the carriage window through barely opened eyes. The sky grew lighter, and in the trees by the road the birds began to chatter and sing. There was a clean edge to the air that one could only discover by getting out of the city.

They came to a stop. She had a glimpse through the window of a massive stone gatepost thickly draped with ivy. There was a murmur of voices, the driver apparently talking to a gatekeeper. After a pause the gate was opened, screeching loudly on little-used hinges, and they drove between the ivied gateposts.

A country place. Of course, she should have guessed that their destination was something of the sort. She vaguely remembered from pre-wedding conversation some mention of a home in the country as well as the townhouse in Paris.

This wasn't so bad, then. The de Grenvilles had a chateau, too, a splendid structure to the south of Paris that was said to rival Versailles itself, and always about this time of year they had fled the heat of the city to spend a month or two in the country. Much as she loved Paris, with all its bustle and glitter, she had to confess that she always looked forward to those bucolic interludes – the lovely swans on the lake, the little pavilion where they sometimes had picnics, the neatly sculptured gardens. It was rustic but all so charming, and when she came back to Paris, everyone commented upon how lovely her complexion looked.

The carriage rolled to a stop again; this time her husband sat forward purposefully, indicating that the long journey was ended. A stranger, an old man with nervous eyes and a stubble of a beard, appeared to open the door, bowing as the baron clambered out. Jean turned and, seeing her eyes wide open, as she had been too curious to continue pretending to sleep, he offered her his hand.

'Welcome to your new home, my dear,' he said.

'Where are we?' She would have refused his hand, but it was a long step from the carriage to the graveled drive and she was forced to accept his assistance.

'The Chateau Brussac.'

She turned to survey the scene, and a look of dismay came over her face.

This was not a splendid chateau like the de Grenvilles'; this was a crumbling ruin of a structure. It looked uninhabited and uninviting, as if it had long since weighed the merits of human society and found them wanting. The house was made of stone and, like the gateposts, was covered with vines. It sat on a little knoll of its own, all but hidden by the massive trees growing around it. To the rear it overlooked shabby outbuildings and, further off, a hillside covered with what appeared to be a vineyard.

She could not resist asking drily, 'Has it been in your family long?'

'That's hardly likely, considering that my father started his life as little more than a peasant. It was given to him in payment for a debt. I believe he spent one night here.'

'But what of Venice? What of our – our . . . ' she nearly choked on *honeymoon* and instead ended lamely, ' . . . our trip?'

'I've changed my mind about that. I believe we'll have more opportunities to get acquainted here. And there will be fewer, shall we say, distractions for you.'

She knew that he was referring to her flirtation with the young officer at their wedding ball, and her face flushed crimson at the memory. She wished she could think of a suitably scathing reply, but nothing rose to her lips.

The old man who had opened the carriage door for them had hurried off at a shuffling gait and disappeared into the house, calling as he went. Now he reappeared, followed by an old woman with a bent back, and a scrawny girl of twelve or so. They formed a ragged line in the drive, heads bowed, the old man holding his cap before him as if to ward off blows. She saw that he had only one hand.

Holding tight to her arm, Jean escorted her to where the servants waited. 'This is your new mistress,' he introduced her. 'This is Christian, his wife Henriette, and the girl – what is the girl's name, Henriette?'

'Katherine, sir.'

'Katherine,' Jean repeated. 'Henriette, you will show your mistress to her bedroom; she is tired from her journey. And you, Katherine, will find me something to eat.'

He started off toward the house, saying over his shoulder to the man, 'Take care of the horses.'

The girl scurried around them and ran ahead into the house. The old man went with the driver to see to the horses, the weary footman following behind. Anne was left in the drive with the old woman; the rough gravel was beginning to hurt her feet through the thin soles of her slippers. They had been intended for dancing and not for hiking in the country.

'Madame?'

'Yes, yes; I'm coming.' Anne followed her toward the house. She was too exhausted, mentally and physically, to argue with her husband now. Later, when she had gotten her strength back, she would make him understand a few things, particularly that she could not live in a hovel like this. He could do as he chose – she would be only too glad to see him stay in the country – but she was Parisian born and bred, and marriage or no marriage, she had no intention of living here like a farm wife.

She remembered then the temper he had displayed the previous night; and yet this morning he seemed his usual self, nonchalant, unconcerned. He acted as though killing a man was an everyday occurence for him.

Perhaps it was; for the first time she realized fully that she did not know her husband at all.

She must have shivered visibly; Henriette asked, 'Madame is chilled?'

'I – no, I'm all right, just tired.'

Jean had followed the servant girl around the corner of the house, presumably to a back entrance, but Henriette led her in through the front, into a large, echoing gloominess.

It was a cold, bare hall, sparsely furnished. Years of treading feet had worn the tiles of the floor to a dull stone color, but she could just make out in the corners a bright floral glaze that must have once brightened the entryway. The wood-paneled walls were warped and cracked, black with age and the accumulated soot from the great fireplace on one side.

Henriette's progress up the great, wide stairs was slow and laborious, giving Anne time to look about, but there was not much to see; most of the doors leading off the hall were closed. She had a glimpse down a stone passageway toward what seemed to be the kitchen area, but that was about all.

'Madame must forgive us,' Henriette said, unlocking a door and opening it to reveal a room haunted with dust covers. 'This is a surprise – we did not know . . . '

'Nor did I,' Anne murmured.

'Pardon?'

'It is nothing.' She walked to the windows. Henriette hurried about her to open the curtains and reveal a little balcony.

Anne stepped tentatively out onto it, half-afraid that it might crumble beneath her, but it felt surprisingly secure. Henriette busied herself whipping covers off furnishings.

'Where are we?' Anne asked.

'Here?' Henriette was surprised. 'Why, this is the Ile-de-France.'

'And that river?'

'The Marne, Madame. Beyond, on the other side, that is Champagne, and there, just through those trees, those are the roofs of Epernay. It's farther than it looks, though.'

Farm country, Anne thought disdainfully; not even the great chateau. country to the south, but a land of wheat fields and woodlands. From here she could see the hills rolling down toward the river, punctuated by hedges and woods. Closer below were the vineyards, larger than she had noticed before, and off to the right, beyond the outbuildings, an orchard of some sort or other.

That was no doubt Henriette's kitchen garden just below, arranged in tidy rows. There were pigs rooting in the grass by the barn, and a family of geese strolled arrogantly across the lawn directly below her balcony, honking heated warnings at any opposing traffic, the goslings echoing their parents in a diminuendo.

It was not at all like the de Grenvilles' chateau with its neat lawns, its expertly placed statuary, the artificial pond for rowing. One could not walk on the grass here without fear of stepping on droppings of one sort or another – human would hardly have surprised her.

Henriette worked quickly. By the time Anne came back in from the balcony, the room had been put to rights, a freshly made bed turned down, a basin and a fresh pitcher of water waiting on the washstand. The girl Katherine came in shortly with hot rolls laden with butter and a steaming cup of chocolate; there were freshly cut grapes as well, red-gold in color and tasting at the same time both tangy and sweet.

Anne ate voraciously, unaware until she began how hungry she was. But as her appetite became appeased and the delicious grapes disappeared from the tray, she began to gaze more fondly in the direction of the massive, old-fashioned bed.

'Do you suppose you could find me a nightgown?' she asked finally, patting her lips daintily with the coarse, oversized napkin that had been brought.

'*Mais oui*, Madame,' Henriette replied. She went out and returned a few minutes later bearing a gown. If she hadn't been so tired, Anne could almost have laughed at the effrontery. It was a rough, woolen gown, a peasant's nightdress. She had never worn anything for sleeping but silk or linen, and under other circumstances she would have ripped the gown in two and flung it to the floor.

But she had neither the strength nor the inclination just now for ripping gowns in two. She meant to sleep – standing up if she must – and she meant to get out of her wedding gown with its increasingly painful stays.

'Thank you,' she said, accepting the gown. 'It will do for now. You may help me undress.'

In a few minutes Anne was naked and slipping into the nightgown. It felt coarse and scratchy on her bare skin, and she thought longingly of the hand-sewn silk gowns that had been part of her trousseau.

'You may tell my husband that I am sleeping,' she said, slipping gratefully into the bed, 'and do not wish to be disturbed.'

She was already drifting off to sleep by the time Henriette quietly slipped from the room.

It seemed to Anne that she had barely closed her eyes when the door crashed open and she opened her eyes to discover her husband standing by the bed, looking down upon her. She sat up, pulling the sheets up to cover herself.

'I am very tired,' she snapped. 'I trust you won't disturb me.'

'Then you're a fool,' he said. 'You are my wife, in case you've forgotten, and this is our wedding night – or rather, our wedding morning. And I have every intention of disturbing you.'

She moved as if she would escape him, but he caught her, falling upon the bed with her. For a few frantic moments she fought against him, raking his skin with her nails.

'You bitch,' he said. 'You think I will let you refuse me what you gave your guardsman, what you would have given that foolish young man tonight if I hadn't intervened? No, by God, I've bought you and paid for you and I'll have you whenever I choose.'

His fingers caught in the rough fabric of her nightgown and he tore it from neck to waist. In a moment it was torn from her completely and she was naked beneath him.

She was terrified by this unexpected violence. Her cheek was crushed against his thick chest and his heart hammered in her ear. She tried to cry out but the cry was muffled. He was a wild man, a stranger, and she was frightened by the arms hurting her.

She threw her head back and tried to scream, but he bent and his savage kiss stifled her scream. She could not escape the kiss and she closed her eyes, seeming to sink into an awesome blackness. There was nothing but the lips on hers and the darkness into which she was sinking, and the feel of his body, trembling, against hers. He was saying something but she could not hear the words and then his lips moved downward, over her bare flesh.

Finally the full weight of his body was upon her and she

could no longer struggle against him; she submitted and was taken, her face wet with tears.

But the body is a weakness, betraying even the strongest mind. In the midst of the pain, the humiliation, the anger, she discovered a sort of wild thrill that she had never experienced before, not even in the moments with Emile. It was fear and ecstasy, surrender and madness – his lips were too brutal, his arms too strong. For the first time in her life, she had experienced someone stronger than she was, someone she could neither bluff nor bully. Somehow, as if of their own volition, her arms found their way around his neck, and the pain and the pleasure became more intense, until they were unbearable and she was sinking into another, a new blackness, but she was falling upward, up, up into a swirling softness . . .

When she opened her eyes, his arms had released her but he still lay over her. She tried to turn away, ashamed of the way she had responded to him, but he cupped her chin in one hand and forced her to meet his eyes.

'Always remember, you are my wife now,' he said. 'And I am your husband.'

With that he turned on his side away from her and went to sleep.

For a long time she lay motionless beside him, bruised and shaken by what had happened to her, exalted and yet shamed as well. At last she fell asleep again.

Some time later she was awakened by the touch of his hands on her again, and this time she did not try to draw away from him.

It was so different this second time that she could hardly believe it was the same man making love to her. He was gentle and tender and, although she did not understand it, she enjoyed the benefit of all the expertise he had acquired over the years in the arms of many other women, high-born and low. Her head swam and at the end incoherent little cries escaped her lips.

Afterward, she fell asleep with her arms about him, his about her, like a frightened child who has been comforted.

When she awoke, he was gone. The soft light streaming through the window told her it was already late afternoon. Had it not been for the rumpled bedclothes and the torn nightgown lying on the floor beside the bed, she would have thought it all an outrageous dream. Her cheeks turned red at the memory and she pulled the covers up to her chin although there was no one there now to see her nakedness.

After a moment, though, she began to smile a little. She thought of what Emile had said – 'Old men make few demands.' That statement was as false as everything else Emile had told her.

Perhaps, after all, things were not so bad. She had had to submit to her husband's mastery, true; but she was sure now that he would have forgotten that innocent flirtation of hers at the wedding ball. Tonight, or tomorrow at the latest, he would beg her forgiveness and they would return to Paris.

She understood him a little better now. For all his coldness, all his aloofness, he was just a man like any other. He desired her, passionately and uncontrollably, and while the depth of his ardor was frightening, it gave her a much-needed whip over him. She had started off on the wrong foot, but now she saw how best to handle the situation in which she found herself.

She got out of bed finally and stood for a moment lazily stretching her arms over her head. My, but she had slept well, though.

Someone – Henriette, she supposed – had put out a dress for her. It was provincial and outdated, but it was clean and not nearly as coarse as the nightgown that she had not needed after all. For the first time in her life, she dressed herself, singing softly as she did so. To her surprise the task was simpler than she had always supposed.

Smiling, she went to the window and, pulling the curtains aside, stepped onto the little balcony. As she opened the window, the day ran to meet her like a kitten bounding up to her feet.

Beneath, the lawns, the fields, the woods all seemed empty, still, as if holding their breath. The sun was radiant in a sky that was a clear, kind blue, not at all harsh; there was a tumble of clouds lazing in the distance. She felt as young as the moment, as old as life.

She was very hungry.

9

She was furious when she discovered that her husband had gone.

'He returned to Paris,' was all Henriette could tell her.

Anne was beside herself; how dare he! He had subjected her to danger, humiliation and the discomfort of an unplanned, unexpected nighttime journey, had brought her here, in the middle of nowhere, and then, thinking her satisfactorily disposed of, had hied himself back to the comforts and pleasures of Paris, while she rotted here.

Never!

'Have the carriage brought around,' she ordered.

'But Monsieur has taken the carriage,' Christian explained timidly.

'Surely there must be another.'

'No, Madame, only the farm cart.'

It was the height of absurdity, to keep a place in the country with only one carriage; why, she happened to know that he kept no fewer than five in Paris, where they were surely less crucial than here.

'Have a horse saddled, then,' she ordered, adding drily, 'I presume there are more horses?'

'*Oui*, Madame, only –' Christian hesitated.

'Only what?'

'Is Madame aware there is a storm coming up?'

'I'm not afraid of a little rain,' she said. 'Have a horse saddled and brought around at once.'

She had ridden through little showers in Paris before; a bit of dampness would not deter her. At any rate, it was not her intention to ride all the way to Paris; she had already formed a plan. She would ride to the village of Epernay, whose rooftops could be seen from her bedroom window. Surely there she would be able to hire some sort of transportation back to the city, which she could pay for when she arrived there. Her husband would not dare refuse to pay, and even if he did, her papa would not.

In fact, the more she thought of it, the more she thought it best to ride directly to her own home. She would fling herself at her papa's feet, tell him how horribly she had been treated. He would know what to do; there must be some way that she could be freed from this evil marriage contract, even if it meant giving back all of the baron's money. Even if it meant living in destitution, Papa would not let her be treated in this manner.

The horse was saddled and brought around to the front of the house. Henriette, wiping her already dry hands on her apron, added her own shy warnings to those of her husband.

'Storms can be very fierce here,' she said. 'They blow up quickly, God knows from where, and sometimes they go on all night.'

'Oh, fiddle-faddle,' Anne cried, mounting with Christian's help. 'A little rain never hurt anyone.'

She snatched the reins from the servant's hands and, kicking her heels into the horse's shanks, went off down the drive with a clatter of hooves.

The gate was closed, but that did not trouble her. She had no intention of going by the road back to Paris. She remembered quite well the lay of the land as she had seen it from her window, and when she was almost to the gate, she turned the horse left, across the fields, in the direction of Epernay.

It was late afternoon; the sun was already sinking behind the treetops and it would soon be dusk. It was already nearly dark, with the ever more ponderous clouds gathering above, and the sky turned an eerie yellow.

Suddenly the clouds obscured the fading sun, and she felt the first few drops of rain upon her face. She was grateful that she was an accomplished horsewoman; she would have to ride hard to reach Epernay before nightfall and without being drenched.

By the time the storm broke in full, she had remembered Henriette's remark about the village: 'It's farther than it looks.'

She had ridden into a different world, a world of darkness and confusion. The howling wind, the rain and the sudden stabs of lightning beset her until she lost all sense of direction. Beneath her, the horse snorted and paused, but she drove him on, spurred by her own demons.

She tried to take shelter in a small stand of trees, but they were no match for the storm. Once-lacy branches clawed and whipped at her, and the leaves slapped wetly. Thinking she had glimpsed the river off to the right, she rode on, the wind tearing at her cloak and threatening to snatch her from the horse. The beast stumbled on the muddy ground, more than once nearly unseating her. It took all her attention to concentrate on clinging to the wet saddle, so that she no longer could even try to find her way but only twisted the reins about her fist and leaned into the horse's wet mane.

Sometime later – she had lost all sense of time as well; it might have been minutes or hours since she had ridden angrily from the house – they came over a rise, and there below was the river, muddy and swollen. She tried to peer into the rain to the other side, but it was impossible to see so far. No village lights penetrated the darkness.

She had come downriver, then. But where was the bridge? It would be impossible to cross in that treacherous current below; she watched a log, torn from some tree further upriver, swept along in the torrent.

Her clothes were soaked, clinging to her. Her flaming hair was a sodden mess, hanging in her face. She was cold through to her bones, and frightened. She might even have returned to the farm, only in the storm she had no more idea where it was than the village.

She urged the horse on again, riding blindly. The beast snorted, his nostrils steaming. She gave him his head, hoping without much conviction that he might find his way home.

She thought of her own home in Paris, of her room with its elegant, familiar furnishings. She thought of a fire, blazing brightly, on the hearth . . . warm . . . the delicious chocolate that Jeanette liked to bring her . . . Mama, playing the pianoforte in the salon below. The images ran together, blurring in her mind, as if washed loose by the rain . . .

She slipped from the saddle, dropping into the wet grass. The horse, freed of its burden, puzzled, stood patiently beside her for several minutes, waiting for her to remount.

Then, miserable himself with the wet and the cold, he began to move on, plodding uncaringly through a thicket. In a moment he had vanished from sight.

Anne lay in a heap in the tall, wet grass, all but hidden from sight.

10

It was cold, so very cold. If only she could escape this icy chill, could reach some warm haven. She tried to sit up, struggling against the weight that held her, and someone spoke to her, softly, soothingly.

'There, there, lie still.'

It was Papa's voice. She opened her eyes, delighted and surprised, but it was not Papa who stood over her. It was . . . but the face faded until there was only the hand on her burning forehead.

'Papa, I – I've come home to you,' she murmured.

'She's feverish,' someone said. A woman's voice, not Mama's, but . . . was that Jeanette?

The voices faded, receding into the distance, then slowly approached again.

'You must marry him,' Mama was saying sternly. 'We need the money.'

'But I don't love him, Mama, I love Emile – oh, Emile, my darling . . . '

'So beautiful,' Emile murmured. He put his arms around her, helping her to sit up. 'Drink this,' he said.

She opened her eyes again. It was not Emile, it was – it was the baron.

'Never,' she cried, struggling against him.

'Drink.'

She drank the warm broth, savoring the warmth that rushed down into her belly. She lay back in the bed. The heat had become unbearable now and she thrashed about, trying to kick away the covers. Something wet and cool ran over her flesh – someone was bathing her, slowly, gently, lovingly. Strong but gentle hands turned her over, bathing her entire body.

'Drink.'

'Is she any better?'

'You must rest, Monsieur. I will stay with her.'

'She's my wife.'

It was Emile, he had come to claim her for his wife after all. 'Emile,' she sighed happily. 'My darling.'

'Sleep,' someone murmured in her ear. 'You will feel better soon.'

She smiled and opened her eyes, but Emile had vanished again. It was her husband who knelt over her. Only she had never seen him look concerned like this before; it changed his features. He looked vulnerable; human, almost; she thought quite suddenly that he looked like Papa when he frowned like that.

His face faded. She was sinking downward into a peaceful darkness, warm and gentle and safe.

She opened her eyes and found herself staring at a ceiling. What had happened to the canopy above her bed? She turned her head and saw Jeanette. For a moment she thought she was still dreaming.

'Jeanette,' she tried to say, but only a croaking whisper came from her lips.

'You are better now, Madame,' Jeanette said. 'The fever has gone.'

She remembered then – her husband, that awful journey to the country, her rage, the ride into the storm. She had fallen from the horse; that was the last she remembered clearly until now.

She sat up on one elbow, her entire body aching. There, on a lounge a few feet from the foot of the bed, was the baron, asleep.

'He hasn't left your side since he returned from Paris,' Jeanette said. 'He wouldn't let anyone else care for you.'

Her husband, by her side – she tried to think, but her mind felt weighted down. 'Papa?' she asked.

'He's here, too.'

'How . . . ?'

'You must not worry yourself for now; you must rest,' Jeanette said.

Anne did as she was bade, sinking once more into the comforting darkness. As she did so, she thought of her husband asleep in the chair, his face unshaven, his shirt wrinkled. This was a different man, one she had not seen before.

When she woke again, there was no one in the room with her but Jeanette.

She looked toward the chaise longue where she had seen her husband before, but it was empty. Had she only imagined him there, dreamed that worried face bent over hers?

'Jeanette,' she said. 'How did you come to be here?'

Jeanette avoided her eyes and began to daub at her forehead with a damp cloth. 'You're not to bother yourself about things just yet, Madame,' she said. 'You've been very ill; for a time it was touch and go, I don't mind telling you, I was that scared . . .'

'Oh, for heaven's sake,' Anne said, pushing the damp cloth away, 'stop prattling and tell me what's happened. What is this all about? Did you tell me Papa is here, or was I only dreaming that?'

'No, he's here. I . . . oh, Mademoiselle,' Jeanette cried, forgetting Anne's new form of address in a burst of emotion. 'It was dreadful, all those awful people, rioting, burning, looting everywhere – no one was safe, it was like all of Paris had gone mad. And most of the servants left, that stupid Bertha was gone in a wink, said it was time the common people got what they deserved – God knows she was common enough – they tore the drapes from the very windows, imagine. I watched them carry the furniture right out the front door . . .'

Anne pressed her hands to her temples. 'Jeanette, in the name of heaven, I'm going to scream if you don't start to make some sense.'

'The revolution,' Jeanette said. 'A second revolution. And then he came . . .'

'He who?'

'Your husband – the baron – he came and said we must leave, it wasn't safe to remain in Paris; he said we must come here while we could still get out of the city. He wouldn't even allow us time to pack, we came with what we had on our backs, although I did manage to get back to my room and get that sock. You remember, I saved some gold *louis*, the ones your papa always gave us for the holidays, and I had them in an old sock, under my pillow, and I fetched that – I've got it under my pillow here now – but that was more than anyone else managed to bring. Why, your dear papa hadn't even time to find his spectacles, and he was still wearing his slippers. The baron practically carried him out of the house, through the kitchen door – imagine – and people carrying furniture out the front. All the servants had gone except Cook and myself. You can imagine how frightened I was.'

Anne tried to struggle to a sitting position. 'I must go see Papa; where is he?'

'Oh, you mustn't. He's directly across the hall, but he's to bed himself since we got here, and anyway, you're not to get up till the doctor says.'

The warning was unnecessary; after a moment of effort Anne sank weakly back into the pillows, struggling for her breath.

'And Mama?' she asked when she could breathe again.

There was an awkward silence. Jeanette swept up the washcloth and the basin of water from the nightstand. 'I'll bring you something to eat,' she said quickly.

'Mama, is she – isn't she here, too?' Anne asked in a whisper.

Jeanette, halfway to the door, stopped and without looking back, said, 'They overturned one of the carriages – the one she was in. It was awful. The baron went back to save her, but they had set fire to the carriage – he did everything. Oh, his hands were burned so badly, and people were shooting at him, I can't think why he wasn't scared out of his wits – but it was no good, he couldn't save her. There's just your papa, and Cook and me – and all the baron's servants. Can you imagine, not a one of them tried to run away and join the rioters! Why, that old fool of a butler of his was right there trying to help the baron save your mama . . . oh, Mademoiselle.'

Jeanette did turn then, and there were tears streaming down her face. She looked both silly and pathetic, standing with her tears streaming into the basin of water held before her.

'It must have been . . . ' Anne struggled for self-control. Her mama – that vain and foolish creature, who'd never harmed a soul – to die so horribly . . .

I mustn't start to cry, she thought. *If I start I shall never stop.* And there was Jeanette, pleading wordlessly for comfort. You must understand servants, Mama had told her time and again, they are like children and that is how you must treat them: firmly, but with kindness.

'Jeanette, I – I believe I am hungry now.'

'Oh, how silly of me.' Jeanette checked her tears with a noisy sniffle and somehow managed to get a corner of her apron to her eyes without overturning the basin. 'I'll just go get something – Cook will be so pleased to know you're hungry.'

When she had gone, Anne bit her lip and pressed a hand to her closed eyes. It was impossible to think – her whole world gone, vanished, all that she had known. Their lovely home, her room with its silks and brocades, and the little gilt tables, the chandeliers that could turn the night into day.

And her mama – she didn't dare think of her mama or she would go mad.

After a moment she struggled up again. This time, clinging to the bedpost, she managed to sit up and swing her legs heavily to the floor. Across the hall, Jeanette had said – she would go to Papa. Darling Papa, he would know what they must do now; he would know how to make everything right.

It seemed to take forever; she found that she must feel her way along the wall, pausing every step or two for breath. Yet somehow she reached the door, managed to stumble across the hall into the room just opposite.

The room was in shadow, the curtains drawn. For a moment she thought the bed was empty. Not until she was almost beside it did she see the little figure buried under the covers, his head propped up on a mountain of pillows.

Why, Jeanette had lied to her; this was not her papa, this shriveled shell of a man whose breath rattled in his throat. Her papa had been strong and confident, in command always. She saw him fingering the gold chain on which his watch had hung, saw his scowl when anyone dared to challenge his word. This was a puppet, a caricature that someone had fashioned. To be sure, there was her papa's nose, and that was the thick underlip that he had liked to thrust forward when he was considering some childish request of hers – but her papa, this? No, it could never be. And yet . . .

As if he sensed her presence, he stirred, turning his head slightly, and opened his eyes, staring up at her. For a matter of seconds they regarded one another wordlessly.

'Is it you?' he whispered. 'Is it really you, then?'

'Yes, oh, yes,' she said, fighting back a sob.

A single tear escaped from one of his eyes, slid over the sunken cheek.

'They told me you'd died in the carriage,' he said.

'Oh, Papa!' The tears did come then, the tears and the sobs she'd fought to hold back. She sank to her knees beside the bed, flinging herself across his fragile-looking chest, clinging to him while her heart poured out all her grief and he, with one trembling hand, stroked her hair.

11

Later, she learned that it was Jean himself, searching for her in the storm, who had found her and brought her back to the house; had it not been for him, she might have died. As it was, it was more than a week before she was able to get out of her bed with ease. She did, however, cross the hall each day, with Jeanette's help, to spend part of her afternoon with Papa. After that first confusion, he had recognized her for herself and not for her mother. By some unspoken consent they did not discuss that scene, nor did they discuss Paris and the tragedies that had occurred there. Sometimes she read to him; sometimes they talked of the past; but it was always of a long-ago past, when she was a little girl. From time to time he spoke of their own chateau, and once or twice she was sure he thought they were there instead of at her husband's farm, but she did not disenchant him.

During this time her husband did not come to see her, so that more and more she was sure she had dreamed his attendance during her fever.

She saw him almost daily, though, from the balcony of her room. He had taken to working in the vineyards that stretched behind the house. At first, seeing him in his shirtsleeves, a scarf tied about his head to keep the sweat from his eyes, she had mistaken him for another peasant.

What a mystery he was. Why should he, with his enormous wealth, work in his fields like a common farmer? She thought of the day he had made love to her – the memory never failed to cause her an odd blush of warmth – how strong and hard his body had been, and his hands all calloused and rough like a peasant's. It was despicable to think that he should demean himself in such a fashion.

And yet she could remember lying in the circle of his arms – how secure they had felt, as if nothing could trouble or threaten her there.

Nor could she forget how he had taken her family, even Jeanette and Cook, within the circle of his protection, had risked his own life, if Jeanette's melodramatic account were to be accepted, in an attempt to save Mama's.

Again and again she puzzled over his character, but she could not reconcile the contradictions. He was hard and ruthless, yet his actions were sometimes selfless. He was violently passionate – she had only to remember his lovemaking to know that; yet since then, although he surely knew by now that she was out of her bed, he had not once come to her.

That surprised her most of all. As the days went by and her strength returned, so that she was more and more able to resume a normal sort of life, she found herself each day expecting him. She had even made up her mind that this time she would not refuse him the gratification of his desires. After all, he had earned some consideration from her, if only through his generosity toward her family. When she thought that without him, her papa might have died at the hands of the revolutionaries as her mama had, she was almost prepared to welcome her husband to her bed.

But it was a welcome that he continued to ignore. At first this puzzled her and in time it annoyed her. There is no frustration greater than being unallowed a self-chosen martyrdom, and she realized that without his co-operation she could hardly make the noble sacrifice she had begun to envision for herself. How could she give the gift, if he would not come to claim it?

She thought that when she began to take her dinners downstairs, things would sort themselves out, but in this, too, she was thwarted, for she found that since her husband had begun to take an interest in the vineyards, he had taken to having his meals at odd times in the kitchen.

'Just like a servant,' she thought angrily, eating alone in the huge dining-room. Cook, having usurped Henriette's place in the kitchen, and learning that her mistress was coming down to dine, had outdone herself, but Anne only picked at the roast pheasant and ignored the pastry confections entirely.

In the end she decided that she would have to go to him. She would wait until she heard him come up to his room that night.

She bathed and, with Jeanette's help, brushed her hair so that it hung about her shoulders like a coppery mist. Her trousseau had been brought from Paris, and she donned one of the dressing gowns, a gleaming honey-colored silk trimmed with yards of fine lace. It plunged to a deep vee at the bodice, exposing the cleft between her breasts; she smiled to herself as she studied her reflection in the mirror.

She had lost some weight during her illness, and if one looked closely, there were dark hollows under her eyes. Still, she thought he would not be displeased by the way she looked.

It was late when at last she heard his tread upon the stairs and the sound of his door opening and closing. She had been half-asleep on the chaise in her own room. Now she dabbed some fresh perfume at her throat and went quickly along the hall to his door, tapping lightly.

He looked surprised to see her. He had been working in the fields and his shirt was open, revealing his powerful chest and a mat of thick hair. He smelled strongly of sweat and the earth, so unlike the perfumed and powdered gentlemen she had known all her life. He exuded power and a sort of animal vitality that was oddly stirring.

'This is a surprise. Come in, please.' He ushered her into the room, closing the door after her. It was an unremarkable room, big and comfortable looking, with few frills. There was a bed, massive and old, and a carved chest. In addition, a writing-table and a chair had been pulled up near the fire. Account books and papers were scattered haphazardly over the surface of the table.

'I was just having a glass of wine. Will you join me?' he asked.

'Please, just a little,' she said, more to be polite than anything else; she didn't really care for wine, except champagne. She was quite nervous now that she was here. If only he didn't always make her feel so foolish.

He poured the wine and brought it to her; it gleamed a deep ruby color in the glass. She could not help but notice as he handed it to her that his hands were scarred, and she realized with a little shock that he had burned them trying to save Mama from a flaming carriage. It made her feel guilty, as if she were somehow to blame, although she could not think how.

'This is from our own vineyards,' he said, toasting her with a a lift of his glass. 'It's not very good, I'm afraid; still, there's something there, a suggestion, if you will. Christian swears that with the right care the vines would produce a first-rate wine. A man could take pride in an accomplishment like that, don't you think? But you did not come to discuss wines, I suppose?'

'I – I wanted to thank you.' She made him a very pretty smile, but he seemed hardly to notice. He sipped his wine and stared into the fire burning on the hearth.

'And what have I done to earn these tender expressions of gratitude?'

'You saved my father's life. I'm told that you were very brave in trying to save my mother's as well.'

'Your father is a very rare commodity, a true gentleman. One should try to preserve such treasures wherever one finds them. I'm sorry I was not able to reach your mother in time. She reminded me of . . . of someone else.'

He paused and glanced down at her, his eyes fastening on her exposed bosom. 'However,' he added, 'it was hardly necessary for you to feel you must pay me for my efforts.'

Instinctively she pulled the bodice of the gown shut with one hand. 'I don't know what you mean,' she said, her voice cold. He did have the most exasperating manner about him; it was really impossible to speak to him as one would to a civilized man.

'What nonsense! You come to my bedroom in the middle of the night, perfumed like a courtesan and with your breasts bare – did you expect me to set upon you like a wild man again, my dear?' he smiled sardonically.

'I should certainly hope not,' she said indignantly.

'That was unfortunate – an impulsive action that I'm afraid flattered neither of us.'

'I was prepared to forgive it.'

Again the smile, but there was a sadness about his eyes. He was the most mystifying man she had ever met.

'I should not have thought it was necessary to forgive a man for making love to his wife, any more than for a man to have to force his wife to make love to him. No matter, though; it will not happen again.'

'Have I your promise to that effect?' she demanded, angered by his haughty manner. How could she not be angry? She had come prepared to – to show him that she was not unreasonable, and he had done nothing but heap insults on her. She was sorry now that she had come at all; she ought to have known he would be as insufferable as ever.

He cocked an eyebrow. 'If you wish it,' he said.

'Good, I'm glad to hear it,' she said, standing to go. To her further annoyance, he seemed as unmoved by her anger as he had been by her invitation.

'As long as you're recovered from your illness . . . ' he said. 'I've been putting off returning to Paris. There are affairs that must be put into order there. I trust you will not be too lonely for me if I am gone for a few days.'

'To Paris?' She forgot all about her annoyance. She came to him, putting a hand on his arm. 'Take me with you.'

'It's out of the question. Paris isn't safe just now.'

'But you're going.'

'And would it grieve you greatly if something happened to me?'

He was laughing at her; she stamped her foot impatiently. 'Oh, I wouldn't care if they dragged you to the guillotine in front of me. I want to go to Paris.'

He did laugh openly then. 'By God, you've got courage, my dear, whatever else you lack in the way of virtues. But it's no use, I am going to Paris, and you are staying here. There are more dangers in Paris than the mobs.'

She tossed her head, her eyes flashing with green fire. 'You think I'll find a man more to my liking? That's why you want to keep me a prisoner here.'

His laughter faded and his eyes narrowed. 'I've no doubt that you could. Almost any alley cat would suit you better, I suppose. Yes, I shall keep you prisoner here if I choose, if I must to keep your thighs unstained. You needn't have me for a lover, if that's as you want it, Madame, but by God you won't have anyone in my place, either.'

'What do you propose to do, chain me to the bed? I left before, you know.'

'And got yourself a good soaking for your troubles. At any rate, your father's here now. You aren't likely to run off and leave him in my clutches – not in his precarious health. Suppose I chose to take my spite out on him?'

She was furious because she knew that he was right; she couldn't leave now that Papa was here, and an invalid. What an unbearably aggravating man her husband was, and to think of how generous her motives had been in coming to see him at all!

'You . . . you . . . ' She stammered, trying to think of a word odious enough.

'Monster?' he suggested, amused again. Suddenly, to her horror, he took a step toward her, and seizing her in his power-ful arms, drew her to him. Her heart caught in her throat as she was crushed against his naked chest. She could feel the pounding of his heart, and the frightened fluttering of her own in response.

'You had other words when I held you in my arms, when you

clung to me,' he whispered hoarsely. She could not speak, could barely move in the crushing embrace of his arms.

Suddenly his mouth fastened hungrily upon hers, his tongue invading her mouth as he had once before invaded her body.

Her head swam. The heat from the fire seemed suddenly to sear her flesh and yet she shivered as an unaccountable chill zigzagged up and down her spine. Her legs were too weak to support her and she lay weakly against him, feeling the length of his strong, hard body pressed against hers.

As suddenly as it had begun, the kiss ended. He released her, holding her arms back from him, and she swayed unsteadily, all but falling into his arms again. Her breasts heaved with the effort of regaining her breath.

'Good night, my dear,' he said, as casually as if the kiss had not happened.

Her hand went to her crimson cheeks. For a moment she could only stare wide-eyed at him, half of her afraid that he might seize her again, the other afraid that he would not. Then, in an agony of confusion, she turned and fled from him, from the room, running until she had reached the safety of her own room and could fling herself upon her bed.

12

Her husband came to her room the following morning, while she was still in bed eating breakfast. He was already dressed for traveling, and so easily, so naturally had he slipped into the role of country farmer that she felt a slight sense of shock to see him again dressed as the Parisian nobleman. Of the two roles, the former sat more gracefully upon him.

'I've come to tell you that I will be leaving the carriage,' he said, advancing no further than the door of the room.

A quick surge of hope flared in her breast, but was as quickly dashed. 'For your own protection,' he added, 'I've ordered the servants to see that you do not attempt to go abroad in it.'

'For my own protection?' she asked drily.

'Of course. The disturbances besetting France just now are

not restricted to Paris. There's been some activity in the country as well. There've been rumors of uprisings in some of the smaller towns, even on some of the estates near here. You have nothing to fear from the servants here – you need have no worries on that score – but not all of the working class are of the same mind. I wouldn't care to have you meet up with a band of revolutionaries from someone else's farm. Suitable brides are not so easy to come by in these troubled times.'

'I can't imagine they'd treat me any worse than I've already been treated,' she snapped. 'If you had an iota of sense, or even kindness, you'd release me from our marriage and send my papa and me back to Paris where we belong.'

'Once a man starts going back on his bargains, he's soon not fit to make any,' he said. The look of mocking amusement had left his face, however, and for a moment his expression was softer, almost sad.

She seized upon the opportunity at once, leaping from her bed despite the fact that she wore only the flimsiest of silk nightgowns, and rushed across the room to him, looking up at him with all the appeal she could manage.

'Then at least take me to Paris with you,' she coaxed. She smiled with her lips parted, her face upturned, an open invitation to a kiss.

And for a moment he weakened; she could see it in the confusion in his eyes. 'But what on earth for?' he asked. 'I've told you, the streets aren't safe, even for myself and my servants. The city's in shambles, rioting and burning everywhere, looters in every house – it isn't the Paris you remember, nor one you'd want to, I'm afraid. Why would you want to go there?'

She hesitated. She could hardly tell him that in Paris she had friends whom she could count on to protect her from him, who would give her sanctuary, tell her how to free herself from this devil's pact of a marriage.

'I want to see for myself,' she said, pouting a little. 'There are things I want to get – even if the city is in an uproar, all the shops can't be closed – and people I want to see.'

She glanced up hesitantly and stopped; his face had gone hard as granite again.

'Such as?' he demanded.

'Why, all sorts of people. I've got relatives there, and girl friends, and – and . . . '

'And your foolish guardsman, Emile. That was his name, wasn't it?'

'He wasn't foolish,' she said without thinking.

'That's it, isn't it? You think you will fly to his arms and everything will be mended?' He turned angrily from her and paced across the room. 'By God, I thought I'd pounded him out of you, at least. I thought I'd taught you what a man was like. But he's still there, isn't he, imbedded in your hot loins. You fool, do you think he'd have you – do you think he'd even want you? He already got what he wanted from you.'

'He would have me,' she cried, forgetting guile in her own anger. 'He loved me; he still does, I know he does. And he's a better man than you'll ever be.'

He suddenly came to her, seizing her shoulders in a grip so tight that it threatened to tear the skin. 'He's not a man at all. He's a trinket, an ornament, a convenient device attached to a rich woman's bed, bought and paid for by her, and by me before that. Do you hear me? He sold you to me for a handful of gold – that's how much he loved you.'

Silence fell between them like a thick curtain. She felt stunned, as if he had slapped her. He released his hold on her, and for a long moment she did not move at all.

'Anne,' he said, his voice dropping to a whisper, 'I'm sorry, I shouldn't have said . . . '

'I hate you,' she said. She brought her hand up and very deliberately raked her nails across his face, leaving bloody furrows that stretched the width of one broad cheek. He neither moved nor flinched. Their eyes met, and for a moment there was an unspeakable sadness in his.

Then, once again, he smiled his mocking smile and, taking a step back from her, he bowed.

'My dear,' he said, 'the field is yours. I withdraw my forces.'

He turned on his heel and left her, but as he went out the door, he said over his shoulder, 'But the war it not over yet.'

The door closed only a second or two before the cup with the still warm chocolate shattered against it.

She wasted no time once he had gone in ordering the carriage brought around for her, only to be informed that it was not in running condition; an axle, whatever that was, had been broken and it would take some days to mend it.

Nor did she take this at face value, but made her own way to the stables, where she found the carriage with one wheel on, one wheel off. She was angry and took it out on poor Christian and Henriette, only to face the truth later that they were only following orders. She spent several days trying to make it up to them by exceptional kindness, but her anger at her husband did not lessen in the least.

For all her anger, however, there was nothing she could do for the present but accept the situation that had been forced upon her. Had she had the use of a carriage, she might have been able to escape to Paris with Papa, but she could hardly set him atop a horse in his present condition, and she dared not go without him for fear of what her husband might do in revenge.

She settled herself to wait for her husband's return, but it was only a temporary surrender. Like him, she found comfort in repeating to herself that the war was not over simply because they had reached a stalemate.

In the meantime, truth to tell, things were not as bad as one might have imagined. For all its primitiveness, the big old house was surprisingly cheery and comfortable. Henriette and her daughter ran it with a silent efficiency. In the de Grenville home in Paris, or even at their chateau to the south, Anne recalled, her mama had been forever after the servants for some neglected chore or some job done badly, but here it was impossible to think of a need or a desire that Henriette hadn't anticipated and seen to already.

Another war of sorts had erupted in the kitchen, where Cook had been reigning since her arrival until the last day or two, when the baron's chef from Paris, heretofore limited by a leg that had been wounded in the flight from Paris, had begun to hobble about, 'making a nuisance', as Cook liked to phrase it.

Their shouted disagreements could be heard plainly from the dining-room. Anne found herself caught in the cross fire just once, and since then had avoided the kitchen as one might a battlefield. When Cook, the first night, came to her room in tears to complain, Anne had told her simply and firmly that she must take up her complaints with Henriette, who, as she understood it, was in charge of running the house. Afterward she had congratulated herself on her diplomacy and pretended not to notice that Henriette was in a temper for an entire day.

It was not quite true, as Jeanette had told her earlier, that all the baron's servants had accompanied them to the farm. Only one of the maids, and she with child and confined to bed since her arrival, had come; his driver and a footman, who had accompanied her husband on his trip to Paris; his butler; his majordomo Philippe; and two stewards; all of whom were now at work in the vineyards, as her husband had been until his departure.

Once she had asked Philippe if he did not resent being reduced to groveling in the dirt like a peasant, but he had only smiled and informed her that he had been raised on a little vineyard in Burgundy.

'Anyway,' he said, 'we're all of us glad to share whatever the master's lot.'

She found the remark baffling, although she had already come to see that the baron's servants were unfailingly devoted to him. Of course, Jeanette and Cook had remained faithful to her through everything, and all her old servants had been fond of her, but somehow it didn't seem the same thing.

Her days went pleasantly enough. She found herself rising much earlier than had been her custom in Paris, and with an appetite that her mama would have criticized as bad manners. The weather was refreshing after the muggy heat of the city, the sky was blue, or sometimes a tender, luminous gray, but never harsh, never too hot. The air had a sweet, fresh scent to it that made one want to swallow whole mouthfuls of it greedily. She spent part of each morning and afternoon with Papa, reading aloud to him, or chatting while she embroidered, a pastime she had resented being forced to learn as a girl, but which now she found enjoyable.

She discovered that Christian and his daughter were accustomed to sitting together in the evenings in the shade of a great old chestnut tree, talking quietly while the old man puffed on a pipe or sometimes whittled, holding the wood between his knees and wielding the knife with his one remaining hand.

She envied them, the old man and the girl. They had in common that the world was not theirs; she was not yet its heir and his reign had already ended.

From Christian and Henriette she learned a little of the history of the place. The main core of the house dated back to the Romans, and even the most recent additions were centuries old. The records did not reveal who had first planted the vineyards – perhaps the grapes had grown wild there at one time – or who had installed the press in the winery; they were said to have been there when an order of monks took over the place in the twelfth century.

For two hundred years it had functioned as an abbey. Then it had passed into private hands, a gift from the church, perhaps to some helpful nobleman. It had changed hands in several wars before finally coming into the hands of the elder de Brussac.

Anne fancied that with a little money and some taste the place could be made quite livable; but, of course, such a project was not for her. She had resolved to return to Paris at the earliest possible opportunity.

But in the meantime, although she'd sooner have bitten her tongue off than tell Jean de Brussac so, she was not altogether miserable in the place.

If only she didn't have such an insufferable beast for a husband!

13

Nearly three weeks went by, and there was no word from the baron. She began to wonder if he hadn't decided after all that he, too, preferred living in Paris. Although the days had gone quickly enough, the possibility that he had left her to gather dust in the country and taken himself off to the more glamorous city life was infuriating, and she began once again to plot how she might engineer her own return to Paris.

Unfortunately, Papa did not seem to have gotten any better, despite the care and attention he was receiving. It was as if something of him had died with Mama; he lacked a critical *elan vital*, a will to live. He was a broken man who seemed to be resigned to spending the rest of his days as an invalid. Paris, his own home, his old cronies, might restore the spark of life to him, but how was she to get him to Paris in his present condition?

She thought and she schemed, but before she could put any of her schemes into action, something occurred that changed everything.

It was afternoon. She was in Papa's bedroom, reading to him from Madame de Staël's *Corinne*, a copy of which she had found in the antiquated library downstairs, when Jeanette burst into the room, beside herself with agitation.

'Madame, Madame,' she cried, dancing about the foot of the bed, 'they're coming, they're coming, oh, we shall be burned alive, oh, Madame!' At this point she burst into tears and began to sob into her hands so that her words were entirely incomprehensible.

'Jeanette, for heaven's sake, stop that blubbering and tell me what's wrong. Who's coming?'

'The revolutionists,' Jeanette cried. 'They're burning everything as they come, oh, we shall be killed. I know it.'

Anne felt a sharp stab of fear. She dropped the book and hurried to the window. Papa's bedroom was to the front of the house, and from here one could just see the rooftops of a neighboring farm.

Or one used to see the rooftops. What she saw now was a column of smoke, billowing upward, and an occasional flicker of flames.

She was so startled by the sight that the breath left her lungs in a gasp. But that wasn't the half of it. Between that fire and the window at which she stood was movement – a swarm of people – men, women, even children – marching. Marching with scythes, hoes, muskets, torches. Marching toward her, along the road, across the fields. As she watched, several of them ran to a field of wheat that grew alongside the road, golden and ready for harvest, and fired it with torches. She saw a curtain of fire and smoke begin to snake across the field in a wild, zigzag pattern.

A mob of rioters, and she was alone in the house with Papa and Jeanette and old Henriette and her daughter. A kaleidoscope of images raced and tumbled through her mind – that horrible drive through Paris on her wedding night; her lovely home in Paris, looted and burned; stories Jeanette and Cook had told her of assaults on helpless women.

Her first impulse was to hide under the bed, to run screaming down the stairs, to do anything to escape. But when she looked again and saw how close the rioters already were, she knew there was no time left for escape.

'Where are the men servants?' she asked, her heart racing.

'They're all in the far vineyard, with Mister Christian,' Jeanette said.

'Jeanette, you must run and get them – hurry.'

'Oh, Madame, I can't,' Jeanette sobbed, sinking into the chair that Anne had vacated and breaking again into uncontrollable sobs. 'I'm too frightened to run, and besides I know they'll catch me and – and . . . oh!'

'In the name of heaven, Jeanette, you must get hold of yourself,' Anne cried. She went to the servant and shook her shoulders violently, but Jeanette only cried the louder, her head jerking limply back and forth until it looked as if it must fly off her shoulders.

Anne let her go. It was hopeless. For a moment she too wanted to fall down and cry with terror, but she fought the impulse. What could she do? If she went for the servants herself, she must leave Papa helpless and unprotected. She thought of all he had suffered already; she thought of Mama, trapped in her overturned coach while they fired it . . .

That thought sobered her, and a flash of anger subdued her fear for a moment. Damn them, they had cost her too much already. How dare they come here like locusts to strip her papa from her as well?

'Daughter.' In all her excitement she had all but forgotten that Papa was there, watching and listening. His voice, a mere croak of a whisper, brought her back to the present.

'In my bag,' he said, pointing, 'in the armoire – a pistol.'

A pistol! She ran to the armoire, flinging the doors wide. The bag – where was his bag – Lord in heaven, if that fool Jeanette had carried it off somewhere . . . she saw it then, pushed to the back. She dragged the bag out, jerking it open. The pistol lay within, gleaming and wicked-looking. She took it in trembling hands. It looked as if it had never been fired; probably it had not. What would poor Papa have needed to fire a gun for in all these years?

'Jeanette,' she said, her voice trembling so that she could scarcely form the words. 'You stay with Papa. If they should come up here . . . ' She stopped; she had no instructions to give. If they should come up here, then it was all over, and by that time she would be – but she mustn't think those thoughts or she would collapse into hysteria like Jeanette.

Jeanette's answer was to shriek and sob all the louder. Her heart pounding, Anne started for the door, holding the pistol down at her side.

'Anne.' It was Papa again. She looked back, meeting his eyes, and saw a determination in them she had not seen since he had fled Paris. 'The sword on the wall, there over the mantel – bring it to me before you go.'

She hurried to the mantel and yanked one of the crossed swords down; it looked more ornamental than useful, but it was better than nothing. She carried it to the bed and placed the handle in her papa's outstretched hand.

'Never forget,' he said in a fierce whisper, 'you are a de Grenville.'

She had a fleeting urge to fling herself across the bed into his arms, but the strength and courage in his look held her back. Biting her lip to keep back the tears, she ran from the room, pattering along the halls and down the broad stairs. ·

As she reached the corridor below, a noise from the direction of the kitchen made her start in terror. She turned and saw Henriette there, an enormous cleaver from the kitchen clasped in one hand. For a fraction of a moment, Anne thought the cleaver was meant for her; after all, Henriette was a peasant, too, of the same class as that mob moving toward the house.

The two women looked at one another steadily. Henriette's eyes dropped to the pistol in Anne's hand and she gave a grunt of approval.

'I've sent the girl for the men,' she said.

Anne gave a breath of relief and hurried on to the front door, Henriette's heavy tread following her.

The intruders were just coming up the drive, shouting and laughing and calling to one another as they came. For a moment they did not see the two women standing in the shadow of the entryway, but Anne, standing with the pistol down at her side, hidden in the folds of her skirt, could see them well enough – the sweat, the excited expressions, even the stubble on the men's faces. Her legs felt as if they could no longer support her and she had a horrible fear that at any moment she might faint after all. There were so many of them and they looked so wild, and against them stood only Henriette with her cleaver and she with a pistol she didn't even know how to use. She tried to remember what her husband had done that night – but the man had been right there before him, at the window of the carriage.

God in heaven, she longed to turn and run, hide, something, she would never be able to stand here and face them; if it weren't for Henriette behind her, she wouldn't stay a second longer . . .

Someone saw her then. A shout went up, becoming a murmur that rippled back through the mob. They came to a stop no more than thirty feet from where she stood, all eyes fastened upon her.

She opened her mouth to say something, anything, but nothing would come out but a tiny squeak of sound. She knew that if anyone moved toward her, she would begin to cry, or even to run.

Oh, why didn't the men come?

The tension seemed to crackle like lightning in the air. One of the men, the leader, it seemed, took a step forward. Anne tried to lift the pistol, but her arm seemed frozen in place.

She was so frightened that at first she did not even hear the clatter of approaching hooves – not until her husband rode into view, followed close behind by the two servants who had accompanied him.

The waiting mob seemed spellbound. They watched the approaching horsemen in silence. Anne watched, too, amazed that her husband could look so unperturbed, riding with only two servants to confront a mob of thirty or forty people. He rode up quickly but with no apparent alarm and swung himself down from his horse, striding toward the leader of the group. Anne saw a few weapons raised, heard a low mutter or two, but the baron seemed not to notice.

He might have been welcoming a delegation of the local gentry to his farm. He grinned, he clapped the leader upon the shoulders; they greeted one another. Her husband greeted the others, seeming to know everyone there by name. Anne could not hear what was being said, but she could sense that the outcome was teetering in the balance. The mob of peasants and farm workers looked unsure of themselves, hesitant. They exchanged glances, shifted their weight uneasily, some of them whispering to one another.

One of the throng approached the baron. Suddenly, to Anne's relief, the stranger grinned at something the baron said. He turned to his companions and spoke, and a ripple of laughter ran through the crowd. It seemed to carry the tension away with it. Anne let out the breath she had been holding.

'Henriette,' the baron called, turning toward the house. 'Call the men in from the fields. Ring the bell; our neighbors have come to sample our new wine. And send the maids out to pour.'

Henriette pushed past Anne and hurried around the corner of the house, no doubt to head off the approaching servants. The baron shouted to the throng and pointed toward the buildings that housed the wine press and the storage casks, and the people began to move in that direction.

He came up to the house then, walking briskly; not until he

was close enough to look into her face did she see the strain in his.

He saw the gun, still down at her side. 'Put that away before someone sees it and gets excited,' he said. He slipped off his cloak and thrust it at her. 'They'll want to meet you. Try to be gracious – and for God's sake, pinch your cheeks, you're white as a ghost.'

He did not wait for a reply but hurried off again to join his guests. For once she was only too happy to do his bidding, although she could not help being a little peeved at being scolded for having a gun; after all, whose fault was it that she was here anyway, with no one to protect her?

It was late by the time the last of their 'guests' had straggled off, some of the men clinging to one another and weaving slightly as they went down the drive.

For Anne, it had been an exhausting, mind-shattering experience. She came into the house and finding a fire already burning in her husband's library, went in and sank gratefully into one of the big, comfortable chairs there. Just now she was too tired even to climb the stairs to her own room.

She was still there when her husband came in half an hour later. Unlike her, he looked actually buoyed up by the experience. He had seemed to have no difficulty rubbing elbows with the peasants as if they were his equals; not that he was so far above them, she added wryly.

He paused when he saw her, as if he were going to speak to her, then went to the decanter of wine that sat atop his desk.

'That was a brave thing you did earlier,' he said, pouring a glass of wine. 'Defending my home and possessions with only a pistol.'

'Pooh, I don't give a hang about your home or your possessions, I just didn't want them burning the place down with Papa and me in it.'

He laughed without rancor. 'You're beginning to talk like a farm wife,' he said, bringing her a glass of the wine. 'Here, taste this.'

She was really in no mood for sipping wine with him and was on the verge of refusing, but perhaps the wine would give her a lift. She took it and swallowed a mouthful, grimacing as it went down.

'Personally, I prefer something sweeter,' she said.

'You have abominable taste, my dear.' He took a sip of the

wine, rolling it about in his mouth experimentally before he swallowed.

'Well, I don't know why that should matter to anyone,' she snapped.

'It might. We're going to become vintners – wine makers. I've been disposing of most of my holdings in Paris – what hadn't already been seized or burned. This will become our world, this farm. We'll call the wine Chateau Brussac, if that suits you.'

'Call it Chateau My Foot for all I care; I have no intention of digging dirt and picking grapes like those oafs who were here today.'

'Perhaps you should, my dear. There's a certain satisfaction in growing things that cannot be found in anything else. Plants, flowers, crops – children, even.' He paused, studying her for a moment with an unfamiliar expression on his face. Suddenly, to her surprise, he put his wine aside and came to her chair, kneeling beside her.

'Anne,' he said in a far gentler voice, 'we've gotten off on a bad footing. It's my fault; I'm too used to acting first and thinking afterward. That's the way it's always been for me, and I can't apologize for what I am. What I'm trying to say is simply, couldn't we make a new start, you and I?'

The nearness of him frightened her. Fleeting images flashed through her mind of other moments when they had been close this way – the morning they had arrived here, the night she had gone to him in his bedroom, their wedding – each time different, and now here he was, in yet another role. What a man of contradictions he was! Each time she thought she had gotten him clear in her mind, he revealed another face. It was like being married to a score of men, and she hardly knew which of them frightened her most.

She got to her feet, afraid to trust the gentle pleading in his eyes.

'You can't apologize for what you are?' she said. 'Do you even know what you are?'

He grinned sheepishly. 'A barbarian, I suppose, in your eyes, at least. Closer to that than an aristocrat, surely.'

'You are a – a savage,' she said, groping for the right word and not quite finding it. 'I don't know what you are. I watched you today with those – peasants, and you might as well have been one of them, and I've seen you in Paris and I know that you have polish and manners and gentility, and you dance beautifully – I suppose you could have done that jig with them that the farmers were doing today – '

'I know it. I didn't think you'd approve if I joined in.'

'You're not like anyone I've ever known – or wanted to know. You might almost have sprung from that dirt you're so enamored with.'

'Is that so terrible a thing?'

'It is for me,' she snapped. 'It isn't what I had in mind for a husband, certainly.'

'What did you want, Anne? What sort of husband would you have chosen? Oh, I know, that young man – but suppose that had never happened either. Suppose you could pick and choose – what then?'

'Well, a gentleman, surely, a real gentleman, someone of aristocratic blood, someone refined and polite and considerate, someone who wouldn't trundle me about like a piece of baggage and make me do things I didn't want to do.'

He had remained kneeling by her chair. Now he got up slowly and dusted off the knees of his breeches. He refilled his wine glass.

'Then I'm afraid there's not much hope for a new start, is there? Because I could never be those things, you see. I am what I am – this man who sprang from the dirt, as you put it. You called me a savage and I'm that, too. I've lived in a wilderness as fierce and untamed as any jungle ever braved by explorers. Those aristocrats you speak of so fondly – how many of them do you think would like to stab me in the back or slit my throat, given half a chance, only they haven't the courage. I have what I have because I've wrested it from them. I've fought and conquered and, yes, even killed, and I will do it all again if I must.'

'Then why did you marry me?' she cried.

He gave a bitter smile and went to the fireplace, staring down into its flames. He spoke without turning, his back to her.

'I'm not a fool, if that's what you're thinking. I had no delusions regarding your feelings for me or your motives – you married me for my money, and because your guardsman had jilted you. You were spoiled and lazy and amoral, like all your class. The de Grenville blood – that aristocratic blood of which you speak so proudly – has long since gone sour, my dear, like – like badly aged wine. I knew from the first that you were thoughtless, even cruel, and that you did not love me.'

'Then why?'

He was so long in answering that she thought he had not
heard, had even forgotten she was there, and when his answer
came, it was not what she might have expected.

'Because you are rare and beautiful, like a precious gem.
Because when you laughed – and that was more often than
you realized, despite your unhappy romance – it was like the
rushing of a brook that has come down from the high, clean
places far in the hills, places I had known as a young man and
could no longer find my way back to.

'Because for all your beauty, for all your willfulness, you
are a child still – a spoiled child, true, but lovely, and with
something yet of innocence. Perhaps even because you were
in love. You were a fool to believe in love, but I found your
very foolishness endearing. I thought you would make a suitable wife for me. I thought I could see to it, that I could shape
you to my will, as I have all the circumstances of my life – as
I did that callow and greedy young man you were in love with.'

It was the longest and most poetic speech she had ever heard
him make. and while it flattered her, it disturbed her too,
because it suggested that he knew her in some ways better than
she knew herself, and because again it roused feelings in her
that she did not want roused.

'Well, I don't know that I care to be shaped to anyone's will,'
she said, taking refuge in haughtiness because she did not
know how else to deal with this situation. 'Like a lump of clay.'

'Anne – ' he began, but she interrupted him, putting her
fingers to her temples.

'Please,' she said, 'I – I'm very tired. It has been a long day;
I want to go to bed now. You . . . no, enough – good night.'

She fled from the room, not even waiting for his reply, and
ran in confusion to her own room.

But when she was there, in her bed, in the darkness, she
found no refuge from her own confusion, from her own longings.

So much had happened to her – her marriage, the move to
the country, the loss of her mother and, in another sense, of
her father as well – all the excitement, the anxiety, today's
terror and yesterday's comfortable existence – they all whirled
about in her mind, bumping into one another, sending her
thoughts reeling.

She felt an unfamiliar ache that she could not quite identify, an oppressive emptiness within herself. She longed for something, someone to cling to. She was lonely and restless, and she would almost have welcomed her husband's embrace. Her bed seemed vast and so – so very empty.

14

She woke feeling sickish in the morning. The weather had turned cool overnight and suddenly there was the sharp hint of autumn in the air. She rose, shivering at the touch of the cold floor upon her bare feet, and dressed herself without ringing for help. She had discovered in these past few weeks that she would as lief do this chore herself as have to listen to Jeanette's silly chatter so early in the day.

After yesterday's excitement, the house seemed much too still. Jean had taken all the available help into the vineyards with him. Cook was in the garden outside the kitchen, selecting vegetables for the day's meals. Only Henriette was in the kitchen, peeling potatoes, which she tossed into a massive pot for a stew to feed the help.

Henriette jumped up as Anne came in and would have begun preparing a huge breakfast, but Anne forestalled her.

'No, please, I'm not at all hungry,' she said, laying a hand over her stomach, which was still queasy. 'Just some chocolate, and I'll have it out here, thank you.'

She had grown bored with taking her meals alone in the large dining-room, and the kitchen was so much cheerier, with its battered old round table and all the cooking smells. She sat in one of the carved chairs and sipped the warm chocolate that Henriette brought her.

At first Henriette had been uncomfortable with this invasion of the kitchen by the mistress of the house, but she had gotten used to seeing Anne at the table, sometimes watching her, sometimes gazing out the window across the fields to the vineyards.

The two women sat in silence for a time. It was Anne who finally broke the stillness. 'Henriette,' she began, 'yesterday, when those people came, why did you not join them?'

Henriette looked dumbfounded by the question. 'Madame?' was all she said.

'I mean, they're your people, your class – isn't that what all this nonsense is about, class against class – those people had masters too, and they turned against them. And why did they stop here? Why didn't they burn this house down the same as the others?'

'The seigneur is well known here,' Henriette said. 'They know what kind of man he is.'

She seemed to think this explained everything. For a moment Anne contemplated the remark. Finally she asked, 'What kind of man is he?'

Henriette looked across at her as if to see if Madame were joking. When at last she spoke, she did not answer the question directly.

'All my life, since I was first married,' she said, returning her attention to the potatoes while she talked, 'I wanted a child, but the good Lord did not see fit to bless me. And finally, they said I was too old for children. But God thought differently, and one day I discovered I was with child. We were very happy, my man and I, even though it meant he must work twice as hard. It was a difficult time for me – my age, you understand.'

Anne had learned that Henriette always referred to Christian not as her husband but as 'my man', and although he was old and crippled and they could not possibly experience what Anne thought of as love anymore, Henriette made the simple phrase ring with pride the way she said it.

'We were serfs on another farm, some miles from here. We worked the soil and gave most of what we made to the master, and if we were lucky there was enough left for us.

'Then one day my man had an accident. The axe slipped while he was cutting wood, and he lost his hand. He was miles from home, and by the time he had gotten there so I could look after him, he'd bled a great deal. For days old Death and I fought one another over him, till he saw how stubborn I was. My man always said I was too stubborn for my own good, but sometimes it pays.'

She paused for a moment, smiling more to herself than to Anne, and shook her head at the memory.

'It was a hard time,' she went on finally. 'He could not work. I scratched the soil as best I could, but in time we lost our holding. There was nothing to do but take to the road.

'It was in the fall of the year – like now, only a bit later – and cold already; I remember the coldness, like a kitchen knife cutting through you. It began to storm, and then my time came. I thought that we must surely die, that God had seen fit after all to punish me for my stubbornness. But my man, he went off for a while and when he came back he said he had found shelter. We came here, to one of the sheds, and hid inside, and there the child was born.

'Your husband found us there soon after. I was so frightened of what he might do, I would have run if I'd had the strength. But he did not even have us beaten. He brought us here – here,' she emphasized. 'Right into this very house, and I was put into an actual bed, the sort the master used to sleep in where we were before. I had never slept on anything but a pallet or the ground.'

She still seemed not quite able to comprehend the wonder of such luxury, and again a soft smile played across her usually stern features.

'Of course,' she added, 'I was not cared for so tenderly as you when you were with fever.'

'Was he really by my side then?' Anne asked. 'I thought I must have dreamed it.'

'He would not leave you until the fever had broken, not even to take a meal. I had to bring food to him there and coax him to eat. And the doctor who came from the village was afraid for his own life if you didn't recover – but there, he wouldn't thank me for telling you this.'

'Perhaps not. But I do,' Anne said.

After a moment Henriette continued with her story. 'Later,' she said, 'when I was able to be up again, he asked us if we would like to stay. He gave us a piece of land for our own. He said the land and what we grew on it would belong to us, all except a small portion we could pay him for rent. But more than that, we could work for him, not as serfs but as . . . ' she hesitated, groping for a word. 'I do not know the word he used; it meant he would pay us for our work, in actual coins, to do with as we wished.

'I had never heard of such a thing, and I told my man this gentleman must be mad, that we should steal away during the night before something dreadful happened to us. But my man was wiser than I. We stayed. And here, God willing, we shall live out our lives – and no bunch of rowdies will harm the master, or what belongs to him, save they kill me first.'

It was a long speech for the old woman, more than Anne had ever heard her say before, and although she had spoken calmly, Anne saw that there was a warning glint in her eyes.

'He is a good man, Madame,' Henriette concluded. 'A fine

man.' Then, as if embarrassed at having expressed herself so openly, Henriette gave the potato in her hand a vicious stab with her knife, almost halving it.

Anne was disturbed by the story, and she found herself remembering it throughout the day. She saw for the first time that she had treated her husband unfairly, and that she was as much to blame as he that their marriage had gone so badly. In the blindness of her love for Emile and her resentment at being pressured into a marriage she had not wanted, she had been unable to really see the man she was marrying. She had misjudged him.

Oh, it was true; he was strong-willed and forceful, violent, even, when danger threatened or his wishes were defied. But he could be gentle, too, and generous to a fault. She owed him her papa's life – for that matter, she owed him her own as well. Had she been in Paris, she might have died with Mama; and later, when her own foolhardy actions had brought her to bed with a fever, he had devoted himself to making her well.

Not only had he saved her and her family, but he had saved her servants, those who wanted to be saved, and his own as well, bringing them to safety and giving them a home, just as he had given Christian and Henriette a home years before. And he had given them more than a home; he had given them pride, opportunity, something of their own to live and work for.

It was little wonder that the peasant mob that had come here the day before had hesitated to do harm, had accepted his welcome and drunk his wine and gone on without burning the house as they had burned other houses throughout the area.

What a fool she had been! She had been selfish and stubborn, blind to reality and cruel where cruelty was not deserved.

Of course, she did not love him. That was out of the question. But Mama had said that love was unimportant in making a good marriage. Perhaps it was even better that she had no such feelings for her husband to cloud her judgment. She saw how love had blinded her toward Emile; but in her marriage she would be able to keep a clear head.

Alone later in her room, she vowed that she would make a success of their marriage. She would be humble and sweet to repay him for all he had done for her. She was no fool; she knew it would mean submitting to his desires as well, but upon reflection she decided that was not such a great sacrifice.

With another shock of self-discovery, she realized that part of the longing she had been experiencing had been physical desire. Of course, it was not he who had awakened that desire, but Emile; still, in the dark she could pretend. And, too, her husband's embraces had not been altogether odious, if she were honest with herself.

She made up her mind that she would see her husband when he came in from the vineyards and, this time without quarreling, let him know she was willing to attempt a fresh start.

She was doomed to be thwarted in her plans, however. With his return from Paris, her husband and virtually all of the servants worked from dawn until long after sundown in the vineyards gathering grapes. The weather had turned cold; Christian was predicting an early and severe frost, and it was important that the grapes be picked before that happened.

Anne waited until quite late, sitting up in bed and trying to read a novel, but at length she fell asleep without hearing her husband come in.

When she woke in the morning, the queasiness she had experienced the day before was even more pronounced. She asked that breakfast be served in her room, and as soon as she had eaten it, brought it right back up again.

Henriette brought her a *tisane*, which she said would make Anne feel better. A hot bath was carried to the bedroom, and while Jeanette helped her bathe, Anne several times discovered Henriette regarding her with a critical eye, as if she had discovered something peculiar about her.

'Is something wrong?' Anne asked finally, impatient with the old woman's scrutiny, but Henriette only clucked her tongue and hurried from the room.

She was right about one thing, though. By the time Anne had drunk the *tisane* and taken a hot bath, she felt much better, although she was puzzled by the nature of her malady. If it continued, Anne decided, she would ask that the doctor be called in from the village. Perhaps this was some lingering after-effect from the fever she'd had before.

When she had dressed, this time with Jeanette's help, Anne stepped onto the little balcony off her bedroom for a breath of air. She was surprised to see Henriette below, hurrying across the field in the direction of the vineyards. If Henriette was going to pick grapes, too, who would run the house?

She shrugged and went back into her bedroom. She had learned since she had been here that it was best to leave the running of the household in Henriette's more than capable hands and not worry herself over such matters.

She went across the hall to Papa's room, but he was still asleep. She stood looking fondly down at him; how little and frail he looked; how had she always thought of him as a towering giant? Why, he could hardly reach to her husband's shoulders when standing.

She felt a sudden pang of sadness. As if a curtain had been held aside for a moment to give her a glimpse of the future, she realized that her father would not stand again. This room, this bed, was his home now, and he would never leave them until he set out on that final journey. And then there would be no one left for her to cling to – no one but her husband.

She was restless and half-toyed with the idea of strolling out to the fields, but she realized she could hardly speak openly to her husband with everyone there to listen. Instead she went back to her bedroom and, making herself comfortable on the chaise, took up the novel she had been glancing at the night before.

She had read only a few pages when she heard heavy footsteps coming up the stairs – two at a time, it seemed – and a moment later her husband fairly burst into her room, pausing just inside the door.

He was dirty and sweat-streaked, and breathing so hard that he must have run all the way from the vineyards, and there was a gleam of excitement in his eyes that was almost frightening.

'Is it true?' he demanded.

She put the book aside and half-rose from the lounge. 'Well, since I don't know what you're talking about,' she said, 'I can hardly tell you if it's true or not.'

'A baby – you're going to have a baby?' he asked. 'My baby?'

'Why, I . . . ' she was so stunned that words failed her. She could only stare back at him and shake her head in bewilderment.

'Henriette told me you're with child,' he said, taking another step into the room.

With child? Lord in heaven, the idea hadn't even crossed her mind, and yet . . . now that the possibility was presented to her, she knew instinctively that it was true, as if at once she could feel within herself that new presence, a new life beginning to flower.

'I – I suppose I am,' she said, still too shaken to know quite what to make of this turn of events.

And suddenly her husband was across the room, had gathered her into his arms to kiss her. But this was not the cruel, the demanding embrace of the past; this was something altogether different. It was gentle, it was loving, it was a silent plea for forgiveness, for fresh beginnings. It was as if the seed within her had created a new thread of sensitivity between them, so that she could feel the feelings of his heart, read the messages of his mind.

For a moment, for one breathless moment, it seemed to her as if their innermost beings had become one, and this time she did not struggle against him but clung to him and returned his kiss, and felt the surge of joy that leapt up within him.

And when he lifted her in his arms and carried her tenderly to her bed, she had a wonderful realization that for the first time they had truly become man and wife.

And she was glad.

15

That night her husband slept in Anne's room for the first time since that day they arrived at the chateau. Surprisingly, it was he who was reluctant, and she, thinking of all the lonely nights she had spent in the vast, empty reaches of that bed, who persuaded him.

'I don't want to harm the child,' he said. 'Suppose I bump into you during the night?'

She smiled and reassured him. 'I don't think we need to worry about that just yet. And anyway, if you go bumping around in the night, I shall give you a kick for your troubles. Besides, later, when the bed gets too crowded, we can always have something moved in for you to sleep on.'

'First I'm ousted from my own bedroom,' he grumbled. 'And now I'm to sleep on a cot – or would you favor a pallet of straw on the floor?'

She wrinkled her nose thoughtfully. 'Umm, a pallet, I think. If you're going to work like a peasant, you might as well sleep like one – unless, of course, you don't want to be close to your child?'

They were in bed still. He sat up and looking deep into her eyes, said, 'Make me a son, Madame.'

She laughed lightly. 'I'm afraid that's out of my hands.'

He was silent for a moment, thinking. Then he nodded and said, 'Yes, of course. And if it's a girl I shall love her as well.' He pulled Anne to him, into a tight embrace. 'Still, I've always wanted a son to carry on the line. I had given up hope, but now . . . perhaps.'

'Jean?' Her husband's name felt foreign to her lips and she said it experimentally, as if tasting a strange new fruit. 'Is this the first – I mean, have you ever fathered a child before?'

He was so long in answering that she thought perhaps he had fallen asleep. At length he said, 'I had a wife before, as you know. She died in childbirth. I blamed myself; I had chided her and told her she was foolish to be frightened. She said to me, "I've given you a son at least," and then she died. But the child followed her to the grave a day later.'

When he had again been silent for several moments, she asked hesitantly, 'Were there – no others?'

He laughed, dispelling the gloom that had descended upon them temporarily. 'I'd be pretty foolish to tell you I haven't bedded any women in the meantime, but to the best of my knowledge, no, none of them has had sons by me, or daughters, either, for that matter. If I'd had any bastard children I'd have taken them in and raised them properly. And as you can see, there's none around.'

'Yes, I can see,' she said, smiling to herself. For some reason she felt glad to know that hers would be his only child.

She snuggled contentedly against him, tracing a delicate pattern with the tips of her fingers in the hair of his chest, and wondered what had happened to the rough brute she had married. He had vanished, to be replaced by this great, gentle bear of a man, who had just made love to her with such fierce tenderness. If knowing that he was going to be a father could do this to a man, what would he be like when the child was born?

In the days that followed she discovered that her husband could truly be a gentle and considerate man. Indeed, so long as his dictates were not violated, he treated her like a queen.

At first they did not have a great deal of time to spend in one another's company. He had gone back to working all day in the vineyards. Once or twice she strolled out to watch the work, but she found that her arrival created so much confusion and so much delay in the work – everyone fussing so about her condition, and Jean stopping everything to find her a shady spot to sit, making her comfortable, hovering over her solicitously all the while she was there – that she had given up such visits and contented herself with remaining about the house.

She soon discovered, too, that her husband's exhausting work schedule did nothing to diminish his sexual desires. Now that he had been welcomed to her bed, he quickly proved himself a man of voracious appetites, as if he wanted to make up for the time that had been lost to them; sometimes the larks would be welcoming the dawn before he at last slept beside her, and she drifted off to sleep savoring the sweet ache that he had left within her.

To her surprise, this undiminished assault did not grow tiresome, as she might have expected; indeed, as night followed night, she found her own sexual appetites increasing, as if a passionate creature hidden within her were gradually being awakened. Jean was a consummate lover who seemed to know a thousand secret places upon her body with which he could rouse her to a fever pitch of excitement that matched and occasionally even surpassed his own.

'By God, I've got myself a lusty wench,' he declared.

She pouted and said, 'That's a pretty thanks I get for accommodating my husband.'

He smacked her bare backside as she tried to clamber out of bed. 'Madame,' he said, 'you accommodate a man with all the enthusiasm of a born strumpet. I think you had a harlot hidden beneath all those aristocratic trappings you used to wear.'

'A harlot?' she cried, offended. 'How dare you, you – you . . . ' Unable to think of a suitable insult, she flung one of her slippers at his head.

He ducked the missile and, laughing, slipped from the room and went off to his vineyards.

He found her bed less welcoming that night, however. She maintained an icy silence when he came in, and when he tried to interest her in lovemaking, she kept her back turned stubbornly to him.

At last, exasperated, he said, 'Very well, my dear, if there's going to be a wall between us, it might as well be a solid one.' With that he got out of bed and went off to his own room.

'Good,' she said when she heard the door of his room close

after him. 'Perhaps now I can get a good night's sleep for a change.'

Luck was against her, though. The night turned positively frigid. She tossed and turned, trying to find a warm spot in her bed, which seemed to have grown in size until it was like a frozen wasteland. She shivered and chattered her teeth and finally, much chagrined, stole along the corridor to his room and crept into her husband's bed.

He welcomed her wordlessly, his apology in the kisses he rained upon her eager flesh. Nor did she fail to notice that he, too, had been awake when she arrived.

Soon the grapes were harvested and the wine making began. Autumn was upon them now with its riot of color, and as the fruit in the orchard ripened, so did the seed within her grow toward its own fruition.

Anne began to show her condition early, a sign which Henriette assured her augured well for a son. 'A big strapping boy he'll be, too, mark my words,' she predicted confidently, which pleased Anne and caused Jean's chest to expand.

One evening in November, Jean surprised her with the announcement that he must be up early the following morning, as he had some special business to attend to. Her curiosity aroused, she pestered him endlessly for some clue to his plans, but he only shook his head and refused even the slightest hint.

'I won't sleep a wink all night,' she said when they were in bed.

'Well, then we may as well make use of the time,' he said, gathering her into his arms.

'Oh, you,' she said impatiently, thinking perhaps she would refuse him his gratification, but his warm kisses soon changed her mind.

Despite her insistence that she would be awake all night, she slept soundly enough. She was awake before dawn, though, only to discover that he was up before her and already gone from the room.

She rang for Jeanette, and by the time he returned Anne was ensconced in a tub of hot water, soaping her body and trying to think what her husband had planned.

'Will you be long?' he asked, standing by the tub and looking admiringly down at her naked loveliness. The bulge of her mid-section only seemed to make her more desirable in his eyes, and her condition had caused her ripe young breasts to swell invitingly.

'Not if you scrub my back,' she said, smiling and handing him a soapy cloth.

He knelt obediently and began to wash her back vigorously, but his hands soon began to move more slowly and to stray from her back.

'Oh, there's some soap there,' she said, indicating a puff of lather on one breast. 'Will you rinse it for me?'

He gritted his teeth, trying to ignore the increasing tightness of his trousers, and brushed the cloth over the offending mound, but a moment later he threw the cloth aside and covered the spot with his mouth instead. She shuddered and her soapy arms came up around his neck.

'Woman, if you keep this up,' he said, 'I'm going to take off my clothes and climb in there with you.'

'Only if you tell me what your secret is,' she teased him.

'At this rate, there isn't going to be any,' he said. 'If I don't get started for Paris soon, I'll never make it by nightfall.'

Her heart sank. Paris! Her husband was going off to Paris again, leaving her to her own devices here in the country, and in her present condition, too. She thrust her lower lip out and shoved him away from her, getting soap on the front of his shirt.

'Well, I hope you have a pleasant journey,' she said coolly.

'If you're going to sulk all the way, it's going to be a very quiet one,' he said, sitting back on his heels.

She could hardly believe her ears. 'Do you mean – are you going to take me with you?' she squealed. He grinned and nodded.

She clapped her hands with delight, but then she suddenly grew sober. 'But the baby – do you think it's safe?'

'I talked to the doctor about it,' he assured her. 'He tells me that so long as you don't overtire yourself, it should do no harm. And I've heard from Paris that things have settled down there, so we're not likely to be in any great danger in that respect, either.'

'Oh, Jean, how wonderful,' she cried, flinging her arms about him again so suddenly that he lost his balance and to the astonishment of both landed half in the tub with her.

They laughed heartily together and then, since his clothes

were already ruined, it seemed just as sensible to take them off
altogether and finish what they had already started, so that
after all it was nearly midmorning by the time they set out on
their journey.

16

'Look, the Café Michel is gone,' Anne cried, leaning out the
window of the carriage to view the burned-out shell of the
once-noted gathering place.

'If you keep hanging out the window like that, you're liable
to be gone, and the baby with you – damn!' Jean swore angrily
as someone emptied some slops out an upstairs window, splash-
ing the sleeve of his coat.

Anne did sit back in the carriage then, but her eyes remained
glued to the windows. They had arrived just as the light was
beginning to fade. It was a soft, gray day with the scent of
winter in the air; it had rained earlier and the streets glistened,
and little wisps of dark cloud drifted overhead in the wet wind.

She was home, in Paris, after what seemed an eternity. And
yet there was something foreign about the city, something that
was strange to her ears. The incessant chatter – had she gotten
so quickly used to the quiet of the country? And so much had
changed. It was not only the burned Café Michel; it was the
many landmarks, scorched or gone altogether; it was soldiers
on every corner, looking ill at ease and ready for trouble –
Jean had explained on the journey that since their departure,
Louis Philippe, the Duke of Orleans, had been proclaimed
King of the French and had managed to restore an uneasy
peace.

'But there are still difficulties,' Jean had warned. 'The radi-
cals are disappointed, although it was they who had him proclaimed king. And the workers are agitating. It will be many
years before France returns to normal, and I'm not entirely
sure Louis Philippe is the man for the job.'

Anne, who hadn't the slightest interest in politics, sat back
in her seat and watched Paris rush by in a cloud of forgotten
impressions that seemed to blot out the past few months as if
they had never existed. The sweet, the painful memories,

things she hadn't noticed, things she hadn't known she'd missed until she saw them now. Tall, severe-looking houses with wrought-iron balconies and shutters on the wet pavements; a huddle of tables beneath the awnings of a café; the smell of wine and cats and sewage . . . it all assailed her senses until she had to close her eyes and sink into the darkness of the carriage.

'We're here, my dear.' Her husband's voice was sympathetic and gentle, his hand light upon her arm as he helped her down.

They were staying at a hotel. 'It's impossible to get servants here in the city,' Jean explained, 'and I saw no point in bringing everyone in from the country for just a few days.'

The manager of the hotel came to greet them and see them to their suite. Anne, beset by emotion, tired from the long drive, saw everything through a blur, and she was more than glad to agree to her husband's suggestion that they have a quiet meal sent up and retire early. He himself looked restless, and she thought that he would rather go out, but she selfishly did not suggest it; she did not want to be alone this particular night, and when they were in bed later she was especially grateful for the feel of his arms about her.

'It's so noisy I'll never be able to sleep,' she complained. 'Can't you close the windows?'

'Dear girl, the windows *are* closed,' Jean informed her. 'You've forgotten what the city sounds like.'

They spent the following day shopping. Anne had brought voluminous lists, not only of things she wanted for herself, but items requested by others as well: Jeanette fancied some eau de cologne that she used to get at a little shop near the Louvre, and Cook had in mind a terrine she wanted to make for the holidays, if only she could get some truffles, and for Papa there were some new books, perhaps by M. Balzac, and some tobacco.

For herself there were nearly a dozen new dresses, with shoes and accessories to match, plus perfumes and scarves and gloves. At her husband's suggestion she bought something new called a 'raincoat', of a rubbery material that was impervious to water, which was not, she thought, very pretty but which would be immensely practical when they returned to the country.

'Especially,' Jean remarked, 'if you decide to go out riding in storms.'

7.

They dined at a restaurant, the Rocher de Cancale on the rue Montorgueil, near the Palais Royal, said to be a favorite haunt of poets and writers, and Anne had a new dish created by the chef there, *sole à la normande,* an elaborate creation in which the fish was garnished with oysters, mushrooms, mussels and a savory wine-based sauce and was finally topped with fried smelts and croutons. Her husband pronounced it excessive, but she thought it delicious.

'Someday, my dear,' he said, watching her as she devoured the rich creation greedily, 'you must learn that more, or more expensive, is not necessarily better.'

She was having much too grand a time to be annoyed by the criticism, and she settled for making a *moue* at him while she speared a smelt on her fork. He smiled tolerantly and shook his head, sipping his wine.

She was pleasantly shocked when one of the more notorious courtesans of the day arrived, trailed by a hang-dog-looking admirer who was said to be one of the most important men in the new king's cabinet.

All in all, she thought it a thoroughly satisfying day. For once she could really appreciate what it meant to be married to a man of unlimited wealth. She thought of the old days, when the de Grenvilles had lived well but not as lavishly as this. If only . . . but she did not let herself finish that thought. It would only spoil an otherwise lovely day.

'Tell me, how do you find Paris?' Jean asked as they were leaving the restaurant.

'It's lovely, as always,' she said; then, more thoughtfully, she added, 'And yet, it's different too. I don't know quite how to say it – cheaper, coarser – all these revolutionaries, people saying whatever they think – no one seems to have any manners anymore, if you understand.'

'The world is changing,' he said, a trifle sadly. 'We see it here especially because of the upheavels. Last year they opened a railroad between Lyon and Saint-Étienne; now they are saying that within a few years there will be railroads everywhere. They say a man will be able to go anywhere in France on a railroad. I was even asked to invest some money, but I turned it down; I can't imagine people will ever exchange good carriages for railroad journeys. Now they're saying that within another fifty or sixty years people will light their homes with this electricity the scientists are all talking about. Think of it!'

Anne, whose scientific knowledge was even scantier than her

grasp of politics, had a vision of homes lighted by great flashes of lightning, as if in the throes of some savage, primordial storm.

'It sounds most unpleasant,' she murmured. She could think of nothing brighter or lovelier than great banks of candles gleaming in chandeliers and rows of *torcheres* – who could want more light than that?

'Oh, Jean,' she cried, doing a light pirouette in the street, 'let's walk back to the hotel.'

'I'm afraid not,' he said, steering her gently but firmly toward the waiting carriage. 'The streets are not yet safe for strolling at night, and anyway, it's time you were thinking of rest. The doctor said not to let you overtire yourself, and it's been a long day.'

Anne, climbing obediently into the carriage, thought sadly of how casually they all had traversed the streets in the old days. All this change, so much commotion – there was something to be said after all for being removed from it, at least until things settled down again.

Jean was off early in the morning to attend to business matters. He left her enjoying chocolate and croissants in bed.

'You'll be able to entertain yourself?' he asked, bending down to kiss her goodbye.

'There's a woman coming to show me some new fabrics,' she said. 'And, oh, Jean, I saw a shop just around the corner with the most delicious-looking hats in the window; do you suppose I could have just one or two more . . . ?' She let her voice trail off coaxingly.

He laughed and said, 'If you buy many more, I shall have to hire a separate carriage to take everything back to the country. Yes, of course, *cherie*, get what you like; tell them to send the bill to me here.'

She laid a hand gently on his and said, 'You're very good to me.'

His eyes gleamed as he regarded her. 'Perhaps you should ask yourself why,' he murmured. He kissed her again, more earnestly this time.

'Regrettably,' he said, 'I must go, or in another moment I shall remove my clothes and rejoin you in the bed, and the bankers whom I am to meet will have their meeting without me.'

'Is it such an important meeting?' she asked.

'It has a great deal to do with our future wealth.'

'In that case, go by all means,' she said, giving him a shove.

He laughed and, standing and readjusting his clothes, said, 'Yes, I forgot. You did marry me for my money, didn't you?' For all his nonchalance, he sounded a little hurt, though she couldn't think why. After all, the reason for their marriage had hardly been secret. Perhaps they had since become friends, but that was another matter entirely. Men were so illogical sometimes.

When he had gone, she puzzled over his suggestion that she ask herself why he was so good to her. She had more or less assumed that it was because of the child, and because she no longer refused his companionship in bed. All in all, she thought they had worked out rather a happy arrangement for them both. Wasn't this trip itself proof enough of that? At one time he would have flatly refused to bring her with him, and she, left alone as she was today, would have been planning how to escape. As it was, she had entertained no such thoughts. Of course, there was Papa still at the chateau, and she was with child, but quite aside from those considerations, she was not entirely sure that she wanted to escape her husband.

Oh, to be sure, she would be glad to live in Paris again someday, but not just now. Having seen a little of it yesterday, she was inclined to think she'd rather wait a bit until things returned to normal. And as for her husband, well, as she had said a little while before, he was very good to her these days.

But she had given up hoping to understand her husband's puzzling, contradictory ways, and when the woman arrived soon with the new fabrics, Anne put his remarks out of her mind and gave herself over to the pleasure of spending money.

After lunch she dressed and started out to find the little hat shop she had noticed the day before, but when she stepped out the door into the street, the familiarity of Paris assailed her once again and she decided to do something else entirely. A carriage for hire was waiting at the street and, stepping into it, she gave the driver the address of the de Grenville townhouse.

She stood on the damp pavement outside the house and stared up at it, hardly able to comprehend that this was the same house she had known, that had been home to her for as long as she could remember. She was grateful now that Papa was not well enough to travel, that he need not come to see this.

There had been a fire, and several of the windows on the first floor still gaped stupidly, their sills and shutters charred black. Someone – the peasants who had taken over so much of the city during the disturbances – had moved uninvited into the rest of the house. There was wet wash hanging on the balcony off her old bedroom, and the shutters there hung awry. Someone had taken the potted geraniums from the garden and put them on the balcony off Mama's bedroom, along with a heap of rubbish that had apparently merely been swept out there to dispose of it.

How utterly stupid of her to have come here like this. She had been warned; Jean had told her that many of the homes of the aristocracy had been burned or taken over by bands of peasants. The former owners had fled the country or been arrested, or in many cases, killed. The authorities had been too busy maintaining order on the streets to bother themselves with disputes over ownership or the eviction of tenants now firmly entrenched, however uninvited.

She had asked the carriage to wait, and she climbed back into it. As it drove off, she took a final look at the house, but it had no ties for her now.

She instructed the driver to take her around Paris so that she could see the sights, and when he expressed some reluctance, she slipped him the gold coins that Jean had provided in case she needed some ready money.

His reluctance thus overcome, the driver proved an apt tour guide. Anne saw the Louvre and the Palais Royale, and the Bois de Boulogne, Montmartre, and the arch that the emperor had had built to commemorate his victories. She saw Paris as a stranger might see the city, and as she did so, she felt as if a great weight were slipping from her. With a sense of shock and relief, she realized that it was the burden of the past that she was shedding. Her future was still hidden and mysterious, but she knew suddenly that it was not tied to Paris and the life she had known in the past. That life was gone from her now, just as Mama and their home were gone. Because of that past she had made herself a stranger to her new home, to her husband, to the life that waited there for her. She had made herself miserable, resenting the life into which she had been brutally forced. Jean was right; she was a spoiled child, refusing to eat because she couldn't have the piece of cake she wanted.

Well, she was never going to have life back on its old terms. She realized that now, and if she was ever going to have a life of her own again, belong anywhere, she must set out to make her place, to fit herself into the life that had been offered her. Things weren't so bad for her; she might have been out on the streets, or in prison, or dead, as so many others were. Instead, she had a husband who was rich and doted upon her, she still had Papa, and soon she would have her child; she had a comfortable home, safe and cheery and removed from the turmoil of the city.

She leaned forward and rapped for the driver's attention. 'I've seen enough of the city,' she said. 'Take me to the Hotel Crillon.'

The afternoon had sped away. Perhaps Jean would be there by now, pacing the floor and wondering what had become of her. She was suddenly eager to see him, to see the way his face seemed to light up from within whenever she came into his presence, to see the slow, out-of-practice grin that formed itself in stages at the corners of his mouth, to come into his arms and feel the weight of his lips on hers.

Her husband was not there, however. Instead there was a note from him, explaining that he had been delayed and that she should have dinner sent up to their rooms if she was hungry.

She lounged about their suite for a while, but she was too restless to want to stay where she was and she did not relish eating alone. Then she remembered that she had not yet visited the little hat shop, and decided that she would go there now; no doubt by the time she returned from her shopping, Jean would be back, and they could have their meal together.

As it turned out, the shop was further than she had thought, although she did find it at last. The owner, a plump, sharp-eyed woman whose true vocation was all too obvious, had been about to close the shop for the day, but she was glad to keep it open for a wealthy-looking customer.

'With your complexion and that hair of yours, you'll want something particularly splendid,' she said, reaching bonnets down from shelves. 'Here's a number that should please your husband.'

She handed Anne a veritable fountain of lavender and green feathers attached to a purple bonnet. Anne looked at it and frowned. It was certainly colourful, and she supposed it must be in the current fashion, as the demimondaine she had seen at the restaurant the night before had been wearing one similar. Somehow, though, she did not think that it would please Jean very much. She had discovered at the dressmaker's yesterday that he had excellent tastes in women's clothes. Moreover, she had observed that his tastes leaned toward the more conservative styles and simple lines, although the dresses he had picked had certainly been expensive.

Her mama had been a flamboyant woman, and Anne had always more or less followed her gaudy lead in clothing; but yesterday she had seen the merit of her husband's suggestions. He had not been afraid of bold colors, but not for boldness's sake alone; he had suggested colors that brought out the green of her eyes or the coppery sheen of her hair or the creamy delicacy of her complexion.

Now, to the shopkeeper's surprise, Anne handed the elaborate creation back and pointed instead to a much simpler hat with a single discreet plume attached to it.

'There, I think that one will do,' she said firmly. 'And let me see what else you have in more understated styles, please.'

Flamboyance, she learned, was very much the mode these days – perhaps, Anne thought to herself, because so many of the people who had had real taste were no longer dictating the styles. Nonetheless, she managed to find an even half-dozen hats that she thought would please Jean as well as herself.

'Send them to the Hotel Crillon,' she said when she had finished, 'and bill them to my husband there – the Baron de Brussac.'

'*Oui*, Madame, I'll have them there first thing in the morning.'

Anne thanked her and left the shop. Outside, she lingered in the doorway. She had been unaware of the passage of time, and now she saw to her dismay that it was nearly dark. She would have to walk the several blocks back to the hotel alone, and at once she remembered Jean's warning that the streets were not safe for strolling at night.

She looked up and down the street, thinking perhaps she might be fortunate enough to find a carriage for hire. It was rather a quiet street. Just across the way was a small café and a cheap-looking hotel, the sort more often used for assignations than for the legitimate needs of travelers. There was a coach parked outside it, but it was obviously a private vehicle, as was the one parked on this side, just down from where she stood . . . why, was that – she stared, hardly able to believe her luck.

Why, it was! There was the crest on the door; it belonged to Louise, the Marquise de Marcheval. Of course, a few months ago she would have declined to share a carriage with the woman who had married Emile, but these were different times, and anyway, it would give her a chance to ask about Emile.

Anne hurried toward the coach. Yes, there was Louise sitting inside; her head was turned just now. She seemed to be staring at the doorway to the little hotel across the street. Good heavens, surely Louise couldn't be waiting to meet anyone coming out of that establishment; it was hardly her sort of place.

'Louise,' she called as she approached.

Then the strangest thing happened. Louise glanced around. Anne was certain afterward that Louse had seen her, had even recognized her. But then, it was dark inside the coach and difficult to be certain, and Louise had turned away again so swiftly. Anne saw her rap for the driver, and at once the carriage pulled away, the driver cracking the whip over the heads of the horses.

'Wait . . . ' Anne called lamely, one hand still lifted in greeting. Louise's carriage disappeared around the next corner.

Anne stood where she was on the pavement, staring after it. 'How utterly peculiar,' she said aloud. Well, there was nothing for her to do now but start back for the hotel before it got any later. Perhaps Jean would have returned by now and, realizing where she must be, would come looking for her.

She turned and once again froze in her tracks. There, across the street, coming out of that shabby hotel, could that possibly be – Lord in heaven, it was!

'Emile.' She breathed his name aloud, touching her fingers to her lips.

17

So that explained it. Louise had been following her husband, spying on him. And with good reason, too, it seemed, for Emile was not alone. There was a young woman clinging to his arm, and it took no great discernment to recognize just what sort of companion she was.

The blood rushed to Anne's face – of all the people to run into in Paris. Of course, she had fantasized such a meeting once or twice, but not like this, in the street, with him in the company of another woman; and anyway, in the cold light of day she had always thrust aside such fancies. She knew well enough how foolish she had been in the past, and she knew too that the man she had loved so passionately had been willing not only to sell himself to Louise but to sell her to Jean for a few pieces of gold. She could never forgive him for that.

And yet, how handsome he was! She had thought herself free of that burden, too, but seeing him now was like a knife wound in the heart. She looked about frantically for someplace to hide before he saw her, but there was no place at hand, and then it was too late – he had seen her. She saw him glance in her direction, saw the little start of surprise.

She wanted to run, but she was unable to move. She saw him say something to his companion; the woman looked in Anne's direction, a hostile expression on her face, but Emile was insistent; he thrust some notes at her, and with a final word, left her and ran across the street to Anne. It was too late to escape him now. She stood and tried to still the trembling that had beset her. The night seemed suddenly to have turned icy cold.

'Anne,' he said, moving as if to embrace her and then, seeing the stubborn tilt of her chin, the rigid line of her shoulders, he caught himself and stopped just in front of her.

'Hello, Emile,' she said, and was astonished to discover that her voice sounded quite normal despite the obstruction of her heart in her throat.

The moment stretched out until Anne thought something within her must snap from the tension. She could think of nothing to say or do, and he only stood and smiled down at her, his eyes seeming to pierce straight into her heart.

'It's been a long time,' he said finally.

'It was not I who dictated our parting.'

He grinned sheepishly. 'Yes, I deserved that; I was a cad. But you must have understood.'

'I'm afraid you give me credit for more wisdom than I possess.'

He did not appear to be particularly disconcerted over what had happened since they had last met. He had the manner of an impish little boy, and of course he was still the handsomest man she had ever seen. Despite herself, Anne felt it difficult to maintain her attitude of cold dignity. She knew what sort he was and she despised him, but she could not prevent the sensual stirring she felt within at this nearness to him.

'Look,' he said, ignoring her last gibe, 'we can't really talk here.' He glanced around, his gaze falling as if by chance on the hotel across the street. 'I've got an idea. Why don't we just go over there. I keep a little room in that place, just for privacy, you understand.'

'And I can take the place of that cheap trollop you just had up there?' she asked drily. 'The bed's hardly had time to get cold, has it?'

He laughed, still unperturbed. 'Well, I can hardly invite you home with me, can I? Louise might be a little surprised.'

Perhaps less surprised than you think, Anne was tempted to say; but she held her tongue. Let him find out for himself that his wife watched and followed him. It was none of her concern; none of this was anything to her, and she was a fool to remain here like this, knowing that with each passing moment she was weakening under the spell of his charm. If only he weren't so handsome . . .

'I must go,' she said hastily.

'But go where? Surely you don't mean to wander around the streets of Paris at night, unescorted. You may find yourself with more men than you can handle.'

She had made as if to go by him, but at his words she hesitated. It was fully dark by now, and beyond Emile the street stretched shadowy and threatening.

'I – I was hoping to find a carriage for hire,' she said, but without much conviction.

'Not a chance. But look, I've got a coach just over there. Won't you at least let me take you wherever you're going?'

'Well . . . ' She glanced indecisively toward the coach. She didn't know what to do.

'Come along,' he said, taking her arm possessively. 'Your husband wouldn't want you walking around at night like this, believe me.'

He was right, of course. Jean would be aghast to think that she was out walking after nightfall, after he had warned her against it. And surely it could do no harm just to ride the few blocks to the hotel in Emile's carriage.

He handed her into the carriage and said something to the driver. 'I'm going to the Hotel Crillon,' she said as Emile climbed in beside her.

'Yes, I've already given the driver instructions,' he said, grinning.

'But how could you, if you didn't know . . . '

But it was too late; the carriage was already moving, and Emile had slid across the seat to sit alongside her. His arm went about her shoulders.

'Don't, please,' she protested. 'I must get back to the hotel, my husband . . . '

'Damn your husband,' he said, holding her despite her protests. 'I can't leave it like this. You know I had no intention of hurting you.'

'I know that you succeeded, whatever your intentions,' she said, beginning to cry in her confusion. 'Please, let me go.'

She tried to tear herself away from him, but he held her too tightly.

'You know that I've always loved you,' he whispered in her ear with the same deep, magical voice she had remembered so well. 'I love you more than ever before.'

'You're lying,' she cried, still struggling, while a confusion of impressions attacked her mind. His perfume, womanish almost – why did Jean smell of sweat and soap and of clean, sweet soil? Emile's arms were so strong, and she seemed to be growing weaker with each passing second.

'I know I was unkind – I was a callous monster – but forgive me, Anne, please.'

She was still struggling and sobbing, trying to break free, but his arms held her fast, and their pressure was oddly comforting. How often she had longed to feel them about her just once more. She was trembling from head to foot; she felt as if the bones within her body were all melting. All the pain, all the passion that she had once felt for him, that she thought dead within her, now sprang to life anew.

'How could you have been so heartless to me?' she sobbed. 'Didn't you know that I loved you with all my heart and soul?'

'My darling,' he murmured. He tried to kiss her.

'No, please,' she said in a faint voice, trying to turn her face away.

He pursued. He spoke broken little phrases of love, and his arms held her so tightly that she felt like a prisoner to the longings he had aroused within her. She gave a faint moan, closing her eyes. Her face was wet with tears.

He found her lips then and the touch of his upon them was like an unholy flame that shot through her. It was an ecstasy that burned her and seemed to glow through her. How often in her dreams had she lived this moment? Now it was here, and she could do nothing but give in to the dizziness and the delight.

What was he doing with her clothes? She did not know or care; she was no longer a woman, but desire personified. She sank back against the leather of the seat, clinging to him, his mouth fastened to hers. She felt the brush of cold air over her bare flesh.

He laughed softly in her ear and his hand slid across the mound of her belly. 'I suppose it's the old man's brat,' he whispered. 'You should have been more careful, pet. Still, who'd have thought he'd have it in him – or in you?'

She stiffened beneath him; his words were like a dash of cold water. She had forgotten the baby, forgotten her condition, forgotten too what the child meant to Jean – how proud and happy he had been, how lovingly he had treated her since they had learned of its coming, and how pleased she had been to have given him what he so desired.

Jean, her husband, who loved her, who trusted her . . . 'Please,' she said, struggling with new conviction, 'I must go.'

'Not a chance,' he said huskily, his hands pawing at her thighs.

'I – the baby, I'm afraid I might be ill.'

That stopped him. 'Good Lord, don't just sit there,' he said, scrambling to a sitting position. 'Hang your head out the window or something, I don't want the upholstery ruined.'

She managed to get the window open; the fresh air was indeed welcome, and she drank it down in greedy gulps, trying to calm her shattered nerves.

'I'll be all right,' she said. 'Just take me back to my hotel, please.'

'I suppose I'd better,' he said sulkily. 'Hotel Crillon, wasn't it?' He gave the new instructions to the driver and then sat across the seat from her in his own corner, pouting with displeasure. Anne did not trust herself to speak but busied herself rearranging her clothes. Then she leaned wearily against the carriage door and tried to still the agitated beating of her heart.

By the time they reached the hotel, Emile had regained at least a semblance of his usual jaunty manner. He handed her down from the carriage and with a great flourish kissed her hand.

'Will you be in Paris long?' he asked.

'No, only another day or so.'

'You must come back when – ' he paused, his eyes twinkling,

and glanced briefly down at her midsection. 'When you've finished your little household chore. I should like the chance to make amends for all our past misunderstandings.'

'That won't be necessary,' she said.

'Not necessary, perhaps, but certainly enjoyable. Till then, *au revoir.*' He climbed back into the coach and a moment later it clattered away, leaving her standing alone on the pavement.

She gave a great sigh of relief and turned toward the lighted doorway of the hotel. As she did so, a figure stepped from the nearby shadows. Her heart gave a jolt.

'Jean,' she said, 'I – I didn't see you standing there.'

'I rather thought you didn't,' he said drily.

His stern expression, his chilling manner only added to her confusion. 'I've been shopping,' she said.

His eyes flickered in the direction in which Emile's coach had disappeared. 'It seems you made a successful purchase.'

'Jean,' she began haltingly, 'it isn't the way it looks. I can explain.'

'That's hardly necessary; I understand all too well. You could hardly wait for me to leave you alone. I could have no more than gotten out of sight before you rushed off to your lover's arms. What a fool I was to want to show you that I trusted you.'

Tears welled up in her eyes again and she put out a hand to try to touch him, but he stepped away from her.

'It isn't like that,' she cried. 'I *was* shopping, at that place I told you about, the hat shop – you can inquire there if you like. And it was getting dark when I left there. I didn't know what to do – I was frightened of walking back here alone, and then just by coincidence I ran into Emile on the street . . . '

'How convenient for you,' he interjected.

'And he gave me a lift back here,' she finished lamely, her face flushing as she recalled the details of that ride. She avoided her husband's searching gaze.

'And put you down with your clothes in disarray and your hair falling over your face. Don't take me for a fool, Madame; any man with eyes could have watched you getting out of that carriage and known what went on beforehand. Can you look into my eyes and tell me nothing went on between you?'

'I . . . ' she began, and stopped, unable to give voice to the lie no matter how much she wanted to do so.

'I said once before,' Jean said, his voice icy cold, 'you were a born strumpet, Madame, and it seems you've proven me right.'

She gave a little cry of pain and threw her hands over her face. How could she ever explain what had happened when she didn't understand it herself? She felt guilty and shamed, and at the same time self-pitying. She seemed to have lost everything at once – her past, Emile, and now her husband as well. She felt suddenly alone, helpless, friendless, terrified.

'I – it wasn't that way,' she sobbed, and then, unable to face him any longer, she turned and fled blindly from him, running she knew not where along the darkened street. She only knew that she wanted to get away from his accusing stare, away from her own guilt and shame, to hide herself in the uncaring darkness.

She stumbled on the rough cobblestones, caught herself, and ran on, sobbing helplessly. She was like a frightened animal running blindly in panic, and how far she ran or in what direction she had no idea. Whether Jean followed her or not she couldn't have said, for the pounding of her heart made her deaf to any other sounds – but surely he would not come after her; what could he want with her now that she had sullied their marriage, defeated his trust in her?

Through her tears she saw two soldiers ahead, standing in the light of a torch. They heard her running footsteps and turned in her direction, and rather than face them she darted down an alleyway to her right.

Out of breath, she began to slow her pace, and as she did so, she became gradually aware of her surroundings. It was so dark here, so frightening, and she could not tell how far the alley went before it reached another street with at least a little light.

She slowed her steps to a walk and glanced fearfully about her. There was nothing here but shadows and dark doorways and heaps of smelly refuse. Something moved in one of those heaps; something small and furry brushed past her foot.

Perhaps she should turn back, seek the aid of the soldiers – but before she could carry this thought any further, two of the shadows had separated themselves from the others, and she suddenly discovered two men in her path.

'Well now, here's a pretty little morsel for our supper, eh, George?' one of them said, giving a menacing chuckle.

'Aye,' his companion said, coming closer. 'Run straight into our arms, too, blast if she hasn't.'

'Please, I – I've gotten lost,' she stammered, more terrified even than before. The two men stepped up to her so that she could see their ragged clothes and their dirty, unshaven faces. One of them grinned a toothless grin, his fetid breath nearly making her faint.

'She's lost, she is,' he said. 'Well now, you ain't lost no more, my lady, not now that we've found you.'

She tried to run past them, but her arm was suddenly seized in a clawlike grip, and then both of them had hold of her and she was being dragged toward one of the shadowed doorways.

18

'Oh, no, please,' she begged, struggling in vain against her captors. 'Let me go!'

'Do as the lady says,' a familiar voice said from behind. 'Let her go.'

The two ruffians released their hold on her and Anne whirled about to discover her husband standing a few feet away.

'Jean,' she cried, trembling with relief; he had followed her after all.

Her would-be assailants blocked her path. They glanced indecisively from Anne to Jean – there were two of them, after all, and only one of him. On the other hand, the stranger had the air of one prepared to back up his commands.

Suddenly a fourth figure, a hoodlum Anne had not seen before, darted from the shadows behind Jean. Something glinted in the dim light as a knife rose and fell. Suddenly Jean clutched his side and staggered, dropping to his knees.

At the sight of her husband wounded and bleeding while his assailant lifted his dagger for yet another blow, Anne's paralyzing fear fled and she rushed forward like an avenging angel.

'Stop that,' she cried, pounding the man's back and shoulders with clenched fists. 'Get away from him!'

The attacker was so surprised by this unexpected assault that instead of merely brushing her aside as he might easily have done, he instinctively raised his arms to ward off her blows.

Remembering the two soldiers she had seen a short distance back, Anne began to scream and cry for help. 'Help, murderers!' she shrieked, all the while pummeling the cowering ruffian ceaselessly. 'Help!'

There was a sound of running footsteps. This was too much for the footpads and they fled in the opposite direction, disappearing into the engulfing darkness just as the two soldiers ran up.

'They tried to murder us,' Anne cried, dropping to the filthy pavement beside her husband and flinging her arms about him.

'Jean, darling,' she sobbed, 'are you all right?'

He turned his face to hers. He was deathly pale and pain was written across his features, yet somehow he managed to smile at her.

'I am now,' he murmured; then, to her horror, he fainted into her arms.

Their assailants had vanished, and the soldiers declined to pursue them through the dark alleyways, but for the promise of a substantial reward they were more than willing to help Anne get Jean back to the hotel.

A doctor was sent for, who examined the wound and afterward gave Jean something to make him sleep. 'He's a lucky man,' the doctor said when he had finished. 'A few inches either way and he'd be dead by now. As it is, a few days' rest and he'll be good as new.'

It was, in fact, nearly a week before Jean felt well enough to travel, and during that time Anne scarcely left the hotel room. She nursed her husband with all the gentleness and affection she could muster.

She was tortured by guilt and shame, not only for what had happened with Emile, but for what had nearly resulted from it. Jean might have been killed, and it would have been entirely her fault.

Her thoughts kept circling back to the question he had posed before – why did he do the things for her that he did? Why, even while consumed with anger, even thinking her unfaithful, had he come after her, risking his life to save her?

She could think of only one explanation, incredible though that seemed. Could her husband actually have fallen in love with her?

Even more puzzling, was it possible that she was in love with him? Oh, she did not feel toward him as she had felt toward

Emile; but what she had shared with Emile he had been only too willing to share with Louise as well, and with that little prostitute she had seen today, and God only knew how many others. It had been thrilling, but it had been vulgar and shoddy, too, like those traveling circus performers who entertained you in cheap, spangly costumes and picked your pockets while you watched the dancing bear.

And what of her feelings for Jean? Was that – could that be love; that deep stirring within her when he was near, that need for his protection, and that desire she felt to protect him, as well; that scorching passion that he knew so well how to rouse in her so that in his arms she did indeed play the trollop. Surely no civilized woman could behave like that in a man's bed unless she were in love with him.

But it was so different from what she'd always heard, what she had always imagined. It was so much richer and fuller and yet, at the same time, more comfortable.

When Jean was better, she told him everything of her meeting with Emile; she did not spare herself, and when she had finished, she flung her arms about him and clung to him tearfully.

'Please forgive me,' she begged, and for an answer he patted her shoulder gently and kissed her hair.

It was a changed couple who returned to the chateau some days later.

It was strange to contemplate at what a leisurely pace the days went by, and yet the weeks and months seemed to vanish in the blinking of an eye.

Christmas came and with it equal measures of happiness and sadness. Jeanette announced that she had become 'most attached' to Peter, one of Jean's stewards, and shyly asked permission to be married, which Anne was happy to give. But Papa's health was clearly declining. Jean had him carried downstairs on Christmas Eve to be with them, but he kept falling asleep and he had difficulty understanding what the occasion was.

'Damned lot of bother,' he grumbled, nodding his head.

Watching him, Anne wondered sadly if he would see another Christmas.

Winter brought its gifts of lamb's-wool hills and carved trees outside her window and then, in a twinkling, it was spring and the whistling of the wind gave way to the bleating of the new lambs and the bursting of buds in the trees.

Her son was born on a fine spring morning, a big strapping
boy, as Henriette had predicted. They named him Claude,
after Jean's father, and Anne, holding her child to her breast
and smiling fondly at the proud swelling of Jean's chest,
thought she had never known such contentment as this.

'I am the happiest woman alive,' she declared one morning
soon after she was out of bed.

'It's bad luck to boast of one's happiness,' Henriette warned
grimly.

'Oh, pooh,' Anne said. 'You can't discourage me with all
your glum warnings.'

Afterward, though, she was to remember Henriette's words
and realize how prophetic they had been.

19

With summer Jean once again devoted most of his time to the
vineyards. He had become quite engrossed in the growing of
grapes and the making of wine. The vineyards had been extended so that they stretched further than the eye could see.
Once or twice Jean made little trips away and came back with
carefully wrapped bundles.

'Cuttings,' he would explain, telling her they were from this
or that chateau, his eyes glinting with excitement.

Anne still knew little about the business, but she made what
she thought were the appropriate remarks and obediently
tasted the wines he brought for her approval. She still had no
great taste for wine, but it did seem as if the samples were
getting better, and anyway, Jean certainly seemed to think so.

It was a long, warm summer, and there was talk of a 'vintage
year'. Toward the fall there was much coming and going
between Chateau Brussac and the other vineyards of the area,
and Jean and the growers looked quite pleased with themselves.

Anne, occupied with the baby, who was already giving
evidence of being an independent spirit, was glad to have her
husband so happily occupied as well. And, of course, they still
had their nights together.

It seemed to her as if her life was full and running over with gladness, and when she thought of old Henriette's glum prediction, she could only laugh.

'I believe Henriette gets sourer with age,' she told her husband.

It was winter again when tragedy struck. Jean had been on a trip to the provinces of Champagne and Burgundy, to buy more cuttings for the vineyards; he was experimenting with many varieties of grapes.

'The province of Ile-de-France has never produced a really first-rate wine,' he was fond of arguing. 'But it's here, waiting to be grown – the soil is right, the climate, everything – it only waits the right man, the right grape.' His face would take on a special glow when he made these predictions, and Anne, sure that he could do anything he put his mind to, hadn't the slightest doubt that he was the right man.

He was gone longer than he had expected, and she, hearing rumors of a cholera outbreak to the south, began to worry. But at last he was home, arriving just as she was preparing for bed one evening. She thought he looked pale and drawn, and it occurred to her for almost the first time since their marriage that her husband was not a young man. He worked so hard and with such seemingly tireless energy that she was used to forgetting his age.

He made love to her with his customary ardor that night, but by the following day it was clear he was not feeling himself. He retired early, to her surprise, and when during the night he woke her with a groan, she was horrified to discover that he was burning up with fever. He was already out of his head with it and did not recognize her at all.

Christian was sent for the doctor in Epernay but it was dawn by the time he arrived. Anne spent the intervening hours bathing her husband's body with rags soaked in vinegar and trying not to believe Henriett's diagnosis until the doctor confirmed it.

'Cholera,' he said after only the briefest examination.

'It can't be,' Anne cried, although Henriette had pronounced the same verdict nearly two hours sooner.

The doctor shook his head and instinctively edged away from the bed. 'Not a doubt,' he said. 'We've had reports of it in Burgundy, but this is the first case I've heard of in this province.'

'He – he just came back – from Burgundy,' Anne said grimly.

The doctor only shook his head sadly. 'What are we to do?' Anne asked.

'We'll start with Julap – seven grams, I think – and about four of calomel; if that doesn't break the fever, we'll try croton oil and mercury.'

Overwhelmed by the medical terminology, Anne could only ask, 'Will – will that cure him?'

'We know of no way to cure cholera, Madame, and very little about it. I can only recommend methods that seem to have worked in other cases. Once we've broken the fever, we'll try alternating medicines – one a blend of tamarind, cassia and cream of tarta, and the other, juice of citron, olive oil and calcined magnesia – it's much the same treatment that's used for yellow fever.'

'Mistress,' Henriette said timidly, 'I have a recipe, a *tisane* . . .'

'Pshaw,' the doctor interrupted her scornfully. 'Those home brews – in my opinion they generally do more harm than good. No, Madame, my best advice is to follow the treatment I prescribe, and to pray a great deal – and, Madame, if there are children about the house, they are especially vulnerable.'

For almost the first time Anne thought of her baby, little Claude, still sleeping at this early hour. He had been turned over to the personal care of Jeanette, who would soon be delivered of her own baby. Little Claude must be kept away from this sickroom, removed to another part of the house altogether. Anne would care for Jean herself, with Henriette's help.

Henriette – the doctor had gone, bidding them a terse good night, and Henriette had resumed bathing Jean's body in an effort to bring down the scorching fever. The doctor had expressed disdain for Henriette's offered *tisane*, but in the past Anne had done well to heed Henriette's homely advice.

'Henriette,' she said, coming to stand by the bedside once again. 'The *tisane* you spoke of – will it take long to brew?'

Henriette glanced up, a grim smile faintly lifting the corners of her mouth. 'An hour or two. I must find all the ingredients –'

'Find them,' Anne said firmly.

When Henriette had gone out, Anne remembered the rest of the doctor's advice; kneeling at the foot of the bed, she prayed long and earnestly.

Anne soon lost track of the hours spent at her husband's bedside. Sleeplessness and fatigue sat upon her shoulders like great stone weights while the hours marched into days, and still Jean lay twisting upon the bed in violent convulsions, his face flushed crimson with the fever.

Soon Anne began to look uncertainly toward the medicines that the doctor had prepared for him, but Henriette, seeing the glance, only shook her head stubbornly and, lifting Jean's head slightly, poured more of her own brew down his throat.

Like a great, roaring brushfire, the cholera swept across France. Reports began to reach them of deaths in the village and on the neighboring estates, and then Philippe, Jean's majordomo for uncounted years, took sick and was dead within the day. Only hours later, one of the housemaids took to her bed with the fever.

'Madame must sleep.'

Anne shook her head and realized that she had dozed off, her cheek lying against Jean's shoulder. She sat up stiffly, feeling the painful ache in her shoulders.

Suddenly there was a distant boom like thunder and the glass in the window rattled.

'What on earth?' Anne cried, leaping to her feet.

'Guns,' Henriette said. 'In Epernay. They think to change the air currents and drive away the evil vapors.'

'In Epernay? It's that bad there?' She got up and went to the balcony, stepping outside to look in the direction of Epernay. What she saw were great clouds of black smoke billowing upward toward a sky already turned gray from their influence.

Great God in heaven, were they burning the city down? But she had no time to wonder, for Henriette, who had left the room a moment before, came rushing back in, her eyes wide.

'Madame – the baby – and your papa, too . . . they're both sick . . .'

It seemed to Anne, stepping out of her husband's sickroom for almost the first time in days, as if the entire estate had been brought to its knees. She discovered to her amazement that virtually all of the servants were either sick themselves with the cholera or too frightened to be of any help. Christian was not to be found, and when Anne inquired about him, she learned that he was busy in one of the distant fields burying those who had already died.

There was no one to send for the doctor, and in the end Anne had to go herself, hitching the horses to the little buggy Jean had bought for her just a few months before.

She set out for Epernay. Along the way she saw fires burning at the chateaux she passed. Katherine, Henriette's daughter, had explained that the frightened people were burning barrels of pitch and tar, which were thought to purify the air; rising columns of smoke were like accusing fingers pointing to the stricken homes. To her dismay Anne saw that hardly a home she passed was unmarked by those sooty fingers.

She had visited the village a few times since coming to live at the chateau and had found it quiet and sleepy. All that was changed now, though. The air, usually so clean and fresh, was rancid with the smell of burning pitch and other stenches that she was afraid to try to identify. As she neared the village, she had to drive past the cemetery. She glanced toward it and nearly cried aloud. There were great open trenches where the bodies of the dead had been dumped unceremoniously; worse, the grave diggers had apparently fled or had died too, for in one spot was a great mound of bodies that had merely been left on the ground because all the trenches were filled and there was no one to dig new ones.

Crows rose angrily into the air as Anne passed by and as quickly settled back down to their grisly business.

She passed an ox-drawn cart going in the opposite direction, and saw one bloated leg sticking from under the cloth that had been tossed across the cart's load – the dead cart, assigned to pick up the bodies that had been tossed into the streets and carry them to the cemetery; she had heard of these carts, but had never thought to see one. Holding a cloth to her nose to ward off the stench, Anne whipped up the horses and hurried by.

Not the slightest breeze stirred, and the sky over the town seemed turned to dark gray. Some houses were boarded up and others stood open, abandoned hastily by those fleeing the city or by those who were too late to flee. And at every corner, it seemed, bodies lay in the gutters, shapeless piles of debris that had once been human beings.

The doctor's office was empty. Anne came back out into the street, wondering what on earth she was to do now, and as she looked up and down the street, she saw a man crossing toward her, stepping carelessly over a body in his path. Not until he was almost upon her did she recognize the doctor himself, his eyes sunken into his head with exhaustion, a stubble of grayish beard giving him an unkempt look.

'Doctor,' she cried, running up to him and seizing his arm, 'you must come to the chateau with me.'

He shook off her arm and continued on as if he had not heard her.

'Doctor,' she cried, running to catch up with him.

'Madame,' he said, hardly glancing at her, 'there are people dead and dying everywhere – in my office, on the streets, in my own home, even. I have not slept in three days or three nights, and even if I were able to come to your house, there is nothing I could do – nothing has any effect.'

'But my father – my baby . . . '

'Your baby is one of a hundred babies dying this very moment right here in Epernay,' he snapped.

She gave a cry of dismay and clapped her hands to her face. The doctor paused then and, seeing her stricken look, he snapped open his bag and brought out a vial.

'Here,' he said, thrusting it at her. 'This is the latest concoction; try it if you like. Perhaps it will work better for you than it has for me.'

He went on then, not glancing back. Anne was left alone and frightened in the smoky street. She watched until the doctor disappeared into his office, thinking all the time that he must change his mind, have pity on her, turn back and . . . and what? He had said there was nothing he could do . . .

The horses attached to the buggy whinnied softly as a cannon was fired someplace not too distant, and Anne heard a rumble of cart wheels. She looked in horror as the dead cart turned a nearby corner and came toward her, dragging one body behind it over the dirty pavement.

Shaking herself out of the trance into which she had fallen, Anne ran back to the buggy. She turned it about and started toward home. Night was already falling; as she came through the center of town, she found it garishly lit by the fires burning everywhere. Flames leaped upward from huge casks of pitch. Suddenly another cannon was fired, this time close at hand. The horses neighed in terror and reared, and Anne cracked the whip savagely, trying to keep them under control as the carriage sped across the village square. The cannons fired again, and Anne could do nothing but cling to the sides of the carriage, bouncing to and fro while the horses ran out of control.

Once someone ran into the street in front of her, waving for her to stop. It was an old man, who pointed toward the steps of his house where three bundles lay wrapped in sheets.

'Please,' he cried as she sped toward him, 'my wife and daughters, help me take them to the cemetery . . .'

She did not hear the rest but cracked the whip again to urge the horses on, all but running the shouting man down. She kept her kerchief clamped tightly over her nostrils, holding her breath until her lungs ached and she was forced to swallow great mouthfuls of air all at once, and then, insanely, hold her breath again.

At last they were out of the town, and the horses, tired by their crazed flight, slowed their pace until she could regain control of the reins. Still she sped them along, eager to put as much distance as possible between herself and the horror of the village. And this was but one small town. What must the larger cities be like? What must Paris be like at this moment?

But there was no refuge from the horror, for still more misfortune awaited her at Chateau Brussac. There was no one to help her with the carriage and, leaving the horses still hitched to the carriage and panting hotly, Anne ran to the house. She met Henriette in the hall.

'Henriette, the doctor can't come,' she gasped out. 'We must do something, we must –'

'Madame,' Henriette said, 'I must go to my own man; he has been stricken.'

'But – oh, Henriette, what . . . ' Anne was beside herself, hardly knowing what to think or say, but there was to be no comfort for her from this quarter.

'God be with us,' Henriette said, and hurried past her.

Throughout the night Anne went from one sickbed to another, feeling utterly helpless at each. Jean was no better than before, and the baby, purple with fever and pain, shrieked ceaselessly until Anne thought she must take leave of her already battered senses altogether. And Papa, he had the look of death upon him already; his eyes were wide open but unseeing, and his breath came in frail gasps.

Sometime near morning Anne fell asleep in the chair beside Jean's bed, but she slept fitfully and was soon awakened by her husband's weak groans. She got up, feeling as if her body were heavy as stone, and as she did so, remembered for the first time the vial that the doctor had thrust upon her in the village.

'Perhaps it would work for you,' he had said.

Perhaps. It was better at least than no hope at all. She took the vial from her pocket where she had thrust it at the time and approached the sickbed with it.

'No,' said a voice from the doorway.

Anne turned; it was Henriette, standing just inside the room.

'We will use my medicine,' Henriette said stubbornly. 'I've brought a fresh batch. Do you think I would have trusted my own man's life to it, and the master's, if there were anything better?'

'Henriette,' Anne started to argue, and then remembered: 'Henriette, your husband, is he – ?' She did not finish the question. She saw the answer in the glint of wetness on the other woman's lashes. 'Oh, Henriette,' she sobbed, beginning to cry despite her efforts not to. 'He isn't – Christian hasn't – ?'

'Our business now is with the living,' Henriette said, her face a mask that made her grief a private business, her pain alone, to be shared with no one. 'Come, help me.'

Biting her lip to fight back her own tears, Anne obediently approached the bed. She helped Henriette raise Jean up to give him the *tisane*. How futile it all seemed; and yet Jean still lived, while Christian, and others, had succumbed almost at once. Perhaps – just perhaps . . .

'Madame.'

Anne lifted her eyes with an effort. How heavy her lids felt.

'Your husband – the master . . . '

Her heart missed a beat. 'What is it?' she cried. 'What are you trying to tell me? He's not – ' She stopped, caught by the expression on Henriette's face.

'The fever's broken,' Henriette said.

For a moment Anne could hardly believe what she heard. Then, cautiously, she put her hand upon Jean's brow.

It was true! The fever had dropped; Jean was going to live. A choking sob tore itself from Anne's throat and she threw herself across her husband's chest.

'I told you, Madame,' Henriette said. 'Old Death is not as stubborn as I.'

Anne felt a quick surge of gratitude, but on its heels came another realization: that while Henriette had grappled for this prize and won, another had been snatched away from her.

20

Little Claude recovered soon after his father, but Anne's papa was buried in the makeshift graves that had been dug beyond the orchards, along with Christian and nearly half the help.

Anne grieved for her father, but in her heart she knew that he had died long ago, on the night he had had to flee Paris and Mama had been killed in a burning carriage. For a year and a half his ghost had lain in that bed and waited for the right moment to depart. Now it was gone, and she knew that he was finally at peace; and in truth, she felt as much relief as sorrow.

As if the powers above wanted to compensate for all the death of that harsh winter, the spring and the summer that followed seemed unusually blessed with life. Jeanette's baby was born, a girl whom she called Danielle, and soon after Anne discovered that she was pregnant again, the child conceived in that long period of her husband's convalescence, when she had surprised even herself with the passion with which she clung to him and took him into her.

It was a vintage year as well in the vineyards throughout France, and everywhere the vintners had to work doubly hard to harvest the bumper crops with fewer hands than before. Jean grieved for the loss of Christian, who had seemed, Jean said, to talk to the soil itself, coaxing the best from it.

The new cuttings that Jean had brought from Champagne and Burgundy, those cuttings that had nearly cost him his life, took to the soil at Chateau Brussac, and Jean began to talk more and more confidently of the wines they would produce.

Late in the fall their daughter, Marie, was born and, true to his word, Jean welcomed her as happily and as lovingly as he had welcomed his son.

Once again Anne could contemplate how happy she was with the life she had found for herself, a life so different from the one she would once have imagined.

They planned on a trip to Paris in the spring, but the unrest that had kept France in turmoil for nearly three years now flared up once again, and Jean and Anne decided to remain in the country.

Sometimes Anne found it difficult to comprehend that she had ever thought such a life boring or longed to return to Paris. It seemed as if the days were never long enough, what with the long season of planting, pruning, tending, harvesting, pressing the grapes; and in the winter there were the long nights with her husband, and time during the warmer days to ride into the woods, where they sometimes made love upon his cloak on the ground or gathered berries or dried plants, from which Anne, with Henriette's patient help, formed decorations to put about the house at Christmas time.

And, of course, there were the children – Claude was already his father's son, it seemed; no matter what sort of temper he might be in or what its cause, he had only to spy his father's doting face and he was happy again. And Marie was so sweet-natured that Anne sometimes wondered if she oughtn't to cry just a little more.

Yes, all in all, Anne thought, she could count herself content.

The political situation grew worse through that summer and fall. Anne listened to her husband's explanations and tried to comprehend them, but politics still remained beyond her grasp. She understood that Louis Philippe still occupied the throne, but it sometimes seemed as if there were more factions opposing him than supporting him. Large-scale insurrections of workers were put down with difficulty, and more and more one heard of secret societies that had been formed to work against the government. The newspapers carried merciless caricatures of the king, most notably by a Monsieur Daumier.

All of this seemed to Anne like distant thunder that rumbled but presented no real threat to her, and she wondered that her husband let himself be so concerned by it, until something happened that brought it all literally to her doorstep.

It was early spring again; still more reports had reached them of violent uprisings in Paris and Lyon, put down with ever-increasing severity by the authorities. The military, it was said, was virtually in charge of those cities, and when the difficulties spread to other cities and towns, even to Epernay itself, Jean began to wear a grim expression and at length even ordered Anne to stay home one day when she had planned on a shopping trip to the village.

'But surely no one around here would harm us,' Anne protested. 'They know you, after all; you're respected by the peasants and the workers.'

'It isn't necessarily the peasants and the workers I'm afraid of,' he said, but when she tried to question him further, he grew silent and only repeated his command that she was not to venture from the grounds for the time being.

As it was, Anne did not have to venture from the grounds to find trouble, because the trouble came to her.

It was April: spring had shown her colors early this year, promising another long growing season, and already the men were hard at work in the vineyards. The children were in Jeanette's care and she had taken them – her own daughter along with Anne's son and daughter – to play out of doors in the sun. Anne, restless after being cooped up through the winter, had brought her embroidery out and sat working it in the shade of the big old chestnut tree, humming to herself and enjoying the happy shrieks of the children, when a new sound intruded itself upon the idyllic scene.

Horses: a great many of them, from what she could judge. She looked in the direction of the road; because of the lay of the land, she could as yet see no one approaching, but she could see a cloud of dust rising into the air, stretching out of sight beyond the trees.

'Jeanette,' she said tersely, 'take the children inside, please. And tell Katherine to fetch my husband.'

Jeanette, who had heard the approaching riders as well, hurried the children into the house over Claude's vigorous protests.

The horsemen came into view – soldiers. Anne saw the sun glinting of shining cuirasses as they started up the drive. Coming here? But why?

She put aside her embroidery and stepped out to meet them. Her gaze went naturally to their leader and as it did so she frowned; there was something familiar about the set of those shoulders, the tilt of that chin.

Mon Dieu, surely that could not be Emile, riding into her life again when she thought she had done with him once and for all.

There was no mistaking him, she knew that at once. She would have recognized him anywhere – but why was he coming here, of all places! Surely he did not think to . . . her face burned at the thought, but there was no more time to think; they were here, and Emile, smiling with wicked delight, was dismounting, coming forward to greet her. Her confused mind registered that he had been promoted, that he was now a captain, and that he rode at the head of more men than she cared to count.

'Madame.' Emile bowed formally before her, although his eyes had the mischievous gleam that she remembered so clearly from the past. 'I'm afraid we've come to intrude upon your hospitality.'

'But I – I don't understand,' she stammered, her senses awhirl. 'My husband is in the vineyards; I've sent someone for him.'

'What a pity,' Emile said in a low aside, grinning. Then, in a more normal voice, he went on: 'We're to be billeted here, my men and I, to put down any disturbances in the area.'

'But – we've had no disturbances.'

'Not yet, perhaps. But government informants have warned of a planned uprising in Epernay. We're here to quell that before it gets started – or crush it, at any cost. And as I was acquainted with you and your husband and we needed someplace to quarter, I assured the commandant that we would be welcomed here.'

'You were mistaken,' Anne said sharply, adding quickly, 'that is to say, we haven't the facilities. Had we known – this is so unexpected. I'm afraid we must respectfully decline.'

'The matter is out of your hands, to be honest,' Emile said, producing a sealed letter from his tunic. 'I have here an authorization signed by the king's minister himself. And in any case,' he leaned closer and spoke again in a lower voice, 'it would hardly do to refuse – it would look as if you were anti-royalists, don't you see? It could make things very hard for you – and your husband.'

What was she to do? Jean had not yet come from the fields, and she could not even begin to guess how he would react to this intrusion. She remembered his reaction to her last meeting with Emile; would he think she was an accomplice to this one?

But there was nothing, really, that she could do. To order them from the property – even assuming that a body of soldiers would heed the command of one frail woman – could bring retribution down upon their heads. Despite her political naïveté, she knew enough to know that the king's 'justice' was swift and merciless.

She somehow managed a weak imitation of a smile and gestured in the direction of the house. 'I'm sure my husband will want to welcome you himself,' she said, sounding surprisingly cool to her own ears. 'In the meantime, Captain, won't you please come in?'

'Very sensible,' he murmured, grinning devilishly.

She did not wait for him but hurried ahead, fairly running across the lawns and up the steps. Behind her, she heard him barking orders to his men to set up their encampment – on the lawn itself!

Henriette was waiting in the hall, her face grim. 'Show the captain into my husband's study,' Anne said. 'See that he has what he wants and tell him – tell him I shall join him and my husband shortly.'

She hurried to her room, racing as if the devil himself were at her heels, and once there, she locked the door after herself, hardly knowing why she did so.

But the fear in her heart would not be locked out. She had carried the past with her like a dead weight into the present. Oh, why were things never as simple as they seemed?

21

What conversation went on between the two men in the study, she had no idea. Like a true coward, she had remained locked in the safety of her room until she had seen Jean striding purposefully across the orchard, until she had heard him come into the house, and until she had heard the door to his study close firmly.

She crept down the stairs then, to discover Henriette, too, outside the study door; the two women had exchanged conspiratorial glances, but neither could know what words the men inside the room were using. Once or twice voices were raised angrily, and Anne half-expected a battle to erupt.

At length it seemed as if the discussion was ending, and when Anne heard someone at the study door, she fled once again to her room. It was there Jean found her a few minutes later.

His anger was evident at a glance. 'It seems we are to have guests for a few days,' he said, his eyes flashing fire.

'I'm sorry,' she said in a tiny voice.

'Are you?' He had been about to pour himself a drink, but

instead he turned upon her. 'Or did you connive at this?'

'I knew nothing of this,' she cried. 'I was as astonished as you to discover him here.'

'But not as displeased, eh?' For a moment his eyes bored into hers; then with a violent gesture he flung the glass in his hand to the floor and strode from the room.

Anne ran to the balcony. She saw Jean emerge from the house a moment later on his way back to the vineyards; he did not hesitate or glance back, and she did not know what to read in that attitude – was it trust in her, or indifference?

In the days that followed Anne went to great lengths to avoid their 'guest'. The soldiers had set up their own camp on the wide lawns, which had turned into a higgledy-piggledy tent town, but Emile and his aide had moved into the house itself, which made things doubly difficult for Anne.

She instructed Jeanette to keep the children indoors; a nursery had been set up for them in the attic, and they spent most of their time confined there. It made the children quarrelsome, and little Claude was inclined to slip away from Jeanette's watchful eye and set out on his own, so that Jeanette and Anne were forever chasing up and down stairs looking for him.

For her own part, Anne kept as much as possible to her room, embroidering, reading, or playing with the children when Jeanette brought them down to break their routine.

Anne had even tried to avoid confronting Emile at the dinner table; the first evening that Emile was in the house, she pleaded a headache and said she would have a tray in her room. But Jean, who had already gone down, returned to insist that she join them downstairs.

'We don't want our guest to think we're frightened of him, do we?' he asked drily.

After that she had dressed hurriedly and made an appearance at the table. It was an awkward meal, although Jean played the part of the host to perfection and, outwardly at least, seemed quite unperturbed. But Anne hardly dared lift her eyes from her food, and whenever she did, it was to discover Emile's eyes watching her, glinting with amusement.

She fled as soon as the meal was ended, again pleading a headache, and this time her husband did not try to dissuade her.

It quickly became a ritual, that stilted evening meal together. The two men talked casually enough together, sometimes of life in Paris, which sounded even more greatly changed than

Anne had discovered it on her last visit; mostly, however, they talked of the political situation, and Anne was left to push her food about on her plate and urge the passing seconds to hurry on.

Even alone with her, Jean showed none of his true feelings toward the situation. He had turned cool toward her in their bed. He came up late and did not try to take her in warm embraces as was his custom. Instead he would lie on his back on his own side of the bed, staring up at the ceiling. Once or twice she slid across to him, snuggling close to the warmth of his body. His arm would go obediently about her, but it was only an absentminded gesture of affection, a prelude to nothing.

She counted the days. Emile had said originally he would be there for a few days only, and since his arrival the news that reached them indicated that the political situation was quieting down again. Certainly the predicted troubles in Epernay had failed to materialize, and with each passing day Anne prayed that Emile and the soldiers would move on.

That her tormentor was the same man whom she had once loved so passionately was a mystery to her. She watched them together, her husband and the captain, and wondered how she could ever have loved Emile. How shallow and false he seemed in contrast to her husband's earthbound manliness. Oh, he was handsome, true, and glib – the sort of man a girl could love – but a woman would know better.

The River Marne bordered the de Brussac property for several miles before passing the village of Epernay and, slightly beyond, Ay. Still further, it turned southward, cutting through the Champagne province and the Franche Comté, till near Auxonne it joined with the Saône in its journey to the sea.

In spots the river ran deep and wide, and where the trees hung far out over its surface, hiding it from the sun, the water appeared dark and bottomless. There were pools in which the young men of the villages came to bathe, and one place where Anne herself had bathed a time or two until Jean had learned of it and scolded her, for beneath the seeming placidity of the dark surface there were rocks and fallen tree limbs about which the fast water swirled and rushed, creating dangerous undercurrents.

It was like that at the chateau. As the days followed one another, things seemed on the surface to be smooth and tranquil. The tensions and difficulties that existed were like so many hidden obstructions. Concealed beneath the dark surface, the dangers could only be sensed or guessed at.

Anne thought she understood the situation, but she did not fully comprehend the depth of Emile's desire for her. He watched for her throughout the day, and each evening at dinner, while he conversed in a civilized manner with her husband, he was consumed with an animal hunger for her.

Who would have thought that that innocent, pretty child he had once seduced would have grown into such a beautiful, desirable woman? What had wrought this change in her? Was it the healthy aspect of country living, or was her husband in some way responsible?

She had put on some weight; she was still slender, but she had an ample bosom and a well-turned hip that suited her very well. A man would have to be blind, he thought, or a fool not to want to spring upon that opulence of flesh and bury himself in it.

Somehow, he meant to do just that. Seeking an opportunity, he had delayed his departure, sending his superior officer one excuse after another for continuing to remain here when the uprising they had been sent to quell had obviously failed to materialize.

Like a hawk circling his prey, he watched Anne, and waited.

'I can't stand this any longer,' Anne cried, flinging her embroidery aside with an impatient gesture and jumping to her feet. The weather had turned unexpectedly sultry, and her room seemed to have shrunk in size with each passing day.

'What are you going to do?' Jeanette asked; the children were having their afternoon nap and Jeanette had been keeping her mistress company.

'I'm going for a ride,' Anne said on the spur of the moment. She started to the door.

'Do you think you should? The soldiers . . . '

'Oh, fie on the soldiers! I'm tired of being a prisoner in my own home. Anyway, I'll ride out the back way, through the woods, down to the river; they'll never even know I'm abroad.'

Jeanette stared after her when she had gone, twisting her hands together anxiously. Should she have interfered? The master had said they were to keep an eye on the mistress at all times while the soldiers remained here.

Putting her own embroidery aside, Jeanette hurried downstairs in search of Henriette. Henriette would know what was best to do.

Outside, the captain's aide, Lieutenant Gabin, was having trouble keeping step with the officer. The captain was dictating a letter while he paced somewhat nervously around the lawns of the estate, and the aide was forced to keep his eyes on the words he was writing, so that he was forever stumbling over some obstruction or other.

Emile was oblivious to his aide's difficulties; at the moment his thoughts were fully occupied with his reply to the urgent message he had received less than an hour ago from the general in Paris, demanding the immediate return of the captain and the troops under his command, or a full explanation for the delays.

'Our own intelligence indicates,' Emile dictated, and then paused. His nervous pacing had brought him about the corner of the house in time to see a rider emerge from the stables and ride off in the direction of the river. He felt a quick, expectant surge of excitement within himself.

'My horse, quickly,' he said to his aide.

'But the letter . . .'

'Damn it, never mind the letter, bring my horse, at once,' Emile snapped.

A few moments later he rode off in the direction that Anne had taken, spurring his horse to a gallop in pursuit of her.

This, he told himself triumphantly, was the opportunity he had been waiting for.

22

At first he was unable to find her, and he was about to give up in defeat and ride back to the chateau when the whinnying of her horse led him to her.

She was on a bank by the river, concealed from the path by a stand of trees. The river was noisy here, rushing and leaping about the rocks that impeded its progress, and she did not hear his approach. He stood for a moment, admiring her.

How lovely she was! Lovely and desirable. She was dressed almost like a peasant, her long hair lying loose about her bare shoulders, the blouse that she wore scooped low to a wide vista of bare, pale flesh. She had removed her slippers and drawn up her skirts, so that her long, shapely legs were bared, too, nearly to the thigh. His heart pounded as he thought of the inviting softness that waited there for him, a prize to be seized and enjoyed.

He advanced toward her. A twig snapped under his feet, making her start. She saw him then and her eyes went wide with fear.

'You,' she said, barely breathing the word.

He made a little mock bow, grinning broadly. 'At your service, Madame. Although I daresay you might have made it a little easier for me to follow you – I was beginning to fear you didn't intend for me to find you.'

She ignored the suggestion and asked coldly, 'What do you want?'

He laughed. 'Hardly a necessary question, is it?' he asked. 'I want the same thing you want. Why else would you have ridden off here to this cozy little retreat in the woods?'

'I rode out here to – to escape from you, if you must know.' Anne tugged her skirt down about her ankles. She glanced apprehensively toward her horse, tethered several yards away.

Emile came closer until he stood directly over her. She found herself staring at the highly polished sheen of his boots, like mirrors, almost.

'To escape from me? What rubbish. Have you forgotten that night with me in your parents' summerhouse? It was I who taught you the meaning of the word love.'

'You taught me desire, but only in its most rudimentary forms'.

'In whatever form, you seemed to have remembered the lesson well. That night in Paris, in my carriage, you were mine for the taking that night, we both knew that. Surely you don't mean to pretend otherwise. And since I've been here, haven't you been haunted by the same desire? Do you think I haven't realized that's why you avoided me – because it was yourself you were afraid of, not me.'

His words frightened her because she could not be sure there was no truth in them. She struggled to her feet, avoiding his mocking eyes.

'I love my husband,' she said huskily. 'That much I do know, and I will not be unfaithful to him. You're wasting your time with all this talk.'

She tried to go past him to her horse, but his fingers caught her wrist in a viselike grip and he jerked her back around to face him.

'Dear Anne,' he said in a low, silky voice that nonetheless sent a chill of fear through her. 'Dear, lovely, foolish Anne, you misunderstand; I was not attempting to persuade or to argue my case. I will have you, for the simple reason that I want you, and because you are too weak and too hot-blooded and still too much in love with me to have it any other way. You see, what you are so afraid to face is that you have always been mine for the taking. You still are.'

She did lift her eyes then to meet his, and for a long moment they regarded one another in silence. Strangely, his words had a sobering effect on her agitated emotions. One may avoid the truth about oneself, but when one hears it from someone else, one must either face it or try to prove him wrong by becoming otherwise. It was true; she had been weak, and hot-blooded, and in love with him, and indeed she had been his for the taking, perhaps until this very moment. Perhaps that was why his visit here had disturbed her so greatly and why she had hidden in her room, avoiding all but the most necessary contact with him.

Perhaps all this was true, but now, faced with the naked truth, she found herself unable, from some vestige of pride or forgotten virtue, to admit it or to tolerate it in herself.

'You're a fool,' she said in a voice that surprised even her with its calmness. 'My entire love for you was a fraud, a sham, because I thought that you were a man, and I was a woman. But I have learned differently since then. I have learned what a man is, and in his arms how to be a woman. Let me go; there is nothing here for either of us.'

Her attack was so unexpected that he did indeed release her wrist. His cheeks flamed at the words she had flung at him, and for a moment he watched her go, tossing her hair haughtily as she went.

Suddenly his anger, his wounded vanity, exploded into fury. 'Bitch,' he cried, running after her, 'I'll make you eat those words. I'll have what I came for.'

She tried to run, but he caught her easily, twisting her about to face him. The horse whinnied nervously as the two humans struggled with one another in the clearing.

She fought him with all the strength and all the indignation that she possessed, and for a while her struggle so surprised him that he nearly let her go.

But no, he had waited too long; he had been too sure of himself, and her words had stung too sharply. Holding her wrists with one of his large hands, he slapped her viciously across the face, once, twice, three times, her head rocking wildly to and fro with the force of his blows.

Only half-conscious, she sank to her knees in the tall grass, her senses reeling from the blows. At once he was upon her, ripping her clothes, forcing her back onto the ground.

She continued to fight and kick, but it was useless; she was bare now from the waist down and she felt his knees between hers, driving her legs apart, and then the sudden brutal thrust of his entry, tearing painfully into her.

Jean paused at the top of a little hill, squinting into the distance. He was breathing heavily; since Katherine had brought her ominous news to him in the vineyards, he had run the entire distance back to the stables and from there had ridden pell-mell toward the river.

He thought he knew where she had gone; there was a spot near the place he had found her unconscious years before. She liked to go there when she was disturbed or unhappy; she said it reminded her of how lucky she had been without knowing it at the time.

He lifted the field glasses he had brought with him, scanning the distant riverbank. He saw her then, striding through the tall grass toward her horse. For a moment he felt a surge of relief.

Then, suddenly, someone else ran into view – the captain! For a moment Jean sat frozen, watching the struggle that followed. He saw and was gladdened by the fury with which his wife fought against her attacker.

But that satisfaction was nothing compared to the rage that boiled up within him. He lowered the glasses and furiously spurred the horse on. It was too far, and barring some miracle, he would be too late to prevent what was happening.

But he would be in time to settle the score.

Anne lay in a crumpled heap in the grass, sobbing quietly. Her body ached with the viciousness of his assault and the blows he had rained on her to overpower her, but those bruises tormented her less than the spiritual and emotional pain she was suffering. She felt wracked and dirtied, as if she could never again belong to herself.

Emile straightened his clothes, frowning at a long scratch across his arm that had drawn blood. Damn, this had been nothing like he had expected. He had been sure that once he'd gotten into her she would stop fighting him, that she would surrender to the desire for him that he was still sure she felt. To his surprise, she had continued to struggle to the very end, even while he was emptying his sperm into her belly.

No woman had ever resisted him that way before. Oh, to be sure, there were those who had offered resistance and had had to be overcome, but always they had submitted at last, while she . . . he felt angered and oddly disgusted by the entire situation.

'At least,' he said, beginning to wish he'd never followed the foolish bitch at his feet, 'you will no longer accuse me of not being a man.'

At that she turned her tear-streaked face up to him and her eyes flashed with a fire he had never seen in them before.

'You – you think you are a man, because you are stronger than I, because you can force your will upon me?' she demanded. 'You think a man is nothing more than brute force and hard flesh? No, a man is heart and mind too, and goodness and love and giving as well as getting. I told you that I had come to know what a man is these past few years, because I have lived with one. And now I know what you are as well, but it is not a man; you are a – a pig!'

She spat at him, and then began to cry into her hands once more. His eyes flashing angrily, he dropped to the grass beside her once more, reaching for her.

'Don't touch me,' she cried, lashing out with her hand and leaving furrows of red across his cheek.

'So,' he said, 'I thought I'd taken the fight out of you. But we've still plenty of time.' Again he reached for her, but his hand suddenly stopped in mid-air.

'On the contrary,' an icy voice said from behind him. 'You have less time than you think, Monsieur.'

Anne could not stop crying. Emile had risen at the sound of Jean's voice, but he now stood directly over her, so that she could not even get up and run to her husband. She tried to say something, to tell Jean that she was not to blame, but her throat felt paralyzed and no sound would come out.

For a long moment they all remained as if in a tableau. The two men seemed to have forgotten that she was there at their feet. Neither of them glanced at her; instead they watched each other, like a pair of dogs circling one another before a fight.

For a sickening moment Anne thought Jean really did blame her for what had happened, that this was why he did not glance at her or speak to her. Then he moved a little further into the clearing and she could see his face more clearly. To another, that placid, expressionless face must have been deceptive, but to her, knowing him now as she did, it was like the ringing of alarm bells.

Emile, who had looked shocked out of his wits at the first moment of surprise, managed to recover at least a semblance of his usual nonchalance.

'So, it's the farmer,' he said, dusting off his trousers as casually as if the three of them had been mere acquaintances passing in the street.

Jean took another step forward. His face was still devoid of any expression. Emile moved slightly backward.

'I suppose,' Emile said when Jean made no answer, 'that you'll want some sort of satisfaction? Do you want to do it formally – seconds and pistols and all that – or do you prefer swords? Pity you didn't bring one along with you today.'

Jean reached inside his shirt and a moment later a wicked-looking dagger clicked into view. 'It doesn't matter what sort of weapon you use,' he said speaking calmly and evenly. 'I'm going to kill you regardless.'

That calm, almost disinterested voice unnerved Emile more than any show of anger might have done. He edged still further away and said, 'Don't be foolish; she isn't worth it, you know.'

Anne saw the quick, sharp intake of Jean's breath, but still he held his emotions in check. She saw, too, the glance that Emile threw in the direction of his horse.

Emile had been sizing up the situation. He hated having to fight the slut's husband, especially since he would no doubt have to kill him, but it did look as if there were no other solution. That he could easily overpower the man facing him he had no doubt – after all, he was in the prime of his youth, a military man, used to combat, in peak condition, while the other man was twenty years his senior. Emile saw only a stockily built man dressed almost like a peasant; he did not see the last several years of working each day in the fields; he did not see the rock-hard muscles beneath the loose-fitting shirt; nor did he understand the depth of feeling seething beneath the placid exterior. Against the other man's dagger, he had a sword. It would be no match at all. Still nonchalantly, Emile drew his sword.

Jean, too, had no doubts regarding the outcome of the fight. Sword or no sword, he meant to kill the soldier; and knowing that, it was for a moment as if he held in his hand the man's entire life. He saw him as a boy going barefoot in the fields, frightening the partridges from their hiding places; as a youngster watching his mother make her way through a marketplace; as a young man laboring over his school lessons; as the poet, the lover, the soldier; all leading him to this final moment when all of that mounting force of life must suddenly and finally flee his body.

Emile moved first, thrusting suddenly with his sword. Anne, still lying on the ground, thought her husband must surely lose such an uneven match, but she had underestimated both his anger and his quickness. He neatly parried the thrust, and before Emile could even recover, Jean had darted inside the sword arm and slashed with the knife blade. A streak of red suddenly sprouted along Emile's arm.

Emile blinked and glanced downward at the spreading stain. The man had moved so swiftly that Emile had hardly realized what had happened, and now once again the farmer was at his distance, the dagger held point up before him. Still his face was blank.

Again Emile thrust with his sword, and again he found nothing but empty air; the farmer had twisted and danced aside with the agility of a cat.

Jean had learned to fight as a boy, in the alleys and back streets of Paris. He had been no more than ten when he had killed his first man, a stinking gutter rat who had wounded and tried to rob Jean's father. There was not a fight trick that Jean did not know, and although he had not used them in many years, they were not forgotten.

Again and again Emile came after him, and again and again Jean either dodged the sword's thrusts or parried them expertly with his dagger. Emile had begun to sweat and his eyes flicked nervously to and fro as he looked for an opening. Twice more Jean had darted in to cut at him with the dagger – not serious wounds, although two of them bled profusely; it was more as if the man were taunting him, exposing his vulnerability so that he could experience fear.

The sweat ran down into Emile's eyes, blurring his vision.

Damn the man, why wouldn't he stand still! It was like fighting a ghost.

Emile lunged, but the man was not where he had been; instead, the sword struck rock. The blade snapped, half of it sailing through the air to land a good fifteen feet away. Emile was left with a useless weapon.

Now for the first time his opponent showed some emotion. He smiled and, with an unconcerned gesture, threw aside his own blade.

'And now, tin soldier,' he said, stepping forward.

Emile made a sudden dash for his horse, but he had gone no more than a few feet when Jean caught him. The two men grappled and swayed, looking almost as if they were doing a grotesque dance together in the grassy clearing.

Emile slipped and fell, bringing his forearm up as he did so and blocking the chopping blow aimed at his throat; he countered with a hard punch at Jean's stomach. Anne could almost see the shock of pain rush through her husband's body, making him recoil. At the same moment Emile lunged. Jean's mouth seemed to explode with blood. His head rocked with the force of another blow and he went down, taking Emile with him. The two men rolled together, the tall grass making it hard for Anne to see what was happening. She could see Emile's arm rising and falling, his fist smashing again and again into Jean's face. The blood seemed to be a mask that Jean was wearing, his whole face dyed red.

Anne struggled to her knees, remembering the dagger. If she could find it, she could bury it in Emile's back and save her husband's life. Jean was so much older than Emile, and he was not accustomed to fighting. She would save him . . . what did she care if she must kill a man. No, what she had said earlier was true – Emile was not a man; he was a beast, who deserved to die like one. If only she could find the dagger . . .

She crawled in the direction in which she thought the dagger had fallen, searching for it through the long grass. Surely it had landed around here, hadn't it . . . no? Then here . . . or . . . God in heaven, where had it gone?

Emile had somehow twisted free of Jean's grip, and now he was leaping away. He saw a rock and his hand closed over it, but Jean was too quick; in an instant he was on his feet, kicking out at the hand lifting the rock. There was a yelp of pain as fingers were crushed between foot and rock. But at almost the same moment Emile's leg came up, his heavy boot catching Jean in the groin, making him double over in pain, and at once Emile had caught Jean's legs and brought him to the ground again, and the two men were clawing and rolling, pummeling one another once more.

Something gleamed in the grass – the knife. Anne seized it with trembling hands, holding it before her awkwardly. Of course she had never used a dagger before, but there was nothing to it, was there? She had only to hold it firmly, to stand above Emile's back and bring the point down, down into . . . she got unsteadily to her feet and staggered toward the two fighters.

But how could she make sure that she stabbed Emile and not Jean? They weren't holding still, and half the time she couldn't even tell who was on top and who was lying underneath, his face being pounded out of recognition, his arm twisted beneath him at an impossible angle.

She caught her breath and stumbled backward. It was Emile on the ground, his breath coming in uneven little gasps as the hands at his throat tightened, tightened . . .

In her search for the dagger, Anne had forgotten the discarded sword, but their struggles had brought the two men close to the place where it had fallen and now Emile's good hand, flailing weakly about, found the broken blade. He caught it, brought it up and down, stabbing into Jean's shoulder.

Jean stiffened and jerked back, the blade pulling free. Emile tried to fling himself aside but he was too weak and his legs were still twisted together with Jean's. Jean's hand found Emile's throat again, tightening, tightening, as Emile's struggles grew weaker.

Suddenly the fight was over. The breath tore out of Emile's throat in a sort of whistle, and he sprawled lifelessly across the ground.

Anne leaned back wearily against the trunk of a tree, closing her eyes and letting the unused dagger fall to the ground.

After a long moment Jean got slowly to his feet and stood looking down at the body. Opening her eyes, Anne watched him, watched the way he slumped with weariness, saw the filth and the blood and the fatigue on his face.

He turned, finally, looking at her, but his gaze was despairing. 'I'll have to turn myself over to the soldiers,' he said dully.

'No!' She sprang away from the tree, hurrying across the clearing to him. 'He isn't worth it,' she said, not realizing she was echoing what Emile had said of her a short time before. 'No one knows of what happened here – no one but you and me.'

She glanced toward the river and then back at him. For a moment husband and wife regarded one another. Then, wordlessly, he stooped down and gathered up Emile's body, flinging it rudely over his shoulder. He straightened, swaying for a moment until he got his balance; then he started with his burden toward the river.

Anne looked quickly around, searching for evidence. She saw the sword and collected the two pieces, and his hat. She took them with her and hurried after Jean.

At the river's bank he stooped down again and slowly lowered his burden into the dark water. It hung suspended at their feet for a few seconds, as if loath to part from them. Then, caught by the swift current under the surface, it slid away, turning, bumping into a rock, hurrying on toward the distant curve that took the river out of sight. Anne threw the hat and the sword into the water. The sword disappeared immediately beneath the surface, but the hat floated, spinning slowly around and then racing off on its master's trail.

She tore off a piece of her skirt and began to bathe her husband's face. There was too much blood, and at length, still wordlessly, they both stripped and bathed in the river's waters, wading into a shallow pool a little upstream. Again and again Anne lowered herself completely into the water, washing away the shame and degradation that she had suffered.

Finally Jean got out of the water and stood drying himself on his dirty shirt. He watched her for a moment and in that moment he realized fully for the first time how much he loved her, and why.

She had been loyal to him, at least in her heart and mind, regardless of what had been done to her body. And perhaps, after all, that was love.

He knew then what had made him want her all along – not just her prettiness, not just her aristocratic heritage, but a force within that perhaps even she had not known she possessed. Until today it had been an undefined something that had drawn him toward her. There were women who loved like that, for whom love meant loyalty, and vice versa – not just the loyalty of the bed, but something more than that. All his life he had looked for this in a woman, and now it was his, in his own wife.

She splashed toward the riverbank, and he gave her his hand to help her out of the water. They stood together, naked, and looking into his face, she saw the love written there, blending with the cuts and the bruises and the fatigue. He took her in his arms.

Some primordial instinct rose within her, the elation of the woman whose man has fought and killed for her, in cave or forest, on barren desert or ship at sea, or medieval courtyard. Blood boiling, she clung to him. Together they toppled into the grass.

The captain's body was not found for three days. It was assumed that he had gone to the river to bathe and, somehow losing his footing, had been carried off by the dangerous current. His horse had drifted back riderless that same night. It was said that the captain's face especially had been badly battered by the rocks.

A brief inquiry was held. The master of the chateau, Baron de Brussac, had been taken with a fever and was unable to leave his bedroom to testify, but it was agreed by all that there was nothing he could contribute to the proceedings, as he had been with his workmen the entire time, as a dozen or more of his servants were willing to testify.

As for Madame, she, too, had been riding that afternoon, but she had seen nothing of the captain. She had, in fact, ridden in the opposite direction, to the vineyards to see her husband. As, again, numerous witnesses were willing to swear.

After two days the inquiry was closed and the captain's death ruled an accident. The soldiers prepared to leave.

On their last night there, the captain's young aide, Lieutenant Gabin, asked to speak to the baron. He was informed that the baron was not well enough for visitors, whereupon he asked to speak to Madame de Brussac.

Somewhat reluctantly, Anne met with the young soldier in her husband's study. After a short while she rang for Henriette, and asked her to ask the baron to join them after all. Jean, his face still purple with bruises, descended to the study, and the three were closeted together for most of the evening.

The following month, Lieutenant Gabin resigned his commission in the royal army. It seemed that a long-forgotten relative had died, naming the young man his heir, and the lieutenant was on his way abroad, possessed of a not inconsiderable fortune.

Two months later Anne faced the unwelcome truth that she was pregnant again. Her third child, another son, was born the following winter, on Christmas night. She named him René. For the first time Jean was not at her side to welcome their new child.

23

'René, for heaven's sake, must you drum on the window like that? It's quite annoying.'

René said, over his shoulder, 'Sorry, Mama.' But in a moment he had started once again to drum on the window glass while he stared out at the lightly falling rain with a petulant expression.

Anne observed him in silence for a moment. What a pretty boy he was, she thought with a mother's pride. At fourteen he was almost girlish, with his long, dark lashes and pale, delicately tinted skin. He had the look of a wounded angel, with his often pouty expression and his fragile build.

'Where is your brother?' she asked aloud. 'Perhaps he's doing something interesting.'

'Claude went riding,' The tatoo of the fingers on the glass increased in intensity slightly.

'In the rain? Oh, dear. Well, anyway, he never gets chills. He certainly has his father's constitution. What about Marie?'

'Same as always, trailing after Claude – her and Danielle both,' René said scornfully, as if to indicate his disdain of trailing after anyone.

'Danielle too?' Anne said, frowning. She supposed one of these days she really must say something to Jeanette; after all, it wasn't exactly right for Danielle to treat Claude and Marie as if they were her brother and sister, when in fact she was a servant's daughter.

Anne sighed; on the other hand, it was not really the children's fault; it was probably inevitable that the children should

grow up as close as they had, having been thrown together
since their infancy. Then, too, they were nearly the same age,
the girls only a few months apart and a year or so younger than
Claude. For some time now Anne had suspected that little
Danielle had a crush on Claude. She supposed she should have
put her foot down long before this.

Oh well, girls of Danielle's age often had crushes that
amounted to nothing, and anyway, Jeanette had confided that
in a year, maybe even sooner, Danielle would be marrying
that nice young man from the village – François, she thought
his name was – and that would settle that.

In the meantime there was the immediate problem of René
– her little darling, as she always teased him when she was
trying to cheer him up – looking most lonely, as he often did.

'There,' she said, relieved. 'I hear your father coming down.
I believe he said he was going into town this afternoon; why
don't you go along with him?'

René's fingers threatened to pound right through the glass.
'You know he won't want me with him – he never does,' he
said.

'Why, René, what an outrageous thing to say – oh, do stop
that drumming on the glass.' She spoke more sharply than she
had intended, partly because his words touched a sore spot
within her own breast. She, too, thought that Jean was distant
toward their youngest son, although she had long since learned
the foolishness of making that accusation aloud.

In a way, she could understand Jean's feelings; but there was
no way of ever really *knowing*. Fortunately, or unfortunately,
perhaps, the child looked most like her. Oh, it was true, sometimes when she looked at him of a sudden, she thought she
caught a glimpse of Emile; but again, there were times when
she thought he looked like no one so much as Jean.

What Jean saw when he looked at the boy she did not know,
as it was a subject he refused to discuss. In the fourteen years
since the boy had been born, Jean had been patient with him,
perhaps more indulgent and generous than he had been with
the other children, and always cordial. But cordiality was not
love, and Jean had never been loving toward the child. Perhaps
it was for this reason that Anne had been especially affectionate
toward him – doting, even. After all, whatever had happened
those long years ago, it was not René's fault.

Jean came into the room, already wearing his cloak. 'There
you are,' he said. 'I'm going to be leaving now.'

Anne put aside her book and jumped up, going to her husband with a bright smile. 'I just finished suggesting that René go with you,' she said. 'I told him you would enjoy the company.'

René had turned from the window with a defiant expression that was at the same time rather pathetic in one so young and frail-looking.

Jean said – did he hesitate just a trifle too long there, surely René wouldn't notice – 'Of course. You'll need a cloak, René, it's still raining.'

'I'll tell Jeanette,' Anne said gratefully, but René said, 'I'll get it,' and left the room. He walked stiffly, but when he had reached the hall, she heard him taking the steps two at a time.

'Thank you,' she said.

'For taking the boy for a ride? After all these years, you still think I'm going to sell him off to the gipsies first chance I get, don't you?' He chuckled and leaned down to kiss the tip of her nose. 'We'll be back by nightfall. Tell my son we still have a chess game to finish.'

She watched them from the doorway until the carriage disappeared down the drive. She supposed it was too much to hope for that some day the two of them might thaw toward one another. Even Jean must see how differently he treated his oldest son Claude. The two of them were forever seeking one another's company, arguing politics – thank God Jean had someone to listen to his political outpourings now and she needn't pretend to understand what it was all about – and Claude had inherited his father's love for the soil. Like his father, Claude seemed to be happiest when tending the vines, although by now Chateau Brussac could well afford to hire all the field workers they needed. Jean's wines had done well, and last year the wine society had given an award to one of his reds. Father and son had gotten drunk together to celebrate that; René, of course, had been too young, even had he been interested in wines, which he was not.

Anne sighed and came back inside. There were times she sorely missed old Henriette's sound, homely advice; it hardly seemed possible that it had been four years now since she had passed away. Of course, the house still ran smoothly. Young Katherine seemed enough like her mother at times to pass for her ghost, and she had slipped quietly, almost unnoticed, into her mother's old role of managing the household.

'And I should be thankful for that,' Anne told herself, re-

membering how often she had heard other women complain of
the difficulties of getting decent employees in these revolutionary times. Well, that at least had never been a problem
of theirs.

Indeed, most of the turmoil of the last decade and a half –
the periodic disturbances in Paris and the other major cities,
even the recent abdication of Louis Philippe and the formation
of the Second Republic, as they called it – had left their day-to-
day lives at the Chateau Brussac largely untouched. And for
that she was truly grateful.

She thought of how much Paris had changed on their last
visit; she hardly recognized the city now. That ugly arch that
Napoleon had begun had finally been completed, she couldn't
think why; and the state of the arts – those garish paintings of
Delacroix that everyone was so enthusiastic about, and the
music – that 'opera', if you wanted to call it that, of M. Berlioz;
she had thought even the title of the piece vulgar: *The Dam-
nation of Faust*, indeed. Why on earth had the Opéra Comique
resorted to playing such works, even if the composer himself
had footed the bill? It didn't benefit the public any to see how
badly music had slipped.

Well, it had all passed them by, thank heaven for that. Her
children had grown up threatened by no more than the ordinary
dangers of growing up. With a husband and a son as hot-headed
as Jean and Claude, she could just imagine what sort of mis-
adventures they'd have had in Paris these last few years. Here,
at least, there was little trouble to get into.

'Claude, where are you taking us?'

Claude, pushing his way through the heavy brush that
blocked their path, answered without pausing, 'I'm not taking
you anywhere, little sister. I merely said I was going to investigate something very intriguing, and you two insisted on tagging
along after me.'

'Only because you made it sound so mysterious – ouch!'
Marie gave a cry as a thistle branch snapped back after her
brother and scratched her hand.

Danielle, who was bringing up the rear, pushed around her.
'Here, let me go in front of you and hold the branches,' she
said.

Marie was only too glad to oblige, although she well knew
that Danielle only cared about moving closer to Claude. Not
that Marie herself was any less in thrall to her handsome

brother; both girls were his adoring slaves. As for Claude, he accepted their homage matter-of-factly, although occasionally he declared it a nuisance to have them ever at his heels.

Fortunately, at least the rain had ended. They had been climbing an embankment, and now they reached the top, only to find their way barred by a stone wall too high to see over.

'What did you expect to see here?' Marie demanded, scrambling up the last few feet. 'There hasn't been anyone living here in years.'

'You'll see,' Claude said, reaching to grab a tree branch and pulling himself up into the foliage, 'if you climb up here.'

Danielle stood on tiptoe, trying to get hold of the branch, but she could barely scratch the wood with her nails. 'I can't reach it,' she said.

'Ssh, not so loud. Here.' Claude dropped back to the ground and, putting his hands about Danielle, lifted her easily into the air so that she could reach the branch. Smiling in secret delight, Danielle pulled herself up into the tree while Claude helped Marie and then joined them.

'But you still haven't said – oh.' Marie started and almost fell from her perch as she suddenly became aware of the muffled sound of voices below. She stared into the courtyard of the chateau, their nearest neighbor and deserted for longer than she could remember.

'They arrived yesterday,' Claude explained in a whisper.

'Who are they?' Danielle asked.

Claude shrugged. 'I haven't found that out yet – look, isn't she beautiful?'

A woman had come into view in an open doorway. Danielle, craning forward anxiously for a glimpse of Claude's idea of beauty, took an immediate dislike to the woman in the doorway. She had, Danielle decided, an overblown quality that had nothing to do with her elegant gown, her perfectly arranged hair, or her graceful carriage. There was something unmistakably sluttish about the stranger; it was in the humid look in her eyes, the frank sensuality of her smile.

'I don't think she's so beautiful, do you, Marie?' Danielle asked.

'Oh, who cares about her; look at him,' Marie whispered intently, staring.

A man appeared behind the woman, talking to her. For a moment they stepped into the courtyard and the three in the tree branches ducked out of sight, but then the woman seemed to remember something and went back into the house, followed by the man.

He was, Marie thought, the best-looking man she had ever seen, with an angular, harsh-looking face and dark, piercing eyes. He walked with an exaggerated swagger that would have been laughable if he weren't so handsome.

'I suppose he's her husband,' she said, a trifle glumly, and Claude, with a sigh of his own, said, 'I imagine so.' Danielle, who found nothing remarkable about the pair below and who had already gotten bored with this adventure, said abruptly, 'Let's go.'

'Don't be a spoilsport,' Marie said. 'I want to get a better look. I wonder who they are . . . ' She began to crawl further out onto the branch that overhung the courtyard.

'Marie, be careful,' Claude whispered, but too late. His sister had already lost her precarious balance, and with a little squeal she toppled into the courtyard.

In an instant Claude had swung himself from the branch and dropped to the ground beside her. 'Are you hurt?' he asked, kneeling.

There was a sound from inside the house and in a moment the man and woman came out, the man leading, a sword in his hand.

'I tell you I heard something – stay inside,' the man barked over his shoulder. 'This may be one of Cavaignac's assassins.'

He stopped short when he saw Marie sprawled gracelessly on the ground, with Claude bending over her. 'What the . . . who the devil are you?' he demanded.

'We're not anyone's assassins,' Claude said, 'we're your neighbors, and that's a fine way to welcome us, at the point of a sword.'

'My neighbors?' The man stared, then pointed with his sword to the face peering out through the tree leaves. 'And who's that?'

'That's our friend, Danielle,' Marie said, getting to her feet and brushing off her gown.

'Well, tell her to get down here where I can see her.' In a moment Danielle dropped lightly to the ground alongside her friends. The man with the sword peered up into the foliage to determine if anyone else lurked there.

'We heard someone was moving in here, so we came to see if we could get a look at our new neighbors,' Claude said, assuming an air of bravado that he did not entirely feel. 'Now be a good fellow and put down your sword, before you frighten the girls.'

'Before I frighten . . . ?' The man's face flushed angrily. 'What do you think you did to us, dropping out of the trees – there are simpler ways of paying calls, you know.'

It was the woman who intervened, coming up to touch his sleeve lightly with one finger. 'Come now, Hector,' she said, her voice a throaty purr. 'There's been no real harm done, has there? And if we're all going to be neighbors, oughtn't we be friends as well?'

She smiled directly at Claude, making his breath catch in his throat. She was the most beautiful woman he had ever seen – not that he had seen so many. Oh, Mama was beautiful, certainly, but she didn't count, and Marie, for all that he was fond of her, was in fact quite plain. As for Danielle – well, she was pretty enough, he supposed, if you liked girls with small breasts and slim hips; she had a little gamin face, with enormous brown eyes that were huge windows to whatever she happened to be feeling at the moment, a funny upturned nose, and an oddly voluptuous face.

Yes, Danielle was pretty when you stopped to think about it, but it was not the kind of beauty you fell in love with. This creature, though – his heart melted inside him when she smiled at him again.

'Permit me to introduce us,' she was saying. 'This is Count Hector de Trémorel, and I am his sister, Antoinette.'

She extended her hand and Claude seized it a bit too eagerly and bowed, pressing his lips to her scented fingers and ignoring the sound of a muffled giggle from Danielle's direction.

'Mademoiselle, *enchantée*,' he said, bowing in her brother's direction as well. 'I am Claude de Brussac, and this is my sister, Marie, and . . . ' he hesitated, then finished a bit lamely, 'Danielle.'

Danielle gave her dark hair a toss and said defiantly, 'My mother is their mother's maid.'

A precisely plucked eyebrow arched upward. 'Really?' Antoinette de Trémorel said. 'How quaint.'

Her brother, looking a bit mollified, said, 'I must apologize for my temper; you gave us a start. We thought – well, never mind what we thought.'

'I'm afraid it's I who must apologize for our untimely arrival,' Claude said. 'But why would you think General Cavaignac would be sending assassins to . . . unless – oh, you don't mean to say you're supporters of Louis Napoleon?'

'Claude,' Marie said, 'you know Papa said we weren't to discuss those things outside of our own home.'

'And quite right, too,' the count said smoothly, giving her a dazzling smile that made her legs feel too weak to support her. 'Let's just say we left Paris for reasons of our health.'

Brother and sister exchanged sly grins. Antoinette said, 'At any rate, we are here, and now that we have all met, we must become the best of friends. Today we are in too much of a turmoil – you must forgive us if we do not invite you to stay – but perhaps tomorrow you'll bring your sister and come for a proper visit?'

Marie blushed and looked confused, but Claude, obviously delighted, bowed again. 'We shall be delighted, Mademoiselle. And now I think we should take our leave.'

'But stop, there's no need to go the way you came. We do have a proper gate, you know.'

'But our horses are here,' Claude said; he reached for Marie and would have hoisted her up into the branches, but to his surprise she pushed his hands away.

'I think we shall leave by the gate,' she announced, her face crimson.

'But why on earth . . . the horses are back here, we shall have to walk all the way around . . . '

'Nevertheless, I think we shall leave by the gate,' Marie insisted, looking daggers at her brother, who finally seemed to grasp her meaning.

'Oh yes, I see,' he said lamely.

'Well, I for one don't intend to walk all the way around,' Danielle said. Without waiting for assistance, she jumped up for a branch and pulled herself up into the tree. In a moment she had disappeared into the foliage.

Claude looked uncertainly from the tree to his sister, but it was Antoinette who resolved the dilemma for him. To his surprise and pleasure, she came and took his arm in an affectionate gesture.

'Come,' she said, 'we'll walk you to the front gate. Hector, do take the young lady's arm, please.'

So brother and sister found themselves at the entrance to the Chateau Trémorel, with a firm invitation to call the following day, and each of them looked forward to the following day with a great deal of eagerness.

When they had gone, the count and his sister strolled arm in arm back to the little courtyard. 'Bumpkins,' the count said in a bored voice.

'I don't know, I thought the boy was rather attractive in a rustic way – quite handsome, if you hadn't noticed – but I don't suppose he's ever been in a proper drawing-room. What did you make of his sister?'

'Shy, rather homely, in fact – but you're right, I suppose; there is something about that sort – a fresh, unspoiled quality . . . '

'That you would enjoy spoiling, hmmm?' She winked and they laughed together. He took her in his arms and kissed her rather hotly on the mouth.

'You know me too well, my pet,' he said finally.

'But of course. And anyway, how else are we to pass the time here in the country? What did you think of the other one?'

'That servant wench? Rather brazen, wasn't she? When the empire is restored under Louis Napoleon and we've gotten rid of that fool Cavaignac and his government, that kind will learn their place quickly enough. But come, I believe you had just promised me a cognac when we were interrupted.'

'Oh, and Hector,' Antoinette said, pausing on their way inside. 'That tree – I wonder if you oughtn't to have it cut down?'

He glanced toward the tree from which Marie had fallen a short time before. 'Yes, I see what you mean. If they can get in that way, perhaps someone else . . . I'll have it taken care of first thing tomorrow. How clever of you to think of it.'

'Well, after all, we did come to the country for our health,' she said.

Laughing, the two strolled arm in arm back into the house.

24

Danielle did not wait for the other two to join her but instead mounted up and rode hard for home.

Gradually, though, she slowed the horse's pace until, by the time they reached the road, he was at a walk. She was still seething, not only at the rude way in which she had been dis-

missed as only a servant's daughter, but especially at the way
Claude had made a fool of himself over that woman. Really,
men were such children sometimes.

She was almost home and so absorbed in her angry thoughts
that she did not see the figure half-hidden in the shrubbery by
the gate until he had stepped suddenly into her path, making
the horse whinny and buck.

'François,' she snapped, quieting her mount, 'how dare you
sneak up on me that way? You might've made my horse bolt.'

'If you weren't out riding with the vintner's son, I wouldn't
have to sneak up on my own fiancée,' François retorted,
taking the horse's reins from her hand and scowling up at her.
He was a good-looking young man in a brutish way, with the
dark hair, dark eyes and olive skin of his native Provence. A
great many girls from the village fancied themselves in love
with him, and Danielle's mama told her repeatedly that she
should feel fortunate François had chosen her, but in fact
Danielle was more frightened of him than flattered.

Just at the moment, though, she was too angry to feel frightened. 'I'm not your fiancée,' she said, trying unsuccessfully to
jerk the reins from his hand, 'and I shall go riding with anyone
I please. Let go of me.'

She brought her quirt down smartly across the back of his
hand, making him swear and jerk his hand away.

'Bitch,' he said, rubbing the welt she had raised. 'I have half
a mind to teach you how a man treats a stubborn wife.'

'I'm not your wife, and I don't ever intend to be. I don't care
what our parents have agreed upon. Now get out of my way.'

François stepped obediently aside, but his coal-black eyes
watched her intently as she started to ride by him. Danielle let
out the breath she had been holding. François was especially
known for his ugly temper, which was one of the reasons she
had made up her mind not to marry him – even if she hadn't
been in love with Claude – and she had not expected to get
herself out of this situation so easily.

When François moved again, it was so quickly and so unexpectedly that he caught her completely off guard. One hand
seized the reins again, while the other caught her wrist. Danielle
tried to hit out again with her quirt but she was off balance,
and when he yanked hard at her wrist, threatening to pull her
arm out of its socket, she slid sideways on the saddle. The horse
whinnied and reared; Danielle had just enough presence of
mind to kick her feet free of the stirrups and then she was

falling into François's arms and the horse was bolting toward home.

'You – you . . . ' she sputtered, struggling against him, 'let go of me!'

'I ought to break your neck for talking back to me that way,' he said, tightening his grip on her.

For an answer she brought up one booted foot and kicked him hard in the shins. He grunted in pain and for a moment let her go. She tried to run, but once more he was faster than she was. He grabbed her arm and, swinging her back around to face him, he slapped her face hard.

They had both been so engrossed in their fight that they had not heard the distant approach of riders until Claude suddenly shouted, 'François!'

François turned and saw Claude riding down hard upon him, with Marie some distance behind. There was just time to give Danielle a shove, sending her toppling into the ditch, and then Claude was diving from his horse, catching François in a bone-crunching tackle, and the two men crashed to the ground together.

Marie rode up, jumping down from her horse and running to Danielle, who was just shaking herself off in the ditch.

'Are you all right?' Marie asked, kneeling to help her friend.

'Yes, I'm fine, but Claude – François is a vicious fighter,' she said.

'Don't worry about Claude, he'll handle that one,' Marie said confidently.

At the moment it was not clear just who was handling whom. The two young men rolled to and fro on the still-wet ground, fists lifting and falling rhythmically. François had the advantage in both age and weight, but Claude fought with the fury of an avenging angel, so that he was soon winning.

François apparently had decided that discretion was the better part of valor. He delivered a blow to Claude's mid-section, stunning him momentarily. In an instant François was scrambling to his feet and running off down the road.

'That's right,' Claude yelled after him, 'run off to your robber friends, and leave decent folk alone in the future.' There were stories that said François was friendly with a band of thieves and smugglers who sometimes made the roads perilous for travelers, although no one had ever accused him directly.

The two girls ran to help Claude to his feet, but he airily dismissed their assistance and got up on his own, holding his side where François had managed to kick him.

'And as for you . . . ' he began, turning on Danielle.

'And as for me, what?' she asked, putting her hands on her hips.

For a moment they glowered at one another, but although Claude felt annoyed with her, he could not quite put his finger on what it was that made him angry.

'Stay out of trouble,' he finished lamely. Turning his back on them, he collected his horse from the ditch where he'd gone to graze and, swinging lightly up into the saddle, he rode on toward the house alone.

He was whistling contentedly, however, by the time he strode into the house. Anne, rising to greet him, was shocked by his appearance. His shirt was in shreds, his trousers mud-stained; there was blood on his face from a gash on his forehead, and one eye had already begun to turn blue-black.

'Claude, what on earth happened?' she asked, rushing to him.

'Don't worry, they look worse than they feel,' he said cheerily. 'Anyway, you should have seen François when I finished with him.'

'François? But why on earth were you fighting with François?'

'Because he was manhandling Danielle.'

Anne had gone to the decanter on a nearby table and poured some brandy onto her handkerchief. Now she came back and began to dab gingerly at the wound on his forehead.

'But Claude,' she said, equally gingerly, 'you know François and Danielle are engaged; you've really no business interfering . . . '

'They aren't engaged,' he said sharply, shoving her hand away. 'Danielle is never going to marry him.'

'Really? Then pray tell who *is* she going to marry?'

For a moment he did not seem to have an answer; then he said angrily, 'She can marry anybody she chooses, just so long as she doesn't marry that horse thief.'

With that he strode from the room, leaving his mother to stare open-mouthed after him.

Neither Claude nor his sister told their parents of their visit to the home of their new neighbors.

For his part, Claude had a pretty good idea how his father would react to the information that the count was a supporter of Louis Napoleon's claim to the throne; his father considered Prince Louis a fool and a danger to the French people.

General Cavaïgnac, who was Louis Napoleon's chief opponent, had been made dictator pro tempore in June, and since then he had cracked down hard on the political associations and especially the secret societies that had fomented much of the upheaval of recent years. Many of the people involved in such societies had left Paris to avoid arrest, and perhaps this explained why the count and his sister had come to the country at this time.

At the same time, however, under General Cavaignac's direction, the national assembly was hard at work preparing a new constitution, which was promised to the people by the end of the year. The general had pledged, too, that free elections would be held, in accord with the new constitution, and then the French people would have the opportunity to choose for themselves between him and Prince Louis.

Notwithstanding the seclusion of the country, Claude, like most young Frenchmen of his generation, had an active interest in politics, having been raised on upheaval and insurrection; in fact, however, when the time came to start out the following day for the Chateau Trémorel, his thoughts were on the beautiful Antoinette.

Had he really seen that look of interest in her eyes yesterday, or had he only imagined it? His inflamed imagination had fed on the prospect the entire night, keeping him tossing and turning upon his bed.

Of course, he knew that girls were attracted to him from time to time – Danielle's were not the only eyes that fastened upon him eagerly whenever he came around – but this was different. Antoinette was sophisticated and beautiful, a woman of the world. He guessed her to be in her mid-twenties – an older woman, with all the glamor and experience that implied, and, like most young men, he found that intriguing.

Marie, for her part, was rather glad that Claude was occupied with his own thoughts, as she was absorbed in her own reflections.

For one thing, she was hurt by Danielle's sulkiness since yesterday's meeting. Marie had even suggested rather tepidly that Danielle come with them today, but the suggestion had met with scorn.

'They made it clear yesterday that they don't care for entertaining people of the servant class,' she said, and flounced off.

Marie, who hated making anyone unhappy, had wrestled with her conscience during the night, while her brother was struggling with his desire. Perhaps she should not go to the Chateau Trémorel again, or perhaps she should tell her mother of their previous visit and get her advice. But when she shyly suggested this second possibility to her brother, he was adamant.

'Stay home if you like; it's nothing to me,' he said. 'But don't say anything to anyone, not until – until we've had a chance to get to know the de Trémorels better. It may be that their political views are not as severe as they seem.'

Marie thought personally that politics had little to do with the situation; she knew that it was the memory of the count's handsome face that was drawing her back, and she had seen, too, how eagerly her brother had responded to Antoinette's flirtation.

Still, the appointed time had come, and here she was riding along silently at her brother's side, and there was the chateau just before them. It was too late now to pay any attention to the inner voice that had been nagging at her.

Antoinette was amused. Not that she wasn't used to having men fall in love with her, even very young men – but this country boy was so different from what she was used to. He had such a charming smile. He was ingenious and naïve at the same time, with all the enthusiasm of youth and the manners of a cavalry officer. Too, the fact that he was good looking did not hurt, with his steel blue eyes and his curly chestnut hair that grew thickly on his neck. He seemed uncertain of what still lay within him to offer to the world.

As for the girl, well, Hector would know how to deal with her. He was quite competent in dealing with virgins, as she recalled, although he had complained recently that they were becoming something of a novelty in Paris.

'You see,' she had said, 'there are compensations in moving to the country.'

He had said nothing, only scratched his chin and smiled, but she saw now that he was displaying some interest in the little goose, at least when he wasn't scowling at Antoinette and the boy – if only Hector weren't so jealous!

Antoinette turned her attention on the girl.

'Tell me, my dear,' she said, 'what do you think of George Sand's books?'

Marie, confused by the unexpected attention, blushed and answered, 'I'm not familiar with them.'

'What! You can't mean it; I thought there wasn't a woman in France who hadn't devoured them hungrily. But you must let me lend them to you – they're delicious. She epitomizes the spirit of revolt against the institution of marriage.'

Marie, who in fact was not sure she favored revolt against the institution of marriage, smiled shyly and said, 'Thank you, I should like to read them.' She did not add that she would have to conceal them from her mother, who almost surely would disapprove of her reading them.

'And you,' Hector said drily, addressing Claude, 'I suppose like most boys you prefer the novels of M. Dumas?'

Smarting, Claude replied, 'Not at all. I've just finished de Tocqueville's *Democracy in America*, and I plan to begin *The Communist Manifesto*, by Marx and Engels – are you familiar with it?'

'I wouldn't waste my time on such rubbish,' Hector said, more sharply than he had intended. 'Communists, democrats, power in the hands of the people – what nonsense! France has had two decades of turmoil because the people have had too much power. What is needed is a strong man, like Louis Napoleon – someone to rule with an iron fist.'

'Why should the people need someone to rule them at all, with an iron fist or otherwise? Why should they not rule themselves, through a democratic process?'

'Hector, darling,' Antoinette said, heading off the impending quarrel. 'Perhaps just for today we could put aside politics and merely enjoy the company of our charming guests? Claude, you must come with me, I have a drawing by Ingres that I'm sure you'll enjoy.'

She took his arm and would have led him from the room, but Claude hesitated, glancing in Marie's direction. It was really not proper to leave her unchaperoned. After all, he was responsible for her.

Seeing the glance, Antoinette reassured him. 'Hector will entertain your sister – unless, of course,' she added, speaking to Marie, 'you don't feel safe in his company?' She laughed to indicate the outrageousness of the suggestion.

'Please, I don't mind,' Marie stammered, embarrassed at being treated like a child.

Claude hesitated a moment longer, but Antoinette ran her fingers teasingly up his arm. 'Or perhaps you're frightened of me,' she said, her eyes searching his. 'It is hanging in my bedroom. I suppose I could bring it down here to show it to you?' She cocked an eyebrow.

'That won't be necessary,' he said. 'We'll be back – ' he said to the room in general, adding, after a pause, 'in a moment.' With Antoinette clinging to his arm, he went out.

The count, pouring himself a fresh drink, scowled darkly after them. His sister was shameless, the way she was throwing herself at that stupid lout. He had a good mind to . . . He turned then and saw the girl sitting stiffly in her chair; he had all but forgotten about her. She looked like a frightened mouse.

But for all that, she was not without a certain appeal; there is a type of innocence that invites corruption, and seeing her there, so timid looking, so vulnerable, he poured a second drink and brought it to her.

'Tell me, my child,' he said, giving her the benefit of his most persuasive smile, 'have you ever been to Paris?'

'I was there two years ago, with my family,' she said, taking the drink hesitantly; she was accustomed to having wine, judiciously watered, with her meals, but she had never been permitted to drink brandy. She took an experimental sip; it burned her tongue and she had to make an effort not to grimace, but the second sip was better.

'Really,' the count was saying; he offered her his hand. 'Come, let us walk in the garden, and you shall tell me everything that you saw and did.'

25

'There you are,' the count said, helping Marie onto her horse. 'But tell me, my little country flower, why do you scowl so fiercely? Is something wrong?'

Marie, taking the reins from him, avoided his eyes. 'I – there is something I wanted to discuss with you,' she said.

'I hope you don't mean to tell me that your parents have learned of your visits here?' The count raised an eyebrow.

'No, it's . . . ' Again she hesitated. 'Oh, it will wait till the next time.'

He shrugged. 'As you wish,' he said. 'Till the next time, then.'

For a moment she regarded him in a curious manner, then she gave him a somewhat troubled smile and rode away.

Hector de Trémorel stood by the gate watching her go. For the past few weeks she had been coming more often alone, as her brother had been busy helping with the harvest and the making of the wine.

All in all, he felt rather pleased with himself. The afternoon they had spent together had left him languid and physically satisfied. In the nearly three months since the affair had begun, the little country wench had proven after all to be a rather spirited lover once he had overcome her shyness in bed. It was a pity that it would all be over soon.

She had reached the turn in the road; she looked back once to wave, then she was gone from sight. Hector turned to re-enter the chateau, and as he did so, a rustling in the bushes caught his attention. He looked and saw the tip of a shoe poking out of the greenery.

'All right, come out of there,' he said, striding toward the bushes. 'Come out before I run you through . . . '

To his surprise it was a boy who crept out of the bushes and stood before him, dusting himself off. The count's initial anger was dissipated by the impact of the almost painfully beautiful face that was suddenly turned up to him. Name of heaven, had Raphael painted that same face on one of his cherubs?

'Who the devil are you?' he demanded aloud.

The boy's sensuous lips formed a pout. 'I'm René de Brussac,' he said sullenly.

'René . . . their little brother? But why on earth are you creeping around in the bushes, spying on us? Is that a de Brussac habit?'

'I wanted to see where Marie's been going so often,' he said defiantly despite the trembling of his lips.

'I see.' Hector nodded. 'And now you know, what exactly do you plan to do with the knowledge?'

'I – I don't know.' It was the truth; René had not thought that far ahead. That the information might give him some power over his brother and sister had not yet occurred to him.

'I must say, you don't look much like your sister,' Hector said, studying him; the boy, in fact, had all the beauty that the rather plain sister lacked. He was a prize, indeed, to tempt a far more virtuous man than the count.

'They tell me I take after my mother.'

'Really? She must be lovely. But come,' he laid a hand gently but firmly upon the young man's shoulder, 'let us go inside. Perhaps we can become friends, you and I – would you like that?'

René, who would have fled had it not been for the hand on his shoulder, steering him deftly through the gate, said, 'I guess so.'

Hector, tightening his grip ever so slightly, smiled down at the boy's curly head and said, softly, 'And so shall I, my pet; so shall I.'

'Marie, are you absolutely certain?' Danielle was so astonished she could not help staring at her friend.

'I don't see how there can be any mistake,' Marie said bitterly, arranging the folds of her dress to hide the slight swelling that had begun in her midsection. 'I haven't bled my last two times and I've been sick every morning this week – anyway, look at this, you think it's just from Cook's pastries?' She patted her stomach.

'God in heaven.' Danielle dropped heavily into the silk-covered settee behind her. 'What are you going to do?' It was all too much for her to comprehend. Marie with child? But that was impossible – Marie was just her own age, and anyway, she had never said she was serious about the Count de Trémorel, only that she found him fascinating.

'I don't know,' Marie cried, wringing her hands. 'I've heard stories – they say there's an old woman with the gipsies, camped across the river – they say she can – can solve problems like this . . . '

Danielle jumped up again and came to her, seizing her shoulders violently. 'Marie, you mustn't. I've heard of her too; she's a butcher. Marie, promise me . . . '

'Good heavens, if you keep shaking me like this, I won't need to see her.'

Danielle dropped her hands at her sides and gave her friend a forlorn look. 'Have you talked to him?'

'I haven't talked to anyone yet, except you, and you swore you wouldn't tell anyone, not even Claude. We – we're going over there tonight. I intend to tell Hector, as soon as I can get him away from the others. I'm certain he'll know exactly what to do.'

She assumed an air of bravado, but her lips were still trembling and it looked as if at any minute she might burst into tears. Danielle forced a smile to her lips, although she personally did not have much confidence in the Count de Trémorel.

'I'm sure that he will,' she said.

Even to her own ears, the reassurances sounded false.

Claude rode as usual, but Marie, wary of her condition, drove the little buggy, giving as her excuse the cold weather. A storm had been threatening all day, the dark clouds gathering ominously. She was glad, too, that sitting in the buggy in the dark gave her time to herself, to try to sort out some of her thoughts.

Mama and Papa were out for the evening, luckily for her, as ordinarily a late visit like this would have been impossible. Somehow she thought it would be easier to tell Hector by candlelight, or perhaps even in the darkness. It occurred to her that they had never been together in the dark; always it had been in the light of day. How strange; in her girlish fantasies she had always linked love and romance with darkness and flickering candles, and now instead it was hard reality that must be faced in those romantic settings.

Mama and Papa had gone to a hastily called political meeting, Mama insisting that she never understood such discussions, and Papa arguing that it was important she hear this one. General Cavaignac had been defeated in the general elections, and Prince Louis Napoleon had been named president of the French Republic. Much of the aristocracy had supported the prince, confident that he would soon restore the empire. Papa, suspecting much the same, had been an ardent supporter of the deposed general, and now it was said that reprisals were being taken already against those who had supported Cavaignac.

The meeting tonight was of those who, like Papa, had opposed Louis Napoleon's election. There were some, frightened by rumors from Paris, who were already closing up their estates preparatory to lengthy trips abroad, while others thought that a united front would discourage any direct action on the new president's part. Papa was one of the latter, but he had thought as well that there should be alternative plans laid, perhaps even some consideration of escape routes, should they be necessary.

Marie had heard all this without really paying much attention; her mind had been too occupied with her own problems. She dreaded the moment when she must face Hector and tell him of her condition. If only he had not been so distant of late! Was it only her imagination, fed by her increasing anxiety, or had he actually been cool to her the last few times she had seen him?

Oh, if only there were someone else she could turn to for advice. Danielle, of course, had been concerned, but Danielle was only a girl, like herself; what could Danielle do?

What could anyone do?

Hector and Antoinette were not alone. A general in full uniform, still wearing his sword, was standing with Hector near the fire. Seated on the sofa beside Antoinette was a woman. Despite her clothes, which were blatantly expensive and clearly the latest fashion from Paris, she was easily the ugliest woman Claude had ever seen.

'Ah, the de Brussacs.' Antoinette greeted them without rising. 'How delightful; you're just in time to meet our friends from Paris. This is the Marquise de Marcheval, and her uncle, General LeFevre. The general, as you perhaps know, has just been named commander of the army.'

Claude bowed to both the general and his ugly niece, placing his lips to the hand the latter offered him.

'Madame le Marquise,' he murmured gallantly.

'My friends call me Louise,' she said, her eyes roving frankly up and down his youthful body.

'So,' she said, 'the young de Brussacs I've heard so much about. I knew your mother.'

Marie gave her an unexpectedly frightened glance. Claude explained hastily, 'Actually, Madame le Marquise, our parents do not know we are here, nor that we are friends of the count and his sister.'

Louise cocked an eyebrow and smiled. 'I see,' she said. 'How interesting.'

Hector had brought drinks; Marie took hers in trembling fingers and sank gratefully into an empty chair. There was a nervous fluttering in her stomach and when the two women, particularly the marquise with her piercing eyes, looked at her, she thought that they must see at once the secret she was bearing.

'Actually,' Louise added drily, 'your mother was better acquainted with my late husband, I believe. He died near here, on the de Brussac estate, in fact.' She paused, then added in a venomous tone, 'They said he drowned.'

Claude, watching her, was startled by the look of hatred that for a moment she flung at Marie, whose downcast eyes did not see it. But as quickly as it had come, the look had vanished, to be replaced by an oily smile, as if the marquise were contemplating some secret victory of which no one else was aware.

'We were about to drink a toast,' Antoinette said, 'to the new president. Won't you put aside your own political ideas and drink with us?'

'To Prince Louis Napoleon,' the general said, raising his glass.

'To Prince Louis Napoleon,' the others echoed. Claude and Marie lifted their glasses in silence.

'I have another toast to propose,' Hector said. 'To Paris, and to our return to the most beautiful city in the world.'

Marie's glass slipped from her fingers and crashed to the floor, the wine staining the rug and the hem of her skirt. She was oblivious to both, her eyes glued to the count.

'You're returning to Paris? But when?' she cried.

'In just a few more days,' he said, unperturbed. 'Now that the reason for our exile has been removed . . .' He shrugged.

'But I thought – ' Marie turned scarlet. Claude was looking at her with an expression of shock and, worse, pity; the others only looked amused.

A storm had been threatening distantly as they had ridden here earlier, and now it approached, the wind striking the house with a violent gust and rattling the windows. It seemed to Marie as if she heard the cries of a horde of phantom riders circling outside the room, calling her: Coward. Coward. Coward.

'Could I speak to you alone for a moment?' she asked in a voice hardly more than a whisper.

'Alone?' Hector asked. 'But that's hardly necessary, dear child – I keep nothing from my sister, and these two are very good friends; you can say whatever you wish to say in front of them – excuse me for a moment, please.'

The wind had pulled a shutter loose, and it was now banging noisily. He went to fix it, leaving her to sit frozen in her chair, the words she needed and wanted refusing to come to her lips. Her sense of anguish mingled with the cries of the wind among the turret tops and the clatter of the shutter, so that she thought she would scream.

The storm broke at last, a rattling of drops against the glass. The count fastened the shutters and again closed the window. The candles had turned the panes to sheets of black marble, and it seemed to Marie, looking in that direction, as if they were a field upon which she could behold the future, a future black with consequences. She saw her parents, heartbroken with shame; the family name, once honored, now a thing of ridicule. She saw herself, homeless, a figure of poverty and humiliation. And she saw the man who had been her lover, striding over the bones of her life, triumphant monster surveying the remnants of the lives he had devoured.

She saw all this before her as if painted upon the darkness of the windowpane, and the outcry of the wind seemed to mock her.

'Now then,' the count resumed, coming back to her, 'you were saying?'

She could not bring herself to look directly at him. She stared down at the reddish-brown stain on the carpet where her drink had spilled, and heard herself say, 'I thought you were going to marry me.'

'But that is hardly possible, even if you were suitable to the life that I shall live in the future as one of the confidants of the new president. You see, I already have a wife.'

She did look up then, in horror; surely he must be joking.

'I don't understand,' she stammered. 'You never said . . .'

'But I thought you knew – I thought everyone knew. Of course, it is hardly a marriage made in heaven, and as you can see, we go our own ways. None the less, she is my wife, and France limits a man, however illogically, to one and only one wife at a time. So you see, marriage had never entered my mind, and to be quite frank, I'm surprised to hear it had entered yours. If you'd mentioned this foolish notion of yours sooner, I would certainly have explained everything to your satisfaction.'

She felt as if she were suffocating. Suddenly she could no longer bear the overheated room, the grinning faces watching her. She leaped up, pushing Claude's hands away when he would have helped her. Covering her face with her hands, she fled from the room. A gust of wind swept through the room as the front door was flung open.

There was an awkward silence in her wake. For a moment Claude was too stunned to do anything but stare open-mouthed. Then, stiffly, he crossed the room and bowed before the count.

'Monsieur,' he said, 'I trust you will give me satisfaction?'

'Just a moment, young man,' the general said. 'Dueling is illegal here, as you very well know, and as a representative of the law . . . '

The count silenced him with a gesture. 'It shall be as you wish,' he said, returning Claude's bow. 'Have you a second in mind?'

Claude could think of no one he could call upon who would not warn his father of the impending duel. 'I have no second,' he said.

'I see. Very well, then, shall we say tomorrow morning at dawn? There is a clearing in the woods, straight back from our stables, half-way to the river – do you know it? Good. We shall meet there. Oh, have you a choice of weapons? Pistols? Or swords?'

Claude, who had little experience with either, said 'Swords.'

'Very well, swords it shall be. It's settled? Until tomorrow morning, then?'

The two men bowed again, and Claude went out; he did not let himself so much as glance in Antoinette's direction; but he could not help hoping that she admired his gallantry.

When he had gone, the four people remaining in the room looked from one to the other.

'What a pity,' Louise said at last, smiling. 'Such a handsome young man, to die so young.'

They laughed, and the tension that had been building for several minutes was broken.

26

Marie drove the horses blindly. The rain had turned into drenching mist, but her soul was already so chilled that she did not much notice the weather.

In her mind's eye she saw the Chateau Trémorel empty as it

had been before, the windows broken out and dark. It was a prevision of the future, and as if to offset it she looked back again and again on those splashed walls and glimmering roofs until they had been swallowed up in the mist.

She felt as if she had lived a lifetime already. She found herself recalling again and again little incidents that had occurred between her and Hector, little phrases that he had spoken to her.

The road went through the woods. It was late and the only sounds were the cries of wild fowl in the wet brush and the rushing and pouring of the swollen rills that fed into the river. Marie listened to the turning of the wheels and it seemed a voice that whispered to her of her shame. She looked at the black window curtains and again she saw a bleak vision of approaching ruin.

Suddenly a new sound intruded upon her misery – a distant hum of voices and the clanking of metal, as if someone were banging cooking pots together.

Then she remembered the gipsies, who had camped for the last several weeks by the river – and one gipsy, the one they called Old Alise. She had heard stories, rumors, snatches of whispered conversations between women in the shops. For a price, they said, Old Alise could help...

She was approaching the fork in the road. To the left the road led straight to Chateau Brussac; to the right was the way to the river, and across the river, to the gipsies' camp.

She jerked the reins, taking the road to the right.

Danielle left the shelter of the kitchen doorway and ran toward the dark smokehouse, cursing herself for her stupidity in forgetting to bring in tomorrow's ham as Cook had instructed her to do hours ago. Now she would have to feel about in the dark and probably she would get a tongue lashing tomorrow for her blind selection.

She had just reached the smokehouse doorway and was reaching for the latch when someone whistled in the darkness.

'Who's there?' she demanded, whirling about. For a moment she could see nothing; then a man stepped from the shadows of a big oak tree and came toward her.

'Oh, François, it's you,' she said. 'What on earth are you creeping about in the dark for?'

'I thought I might see you,' he said. 'I thought with your

good friends so busy of late, maybe you'd have time for a stroll with me.'

She laughed and said, 'A stroll, in this weather! François, you do get the funniest ideas.'

'I know a place where it's not wet. There's plenty of warm straw and no one around to see or hear . . . ' He put his hand tentatively on her arm, but she shook it off.

'Stop that,' she said. 'Someone will come.'

'Who will come?' In the gloom she saw his eyes narrow suspiciously. 'Are you out here to meet someone?'

'What if I am? It's none of your business.'

He caught her wrist in his hand and pulled her close, studying her defiant expression. Finally, his lips curled in a cruel smile.

'Not the young mademoiselle, at any rate,' he said. 'She won't be home for a long time.'

'What do you mean by that?'

'Only that I saw her buggy – sitting empty.'

'Listen,' she said, poking his chest with the tip of a finger, 'don't you go spreading any gossip. It's none of your concern if she happens to pay a visit to the neighbors.' She turned from him and would have gone on into the smokehouse, but his next words stopped her.

'So, now the gipsies are neighbors?' he asked.

She turned to face him directly again. 'François, what are you talking about? If you don't come to the point at once, I shall start screaming, and tell everyone that you molested me when I came outside.'

'The point is, there's only one reason I can think of why a girl like her would be going at night to the gipsy camp – to Old Alise's wagon.'

She stared back at him for a stunned moment. 'Name of God,' she breathed. 'François, you must come with me, we must go there and get her, before . . . '

'Not me,' François said, shaking his head firmly. 'I've heard too many stories about gipsy hospitality. And if you want my advice, you'll stay out of there, too.'

'Oh . . . ' She decided it was a waste of time to argue with him. For all his bravado, François was a coward. She would have to go alone and pray that she was not too late. She shoved past him.

'Hey, where are you going?' he called after her, but she was already running along the path that led toward the river, and she did not waste breath in answering him.

The bridge was too far to go on foot, but there was a path and a footbridge. Danielle slithered and clambered along the river embankment, her eyes fixed on the lights that glowed across the river. You could hear and even smell the gipsies long before you reached their camp – the singing, the babble of voices, seemingly always excited, always passionate – and the smells, of cooking, of smoky fires, and unwashed bodies. Danielle was afraid of the gipsies; there were so many ugly stories, tales of things that happened to girls who fell into their midst – but she was more afraid for Marie.

The path was easy enough to see, even in the dark, but it was muddy and treacherous in the rain like this, and the wind whipping at her skirt made it rough going indeed. She had kicked off her shoes because she trusted her footing more with bare feet, but even so she slipped several times and was in danger of falling into the turbulent waters below.

Hurry . . . hurry . . . now she was at the very edge of the water, the wind whistling through a gully above her and the water roaring at her feet with demoniacal fury, through crevices and clefts, hurling and twisting and lashing out at her feet as if to seize them and draw her down, down . . .

She was gasping for breath. The lightning flashed, bringing all the elements – fire, water, air, earth – into play, slowing her down and at the same moment urging her on.

Finally she was at the 'bridge', which was nothing more than a felled tree extending across the narrowest part of the river, but the narrowest part happened also to be at the falls, where the water plunged over a steep shelf of rock in a swirling, clamoring cascade so that the log's surface was washed smooth with the water's endless buffeting. In the light of day, buoyed by the company of Claude and Marie, Danielle had taken her heart in her hand and crossed on the log once or twice; but alone, in the darkness, in the rain – she paused at the edge, her eyes drawn of their own volition to the turbulence at her feet. One slip, one misstep, and those muddy depths would be her grave. She took a deep breath and stepped onto the log.

The log seemed to tremble with the roar of the water. It felt as slippery as glass under her feet, and again it seemed almost as if the water were reaching for her, clawing at her skirt with watery fingers. She tried to concentrate on the opposite end of the bridge but it lay in shadow, and she might have been stepping into eternity. Slowly she put one foot before the other: a step, another step . . . she was half-way now, in the very center; only a little way to go and she would be safe.

There was a sudden, violent burst of lightning. It startled her, making her draw up suddenly. The wind caught at her wet skirt, whipping it out from her body with such force that she swayed. She threw her arms out for balance, tilting precariously on one foot while the river screamed its approval below.

Somehow she caught herself, got both feet again on the log. She was drenched from the spray and shivering as much with fear as with cold, but she went on, a step at a time, inching her way across the bridge. She could see now into the darkness at the opposite end, could see where the log lay firm and steady on solid ground, could even see the tall grasses whipping in the wind. Almost there . . . almost . . . she dared not think, dared only to move forward.

Her foot slipped again, and she lurched off balance, knowing in that precarious instant that this time she could not check her fall. She staggered to the left, trying vainly to regain her balance, but her foot missed the log altogether – and came down on a grassy embankment.

She had made it. She was across the river.

And now her journey had just begun.

The gipsies saw her coming. By the time she was fifty yards from the camp, a crowd of them had lined up to watch her warily. One of the men separated himself from the others and strolled out to meet her. Unsure of herself, Danielle stopped and watched him come closer. He stopped, too, a few feet in front of her, and looked her up and down with a bold leer.

'I – I want to see Old Alise,' she said, giving her head a toss.

'What do you want with her?' She saw that behind him two or three other men had begun to slink toward her, circling about as if setting a trap. Instinctively she took a step backward; her questioner took two steps forward.

'There's a girl here – the girl with the buggy – I want her.'

'There's no one here; no one but us gipsies.'

Danielle's eyes darted to the buggy, still tied to a tree at the edge of the camp. His gaze followed hers.

'That is ours,' he lied. He grinned and took another step toward her. 'But maybe that is only a story to explain your visit – maybe you come because you have heard that gipsy men are fine lovers, eh?'

She glanced over her shoulder – the other men had moved about her until escape was cut off. Her heart hammering, Danielle looked from one to the other. What would she do if they seized her? She had heard of the gipsy men, all right, and what they did to helpless women who came their way.

A cluster of women left the fire and pushed through the men, coming quickly toward her. The one who led them was tall and buxom, and as she came close, Danielle could see the savage gleam in her eyes.

'We will handle this,' she said, pushing past the man. He grunted something that Danielle could not hear, but the gipsy girl ignored him and came to stand before Danielle, her hands on her hips.

'This is not a good place for you,' she said. 'Go away, quickly, before the men decide to have their way with you.'

The other girls who had followed her crowded around Danielle, eyeing her with unabashed curiosity. One of them even reached out to feel the fabric of her skirt appraisingly. Oddly, Danielle felt even more frightened of them than she had of the men. The eyes examining her were hard, utterly cruel, and one or two of the women grinned mockingly.

'I must find my friend,' Danielle managed to say, despite the dryness in her throat.

A knife appeared as if by magic in the gipsy girl's hand, and she leaned closer to speak through clenched teeth.

'Little fool,' she said, 'that is my Juanito who is smacking his lips over you. He is a man used to taking what he wants and in another minute he will take you – I know him well – and if he does then I will kill you when he is finished. *Comprende?*'

She brought the blade up until the tip was pressed against Danielle's trembling breast. The others were all grinning now, maliciously delighted by the fear that was all too evident in Danielle's eyes.

Slowly Danielle began to back away, her eyes never leaving the gleaming knife. The gipsies watched her, some laughing and chattering in Spanish. The rain had dwindled, but even so Danielle's clothes were soaked and her hair hung like a wet mop over her forehead.

Marie – she was here, perhaps at this very moment dying at that butcher woman's hands – and Danielle could do nothing to save her. It would take too long to go back the way she had come – across the log bridge again, all the way through the woods; too far, and the road was even longer. It would be an hour, perhaps two, before she could return with help, and by then it would certainly be too late.

27

Something moved unexpectedly behind her, making her jump and squeal. It was only a donkey, unconcernedly feeding among the dried weeds; the gipsies' horses were tethered among the trees, but the donkey had been allowed to roam free. The gipsies laughed among themselves at the scare the little animal had given her.

In an instant, Danielle knew what she must do. The gipsies were several yards away now, and here close to her was the donkey – close enough that she had only to reach out a hand, put it gently upon his neck . . .

She was upon him before the gipsies, or even the startled donkey, for that matter, knew what was happening. There was a shout from the camp, but she had already dug her heels into the donkey's flanks and, despite his surprise, he ran obediently forward into the woods, with Danielle clinging precariously but stubbornly to his neck. Wet branches slapped at her and she heard continued shouts from the gipsies, but in a moment she had disappeared into the woods and was gone from view.

For Anne it had been a long and tedious evening – all this talk of coups and revolts and elections and districts; what did it all amount to, anyway? All this talk and all these meetings, and Prince Napoleon had been elected anyway. And what made them so certain that they needed 'escape routes'? Oh yes, there was talk of arrests and difficulties in Paris, but when in the last twenty years hadn't there been difficulties in Paris?

'But aren't you frightened, Madame de Brussac?' one of the women had asked her.

'Good heavens, but of what? We are a full day's journey away from Paris; who would bother us here? And anyway, there are far bigger fish in the sea, if Napoleon wants to arrest his political enemies. He'd hardly bother with us provincials.'

The woman had given her a peculiar look, but someone had interrupted them just then and shortly afterward Jean had come for her.

Then, afterward, on the way home, Jean announced that he had yet other calls to make, on neighbors who hadn't attended the meeting.

'Some of them just couldn't make it,' he explained. 'Geriot, for one, can't get around now since he hurt his foot.'

'Heavens, you don't mean to say you're going to call on all those who didn't attend the meeting?'

'Not quite all. I don't think the Count de Trémorel and his sister would welcome me – I hear, by the way, that they're leaving soon for Paris.'

'Oh?' Secretly Anne was a little disappointed that they were leaving and she had never gotten to meet them; once she had made the mistake of suggesting just that, which had made Jean furious.

'That nest of vipers!' he had exclaimed. 'It's just such as they that will be running the country if the prince is elected.'

Anne had avoided bringing their names up again, but just the same it would have been nice to hear the latest from Paris. They almost never went themselves anymore; there were numerous good reasons for not making the journey, but she suspected the chief reason was the trip itself. Jean was getting old; he would be sixty soon, and although he still worked as hard as any of his employees, the signs of advancing years and declining vigor were becoming plainer each year.

Thinking of that, she asked, 'But is it so important that they hear all about this tonight? Wouldn't tomorrow do as well?'

Jean had kissed her and said, 'The sooner the better, my love; there's no telling when any one of us may need to make a hasty departure.'

'All this talk of hasty departures – I feel certain Madame Marquette, for one, couldn't get ready to go to the privy in less than a week.'

Jean had smiled and patted her hand, but his thoughts were already elsewhere, as they had been since the news of the election had reached them.

Well, so be it; she had long since ceased trying to understand his passion for politics; at least he did not expect her to trudge around the neighborhood with him but had brought her home, and glad she was of it. She could think of nothing so appealing as a cup of chocolate and then off to bed.

And now, just when she had thought the long evening ended, here was everything in a muddle. First had come the news, delivered by a nervous Jeanette, that Claude and Marie weren't home.

'They dressed for paying a call,' was all Jeanette could offer in the way of explanation. 'The young miss drove the buggy and he rode a horse, and they rode east.'

'But I don't understand – everyone who lives in that directtion was at the meeting tonight – everyone except the de Trémorels – and they'd hardly have been calling on them. They don't even know one another.'

Even as she voiced that opinion, though, something stirred uneasily within her: the de Trémorels, living just to the east of them; all those rides her children had taken together of late, nearly every day . . . but surely if Claude and Marie had met the de Trémorels, they would have mentioned the fact, wouldn't they?

Or would they? Jean had made no secret of his distaste for their neighbours; the children had been present when he had forbidden her to pay a call. Perhaps . . .

She was still puzzling over the situation when Claude came in, but he looked so ferocious that his appearance fanned her fears rather than calming them.

'Claude,' she cried, hurrying down the stairs to meet him. 'Where have you been? Where's Marie?'

'Isn't she home? But she left long ago; I've been riding about –'

There was an interruption; Jeanette came in from the kitchen, looking even more alarmed. 'Madame,' she said, 'Danielle . . . she says . . . oh, Madame!' Jeanette stopped and wrung her hands together.

Danielle, hovering in the kitchen door, pushed past her mother and hurried to where Claude and Anne stood at the foot of the stairs. Inconsequentially, Anne noticed that the girl was tracking mud across the floor, and her clothes looked as if she had been bathing in them.

'Madame,' Danielle cried breathlessly, 'you must stop them, they'll kill her, they're nothing but butchers . . . '

'Good heavens, child, what are you saying? Where's Marie? Who will kill her?'

'The gipsies! She's gone to that woman, Old Alise. I tried to go to her, but they wouldn't let me. You've got to stop them!'

It took a moment for full comprehension to come to Anne. The gipsy woman; she, too, had heard the stories. It was the sort of thing women liked to gossip about when husbands and children were not around. But Marie, gone there; 'Mother of God,' she breathed aloud, clapping her hand to her bosom.

Claude, almost as stunned as she, moved to go. 'I'll get her,' he said.

'No.' Anne tried to think, tried to make some sense out of the muddle of her thoughts. 'We must wait for your father; he'll know what to do.'

'There isn't time,' Danielle cried. 'They'll kill her, I know! There was a girl from the village, the gipsy woman helped her, too, and the girl died.'

Anne felt the blood draining from her face. She looked from the frightened face of the girl to the anxious, angry one of her son.

'We'll both go,' she said. 'Jeanette, bring my cloak; Claude, saddle the horses.'

She ran to her husband's desk and scribbled a brief note, telling him where she had gone, and to follow her there at once; she did not tell him why – there would be time enough later for explanations.

Or perhaps no time at all.

Afterward Anne was to wonder how Danielle happened to come with them, riding along at her side as if she belonged there, but at the time it seemed right, as if there were strength in their numbers.

The unexpected arrival of three riders upset the gipsy camp, and for some seconds they did not recognize Danielle as the same girl who had visited them earlier and stolen their donkey. People clambered from their wagons and men left the camp-fire to form a line and stare at the intruders.

Anne, her eyes raking the camp, saw the buggy and mare, still hitched to a tree, near a wagon set off from the others. It was larger than all but one or two of the other wagons, and garishly painted; Anne saw the healing sign of the gipsies painted over the door, and although lights gleamed from beyond the curtains, no one rushed from this wagon to investigate the tumult.

'There,' she said, pointing to the wagon.

Claude and Danielle leaped down from their horses and

started toward the wagon, but they had gone only a few feet
before the gipsies, recognizing Danielle at last, had rushed
forward and seized them.

One of the gipsy men came toward Anne and moved as if to
seize the reins of her horse. She made the horse rear, kicking
out with his front hooves until the man had ducked and run
out of the way.

'I am the Baroness de Brussac,' she said, suddenly too angry
to be frightened. 'And if you lay a hand on me, I'll have you
one and all arrested and whipped. Get out of my way.'

She swung down from her horse and started for the lighted
wagon. The sea of gipsies parted before her, but when she
reached the steps of the wagon, the door opened and she found
her way blocked by an enormous hulk of a woman whose hard
eyes challenged her boldness.

Anne saw in a glance the blood on the woman's hands and
her heart all but stopped within her, but the steel in her voice
did not tremble.

'If you have harmed my daughter,' she said, 'I shall personally see you beaten and hanged.'

They faced one another. Although the gipsy woman was
hardened by the cruel life she had led, it was she who yielded
first. She glanced away, nodding toward the men who still held
Claude and Danielle, and at once the men released them. With
a final venomous glance Old Alise stepped from her doorway
and strolled with an affected nonchalance toward the campfire.

Danielle, crowding in behind Anne and Claude, saw blood –
blood seemingly everywhere – on the dirty, unmade bed, on
the floor, even on the walls – and thought, *We are too late then.*
She slumped against the door frame, the hot tears scalding her
eyes.

'Oh, God,' Anne murmured in front of her, but Claude had
rushed to his sister and now he said, in a voice that broke,
'She's alive!'

Claude carried Marie gently to the buggy; Danielle drove and
Anne sat with her daughter cradled in her arms, while Claude
rode and led the other horses.

As they left, Anne saw the gipsy woman by the fire, gnawing
at an old bone – like a dog, she thought angrily.

'If you are still here in the morning,' Anne said, 'you will
regret it sorely.'

With that they rode toward home. Claude, riding alongside the buggy, was already thinking of the coming morning and his rendezvous with the Count de Trémorel.

There was much to be settled between them!

28

Claude was at the clearing long before dawn, dragging a reluctant René with him.

'But what has any of this got to do with me?' René wanted to know as they rode through the still-dark woods. The weather had turned cold, and the previous day's rain had become an icy slush. In the forest, where the trees had provided some shelter, the ground was already hard and crackling beneath their horses' hooves.

The frost had bound the air windless and the blackness was like a roof over their heads. The cold of the night descended upon them as if they had been doused with cold water.

'She's our sister,' Claude explained yet again, 'yours as well as mine, and she's been dishonored by this swine.'

René's trembling grew worse as they neared the clearing. They arrived and, dismounting, tied their horses to trees. 'Will we have long to wait?' René asked, looking about apprehensively. He hated himself for his fear; cowardice is a form of slavery, though, and even as he hated himself, his knees trembled and his hands were so unsteady that he forced them into his pockets so that his brother would not see them shaking.

'I think not,' Claude answered. 'There's a light coming along the path just over there.'

In a moment the count appeared, accompanied by a servant bearing a candle. The count acknowledged René's presence with a tilt of one eyebrow, but René avoided his glance.

'This will do,' the count addressed the servant. 'Put the light down.'

The servant set the candle on the ground; the flame flickered once, then steadied and rose as if in a chimney. All about them the trees were glinting with frost. The two antagonists faced one another. Claude had taken his father's old sword from the wall of the library, and the count carried a gleaming weapon with a jewel-encrusted handle.

'I think you're a fool to want to go through with this,' the count said. 'Or perhaps even now you'd like to change your mind?'

'I mean to avenge my sister's honor,' Claude said, giving a fencing salute. 'I shall kill you or die in the attempt.'

The count smiled sardonically. 'It seems such a paltry reason for giving up one's life. I can assure you that at the time your sister did not mind at all giving up her honor – any more than her pretty little brother did, eh, René?' He gave the boy a lewd wink.

The boy looked from the count's grinning face to his brother's horrified one. He blushed crimson, but no words would come with which to defend himself, and with a strangled cry, he turned and ran into the woods. For a moment they could hear him crashing through the foliage; then an ominous stillness descended once more.

With a violent oath, Claude lunged his sword and the duel had begun.

Danielle had missed the brothers by only a few minutes. She had learned of the intended duel in a whispered conversation with Claude the night before, and had tried in vain to dissuade him from going. She had seen the few times his father had tried to teach Claude to handle a sword; even to her inexpert eye it was clear that Claude handled the weapon well enough but without finesse, and most of all without the sort of boldness that carried the enemy before one's point.

She had risen early, hoping to try once again, only to find that Claude and René had risen even earlier and had already stolen from the house.

Filled with dread, she had flung a cloak about her and set out through the woods, but in the darkness the clearing eluded her. She was about to give up and return to the house when she heard the crash and slap of someone running blindly through the brush, and a moment later René had fairly run into her arms. His clothes were torn and his face and hands bleeding from his headlong flight, and his breath came in sobbing gasps.

'René, for heaven's sake, what's happened?' she cried, trying to hold onto him, but he tore himself free from her embrace.

'Let me be,' he sobbed, and before she could stop him he had darted past her and was gone once again into the darkness of the woods.

Stark terror swept over her. She imagined the worst – Claude already dead, the count gloating over his easy victory. Danielle began to run in the direction from which René had come, racing almost as blindly as he had.

Suddenly she saw the light of the lone candle gleaming with startling intensity in the still air, and in its glow she saw two men still fighting. Her relief was so intense that for a brief time the scene seemed to swim before her eyes.

The fight had not gone at all as the count had imagined. True, the young man opposite him was not an accomplished fighter, but from the first Claude had taken the upper hand, fighting with a glowing but contained fury. Right was on his side. It was his strength, that unambiguous anger. It wasn't the fair-minded who survived in conflict and had a chance of winning; anger, total anger, was the necessary ingredient. Claude crowded in on the count with an almost reckless determination, and what he lacked in subtlety he more than made up for in the sheer force of his drive. The sound of their blades was like the cracking of ice on a thawing lake.

Danielle saw that the fight was not going as expected. Even to her eyes it seemed that Claude was gaining. Nearer and nearer he came to his opponent, forcing the count to leap back time and again with low oaths. Danielle saw the count squint as if the light were now in his eyes, but he could not seem to maneuver to a better advantage. Claude was now pressing him outrageously, and it was plain that the count's confidence was badly shaken. For the first time he seemed to be tasting the cold agony of fear.

It was true that the count was afraid, but it was not of the other man's steel. He had always been terrified of doing the wrong thing, and he had let this become the guiding force of his life. He had lived his entire life as if walking a tightrope over a yawning chasm, fearful of each step, not daring to look around or down.

Now it seemed as if his trip was ending, but when he looked down into the chasm he had traversed, he saw with a shock that there, in that chasm, was life; not in this rarefied air through which he had inched his way, but there, amid the rocks and crags, where the rare flowers bloomed in tiny crevices and a thousand dangers waited at every step, and somewhere, near enough to be heard but too far to see, a stream ran fresh and clear.

He had never been afraid of death, but now suddenly he was afraid of not living, of never having lived. He was leaving behind years of hurt and hatred and bitterness, of frustration and despair and loneliness; of passion, even, and lustful encounters; but of happiness there was nothing. Frantically he raced through the corridors of his memory, seeking one golden moment, one treasured memory he could clasp joyfully to his breast.

There was nothing!

It was at this crucial juncture that the count showed his true colors. With a sudden, swift movement he had seized Claude's blade in his left hand, violating all the rules of combat. For a second or two he had the advantage, and by every expectation it should have ended in those seconds.

But it may have been that Claude was expecting something of the sort, or perhaps the night, the cold air, or the heightened emotional sense had made his reflexes quicker. He leaped aside, avoiding the sword that would have opened his stomach. At the same time the count, lunging, stumbled and fell upon the blade he had unfairly seized. It went through his body.

Danielle gave a cry. The count fell to the ground. For a moment he writhed like a trodden worm; then he lay motionless.

Both Danielle and the count's servant rushed forward to kneel beside the wounded man. Their breath and Claude's were visible in little clouds each time they breathed, but no breath issued from the lips of the fallen man.

'God help us,' Danielle said in a whisper. 'He's dead.'

The count's servant stared from one to the other in horror. Then, without a word, he leaped up and ran off along the path, leaving them alone in the clearing.

'Dead?' Claude stared with a stupid expression on his face. 'Dead?' he asked again, and suddenly flung his sword upon the ground. It was red halfway up the length of the blade.

'What are we going to do?' Danielle asked. She had never been more terrified. The candle still burned steadily, casting a broad circle of light upon the ground. It was still dark, but within that ring of light it seemed as bright as day. The frozen ground was mute, the night as empty as a deserted church. You could have heard the faintest sound a mile off.

She bent and put out the candle; the gloom fell about them

like a mob closing in. Claude still looked stunned by what he had done and, rising, she took his arm and said, 'Come, we must return home; your father will know what to do.'

He said nothing but helped her mount the horse that René had left behind, and they started for Chateau Brussac, Danielle looking over her shoulder as if expecting to see the bloody specter of the dead man in pursuit.

It was not yet light, but there was the scent of morning on the air. The branches of the trees had begun to toss so that they sounded like a gentle sea, and the still air had begun to puff a little against their faces. Even as they rode, there was a gust of morning air.

Danielle could not stop thinking of the dead man they had left behind and the servant who had run off to spread the news. By now the count's sister knew the outcome of the duel. Even at this moment soldiers might be on their way to arrest the man beside her – the man she loved – and she could think of no way out of their predicament.

She soon learned she had not overestimated the swiftness with which Antoinette de Trémorel would avenge her brother's death. By the time Danielle and Claude rode up to Chateau Brussac, the man whom Claude knew as the general was already waiting with a party of soldiers to arrest him.

29

The mayor of Epernay himself, at Jean's request, made inquiries regarding Claude's release, but the effort was in vain.

'It's out of the question,' he informed them later that day. 'He's being held incommunicado, on direct orders from Paris.'

'Prince Louis will have his pound of flesh,' Jean said wearily. For perhaps the first time in his life, he truly felt his age; so much had happened in the past few hours, so many shocks – Marie, still critically weak from the crude abortion; and now Claude, arrested and taken, not to the little jail in Epernay, but to the old fortress at Reims. He had known when he learned this second piece of information that Claude's arrest was not simply routine.

'But why?' Anne asked. 'Oh yes, I know, you supported the general in the election, but so did many others; there are surely bigger fish in that pond.'

'I was rather generous in my support,' Jean said.

'How generous?'

'Nearly a million francs. So you see, we are the "big fish". Louis Napoleon will want revenge, and now he has it – a legitimate reason to arrest and hold my son. It has worked out very conveniently for him.'

'What will happen to Claude?' Anne asked.

'They'll hang him.'

'Oh, no!' Anne ran to her husband, but the despair on his face offered her no consolation; she turned to the mayor, but he only nodded grimly.

'I'm afraid it's true,' he said.

'Unless,' Jean added, 'we can think of a way to save him.'

'What if Claude were to escape?' Danielle asked from the corner where she had been huddled in the chair.

Jean had all but forgotten the girl was there. In the last night and day, he had gotten so used to seeing her with them that she seemed almost a member of the family.

'Impossible,' the mayor said. 'Escape, from the fortress at Reims? It's impossible.'

'But if it were possible,' Danielle persisted, 'what then?'

Jean stared toward the shadows, but he could not see the girl's face clearly. He said, 'There are ways – a route by which a man could reach the sea, and boats waiting there to carry him from France.'

'But where would he go?' Anne cried.

Jean was silent for so long that she half-thought he hadn't heard her at all, and when he replied, his answer was so unexpected that she could hardly believe she had heard correctly.

'Mexico,' he said.

'Mexico?'

'Alta California. We have a land grant there, a gift years ago from the Spanish ambassador. They say men are carving out a New World there . . . ' His voice trailed off thoughtfully.

'But – but that's so far,' Anne said, without really knowing where those places were.

'Yes. Too far for Louis Napoleon to reach. But,' he sighed, 'as the mayor says, it is impossible to think of escape from the fortress. No, I must find someone who can help, someone who will listen to me but who has influence with Prince Napoleon as well.'

In the corner Danielle drew her shawl closer about her shoulders and stared into the fire, making her own plans.

'François?'

At the sound of Danielle's voice, François stepped from the woods into the clearing. 'Mademoiselle, this is an honor,' he said, giving her a mock bow and a cocky grin.

'Oh, François, don't try to be funny; I'm in no mood for it,' she snapped. 'I need help, and you're the only one I know who can give it to me.'

'And what exactly is it you need, *ma petite*?' François was enjoying himself; the one girl he wanted, who had so far spurned him, was finally seeking him out.

'I want to get someone out of jail.'

'Someone out of jail? But there is no one . . . ' He paused and suddenly his eyes went wide. '*Mon Dieu*, you can't mean the vintner's son?'

'François, I know your friends are thieves and highwaymen. If anyone can get him out – '

'You must be crazy,' he said angrily, seizing her and shaking her till her hair fell about her face. 'Even if it were possible, do you think I'd lift a finger to help that one?'

'I – I didn't mean for you to do it out of love for him. I thought – the baron has enormous wealth and – and you always said you loved me . . . '

He let her go so suddenly that she staggered backward. His eyes narrowed as he stared down at her.

'Great wealth – yes, that's something, of course – there are always men to be bought, if the price is right.'

She could see ideas beginning to turn about in his mind. He looked through her for a moment, frowning at some unnamed obstacle, then smiled slightly as he saw his way around that.

He took her arms again, drawing her closer to him. 'And you, *ma petite*,' he said, grinning again. 'What price would you be willing to pay to save your aristocratic friend, eh?'

She shivered slightly, but she forced herself to meet his gaze unwaveringly.

'You've always said you – you wanted to marry me,' she said. 'If you'll do this, I'll marry you whenever you say.'

'But there are plenty of girls willing to marry me, without the necessity of risking my neck in such a dangerous fashion.'

Her heart sank; so he was not going to take her offer after all. So much for his professed desire.

'Still,' he added, grinning at the despair that had flashed across her face, 'it would be nice to have a woman of my own, to use when I wanted – without all that bother of getting married.'

The silence stretched between them. This time she could not raise her eyes to look into his. She could feel her face burning crimson. He was proposing to make her his whore, a slave to his desire so long as it pleased him, and when he had grown weary of her, or when she had gotten pregnant, he would cast her off, but then no decent man would want her again. She would be ruined, doomed to a life of prostitution, and Claude – Claude would be thousands of miles away, in a wilderness she could not even imagine, gone from her.

But still alive, wherever he was, and his life would be her gift.

'I – will be your – your woman,' she said falteringly.

He crushed her to him and his lips found hers, hotly, exploring. His hand came up between them, fumbling at her breast, crushing it in brutal fingers.

She struggled against him, freeing her mouth at last. 'No,' she said, 'first, he must be free. Then – then I'll do what you wish.'

'You'll do anything I say? No arguments?' he demanded, staring down at her.

'Yes.' Her voice was a mere whisper. 'Anything you say.'

He laughed, and the coarse sound sent a shudder through her.

30

It was astonishing, Danielle thought, what could be done if one had money enough.

At first the baron had been doubtful of her story, but he had agreed to talk to François, and afterward what seemed to her like a vast fortune had changed hands. But that was only a start; that had been to persuade François's friends to join him in planning the enterprise.

Then a young army officer was found who was on duty at the fortress in Reims and who also happened to have an expensive mistress and an accumulation of debts. Yet another fortune changed hands.

Mysterious visitors came and went late at night – arrangements must be made for a hard two-day ride, discreet lodgings found, fresh horses arranged and paid for; an English sea captain came and was closeted with the baron most of the night.

The days inched by, and with each one Danielle's fears grew. What if they transferred Claude to another prison? What if they proceeded with the hanging? She urged François to hurry and refused to think what would happen to her when the event was accomplished.

For Jean the days were speeding all too fast. There was much to be done and little time in which to do it. How long would Louis Napoleon and his friends allow Claude to languish in prison? Not long, surely. And in the meantime there were arrangements to be made, countless details that must be carefully planned.

Timing was critical. Horses could not be kept saddled and waiting forever; they must be at the appointed places at just the right time. The ship that would wait for them near St Valéry-sur-Somme could put in only at high tide; if they missed the rendezvous, the ship would go without them.

Like Danielle, Jean tried not to think of what might happen after. If it had been possible, the entire family would have gone, but although Marie was recovering gradually from her misfortune, it was clear that she would not yet be ready for such an arduous journey, and they could hardly go and leave her behind. So Claude must go alone, and they must remain to weather the storm of Napoleon's anger. At least it would be directed at him alone. It was unlikely that Napoleon would take revenge on Anne or the younger children, particularly since it would be clear that they knew little or nothing about what had transpired. The children he told nothing of what was being planned, and Anne only the barest essentials – that an escape was being planned, and a route by which Claude could leave for Alta California.

To know more, he insisted repeatedly in response to Anne's questions and pleadings, was dangerous.

Finally he took the boldest step of all: He wrote to Prince

Napoleon himself, asking for an audience with him in Paris to discuss an urgent and personal matter. It was an appointment he did not mean to keep; it was a false trail intended as an alibi, but by the time Napoleon realized Jean was not going to show up, Claude would be out to sea, out of reach of Napoleon's agents. And in another day's time Jean would be found to be ill at the house of a friend, too ill to have kept his appointment – and too ill to have had any part in any escape attempt.

Napoleon would be furious, but there would be people enough in Paris to swear to Jean's story. Despite his grandiose schemes, the prince was nonetheless bound by law. He would not dare arrest Jean without charging him with a crime; there must be a trial.

Afterward, if all went as planned there would be time to remove himself and the rest of his family out of Napoleon's reach.

If. If all went as planned . . .

'You are certain they will be captured?' Antoinette gave the handsome young man before her an appraising look.

'Absolutely,' François assured her. 'My men and I will go along to escort them to the coast. There is a garrison of French soldiers here,' he said, tapping the map that they had spread on the desk – her brother's desk. Since his murder, she had thought of nothing but how to avenge herself on the de Brussacs; it was not enough that the boy was arrested, as Louise de Marcheval had been firm in pointing out to her; the entire family must pay. They must suffer as they had made others suffer.

'At the right time,' François was explaining, 'one of my men will inform the officer in charge of the garrison that an escaped political prisoner and his accomplices, personal enemies not only of France but of Louis Napoleon, are virtually in his hands. They'll waste no time making the capture.'

'The de Brussacs are clever, and powerful,' Antoinette said. 'Suppose they elude capture?'

He gave her a confident grin. 'They won't. I'll be with them, don't forget, and they trust me.'

'I wonder why,' she said with a lazy smile. Although their relationship thus far had been a business one, beginning when the young peasant had approached her with his proposition, she was far from unaware of his good looks. Nor was he unaware, she was certain, of the effect that he had upon her.

He came now to stand directly in front of her, and his eyes were bold as they gazed down into hers. There was nothing servile in his manner, despite the difference in their stations. She found herself wondering, not for the first time, what it would be like to be loved by a peasant. It would be rough, she supposed, unsubtle, perhaps even coarse.

But of course that could be thrilling, too, with the right partner.

'And when I return . . . ' he said, running the tip of one finger teasingly up her arm.

'You shall have your reward – the sum we agreed upon,' she said. She attempted to turn away, thinking he was really too presumptuous, even for one so young and handsome, but he clasped her shoulders and turned her firmly, even roughly, back to face him.

'I wasn't thinking only of money,' he said.

She arched an eyebrow in mock innocence; despite her intention of remaining in full control of the situation, she found her blood pulsing dangerously. This was a young man with no scruples, dangerous and not to be trusted for a moment; but he was also undeniably exciting.

'Perhaps a little something on account,' he said, lowering his mouth to hers.

He wore a peasant shirt, open to the waist, and she could feel the coarse hair of his chest against her flesh. He smelled of sweat and dirt and stables. Her arms seemed to lift of their own accord about his neck.

'I could have you hanged for kissing me,' she said when his lips had left hers.

'Or rewarded,' he said with a devilish grin. 'But I'll take my chances on how you feel when I'm finished.'

He took her then, on the sofa, in her brother's study – took her harshly, masterfully, a devil's caresses to seal a devil's bargain.

The cell was silent. There were no furnishings, not even a bucket for toilet purposes – only a pallet of dirty straw on the floor. Claude had grown up knowing nothing but the finest in furnishings, clothes, comforts; at first the cell into which he had been thrown had been a shock to his sensibilities, but with the resiliency of youth he had accustomed himself to it well enough. He knew that he could pace exactly five steps in any direction, and that if he put his face to the bars and yelled, no one would answer. There was no window to the outside, but some small portion of light managed to filter into the corridor so that he could differentiate between night and day.

He had been here a week. He had experienced that boredom that is indistinguishable from despair. There was no moment's pleasure in the day – no pain, but discomfort, the drag of the body – day after day with nothing in any of them. He sat on the dirty pallet with his chin on his knees and wondered how long a man could endure the silence and the aloneness before his mind began to fail. That he might ever again be free to enjoy the company of men did not occur to him. He had killed a man in an illegal duel; worse, he had killed a man favored by the new president himself. He had no doubt that he would be killed in return.

Even so, he did not regret what he had done. There were other regrets: for the pain he knew he had brought to his family; and for Antoinette, whom he still loved. Would she understand the necessity of what he had done? He would have liked a chance to talk to her, to explain that it had nothing to do with her. He would have liked once more to hold her silken body next to his, to kiss her honeyed lips and thrill to the feel of her fingers, teasing, toying with him . . . Sometimes, when he had been away from her, he had tried to come up with the words he would need to explain his feelings to her. But when he actually saw her, the words never came out as he had formed them in his mind; just as, when he tried to imagine their next time in bed, it never turned out quite like that, as though their bodies had wills of their own.

But he thrust these thoughts from him angrily. To remember, to yearn, to torture oneself with longing – these were the paths to madness.

He stretched out upon the straw. He could do that now without minding the vermin he knew were there, just as he had learned to eat the food without minding what was crawling in it. The time would come soon enough when he would have no need of food or beds. He had a conscious awareness of things trickling off into nothingness.

It was strange to contemplate that what he had done had seemed almost innocent at the time, a right, a duty that could not be avoided, and the consequences, had he thought of them at all, existed apart from it. Acts themselves were so innocent – a sexual union; words spoken in a moment's heat; a stroke of a sword – they were all so simple, so self-contained, disconnected from the results that flowed from them. His generation, raised on revolutionary action, had not been trained to think in terms of the consequences of their actions. They lived in a present that changed so swiftly that it seemed foolish to think of tomorrow.

There was a sound in the corridor; someone was approaching. It was not time, he was sure, for the daily meal, and he sat up, scratching at the lice in his hair, listening.

The sound stopped outside his door. Claude rose to his feet as a key grated in the lock, and a moment later the door swung open to reveal three uniformed soldiers.

'Come with us,' one of them ordered; before Claude could comply he had been shoved roughly forward into the corridor. With a guard on either side and one walking behind him, gun drawn, Claude was escorted along the musty hallway. He had not realized how weak just a week of confinement had made him; his legs felt shaky beneath him, and once or twice he staggered slightly, making the guards start nervously.

They had to cross a courtyard, and the sudden shock of bright sunlight was excruciating. He cried out from the agony and covered his eyes with his hands, stumbling along blindly with the guards prodding and shoving him.

He was taken into a room. The light here was not so intense, and after a moment he was able to open his eyes to a squint.

What he saw was General LeFevre seated at a desk, scowling at him. In addition there was a lieutenant who stood respectfully behind the general, and a third man – if this one could still be called a man. He wore nothing but trousers, and the crisscross marks of the lash could be seen everywhere across his shoulders, his chest, his arms, even his face. Many of the cuts were purple and festering, and one arm hung awkwardly, mangled and broken.

'Do you know this man?' the general asked. At a signal from him, one of the soldiers seized the man's hair and yanked his head back so that Claude could see the disfigured face.

'No,' Claude said, surprised to discover that he was hoarse; he hadn't spoken more than a few words aloud in a week.

'You lie,' the general said. 'He has confessed to belonging to a secret society of which you are a member. He has confessed to plotting with you and others against the government of France.'

'As badly as this man's been tortured,' Claude said, 'I'm not surprised that he would confess to anything; but the charges you have just made are not only false, they are ridiculous.'

The general's angry frown deepened. He motioned with his hand, and suddenly one of the soldiers who had brought Claude here stepped before him and slapped him full across the mouth. Claude reeled backward, barely able to keep from falling.

'You will talk,' the general said. 'In the end you will be grateful to be allowed to crawl on your knees and confess your guilt – yours, and your father's.'

It was this last that chilled Claude to the bone: his father! Good God, they meant not only to kill him, but to use him to implicate his father as well, perhaps even his entire family. This was not merely an arrest for killing a man during a duel; he had become a pawn in a political persecution.

Oddly enough, it was this knowledge that gave him the strength to withstand the beating he was given. Had it been only a question of himself, he would no doubt have quickly confessed to whatever they wanted. After all, if he was going to die anyway, it could hardly matter whether he died for dueling or for treason. But he had already done enough harm to his family; he would not – he could not – confess to anything that would endanger them.

At last he was taken back to his cell; he could never have imagined that he would be grateful to see that dreary tomb, but now he was. The guards had virtually to carry him, and when the cell door was open, they gave him a shove and he toppled to the floor inside. The door clanged shut after him and once again he was alone. He vomited until his stomach ached from the retching; then, too weak to move, he lay in his own filth until he sank mercifully into unconsciousness.

He had no way of measuring how long he was unconscious. He was awakened by the squealing of the cell door upon its hinges; the sound sent a shudder of horror through him. Not so soon, surely! He did not think he would be able to withstand another beating so soon after the first one; he needed time to pull himself together.

'On your feet,' a rough voice barked. When Claude continued to lie where he was, he was seized and dragged to his feet.

This time it was the lieutenant who had stood behind the general during the previous 'questioning', along with a single soldier, who now held Claude's shirt front to keep him from falling.

Once again he was taken into the corridor, the soldier holding tight to his arm. Claude shuffled along as best he could; this time he knew to cover his eyes before he was taken into the courtyard, but that proved to be unnecessary – it was no longer daylight. Overhead only an occasional star relieved the solid blackness of the sky.

They did not take him across the courtyard as before but skirted it and took yet another corridor that led off to the right.

'This way,' the lieutenant snapped when the soldier seemed to hesitate.

This corridor was unlighted; once they had rounded a corner it was almost impossible to see in the gloom. Claude stumbled repeatedly, and only the firm hand on his arm kept him from falling. They marched along in silence, the lieutenant bringing up the rear.

Another corner, and here a single torch was burning, revealing a door at the end of the corridor. They approached it and came to a halt.

'Open it,' the lieutenant ordered.

'But sir, this goes –' the soldier started to object.

'I am well aware of where it goes, soldier,' the lieutenant said. 'I have my orders, and you have yours. Open the door.'

For a moment more the soldier hesitated. Then, giving a shrug, he let go of Claude's arm and turned to the door, producing a heavy ring of keys. He selected one and fitted it into the rusty lock.

The lieutenant had been carrying his pistol in his hand. Now, to Claude's astonishment, he stepped up behind the soldier at the door and, putting the pistol to the back of the man's head, fired. There was an explosion of bone and flesh that spattered Claude's already bloody clothes.

'Merciful God,' Claude breathed, too dazed to comprehend what was happening.

'Quick,' was all the lieutenant said. The body of the soldier had slid to the floor and now the lieutenant kicked it roughly aside and shoved on the iron door. It swung noisily outward. Grabbing Claude's arm, the lieutenant pulled him through the opening.

They were outside the prison. Claude wondered if he were only dreaming this. Outside? And there, stepping from the shadow of the trees, surely that could not be – but it was – his father, and there, François, and others that he didn't know.

His father embraced him, but François said, 'Hurry,' and shoved them in the direction of the trees.

Hardly realizing what was happening, Claude stumbled over the rough ground. In a moment they were in a wood, and there were more men, horses and – good heavens – his mother and Danielle.

In another moment Claude had been helped into a saddle, and as swiftly as that, the entire party had started up and they were riding hard away from the prison, and Claude was a free man.

31

Jean would never have brought his wife and Danielle, but nothing he said could sway the women from their decision.

'We can ride as well as any of the men,' Anne had argued. 'And I've already put out the word that I was going to Paris with you.'

'And what of the children?'

'Jeanette will look after them. Claude is my son, too. If we must, we'll follow on our own.'

To that he had had no argument. And in fact the women had been no real hindrance. It had been a hard journey, changing horses at prearranged points along the way, resting no more than an hour or so at a time. He himself was feeling the strain of fatigue, every mile reminding him that he was no longer young.

Now they were within two hours of the coast and the ship waiting there. Their last change of horses had been several hours before; despite the impatience that drove them, it was necessary to stop for another rest.

François's men started a small fire, and Danielle brewed chocolate over it; that, and the hard rolls that were passed around, were the first meal any of them had eaten since midday of the day before.

Jean rose from his place near the fire and walked around to his wife. She was huddled in a blanket, her hands stretched out toward the fire. It was hard for him to believe that this was the same spoiled creature he had wed so long ago; her face looked tired and drawn, but she had not complained once throughout the long trip and, as she had promised, she had ridden as hard as the men.

She gave him a wan smile as he sat beside her. He put an arm about her shoulders and drew her close. Claude was asleep; Jean had worried about him most of all. Clearly he had been in no condition to begin so difficult a journey, but the boy had shown his mettle.

The boy. Jean smiled at his choice of words; surely his son had proven himself a man in the past week. And Jean could only guess at the challenges his son would have to face in the weeks and months to come.

'Is it time?' Anne asked. A breeze had come up, hinting of the morning to come.

'Soon,' he said, unable to keep the weariness from his voice. This, he knew, would be his last adventure. His body ached, seemingly from deep within. He was grateful that the end of their journey was near; yet it meant the end of so much more as well.

'Soon,' he repeated.

A single light flashed among the trees – once, twice, three times. François crept from his hiding place and hurried toward the signal.

The man he was to meet, one of his own highwayman friends, came out of the woods. François cast an apprehensive glance over his shoulder, but there was no one else about; all the others were still resting about the fire.

'It's all arranged,' his man told him. 'There was a corporal in command of the garrison. He was happy as hell to hear what was in store for him.'

'How much time?'

'They're about half an hour behind me, no more than that.'

'Good. You'd best start back, then. Wait for me at Amiens.'

'Aren't you coming? Those soldiers are liable to shoot first and ask questions later.'

'I'll be behind you. I have to get the girl, that's all.'

When the man had gone, François stole back to the camp, following a roundabout route. So far everything was going exactly as planned. By now all of his comrades had crept away while the others rested, and in a few minutes he would follow.

But first he must kill the lieutenant who had brought the young de Brussac out of prison; he was the last one who could link him and his associates directly with the escape – other than the de Brussacs themselves, and even if any of them survived the trap that had been set for them, their word was not likely to be believed.

The girl was a problem. He had not counted on her being along, and when he had first seen her and the wife accompanying the old man, he had objected, but his objections had been overridden.

So be it, then. Somehow he must get the girl to go with him – by force, if necessary. Once her would-be lover was dead, she would come around quickly enough; he was sure of that.

He paused in the shadow of a tree. There, off by himself, was the lieutenant, still sleeping. The others were either sleeping also or huddled around the fire. The sky had just begun to turn gray, but it was still too dark for anyone to observe him. He drew his dagger and, crouching down, stole toward the sleeping figure.

One swift motion, and it was done. The man made a low gurgling sound in his sleep; he would waken no more.

'What are you doing?'

The unexpected question made him jump. He stood, whirling about as he did so. Danielle was there, just a few feet away; she had come upon him unnoticed.

He stared stupidly back at her. She moved closer and her eyes went to the bloody dagger still in his hand.

'François, it's you! But what are you doing with that dagger? The lieutenant, is he . . . ?'

'Come with me,' François said, seizing her wrist. He thrust the dagger into his belt.

'I don't understand – where are you taking me? What's going on?' She tried to resist, but he yanked her roughly along with him to where two horses were already saddled and waiting.

'It's time to collect on our bargain. I kept my part of it – your lover is free – now it's your turn.'

'No, not until Claude is safely away. Wait, where are the rest of the horses?' Her eyes raked the animals and then went back to the campfire. She began slowly to comprehend.

'Your men, they're all gone,' she said, turning back to François. 'And you've killed the lieutenant – what does this mean?'

'It means you're coming with me,' he said angrily. He seized her and tried to lift her onto the horse, but she fought him, kicking him hard in the shins.

'You little vixen,' he cursed beneath his breath. 'Don't you understand, I'm saving your life! If you're still here when the soldiers come, they'll kill you along with the others.'

'Let go of her.' It was Claude's voice, cold and commanding. He had seen the scuffle going on and come to investigate.

Startled and dismayed by the turn of events, François let her go. Danielle ran into Claude's arms.

'Claude, it's some kind of trap,' she sobbed, clinging to him. 'His men have already gone and he was trying to take me away, too – he says there are soldiers coming . . .'

For the moment Claude's attention was concentrated on Danielle; François seized the opportunity. He leaped for his horse, bounding into the saddle. Claude drew his pistol, thrusting Danielle aside, and fired after the fleeing horseman, but he was too late. François vanished into the darkness, the sound of galloping hooves fading rapidly.

The de Brussacs and Danielle found themselves alone. François and his men were gone, the lieutenant was dead, and from somewhere beyond the shadows, soldiers were approaching.

'What are we going to do?' Anne asked.

It was Claude who answered; the frightened question had broken the spell that held him rooted to the spot.

'We're going to get the hell out of here,' he said.

They rode as if Death himself were at their heels, and for all they knew, he was. They were all excellent riders, and they wasted no time on hedges or marshes but leaped them swiftly, gracefully; nor did they waste breath on talking.

Danielle was cursing herself for a fool; she ought to have known François could not be trusted. She ought to have foreseen that he would attempt some sort of trick and been ready for it.

Their pace was brutal. The beast beneath her was drenched with sweat and the foam from his nostrils flew back into her face, but they dared not slow their flight. It was morning now, and somewhere close ahead was the ocean; already she could smell its tang on the cold wind that whipped her cloak behind her like the wings of a giant bird. Before them wood fowl leaped up, crying shrilly, frightened by the sudden, swift approach of horses' hooves.

'Look!' Claude shouted.

They all glanced back. There on the crest of a hill they had covered earlier was a flash of scarlet and blue – soldiers, in pursuit! The soldiers were gone in a moment, dipping down into a little valley. François's trap had nearly succeeded; had they remained at the camp just a little longer . . . And even now, the soldiers might catch them before they reached the sea.

It seemed to Danielle, looking back a moment later for yet another glimpse of their pursuers, that the soldiers had gained on them. She dug her heels into her horse's flesh, urging him on. The wearied beast's nostrils were like pits of blood, his eyes circles of red, yet still his hooves broke the stubble of the field beneath them and his neck stretched till the tendons were like bowstrings.

And suddenly they had topped another rise, the ground fell away before them to the ocean – and there, tossing fitfully on the waves, was a small boat. Further out, beyond the threat of rocks, lay a sailing ship, her sails puffing impatiently.

A man – the captain of the ship – stood on the beach and waved frantically. A narrow path led down to the beach; they took it single file, picking their way, with Jean in the lead, and at last they were there, the horses' hooves sinking into the wet sand.

'Here, help me with these,' Jean said, leaping to the ground and struggling with the burlap bags tied to his horse's saddle.

'What're these?' Claude asked, helping him.

'Cuttings, from all the best vines. They tell me they're already making wine in the New World; wherever there are men, there'll be a need for something to soften the harsh edges. Keep them moist and always remember they're living things. I give you a living legacy.'

The bags were tossed into the little dinghy. 'This man,' Jean went on, indicating the captain, who was already shoving the small boat into the surf, 'will take you to London. There's a ship sailing for the New World in a week's time. This gold will get you there, and this letter is to our London representative. He'll see you have whatever funds you need.'

'Mister!' It was the ship's captain; Jean followed his pointing finger and saw the scarlet and blue on the crest above them. 'Soldiers – looks like a whole damn army of them.'

'You'll take the women with you,' Jean said. There was a stunned silence that followed this pronouncement.

'Jean, no,' Anne said, taking a step toward him. 'We – we must all go.'

'Impossible. Marie and René are still here – someone will have to look after them. Claude, help the women into the boat.'

Danielle was already clambering into the dinghy with the help of the captain, who kept glancing anxiously at the line of soldiers already making the difficult descent down the face of the cliff, but Anne gave a stubborn toss of her head.

'I won't go,' she said.

'Don't you understand,' Jean said, 'he's not likely to harm the children, at least I pray not, but they will certainly arrest me, and you, too, if you remain. I can look out for myself – I'm still not entirely without influence in Paris – but I couldn't bear to think that you . . . '

She came to stand before him, head held high; he thought she had never looked more beautiful, more desirable, and suddenly his love for her was like a flaming sword that pierced his breast, and he knew he would bear its pain forever.

'My darling,' he said, seizing her and crushing her to him.

The kiss was as brief as it was violent. One moment his lips were fastened hungrily upon hers and the next they were gone, he had taken a step back from her, and suddenly his fist was crashing into her jaw. She gave a single low moan and collapsed into his arms.

Swiftly but with infinite tenderness, he lifted her and carried her to the boat. Danielle took her with a sob, cradling Anne's head against her shoulder.

'Mister, we've got to go,' the captain said, grabbing an oar. Even as he spoke a shot rang out from above.

'Father,' Claude tried to say, but even that word refused to come. He could hardly see his father for the tears filling his eyes.

He knew that he was saying goodbye to more than his father, to more than his homeland; he was saying goodbye to a great part of himself as well. He had been a boy until this chain of events had begun, never mind his years; years didn't matter. He had lived in a child's world, sheltered, loved, cared for, protected. He had never known until a week ago a world of pain, a world of disappointment and failure; a world in which you could hunger and weaken, suffer and die and live to suffer again.

He had never known the real world at all.

'There's no time,' Jean said. He embraced his son, kissing his cheeks. Somehow Claude found himself in the boat, the distance between the boat and the shore growing wider. His father did not move from where he stood, nor even turn to look at the soldiers swarming onto the beach, rushing to surround him. He remained motionless, his hands at his side, staring after the little boat that rose and fell with the swell of the ocean, until the soldiers had seized him and taken him prisoner.

PART II

The
HARVEST

32

'Ah, Madame, there you are.'

Anne turned from the rail where she had been gazing out at the unrelenting vastness of the ocean – so much water, as if the world had turned liquid. Would they ever see land again?

'Danielle,' she said in English, 'I thought we had agreed to practice our English among ourselves.'

English had been a part of Anne's education as a girl, and in educating her children and Danielle, she had imparted her somewhat shaky knowledge of the language to them. Since they had sailed over a month ago from England they had, with the help of the captain's cabin boy and some books they had brought from London, progressed to a fair fluency with what was to be their new tongue.

'Yes, Madame,' was Danielle's meek reply.

Anne, somewhat abashed at having spoken so sharply, said more conversationally, 'Where is Claude?'

'He's with the captain, in his cabin.'

'No doubt telling the captain how to run his ship,' Anne said drily. 'God knows, someone should.'

They had long since made the discovery that the ship on which they were sailing was not the best-managed vessel afloat; the potatoes that had been loaded as the staple food for the passengers had been bought in such excess that they now filled the ship with the stink of their rotting, while drinking water was in such short supply that it had been rationed for over a week now.

'Claude could, if anyone could,' Danielle said, her face lighting up as it always did whenever Claude's name came into the conversation.

'You're in love with him, aren't you?' Anne asked, her eyes narrowing shrewdly. 'No, don't blush and look away. We might as well be honest with one another, you and I, since our lots seem to have been cast together.'

Danielle managed the courage to say, 'I've always loved him. I think I was born loving your son.'

'Yes, well, some girls start earlier than others,' Anne said.

Danielle remembered why she had come out, and said, 'It's getting cool – shall I bring you a shawl, or will you be coming to the cabin?'

'No, I'm all right, thank you; you go in and never mind about me. I'll be in shortly. Oh, you needn't look at me like you were weighing up a fish; I don't mean to fling myself overboard, although God knows I'm thirsty enough.'

'I've saved some water,' Danielle said. 'We can share it when you come in, if you like.'

Anne made no reply, and after a moment Danielle left her. Watching her go, Anne could not help resenting the girl's efforts to be friendly. She knew it was not friendship Danielle wanted, it was approval – approval of her designs upon Claude, and that she had scant likelihood of obtaining.

It was true, Anne conceded, that she had much to be grateful to the girl for; it was she, after all, who had contrived Claude's escape from prison (although in a manner that had landed them on this stinking ship while Jean was somewhere under arrest in France), and there was no denying that the girl had courage. Danielle had shown a dignity thus far in their difficulties that many women of noble birth would have done well to emulate.

Still and all, Anne did not intend to see her son wed to a peasant girl, and she thought it presumptuous of Danielle to be in love so far above her station.

At the moment, however, Anne did not take these matters seriously. For the present, Claude clearly had nothing on his mind but the cuttings his father had given him, and getting them all to this California, which apparently was somewhere beyond the ends of the earth. He hardly seemed to notice Danielle, and Anne was sure he was unaware of the girl's infatuation.

Alone on the deck – or at least as alone as one could expect to be on the deck of a sailing ship – Anne turned her gaze once more in the direction from which they had sailed. There, beyond those crested waves, lay France and home and all that she knew and was dear to her.

And Jean.

At first she had raged in anger and grief and frustration, swearing that she would not go to this New World to which she had been sent so unceremoniously, threatening to return to France, even threatening to take her life.

But in time Claude's arguments had prevailed. This was what

Jean had wanted, the only way he had felt that he could cope with what was ahead of him. He had promised to join them as soon as it was possible. Returning to France could accomplish nothing but certain arrest, and in any event, there was no one to return to – their English attorneys had made discreet inquiries: Chateau Brussac was empty, save for some guards that had been posted there. Jean, Marie, René, even the servants had all disappeared, no one could, or would, venture a guess where.

At length Anne had resigned herself to the fate that had been thrust upon her. She remembered something that Jean had said once: that survival often meant nothing more than knowing when to change one's habits. They had taken the money from their English accounts, leaving enough to pay for the passage of Jean and the children when they obtained their freedom; booked passage; and departed.

But to what she couldn't even guess. They had learned while they were in England that a war had been going on over this place called California, between the United States and Mexico. Mexico had lost the year before and California was now an independent territory, soon, apparently, to become one of the United States of America. Whether that augured well for them or badly no one could say, nor even whether their ancient land grant would still be honored.

A shattered past, an unknown future – it had been like that for her once before, when she had lost Emile, whom she had thought she loved, and married Jean, whom she had thought she hated; only this time she would not have Jean's strength and wisdom to guide her.

Oh, Jean, Jean, she cried silently, the ache in her heart as bitter as when she had first awakened in that rocking boat and realized what had happened, *how am I to go on?*

'I tell you, Captain, I must have water or my cuttings will die.'

'And I tell you again, Mister de Brussac,' the captain replied, 'that if I give you the water for your plants, the people on this ship may die. We've at least a week of sailing before we reach New York harbor and barely enough water even with strict rationing to last us that long. It's out of the question. Your request is denied.'

Claude glowered angrily across the desk at the red-faced man opposite him. Why couldn't he make the old fool understand – virtually the entire de Brussac fortune was riding in the cargo hold of this ship. Since his father's arrest, the bulk of the de Brussac holdings, still in French banks, had been closed by governmental order; the once seemingly limitless de Brussac resources had been reduced to their English holdings and the money that his father had been providently transferring to English banks in the weeks before their escape and his arrest.

There was money enough, if he was cautious, to take them to California, but once they got there it was upon the cuttings he had brought with him that their fortunes would rest.

Only those cuttings were already perilously dry. Another week without water and they would be worthless; the de Brussacs would arrive at their new home empty-handed.

'Captain, what can I do?' he asked wearily.

'You can pray for rain. Mister de Brussac,' was the reply.

33

Danielle was tormented by a worry that had nothing to do with Claude's cuttings. In the weeks and then months since they had fled France, she had become increasingly aware of one fact.

Claude was a man now; he had cast aside the last vestiges of his boyhood on that icy morning in the forest when he had avenged his sister's dishonor.

Since then he had been occupied with taking on the responsibilities of his particular manhood, providing for his mother and her, arranging for their transport to the New World, negotiating with men in that peculiarly masculine world of affairs.

But there were other burdens of manhood. Here, on this ship, there were few reminders; the only other women were those unfortunate creatures below in steerage and they were expressly forbidden on deck, so they were unlikely to awaken any interest on Claude's part; and though the ghost of Antoinette might still haunt him, she was further behind with each passing day.

Soon, though, they would be arriving in New York City. She had only a vague impression of what would greet them there, but nothing that she had heard had indicated that it was a womanless city. There would be women enough there to remind Claude of his manly needs. And once he had turned from her to them, would he turn back again?

She had gotten so used to him in the weeks since they had fled France; his mother's resentment, all the shock of leaving family and homeland, all the things that had happened, had paled beside that one consoling fact; she was with Claude.

But would she be with him for long, or would he, once he had found himself a woman, look upon her as an unnecessary burden, to be discarded at the first convenient opportunity?

'Sooner or later,' she told herself, 'he's going to need a woman . . .'

But I am a woman, Danielle thought, *and I love him. Why should I stand idly by and watch another woman take him from me?*

At once her mother's admonitions came back to her: 'A man loses respect for a woman'; 'your husband will want you untouched'. What she was contemplating was a sin against God and church. It would have been bad enough under any circumstances, but when you added that he was an aristocrat, and she merely the daughter of his mother's maid, her effrontery was scandalous.

And yet she wanted him. In the face of all her provincial upbringing, she longed to feel his arms about her, not as friend embraces friend but as man embraces woman. She was shamed by her own boldness, dismayed to think that after all she was only a wanton creature unworthy of her parents – and still she wanted him, wanted to cling to him, wanted to bind him to her, wanted to make him hers in the way that a woman could possess a man.

The sunny, rainless days wore on. There were no opportunities for privacy between them; she and Madame shared one small cabin, while he slept in the mate's quarters, and the deck was never quite free of watching eyes.

The city of New York loomed ever larger on her mind's horizon until it seemed that she could actually see its outline across the water, although they were still several days out of harbor.

The captain had ordered the rotting potatoes dumped into the water. Danielle stood by the railing, watching a seaman with an obvious lack of relish for the job slowly shoveling the smelly produce overboard. The potatoes formed a bobbing trail in the ship's wake, like an accusing finger that marked their passage.

Despondent because she had still found no solution to her conflict, Danielle turned her back on the sight and returned to the cabin. Madame was eating the midday meal. Danielle sat at her own place but she had no appetite for the food that had been set out.

'Aren't you hungry?' Anne asked.

'I'm worried about Claude,' Danielle said, toying listlessly with her food. 'He thinks the cuttings will be lost.'

'It's too bad they can't eat potatoes,' Anne said, putting down her own fork and pushing aside the bowl of boiled potatoes that had made up the better part of their meals since they had sailed from England. 'Personally I don't think I'll ever be able to endure them again.'

'*Mon Dieu!*' Danielle brought her hand down on the table so hard that the dishes clattered.

Anne gave her a startled look. 'Danielle, what is it? You look as if you've seen a ghost.'

Danielle seemed hardly to have heard her; she stared past her, at the open porthole, and said, as if to herself, 'But they can.'

'Danielle, what on earth . . . ?'

Danielle jumped up, knocking her chair over. 'But of course they can,' she cried, and with that she ran from the cabin, leaving Anne to stare after her in bewilderment.

'Claude! Claude!' She burst into his cabin without knocking. The mate, who shared the cabin, was in the process of shaving in front of a cracked mirror and he was shirtless; at the sight of the girl bursting unannounced into his cabin, he seized the first thing at hand, a blanket from his nearby bunk, and flung it about himself like a shawl.

'Young lady!' he cried, shocked at this breach of conduct, but in fact she hadn't noticed him at all.

'Claude, you must stop him,' she cried, running to him. He had been reading on his own bunk, but at her entrance he had jumped up.

'Danielle, what on earth are you doing here, and what are you talking about – stop who?'

'That man, he's throwing the potatoes overboard.'

'But of course he is; they're no good for anything now but stinking up the whole ship –'

'Water,' she cried, laying a hand on his arm and staring up

into his face eagerly. 'Moisture – when potatoes rot, they turn to water.'

For a moment he could only stare incredulously at her. Then suddenly he gave an excited whoop and, seizing her by the waist, lifted her into the air and spun her wildly about to the further consternation of the ship's mate, who thought the two 'Frenchies' had gone mad.

It was an opinion that the captain was inclined to share, especially when Claude burst into his cabin, the girl at his heels, and said unceremoniously, 'I want to buy the potatoes.'

'Young man, have you taken leave of your senses?' the captain replied.

'There's no time to argue,' Claude said. 'There's a man shoveling them overboard right this moment. You've got to stop him.'

'Good heavens, what are you talking about?' The captain rose from his desk, wondering if after all he had been wise to take these foreigners aboard; of course they had paid dearly, but still, if they were actually mad . . .

'I want to buy them, all of them, here – ' he tore a packet of pound notes from his coat and flung them on the desk ' – if that's not enough, I'll bring more.'

'What . . . why . . . ?' the captain sputtered, but before he could even think of a suitable reply, the pair had gone as abruptly as they had come, and he was left to wonder why they should want to pay so much money for a load of rotten potatoes.

The money lay scattered across his desk. It was true, of course, that he could use the money; and after all, if they wanted to throw good cash away on bad potatoes, well, it wasn't as if he hadn't tried to argue with them.

He began to collect the notes, smiling to himself as he counted them.

Had the Frenchman actually offered to bring more later?

They worked through the afternoon and into the evening, Danielle and Claude together, cutting slits in the potatoes one at a time and sticking a precious vine cutting into each one. It was dirty and smelly work; the stench was so bad in the hold that Danielle thought she must surely faint, and more than once her stomach threatened to rebel, but somehow she managed to endure. She learned that afternoon that, given time enough and motivation enough, one can get used to almost anything, even the stink and the slime of rotten potatoes.

'There, the last of them,' Claude said at last. He wiped the back of his hand across his forehead, leaving a blackish streak.

'Will they be saved?' She leaned back wearily against the damp wall.

'Too early to say, but I'm betting they will be.' He turned to smile down at her. They were alone in the hold, the only light the flickering glare of a lantern. 'Thanks to you,' he added.

'Claude, I . . . ' but she could think of no words to say. She felt a tightening in her breast. How handsome he was!

He took her in his arms, drawing her slowly toward him. Leaning down, he kissed her.

It was a gentle, a brotherly kiss at first, and then all at once, as if he had suddenly been struck with a realization of her womanhood, it became something else. The lips that had brushed hers gently were fastened upon her hungrily, and she was swept into a passionate embrace, crushed against the hardness of his lean, young body. She clung to him, her heart pounding, and in that instant the conflict ended for her and she knew what the outcome must be.

Never relinquishing her lips, he lowered her to the rough wood, covering her body with his own, and there, amidst the flickering shadows and the stench of rot, he became her lover.

Afterward she lay in a sort of dazed wonder in the crook of his arm. Her body felt bruised and torn, yet deliciously languid. She turned her head to look up at him, studying the somber line of his profile in the flickering light.

'A penny for your thoughts,' she said.

He said, without looking at her, 'I was thinking what a rotten place this is for a girl's first time.'

'Is it?' She sounded genuinely surprised. 'I hadn't noticed.'

He laughed at her innocence, and after a moment, because she was still as much a girl as a woman, she laughed with him. The sound of her laughter dispelled some of the gloom and exorcised, at least for the moment, the ghost of Antoinette.

34

'You see, Mother, it isn't nearly as bad as you expected, all this talk about half-clad savages.'

'You're quite right,' Anne agreed. 'I can see for myself they're fully clad.'

Actually she was surprised to find that there was a modicum of civilization in New York – at a barbaric level, true, but better than she had expected. She was all for staying here, at least until Jean and the other children could join them. She was uncomfortably aware of the new relationship that had sprung up between Claude and Danielle, and she thought it more likely to resolve itself here in New York than on yet another journey. Claude, however, was all for pushing on.

'There's no telling how long we might have to wait,' he pointed out. 'And if we stay too long, our money and the cuttings will both be gone. They won't survive forever out of the ground.'

'But I'm so tired with all this traveling – how much further is it anyway to this California?'

'Just a short journey, I think – a few more days and we can be on our own land.'

'Or in it,' Anne added drily.

Danielle, who was suffering a nagging suspicion that Claude was not quite as happy with their new relationship as she was, eyed the rather elegant women of New York and sided with Claude.

'At least we won't be crammed into any more ship cabins,' she said optimistically, words she was to regret over the weeks and months that followed.

Once he had gotten them established in a hotel, Claude went to a travel agent to arrange for the final leg of their journey. At first Mister Dawes, the agent he visited, did not seem to understand where it was they wanted to go.

'El Pueblo de Nuestra Señora la Reina de los Angeles de Porciurncula,' Claude repeated the name, coping with the

Spanish tongue as best he could. 'It's in California,' he added.

Recognition dawned in the man's eyes. 'Ah, you mean Los Angeles,' he said. 'But that's not where you want to go.'

'It isn't?' Claude asked, puzzled.

'No, the gold is up north, place called Sutter's Mill mostly, but they say it's all over the place, nuggets as big as hen's eggs lying on the ground, all you got to do is walk around and pick 'em up.'

Claude stared back at him. 'But our land is at Los Angeles,' he said.

'Land?' Dawes gave a disdainful snort. 'Nothing there but a passel of desert and some scrub brush. Nobody but a fool'd want to go there when there's all that gold to the north.' He gave Claude a look that said he hoped he wasn't such a fool.

Claude hesitated. Gold – if it were true, perhaps he could renew their fortune; perhaps by the time his father arrived, the de Brussacs could again be a family of wealth and importance, living the sort of life they had been accustomed to living before he had brought disaster upon their heads. And Antoinette – if he were a rich man again, perhaps Antoinette would come to him . . . he felt a pang of guilt as Danielle flashed into his mind. Danielle, dear little girl, so childlike, so devoted; he supposed he loved her too, but it could never be the fiery passion that he had known with Antoinette; that was the real thing. And perhaps with the gold he could regain it.

And yet there were the vines, vines his father had treasured, the legacy he had passed on to him. These were their fortune, his father had always told him, a living treasure, not just rocks hacked out of the ground.

And there was the land itself; it had been his father's and his grandfather's, notwithstanding that neither man had ever set eyes on it. His father had given it to him, charged him with beginning a new life for the family there, and the remnants of the de Brussac pride made him bristle to hear it disposed of in such a disparaging fashion. Desert and scrub brush it might be – and in fact he had never seen a desert and had no idea what a scrub brush might be – but it was de Brussac land, it was *his* land now.

'Nevertheless,' he said aloud, 'I want to go to Los Angeles.'

'Well.' The two men studied one another across the wooden counter. 'If that's what you want . . . it'll take some doing, though. There's not many trains setting out for there; most people want to go up north. You better come back in about a week. Maybe I'll have something for you by then – that's if you haven't come to your senses.'

During the following week Claude's determination began to waver. For one thing, in asking about he had come to the realization that Los Angeles was much further that he had anticipated; what he had thought was to be a journey of a few miles now appeared to be two, perhaps three thousand miles; worse, there was no organized transportation across that vast distance. There were railroad lines, riverboats, even canals scattered about the eastern portions of this enormous country, but to reach California one had to travel by horse and wagon. Because much of the area was still wilderness, peopled in some places by unfriendly savages, most travelers joined up with the wagon trains that made the westward journey with increasing frequency. Still, even these sometimes lengthy caravans were not entirely safe from Indian attacks or the other dangers that lay along the way.

The men he asked gave him widely varying estimates of the time it would take to make the journey; some said two months; others said it would take them a year, if they made it at all.

Yet for all the dangers and hardships, he found that they were not alone in their desire to go west. Everywhere the eyes of men seemed to be turned to the new frontiers that lay beyond the distant horizon. Men and women, young and old, the brave and the bold of every class and generation were pulling up roots, settling their affairs and gathering in cities like Saint Louis, where wagon trains were forming, to begin the westward trek. A new land was opening before them, peopled so far with little more than legends and dreams, and at length the fire of adventure was kindled within Claude's youthful spirit and he found himself looking forward to what lay ahead.

Anne, having argued and lost, maintained a resigned silence. Danielle, to whose arms Claude came less often now that they had reached New York, secretly looked forward to being isolated with him once again, and insisted aloud that she was not in the least afraid.

The first of May, a month after their arrival in New York, they set out by Concord coach for Saint Louis, where a surveying party was preparing to travel, with military escort, to a place called San Antonio. There, according to the information Mister Dawes had obtained, a wagon train was being formed to make the trek to California.

14

It took two weeks in the bumping, swaying coach to reach Saint Louis. By the time they arrived there, Danielle had become afraid after all, not of what might happen on the journey, but of what was already happening within her body. She was sure that she was pregnant.

She questioned Claude cautiously about the length of the journey before them, but his answers were necessarily vague.

'They tell me the survey party will take about two months to reach San Antonio,' he explained. 'Dawes wasn't sure just when the wagon train would be leaving for California or how long it will take to reach there – two or three months, perhaps.'

'Maybe we should wait in Saint Louis until there's a train going through directly,' Danielle suggested.

'No telling how long that might be. No, the survey party is our best bet, and we'll be with a military escort, at least for the first half of the trip.' He gave her a quizzical look; generally she was inclined to go along with whatever he arranged without question; if anything, he found her too subservient to his wishes, too eager to please him, which only made him feel guilty because he knew that he couldn't fully return the love she felt for him.

'Not getting tired already, are you?' he asked. 'We've just gotten started, you know.'

She looked away from the questions in his eyes. For a moment she had toyed with the idea of telling him the truth about her condition, but now that the moment to do so had come, she found herself unable to speak. What if he decided she would have to stay behind until the baby was born? What if he were angry at this additional burden he would be saddled with? She could not guess how he would react to the news and was too unsure of her place in his affections to risk finding out.

'No, I'm not at all tired,' she said.

35

They set out early in June on a thousand-mile leg of their journey that would take them from Saint Louis through the new states of Missouri and Arkansas, across a stretch of Indian territory, and finally across the state of Texas to the city of

San Antonio. Although there were only about a dozen wagons in the train, the military escort that they had been promised turned out to be some one hundred and fifty strong, so that with the addition of guides and scouts, they made an impressive and colorful company as they wound their way through the rolling hills west of Saint Louis. Claude had bought two wagons for the trip, one to carry them and their provisions, the other filled with the growing plants.

Like everyone else involved in the wagon train, Anne and Danielle had to practice 'wagon drill' and learn, too, how to fire a rifle and a handgun. Anne, gritting her teeth with steely determination, had surprised everyone, even her son, with how well she had done.

'By God, mother, you're pioneer stock after all,' Claude had said proudly.

'I hope that isn't intended as a compliment,' she had said drily, but she had looked a bit pleased with herself.

Danielle had a dreadful time learning to drive the horses and argued that she ought to be allowed to ride them instead, but in the end she had finally gotten the hang of it. Her shooting was erratic at first – 'No telling who she's liable to shoot,' one of the scouts grumbled – but she eventually learned that too.

It was slow travel, rarely more than twenty or thirty miles a day, and as they began to descend into the flat, barren plains, it grew increasingly hot and dusty.

For all of that Danielle found the experience awesome, even exhilarating. She could hardly believe the vastness of the land unfolding before her eyes; it seemed an ocean of land, with great, broad vistas as wide and unmarked as the ocean across which they had sailed from England. The sun seemed to shimmer in waves, and sometimes in the distance she could see the dust, whipped by the wind into little funnels that looked delicate and harmless but could, she was told, grow to such size and ferocity that they could flatten a house in seconds or lift a wagon, horses and all, into the air and drop it again miles away.

'When the sky turns yellow,' Jim Rumford, their chief guide, told her, pointing to the little dust funnels, 'and the clouds seem to form downward, that's the time to start worrying.'

For a day or two after that, she watched the sky anxiously, but it had remained cheerfully blue and the few clouds that appeared were so innocent and upward-turned that she soon put that worry out of her mind.

Indeed, her only persistent concern was with the new life growing within her. She was frightened that her child might be born on this long and arduous journey. Far more worrisome to her, though, was the fear that Claude might find out and not let her continue on from San Antonio.

She and Anne had exchanged their French and English gowns for the loose-fitting cotton dresses and sensible poke bonnets worn by all the women in the train. Even when she began to 'show', the looseness of the gown would hide the truth from Claude for some time. If only they were not delayed too long in departing from San Antonio! Once they were on their way, there would be little he could do but let her go on.

Still, she wished with all her heart that they could be married so that their son needn't be born out of wedlock. Since they had set out from Saint Louis, Claude had again begun to turn to her for relief, but opportunities for privacy on such a journey were few and brief; when he came to her at night and took her to lie with him beneath the wagon, he used her with urgency and haste and with a minimum of conversation. These little comings-together, as she labeled them, both pleased and depressed her: pleased her because she could be, however briefly, in his arms, and depressed her because they were so unemotional and because each time she was reminded that the goal she had thought she had achieved had yet eluded her – he was still not hers, not even in those moments when, encased within her flesh, he shared his life's stream with her; for she sensed, knew in her woman's heart, that he took more than he gave.

At first these thoughts and her awe of the land they were traversing so occupied her mind that she rarely had time to think of anything else, but as the days and then weeks passed and the land settled itself into the monotony of the plains, she became gradually aware of other matters.

One of these new discoveries was that their chief guide, Jim Rumford, paid considerably more attention to her than he did to the other wagoners. Jim was handsome, blond and lean with a neat little mustache and skin like fine leather. He seemed always to be riding alongside the wagon, pointing out some sight to her, explaining something that had puzzled her, or just offering kindly advice.

'You looked peaked, ma'am,' he would say, eyeing her with

friendly concern. 'You oughta ask someone to spell you and climb in the back to rest for a while.'

Or another time, 'You oughta be wearing your gloves, ma'am; them reins will be the ruin of them pretty hands of yours.'

For a time Claude seemed not to notice the attention Jim was paying her; when he did, he grew a bit peevish about it.

'Looks to me like that Rumford spends more time chattering with you than he does guiding the train,' he grumbled on one occasion when they were camped for the night.

'It's a long journey for a man without a woman,' Anne said, giving her son a meaningful look. He clamped his jaw shut and went to check the plants.

Danielle was surprised at this interpretation of Rumford's behavior and pooh-poohed the suggestion at first, but over the next day or so she paid more attention to him and came to the conclusion that Madame was right. Now that she looked, there was that unmistakable something in the way the guide's eyes rested on her, however briefly or casually.

Of course, she couldn't be less interested; she was in love with Claude, however callous he might be toward her. But the truth was, of late he had treated her rather like another piece of equipment brought along for his use to make the journey more tolerable. It was pleasant to be noticed as a woman, particularly by a handsome, agreeable man, and as the days wound on she began gradually to respond to him, more unconsciously than consciously, in a mildly flirtatious manner.

Claude, for his part, became less talkative than ever and began to pay more and more attention to his plants. On the few occasions when he did come to her now at night, he took her with an angry violence that both thrilled and frightened her.

There was a bonus to her tenuous relationship with Jim Rumford. He had spent most of his life, he told her, traveling the plains, first as a boy accompanying his parents in a wagon train to their home in what was now Texas, and later as a guide. His knowledge of the plains was encyclopedic, and he was more than happy to share it with her as he rode alongside the wagon.

It was the Indians that interested her most, the savages of whom the other women spoke with such trepidation.

'What if we should meet up with them?' she asked her mentor.

'They'd probably take a shine to you all right; a plains warrior needs all the wives he can get to do all the work for him, so a healthy woman is always in demand. They even got men that dress up like women, *berdaches* they call them; some of the warriors take them on as wives too, to help with the work.'

'And what do they do with men they capture?'

'Don't often capture any – that's a lot of bull about them capturing and torturing white men. The plains Indians kill quick and get it over with. They don't even cotton to our idea of hanging – say it takes too long to get it over with.'

'But – I heard that they scalped their victims.'

'Some of them do – after they kill them.' Rumford paused and spat a stream of brown tobacco juice onto the ground. 'But they learned that from the white man. The settlers used to pay bounty for Indian scalps.'

Listening to Rumford, Danielle got the impression that the so-called savages of the plains were in many ways less savage than many so-called civilized men of Europe and America.

Rumford's most familiar companion was one of the train's scouts, Carl Betts, a swarthy half-breed with yellowed, rotting teeth and a drooping mustache that hung below his jawline.

Danielle found Rumford pleasant to talk to, but Betts frightened her. Sometimes she would glance in his direction to discover his hard, dark eyes on her, studying her in a way that invariably made her feel suddenly chilled. He rarely spoke to her, and on those occasions when she spoke to him, he would merely nod and ride on, leaving her to wonder at the friendship between the two seemingly different men.

They were three weeks out of Saint Louis when the detachment of soldiers leading the train crested a low ridge and came to a halt. The word came back to set up camp for the night, although it was only early afternoon at the time.

'What is it?' Danielle asked of Claude, who was as ignorant of the reason for the unexpected stop as she was. She asked the same question of Jim Rumford when he came by, directing the wagons to a campsite on the low hills to their right.

'You'll see in a minute, when you reach the ridge,' Rumford said, grinning and displaying teeth stained by the tobacco he liked to chew.

Danielle was driving one wagon, Anne the other, while Claude rode horseback. Danielle followed the wagon before her, and as she came to the ridge, she saw another of the broad, open vistas that had made up most of the scenery of the journey so far, but with one difference – the valley below was alive; a cloud of dust partially obscured the view, and through the cloud she could see a rippling movement like the waves of an ocean.

'What – what is it?' she asked, astounded; it was like nothing she had ever seen before.

'It's what we came for, ma'am,' Rumford said. 'Buffalo – biggest herd I seen yet.'

A gust of wind briefly whipped aside the curtain of dust and she had a glimpse of the distant creatures themselves. They were like cows, but huge, with great shaggy manes and powerful shoulders and haunches. The herd stretched as far as she could see, hundreds upon hundreds of the animals, impressive in a grand and terrifying way.

'Buffalo? But I thought this was a surveying party?' Danielle said.

Rumford threw back his head and laughed. 'Surveying party? Have you seen any surveying going on? No, ma'am, that's the story that was put out – you'd be surprised how many Indian sympathizers there are, even in Saint Louis – but the true story is, we came for the buffalo.'

'What do you plan to do with them?' It was hard for her to imagine what anyone *could* do with so many animals.

'Why, kill them, of course,' Rumford said.

'But why? Surely we have provisions enough?'

He sat back in his saddle and spoke as if to a slightly ignorant child. 'The plains Indians live on the buffalo herds. That's their meat and oil out there, as well as the skins for their clothes and their tepees. They even make tools and such from the bones.'

'But if you kill the buffalo, what will the Indians live on?'

'That's the idea, ma'am. It's the government's new policy, came down direct from Washington. Kill off the buffalo, you kill off the Indians.'

Someone shouted his name then, and with a tip of his hat in her direction, he rode off, leaving her to stare in dismay after him. It seemed almost incredible to her that his explanation could be the right one, and yet, looking now at the soldiers, it was not hard to see that they were indeed preparing for a slaughter. The men were checking their rifles, and extra ammunition was being passed around.

She looked down again at the herd below and could not but think that the entire scheme was barbaric. What a splendor there was to the sight of the majestic beasts below; to slaughter them was surely an obscene gesture. And what a horrible way to deal with the Indians. Of course, she had heard tales. Since they had descended onto the plains, there had been talk about the red man and wild savages, but in truth she had been more curious than frightened by the prospect of seeing these people, particularly after Jim Rumford's remarks. She remembered, too, passages Claude had read to her from the writings of Rousseau, in which he had expressed his admiration for these 'noble savages', as he had termed them, and from Montaigne, who had also admired these men so removed from so many of the vices and crimes of civilized man. Even if the tales that were told of cruelty and torture were true, and some of them beggared the imagination, surely there was some more honorable way of dealing with the native Americans than this.

She got down from the seat and, leaving the horses to graze, she wandered along the line of wagons, but to her surprise no one else seemed particularly displeased with the revelation of the real nature of the soldiers' mission. Indeed, there was almost a carnival atmosphere as everyone waited for the action to begin.

The animals themselves seemed as yet unaware of the activity on the ridge above them, although once or twice she saw a wary beast lift his head and turn in their direction, as if sensing the danger.

'We're upwind from them,' one of the women explained, and another pointed to a distant gully into which it was intended to drive the beasts, where they would be trapped and could be shot more or less at leisure.

'Oh, Claude,' she said, seeing him approach with rifle in hand, 'you're not going to take part, surely? Can't you talk them out of it?'

'All the men are to help,' he said, speaking rather sharply because, in actual fact, he too thought the newly revealed scheme a rather shabby one; he had even come close to refusing, but had decided after all on discretion – to refuse to follow the orders of the train's leaders could result in their expulsion, which would be disaster for them. 'For heaven's sake, Danielle, get those horses tethered before the shooting starts or we're liable to lose them.'

She was stung by the sharpness of his tone, but he did not

give her the opportunity of arguing further; he hurried on to where the men were already mounting their horses.

There was nothing she could do but return to the wagon with a heavy heart. For the first time she actually regretted having begun the journey. Was this what men were like in this raw, new land: deceitful, dishonorable, cruel?

She discovered that hers were the only horses still hitched to their wagon instead of tethered to the thick stakes driven into the ground for the purpose. Since she had left, the other wagons had been brought around into the circle normally used when they camped at night. Anne was standing by the still-hitched wagon, looking about impatiently.

'There you are,' she snapped. 'I didn't know what had happened to you. Everyone's been making such a to-do; we've got to get the wagon in the ring, and get the horses unhitched before the men start . . . '

'I know, I know,' Danielle said angrily, grabbing the reins and climbing up to the driver's seat.

Afterward, no one was sure exactly how the shooting had begun – some overly excited soldier, perhaps, firing out of turn, or perhaps the man in charge simply hadn't seen that her wagon wasn't yet in place.

But suddenly a shot had been fired, and the men on horseback, taking it for their signal, all began to fire at once, the advance wave sweeping down the hillside toward the buffalo grazing below.

Danielle had just snapped the reins for her horses, and the horses, starting to move, were frightened by the deafening roar of gunfire. They leaped forward so violently that she was lifted from the seat and all but toppled off the wagon altogether. The terrified animals charged straight over the ridge and down the hillside into the valley below at breakneck speed.

Everything swept by in a blur; Danielle had a glimpse of men on horseback trying to head her off, but it only made the horses veer so sharply that the wagon rocked violently to and fro, threatening at each lurch to overturn. Then the dust rose around her so thickly that she could hardly see at all. She fought to hold onto the reins, jerking them back until she thought her hands would be snapped off at the wrists, but it was useless. The horses were in a panic now and completely out of control. She was flung about like a rag doll, so terrified that she could not even manage to scream or cry out.

The wagon struck a rock, actually bouncing into the air and

coming back to earth with a wood-snapping crunch, and she realized with horror that they were at the bottom of the hill, and there to the right, the dust cloud trailing like a bridal train, was the herd of buffalo, driven into a stampede by the gunfire, a brown sea of shaggy, charging beasts, and she was in their path!

She screamed then until there was no air left in her lungs and she was forced to swallow great mouthfuls of air, but the scream was noiseless, drowned out by the thunderous roar of thousands of hooves on the hard ground.

Again the horses veered, again threatening to overturn the wagon, and now they were running before the buffalo, but the great beasts were overtaking them in mighty bounds; the earth trembling beneath their charge, they came like gray-brown messengers of death.

'Holy Father,' she tried to pray, but the words stuck with the dust and the terror in her throat.

The buffalo were alongside the wagon now, the leader of the herd running so close that she might have reached out and touched those heaving shoulders. She could smell the sweat and the animal scent and see the blood-flecked foam that fanned from his nostrils. The mighty beast rolled his eyes, his tongue lolling to the side of his mouth, and for an electrifying moment it seemed that he looked directly into her eyes.

It was madness, and yet in that instant it seemed to her that she could read in his eyes not only the blind terror that drove him, but something more, as if that thoughtless beast beseeched her for . . . for what? Mercy? Understanding? Or perhaps forgiveness for the fate that had befallen them both.

For a crazy moment she seemed to know what he felt, that horrible panic that man and beast alike may feel in the face of a nameless and unstoppable horror; she knew because she shared it with him. Woman and animal, pounding heart and pounding heart, charged in terror over the shuddering prairie earth with but one driving instinct in their breasts: Flee! Live, if life be yet possible!

And for her, she knew, it could not long be possible. Her arms felt as if they were being torn from their sockets, and all about her was the sound of wood being ripped from joints. They struck a rock and suddenly she had a glimpse of a wheel come loose before it was crushed to splinters beneath those thundering hooves. The wagon shook, as if to free itself from its burden; the other rear wheel broke loose, the rear of the

wagon crashing to the ground. Boards and planks were flung
about like straws as the wagon began to break up around her.

With a gasp of despair Danielle let go of the reins and gave
herself up to her maker.

36

But it was not her maker into whose arms she was lifted; these
were the arms of Jim Rumford. Through the tears and the dust
she saw him as if in a vision, threading his way between her
and the buffalo. He leaned down from the saddle, stretching
his arms toward her.

'Jump,' he shouted, his voice a mere whisper above the roar.

She did, springing from the crumbling wagon as best she
could, and felt his arms close about her, hauling her up onto
the saddle with him.

For a time she thought that she had doomed him too, for the
stampeding buffalo were all about them, but somehow he
seemed to find a path, and his horse raced as if on winged
feet. Little by little they outdistanced the beasts until suddenly
they were before the herd, breaking through the cloud of dust,
and she could see the barren plain before them and the hillside
to their left; his horse charged up it, and seconds later a tidal
wave of flesh and sinew swept by them with a roar, and she
knew that they were safe.

Danielle gave a whimper, like a child in his sleep, and sank
against his chest in a dead faint.

She woke lying on the ground in the shelter of a wagon. Claude
and Anne were bending over her, and Jim Rumford, and
beyond them she saw a number of people from the wagon
train.

For a moment, as her eyes darted to and fro, the fear was
still alive in her; she seemed to hear the thundering of hooves
and the terrified bellows of the animals.

'It's all right, you're safe now,' Claude said; he reached for
her as if to put his arms about her, but he froze when Jim
Rumford spoke.

'You sure gave us a big scare there, little lady,' Jim said. 'Good thing for you my horse could outrun the devil himself.'

'I – I owe you my life,' Danielle said, managing a wan smile for his benefit. Claude sat back on his heels.

A young colonel from the military detachment rode up and approached Claude. 'We found one of your horses, sir,' he said. 'The other one must have gotten shot with the buffalo.'

'And the wagon? Our supplies?' Claude asked.

The man gave his head a solemn shake. 'Not enough pieces to bother picking up,' the soldier said.

'Oh, Claude, and it's my fault,' Danielle cried out, bursting into tears. 'I wish I'd died out there.'

'Hush,' Anne said quickly, and Claude, who had risen when the colonel rode up, said, 'It's all right, we'll get by.' But he did not kneel down to try to comfort her, and as she watched him move away with the colonel, she saw that his face was weary with disappointment.

It was Jim Rumford who knelt and offered her a none-too-clean handkerchief with which to dry her eyes.

'Couldn't have let you die,' he said, low enough that only she and Anne could hear his words. 'Ain't enough pretty girls in the West as it is.'

Danielle, occupied with her own misery, scarcely heard what he said to her, but Anne leaned back and gave the cowboy an appraising look before she rose and followed her son.

They had lost, as it turned out, nearly all their provisions. A few things that had not found room in the front wagon had been stored with the plants in the second, and these were still intact, but for the most part they were left with little more than the clothes on their backs and the cuttings, which had now become doubly precious.

The other wagoners were generous in their offers to share what they had, but Claude insisted on paying for everything, with the result that his already meager cash supply shrank even further.

It was a much subdued trio that moved on with the rest of the caravan two days later. They had managed to buy enough on which to subsist until they reached San Antonio, and somehow Claude had found room for the two women to sleep in the wagon with the plants. Claude was already thinking ahead to their arrival in San Antonio; in order to set out with the wagon train headed for California, they would have to buy a new wagon, new provisions, new horses; even if the money he had left were enough, it would mean arriving in California virtually penniless.

The buffalo kill had been successful, at least in the opinion of the hunters; virtually the entire herd had been wiped out. Some meat and skins had been taken—Claude had even cut some steaks from one carcass, although Danielle flatly stated that she could never eat them – but for the most part the carcasses had been left to rot on the plains, an extravagant display of the will of the United States government. As the train rolled out once again, Danielle could not help peering down into the valley, strewn now with rotting flesh and already black with the vultures who had come to feast, strutting in a military fashion among the carcasses of the once-proud denizens of the plains.

Claude and Anne had insisted that Danielle remain in her bunk in the wagon, but after a day of resting she had become too restless to remain abed and had gotten up again.

Her initial fear, once she had gotten over the shock of the tragedy, was that she might miscarry, but it seemed the life within her was as strong as ever, and as the train continued to roll southward and westward into the Indian territory that bordered Texas, she began once more to worry about her unborn child.

Now more than ever she felt that she was lacking in Claude's eyes, and she dreaded the moment when she must tell him the truth. At the same time, she could not bear the fear that her son – Claude de Brussac's son – might be born illegitimately; and that she should be the one to bring such a shame to the family that she loved as her own was enough to bring tears to her eyes each time she thought of it. And the fact that Claude, ever more occupied with his concern for their financial plight, no longer came to her arms at all, only added to her unhappiness.

Once they had reached Indian territory, the soldiers in command of the train were eager to push on, and the pace was quickened. Travel began even before daybreak and continued until the last traces of daylight had vanished from the sky. The days began to run together, a seemingly endless blur in which the terrain and the day's routine varied hardly at all and their activities became almost mechanical. The heat had become more intense, the land more arid; the long, dusty trail had ceased to be an adventure for Danielle and had become an ordeal to be endured.

And with each day she seemed to feel her child growing within her.

She was more conscious now, too, of Jim Rumford's attentions. She was grateful to him and knew that she owed him her life, and yet the ever-growing interest that she saw in his eyes had begun to make her uneasy. It had been a month now since the soldiers and guides had seen any women except those in the train, and with the exception of herself and Anne and one girl of ten, these were all married women traveling with their husbands. She was sure from the raucous laughter that drifted from the campfires that the men's conversation often turned to women when they were alone, and now when Rumford rode alongside the wagon or paused to speak to her in camp, it was impossible not to recognize the sexual tension behind the long looks he cast at her. Danielle began to regret the innocent flirtation she had permitted earlier and to wonder if and how he expected her to pay her debt to him. Even Carl Betts, the scout, seemed to look at her with a new boldness.

That Claude, too, was aware of Rumford's interest in her was fairly certain. More than once she saw him scowling after the guide as Rumford rode away, and whenever he had seen her and Rumford together for even a moment, his manner toward her became particularly curt, even surly. But she did not know how to make him understand that she had no interest in the other man, any more than she knew how to interest him in making love to her again. If they were at home, perhaps, or someplace where she could make herself more attractive – where she could bathe and dress her hair, and put on something besides one of the two dresses she now owned, and which often had to go dirty and unmended because there wasn't time to wash and sew every day while they maintained this murderous pace – perhaps she could renew his desire for her; but as it was, the end of the day meant nothing but filthy exhaustion for both of them, and if he felt the absence of a woman's body in his life, he did not show it toward her.

At last they reached the Red River, which formed the border between the Indian Territory and Texas. They had crossed the territory, Rumford told her, in record time, but now, even though they were not out of danger from the savages, it would be necessary to stop and rest the animals.

'Else we'll never make it to San Antone,' he added, dropping the last two syllables of the name, as she had noticed the westerners did.

Danielle went with the other women to refill water kegs from the river, which ran surprisingly clear here in contradiction to its name. She found herself looking longingly at the cool, refreshing water. If she could only bathe and wash her hair – with the water supplies running low, for a long time they had been unable to give more than the most cursory attention to cleanliness.

Of course, they had been warned more than once about going off anywhere by themselves, but after all, they had been on the trail for several weeks now and had not seen a single Indian; besides, since the buffalo slaughter she felt a compassionate curiosity about these 'savages'.

At any rate, all other considerations paled beside the possibility of making Claude desire her once again; and as they were going to be camped for a full day before starting off again, there might actually be time . . . She made up her mind to steal away while everyone else was busy in the camp and find a spot where she could bathe in privacy.

She had only just started to make her way toward the river, however, when Anne, who had had much the same idea and discarded it as unwise, intercepted her.

'Danielle, you can't mean to go off by yourself,' she said. 'You know what the men have told us.'

'But Claude, he hasn't . . . ' Danielle stammered and then paused. 'I wanted to look nice for him, tonight especially – and you can see it's safe, there's no one for miles.'

Anne glanced toward the river. There were pecan and willow trees growing along its banks, providing a screen of privacy from the camp, but beyond them the plain stretched flat and open as it had for miles upon miles; surely no one could approach without being noticed while they were still far off.

Even without Danielle's particular reasons, Anne was unhappy living in filth. After all, though Danielle had grown up as a peasant, she herself had lived a life of luxury until the past few months. It would be wonderful to bathe again, to be free, however briefly, from the sweat and the trail dust and the flies.

'Very well,' she sighed. 'But wait until I get a gun and I'll come with you.

'Well, now,' Carl Betts said some minutes later, 'that's an interesting sight.'

Jim Rumford, busy with his horse, followed Betts's gaze and saw the two women slip away toward the river. Rumford glanced around to see if by chance Claude had noticed the departure.

He hadn't.

'Looks like we're the only ones know they're down there,' Betts said, reading his thoughts.

'Looks that way, doesn't it,' Rumford agreed.

The two men exchanged pleased looks, grinning.

37

Despite the confidence with which she had persuaded Anne, Danielle could not help feeling a certain apprehension as they made their way through the grasses at the river's bank.

They found what appeared to be a perfect spot only a short distance downstream from the camp, where a little inlet made a pool half-shaded by a willow and dappled with sunlight. There was no sound except for the soughing of the wind in the trees and the occasional flutter of a bird taking flight at their approach. The banks rose high on either side of the river, screening them from any possible observation from camp.

It occurred to Danielle for the first time that the high banks of the river at this point might screen someone else from camp as well; it would be possible for savages to steal along this little ravine without actually being seen.

She shivered and at once scolded herself for being foolish; whatever might or might not be possible, one thing was quite evident: There was no one here now but the two of them and they might as well take advantage of the fact.

She began to remove her clothing. 'Aren't you going to bathe?' she asked, seeing that Anne had seated herself fully clothed in the tall grass on the bank.

'No, you go ahead,' Anne said. 'I'll just keep an eye out until you're finished.'

Danielle quickly stripped down to her petticoat and, laying her clothes down within easy reach on the bank, she waded into the water. It felt delicious as it rose about her legs, and when she was far enough out, she lowered herself into the water, even ducking her head beneath the surface.

'It's wonderful,' she called aloud, reveling in the feeling of being reborn after days and days without more than a dab and a pat with a damp cloth. Although they were dangerously low on soap, she had nonetheless recklessly shaved off a small sliver, and now she began to soap herself.

'What's that song Jim Rumford's been singing?' she asked aloud.

Anne thought for a moment and then began to hum the tune.

'Yes, that's it,' Danielle cried. ' "Come and sit by my side 'ere you leave me," ' she sang. ' "Do not hasten to bid me adieu." ' She smiled to herself at the way the cowboy pronounced the French word. ' "Just remember the Red River Valley, and the cowboy who loved you so true . . ." '

Danielle began to clamber out of the water. Both women had been so absorbed in their own thoughts that neither of them was actually aware of the two men who had approached until Jim Rumford, with Carl Betts at his heels, stepped from the shade of a willow tree.

'I hope you're singing that song for me,' Jim said, grinning.

Danielle gave a little squeal; she was all but naked in a wet petticoat that revealed more of her body than it concealed. She grabbed for her dress, holding it up before her.

'What are you doing here?' Anne demanded, jumping up. 'We didn't hear anyone approach.'

'It isn't safe for you ladies to wander off by yourself like this,' Rumford said, strolling toward Danielle as casually as if they were in camp and she weren't practically unclothed. 'We thought maybe we'd better come down and keep an eye on things, just in case.'

'Yeah, you never know when them Indians is liable to show up,' Carl said.

'That's – that's very thoughtful of you,' Anne said. 'And you're right, it probably isn't safe. If you gentlemen will just turn your backs, Danielle will get dressed and we can all go back to camp.'

'It will only take me a moment,' Danielle added.

'Say, there's no hurry now, as long as we're here,' Rumford said.

'We kinda thought maybe we could have us a little party,' Carl said. 'Just the four of us.'

'No,' Danielle said quickly, and added, 'I'd like to go back to camp, please.'

Rumford's eyes narrowed and the smile vanished from his lips. For the first time Danielle noticed what a hard-looking man he was, cruel even. He had spent a great part of his life in this wilderness; why, he was nearly as much a savage as the Indians he was forever warning her about. And Betts – at one time she had wondered about the friendship between the two, but now suddenly she saw that they were two of a kind, only Rumford concealed his true nature better than his friend.

'Seems to me like you owe me,' Rumford said.

'Why – I'm obligated to you, of course, and deeply indebted for saving my life, but that doesn't mean – I didn't agree to do whatever you want.'

'I didn't agree to rescue you either, I just did it because it needed doing, isn't that right?'

'Well, yes, but . . . '

'So now it's me who needs rescuing and you're the only one around who can save me,' he said, grinning again.

'What do you mean, rescuing from what?' she asked, wishing he would not stand so close or look her up and down the way he was doing.

'Why, I'm drowning in those big brown eyes of yours, little lady,' he said with a chuckle. Suddenly the smile vanished again and with a lightning-fast movement he had taken another step forward and grabbed her arms. She was yanked violently against him, and before she could struggle or protest, his lips had fastened hungrily upon hers and she felt his hands upon her body, fondling her intimately through the wet cloth that was all she wore.

She struggled against him, pounding upon his shoulders with her fists, but he seemed not to notice at all; his arms were like bands of steel, imprisoning her, crushing her helplessly to him.

'Let me go,' she cried.

'Yes, Mister Rumford, let her go,' Anne said, drawing the revolver that she had concealed in her waistband. She held it aimed directly at Rumford.

Rumford gave a low whistle and released Danielle, who quickly began to struggle into her dress, disregarding the still-wet petticoat.

'You know,' Rumford said, taking a couple of slow steps toward Anne, 'a nice lady like you ought to be careful who she points a gun at; someone could get hurt.'

'Someone will get hurt if you don't stop where you are,' Anne said. 'I mean what I say – don't come any closer or . . . '

So intent was she upon Rumford's nonchalant stroll in her direction that for the moment she forgot all about Carl Betts. Suddenly, like a cougar, he had sprung toward her. The gun was torn from her fingers and she was flung to the ground with such force that for a moment the ground seemed to tilt and reel about her.

'Sorry we had to play rough,' Rumford said, 'but you shouldn't ought to have threatened us. Like I was telling the young lady, there's something we got to do, and we don't mean to have any trouble doing it. Tie her up, Carl.'

Betts produced a piece of rope, and with a few deft movements he bound Anne's hands together.

'Now you just sit there and don't make no fuss till we're finished with this little lady,' Rumford said with a lecherous grin, 'and maybe you'll get your turn too.'

'My son will have you shot for this,' Anne said angrily.

'Well, now, I just doubt that, lady. In case you've forgot, I'm a guide to this wagon train, and I expect if it was put to a vote, the folks would all rather lose three Frenchies than lose one guide, now wouldn't you agree?'

The logic of what he said startled Anne into silence. From what she had seen so far of the people in this wild land, it was entirely possible that he was right.

'And now, where was I?' Rumford said, turning back to Danielle. 'Carl, you go stand back that way and watch to see nobody comes down from the camp.'

Betts obediently went part way back the way they had come. Danielle, overcoming the fear that had frozen her in place, tried to run past Rumford, but he seized her wrist and, jerking her violently around to face him, kissed her, tearing at her dress like a madman.

Suddenly Rumford's body stiffened against her. For a moment she thought that he had prematurely reached his peak and that perhaps after all she was to be spared what he had planned. Her hand had been pinned between them and she pushed against his chest with it, scraping her hand against something hard and sharp as she did so.

Rumford's grip on her slackened slightly. She shoved herself free of him and took a step backward. As she did so, she saw the blood on her hand.

She took another step backward, her eyes going from the expression of pain and horror on Rumford's face to the hard object protruding from his chest on which she had scraped her hand.

At first she did not understand. Not until Rumford took two or three odd, shuffling steps and slowly turned away from her did she see the arrow that had struck in his back and penetrated all the way through him.

He sank slowly to his knees as if to pray, then toppled forward on his face.

But Danielle was no longer looking at him, she was looking beyond him to the five men standing just a few yards along the riverbank. They were half-naked, with feathers in their hair and grotesque designs painted on their faces.

She realized with a shock that she was finally seeing the savage Indians she had heard so much about.

'Don't scream,' Anne said in a tight little voice, 'and don't try to run; you may panic them.'

'They're going to kill us,' Danielle said. Betts had disappeared, apparently having seen the Indians in time to hightail it for the camp.

'No, I don't think so; if they wanted to do that, they could have shot us the same as they shot Rumford.'

Three of the Indians had arrows in their bows and it was clear they were trained upon the two women. The Indians, however, were engaged in a low-voiced discussion among themselves, their dark eyes glued all the while upon Anne and Danielle.

Her hands still bound, Anne managed to get slowly to her feet and come to stand by Danielle. She had to resist the urge to run screaming in the direction of the camp; she was sure she would not go more than a few steps before the Indians killed her for the attempt.

Some decision was apparently reached among the savages. The bows were lowered. Two of the warriors ran forward, and the women were lifted unceremoniously and flung over their shoulders. The Indians began to run with them, following the riverbank.

It seemed to Danielle as if they must have run for miles, but the reasoning part of her mind told her it was no more than a few hundred feet till they came to some horses tethered among the trees. Anne and Danielle were set upon the horses; the

Indians swung themselves up behind them and they rode off, still following the river, concealed by the banks and the vegetation from all but the keenest eye.

38

They slept on the ground that night, huddled under an animal skin, while nearby the Indian warriors carried on an incessant discussion in low voices.

Danielle strained her ears, trying to catch a familiar word. One thing she was sure of, the Indians were discussing them. At first she had been terrified of what would happen to her and Anne when they had finished their ride, but nighttime had fallen; the Indians had stopped to set up a crude camp. They had given the two women some sort of dried meat to eat and water to drink. An animal skin – buffalo, judging from its size – had been brought to keep them warm; then the discussion had begun. It was still going on when she fell asleep at last, exhausted.

In the morning, unmolested, they again mounted up. This time they were allowed to ride behind the men. It gave her an odd sensation to have to hold onto the half-naked body of the savage before her, but she had learned after a few yards that it was hold on or fall off, and as the morning wore on and she grew tired, she actually found herself grateful for the strong back to lean against now and then.

Having begun the day's ride, the Indians spoke hardly at all, neither to one another nor to the women, except to bark an occasional command, accompanied by sign language that made their point clear enough.

There was little need for direct communication between them, actually. Sometime about midday they had stopped to eat and to rest, although she realized as she sat on the ground watching the restless Indians that it was she and Anne whom the Indians had felt needed rest, and not they themselves. The Indians spent the time again in ardent discussion, punctuated by quick glances in the direction of the women; from time to time one of them would clamber up a rock to peer in all directions over the plains.

They had one really difficult moment, shortly before mounting up again, when the Indian men had relieved themselves without any pretense of modesty. It had embarrassed her, but not nearly so much as the realization, immediately afterward, that they were waiting for her and Anne to do the same – and waiting none too patiently, making gestures which needed no translation, urging them to be done with it. Both she and Anne shook their heads vigorously, and after some deliberation the Indians again hoisted them up onto the horses and they were off once more. By the time they had gone a few miles further, Danielle was beginning to wonder if her modesty hadn't been a mistake, but by then it was too late and she could do nothing but cling to the man before her and hope that it would not be nightfall before they stopped again.

Strangely enough, by this time Danielle had begun to lose a great part of her fear. Of course there was no telling what lay in store, for them when they reached their destination, but it had become evident by now that until then these men did not intend to harm them. Indeed, in their gruff and primitive way, the savages had been surprisingly considerate of them. She thought of Jim Rumford and Carl Betts and what they would have done in similar circumstances, and could almost be glad that she was a prisoner of these red men instead.

'Where do you suppose they're taking us?' Anne asked late in the afternoon.

'They must have a camp somewhere,' Danielle said. 'There's surely more to their band than this. I suppose once we're there we'll be married off to someone or other.'

Anne gave her a startled look. Danielle told her briefly what Jim Rumford had said about the Indians. 'If they're as short of women as all that, it's unlikely that they'll do us any serious harm,' she concluded. 'Unless we anger them. Damaged wives probably aren't as valuable.'

They reached the Indians' camp that evening. The two women were exhausted from the long ride on horseback, their unprotected faces burned by the sun, their hair hanging in dirty strands about their faces.

'We look like savages ourselves,' Anne said wearily; a passing acquaintance would never have recognized her as the aristocratic woman who had so recently been mistress of her own chateau in France.

Their arrival at the Indian camp occasioned no small commotion. Danielle was aware of it all through a blur of exhaustion – the wide-eyed children; the chattering women who stared and poked and even pinched them until one of the warriors barked a rough command and soundly boxed the ears of an overly inquisitive squaw; the men, aloof, proud, but no less interested in getting a look at the prisoners. There was even a ragtag collection of dogs that chased around them, yapping excitedly.

Anne and Danielle, stumbling with fatigue, were shepherded into the center of the camp, where for a few minutes they were the focus of all attention. Suddenly the throng around them parted to make way for an imposing figure in an elaborate headdress. Both his costume and his demeanor made it evident that he was the tribe's chief. He came to stand before them, studying them with an emotionless face.

He issued a command, and two of the squaws came forward and began to rip Anne's and Danielle's clothing from their bodies.

'Stop that,' Anne demanded, but her objections were ignored, and when she continued to struggle, a warrior came and held her hands pinned behind her back while the women continued to rip at her clothes until she was naked; Danielle was too tired to struggle and too frightened to protest. She stood mutely, trembling, while she, too, was stripped.

There was a great deal of discussion among the men, some of it heated. Once or twice a brave would approach to examine them more closely, but their interest seemed more anatomical than prurient – it was the muscles of their arms and thighs in which they seemed most interested, although one warrior ran a wondering hand over the smooth flesh of Danielle's breasts. Glancing around at the filthy women with their skin hardened like leather from their lives in the outdoors, she could well imagine how different the two of them must seem. Would it make them more valuable as wives, or would their softness and lack of muscular development count against them? And what if they were judged unsuitable as wife material; what would happen to them then?

Finally the chief gave some new command. Anne and Danielle were herded along by the women to a huge tepee some fifteen or twenty feet in diameter. They were ushered inside and, for a few minutes, left alone.

'Filthy beasts,' Anne swore, rubbing her bruised wrists. 'Examining us like we were so many cattle at a market.'

'In a way, I think that's the way they see us,' Danielle said.

'I think the arguments are about who we are to belong to. There were five men who captured us, and only two of us, and I think each of them is claiming us.'

'Well, I don't claim any of them,' Anne said. 'I'd rather die than be married to one of those savages.'

Danielle nearly said, 'We may not have any choice either way,' but held her tongue at the last minute. It was pointless to frighten Madame any more than she was already. Anyway, so far, except for the rigors of the journey across the plain and the indignity of being stripped and examined by the men, they had not suffered greatly at the hands of their captors. And they were still alive, at least.

The previous night, while huddling under the animal skin they had been given for a blanket, they had discussed their chances of being rescued.

'Claude will come for us, I know it,' Anne had said confidently.

But with each mile that had passed today, Danielle's hopes of that prospect grew a little dimmer. That Claude would try to save them she had no doubt, but how could anyone follow the Indians' trail so far across the barren plains? And would anyone else be willing to come with him to try to rescue two insignificant members of the train from the Indians, with all the dangers that suggested? The soldiers had already indicated their desire for speed in crossing the Indian territory – would they now voluntarily spend several days crossing it again in search of two women taken captive?

The Indian women returned, bringing dresses like their own, made of animal skins. They indicated that Danielle and Anne were to wear them.

'I suppose it's better than going naked,' Anne said, making a face and sniffing at the skin. The Indian women watched them and talked among themselves, giggling to one another. One of them reached out tentatively to stroke Anne's coppery hair.

'Leave me alone,' Anne snapped, slapping the hand away.

Some of the women left and came back with food – more of the dried meat, this time mixed with fat and some sort of berries into a malodorous blend.

'Ugh,' was Anne's reaction, but when it became apparent that there was nothing else forthcoming, they set upon the unappetizing meal ravenously.

The squaws watched them until they had finished eating; then, apparently satisfied, they left and returned once more, this time with more animal skins intended as bedclothes.

When they were finally alone for the night, Anne and Danielle huddled together in the far reaches of the tepee and considered their plight.

'We might be able to escape,' Danielle suggested. She had found that by lying on the ground she could lift the hide covering of the tepee enough to see underneath. From her awkward angle she could see little but more tepees clustered in a seemingly random pattern, but there was less activity in this part of the camp, and not too far distant it appeared there was a protective ridge with a few trees on it.

'But escape to where?' Anne asked. 'We must have come fifty, maybe a hundred miles, and God alone knows in what direction. We could spend months wandering on those plains on foot and never find our way back to civilization. More likely by far we'd find more of these savages.'

'If we could get horses,' Danielle thought aloud.

'Of course – the next time we're disrobing for the chief, I'll ask if he couldn't loan us a couple,' Anne said drily. 'Oh, don't you see, it's hopeless; we'll end up either dead or, worse yet, married to one of those monsters.'

Danielle sank into a somber silence; try though she might, she could see no other alternative.

At last fatigue had its way with them, and despite their predicament the two women slept, their sleep peopled by strange and frightening dreams.

39

They were awakened at dawn by the arrival of the Indian women. Food was brought, and this time instead of water they were brought a bitter-tasting liquid that made Danielle thirstier than before she drank it.

'Probably some sort of spirits,' she said.

'Not a vintage year,' Anne said, but at the insistence of the Indian women, she drained the cup.

They were brought different dresses too, these embroidered and fastened with beads and feathers, and treated with such reverence that it was evident they were reserved for special occasions.

'Perhaps they're wedding dresses,' Anne said. 'It's a far cry from Madame Grisolde to this. Oh, good heavens, is that a man – no, no, I mean here, with the women?'

Danielle stared at the individual in question. 'Yes, Rumford told me there were men like that, *berdaches*, he called them,' she said. 'They actually live as women, dress as women, do women's work. He said the warriors sometimes even marry them as extra wives.'

The *berdache* was perhaps the oldest of the 'women' present, and except for a few obvious differences, hardly distinguishable from the others. He must have sensed that they had discovered his nature, for he said something to the others and they chattered quickly together, laughing. Far from being embarrassed by his peculiar state, he seemed quite proud of it. He spoke to Anne directly and gestured as if to lift his skirt.

'I think he wants to show you,' Danielle said.

Anne shook her head vigorously and said in a firm voice, 'No, thank you, oh good heavens, tell him not – '

They were interrupted by a sharp, masculine voice from outside, giving some command. At once all the chatter and giggling ceased and the squaws set to braiding the hair of the two white women. The brew they had consumed earlier had made Danielle light-headed, and she sat quiet and docile while her hair was arranged in Indian fashion.

At last headbands trimmed with beads were placed around their heads. The Indian women stepped back and engaged in a brief discussion among themselves. Finally, when it seemed that they were satisfied, Anne and Danielle were led outside.

Seemingly the entire village had been assembled. They stood or sat in a great circle in the center of the camp, the chief and some rather imposing companions sitting to one side by themselves. Anne and Danielle were brought to a spot directly opposite the chief, where the women signaled for them to be seated on the ground.

There were what appeared to be speeches of some sort, followed by prayers. Finally two warriors appeared on opposite sides of the center clearing; they were dressed in nothing more than loincloths that hung from thongs at their waists and gave only a passing nod to modesty. Both men carried wooden clubs.

'Why, those are two of the men who captured us,' Danielle said. 'They must be going to fight over us.'

She and Anne watched fascinated as the two warriors approached to meet one another face to face. Some words were spoken; then, at a signal from the chief, the two men suddenly began to fight, striking at one another with the heavy clubs, dodging and ducking as they circled about the clearing.

Danielle felt flushed and a trifle giddy; the primitive spectacle being staged before her eyes was oddly stimulating. The audience seemed mesmerized; there was no sound save the breathing of the combatants, an occasional grunt as a blow was landed, and the thud of wood on flesh.

She knew that she should be frightened or contemplating some way of escaping from their predicament. Soon this fight would be ended, and one of these savages would be claiming Anne or her for a bride. She would become one of those pathetic, filthy creatures they had seen here in the camp, living as a virtual slave to her 'husband', existing as a savage herself in this wilderness. Yet she could not bring herself to be frightened. Like the savages themselves, she watched the brutal combat with glassy eyes, her nostrils dilating with excitement as one or the other of the warriors was brought to his knees.

On the ridge beyond the camp, Claude crouched alongside the sergeant in command of the soldiers who had accompanied him on the search. They had been given a week by the commanding officer of the military detachment – a week to find the captured women and return to the wagon train.

From the moment when Carl Betts, wide-eyed with fright, had stumbled into the camp, saying that there were Indians down by the river, the camp had been in an uproar. Betts's story was that the Indians had killed Rumford and the two Frenchwomen, but when the riverbank had been searched, only Rumford's body with the arrow still in it and a torn scrap from Danielle's dress had been found. It was obvious that the Indians had taken the women captive instead of killing them.

Claude had been horrified at the thought of his mother a prisoner of savages, but, confusingly to him, it was Danielle who had haunted him since – with her street-urchin face and wide, innocent eyes. Perhaps it was because he felt guilty over the way he used her, knowing that she wanted and hoped for so much more from him than he was prepared to give.

If only he could bring himself to marry her. He knew it was her dream; he knew it would be the fair thing to do. And it wasn't as if he didn't love her, in a way. He felt a deep and abiding affection for her that, when they were locked in one another's arms, flamed into a giddy passion.

But she was not, of course, Antoinette. How could he marry Danielle, or anyone, for that matter, without sacrificing the dream that he still had of someday regaining the glorious love he had lost.

Yet since she had disappeared, he had been terrified lest he find that Danielle was gone from him forever. As the trail, painstakingly picked out by one of the train's scouts, had led them further and further into Indian territory, Claude's despair had grown. Once or twice it had seemed as if they had lost the trail altogether, and then, just the evening before, they had found his mother's lace handkerchief caught on a branch of scrub brush – had she lost it accidentally or left it as a marker? Impossible to say; but it had spurred them on, and just a short time before the scout had guided them to this camp.

He had been crouched here for nearly an hour, watching as the special ceremony was prepared. He had seen the two women in Indian garb brought from the one large tepee, and at first he had not recognized his mother and Danielle. Then Danielle had turned, for a moment actually glancing in his direction as if she knew he was there, and his breath had caught in his throat.

They were alive then! He had not dared to think what might have happened to them since their abduction; his imagination had conjured up all sorts of horrible fates for them, and now here they were, not a hundred yards away from him and apparently unharmed.

'Almost set,' the sergeant whispered. They had been waiting for his men, some fifty strong and all volunteers from the main group, to surround the Indian camp, a slow and risky process because of the lack of cover. Claude had had time to make his own estimate of the Indians' strength; there were, he calculated, no more than thirty-five or forty in the camp altogether, of whom about half were braves, the rest old men, women, children. And the element of surprise was on the side of the soldiers. His only fear was that Anne or Danielle might be hurt in the cross fire; his own plan was to reach them as quickly as possible, going straight through the mêlée when it began, and to try as best he could to protect them until the fighting was over.

There was a distant whistle that might have been the call of some prairie bird. Claude saw one of the Indian warriors stiffen and turn his head suspiciously in that direction, but his suspicions came too late.

'Now,' the sergeant cried aloud, and with that the soldiers rose and began firing.

The Indians were caught in a murderous trap. A few of the braves carried knives or bows, but most of them were unarmed, trusting on warnings from the sentries the soldiers had already ambushed and killed.

It was hardly a battle; it was a slaughter. Claude, racing down the slope and into the camp, saw Indians, not only warriors but helpless women and even little children, dropping all about him. A few men reached the rifles in their tepees, but they were cut down before they could use them; others tried to escape, but there was no direction in which to do so; the soldiers were everywhere. Claude was only grateful that no stray bullets found him.

One brave, his face a mask of rage, came at him with upraised knife, but before Claude could even fire, another man's bullet had blown away most of the Indian's face, rage and all.

The two captive women seemed too dazed to fully comprehend what was happening. 'Claude!' his mother cried. 'But how . . .'

'Never mind, get down,' he ordered, shoving them both roughly to the ground. 'Stay down until the shooting stops.'

When the first shots had rung out, one of the warriors who had captured her had tried to seize Danielle. Whether he had intended to protect her, to escape with her, or perhaps only to use her as a shield she couldn't say. He had died with his hand on her arm and had fallen at her feet. Now she found herself lying nearly face to face with him on the ground. His unseeing eyes seemed to stare accusingly into hers until she could no longer bear the sight and covered her face with her hands.

It was over in minutes. The entire band, even the dogs, were slain. A few of the women were spared for a time, and Danielle watched in horror as they were set upon by the soldiers, ravaged mercilessly before they were slain, sometimes actually butchered. She saw two soldiers playing ball with the breasts they had severed from the body of an Indian maiden.

I have seen the gentleness of the savage, she thought, and the savageness of gentlemen. They were lessons she would long remember.

'Were you badly mistreated?' Claude asked of her on the

journey back to rejoin the wagon train.

'We weren't harmed,' Danielle answered simply.

When he pressed for more details, however, Claude found her strangely evasive. Nor was his mother any more inclined to discuss what had happened to them.

It was as if the two women had made a pact between them.

40

San Antonio was already an old city by American standards; it had been founded long before by the Spaniards, when the land that was now the state of Texas had still been part of New Spain. But compared to the cities of Europe or even New York City, this was still a frontier village: dirty, raw and dangerous, filled with gamblers, cowhands, renegade Indians, loose women and opportunists of every sort. Its hot, dusty streets were lined with wooden storefronts and old adobe and brick structures, and from within the dingy saloons came loud music and the raucous laughter of lusty men – and women – unwinding after long weeks on the trails.

There had been one postscript to the misadventure with the Indians. On the evening that the soldiers with Claude and the two women returned to the camp, Carl Betts had disappeared, obviously afraid of the story they would tell. He had stolen an extra horse and some supplies from one of the wagons and disappeared into the plains night.

The capture and subsequent rescue of the women had delayed the wagon train a full week, and despite the murderous pace they had kept since then, they had not been able to make up the time. They arrived in the city late, to be greeted by some unpleasant news: The train they had expected to join for the trip to California had gone without them two days before.

'When will there be another train?' Claude asked the agent he had gone to see.

'To California?' The man scratched his head doubtfully. 'Hard to say. Not much traffic out of here heading for California. Most folks going there take the northern trails, the Old Spanish or the Mormon Trail. They're heading for the gold fields, you see.'

Claude started to leave, but a thought occurred to him. 'The train left two days ago, you say? Would it be possible to overtake them, do you think?'

'Would be, I suppose, on horseback.'

'No, no, I mean in a wagon.'

'Well, I don't know.' The man looked doubtful again. 'I suppose if a man had a fast team, and if he was to get old Gus Barnett to guide him . . . ' He hesitated, then shook his head. 'No, he'd never do it.'

Claude asked, 'Who is this Barnett? Maybe if I talked to him . . . '

'Old Gus is the best guide in this part of the country, knows the land between here and there like he knows the back of his hand – but talking to him wouldn't do any good.'

'Why not?'

'He says he's through with living on the trail. That wagon train that just left, the wagon master tried to get Gus to guide them, but Gus didn't want to do it – finally put his price so high they quit asking him.'

'What was the price he was asking?'

The agent smiled a trifle condescendingly. 'Fifteen hundred dollars,' he said.

Claude's heart sank. It might as well have been a million. He had less than three hundred dollars left, and a large portion of that must go to replace the provisions they had lost on the journey here.

He returned to the rooms he had rented for them, not in the best hotel, but over a noisy saloon. They had been far less expensive, and after the long weeks on the trail, even these shabby quarters seemed luxurious. Anne and Danielle listened in sympathetic silence.

'We could wire London,' Anne suggested, 'and ask them to send some of the money we left there. I know Jean would want us to use it, and there's no telling when he'll be able to leave. We can always replace it later.'

'But that would take weeks,' Claude said. 'It would be too late by then to try to catch the train. We'd have to wait here for another one and that could be months, even years.'

'We couldn't go on alone?' Danielle asked.

'Too dangerous. One wagon, no guide – we could wander around forever out there, if the Indians didn't get us. No, this Barnett was our only hope.'

'Then we shall have to have him,' Anne said matter-of-factly.

Claude gave a bitter laugh. 'Oh, sure, all we have to do is persuade him to do for us free what he asked fifteen hundred dollars for a few days ago.'

'We can try,' Anne said. 'And we needn't ask him to do it free.'

She got up and went to the room's chipped dresser, removing a small box from a drawer.

'I had this with me when we left France,' she said, bringing the box to Claude. 'I – I didn't know at the time that I would be leaving, too. When we started across country, I hid it with the plants, thinking it would be safer there. So, as it turned out, it didn't get lost when we lost the other wagon.'

She opened the box. In it was a brooch. He recognized it at once; it had been her Christmas present from his father their last year in France, and always afterward she had used it to fasten her cloak when riding. It was an emerald, not overly large but flawless in quality, surrounded by a ring of small diamonds.

'This too,' Anne added, removing her wedding ring from her finger with so violent a yank that it made him wince. 'Even here these should bring something.'

'But I can't let you sell these,' Claude cried, staring at the jewels she had dropped in his hand. 'They're precious, and anyway, they're the last things you've got left that father gave you.'

To his surprise she drew herself up in a gesture that told as words could not – despite the new-formed calluses on her hands, despite her mended dress and the shabby room in which they stood – of the generations of aristocratic blood that flowed in her veins.

'No, you are mistaken,' she said, looking down at her son as if from an unscalable height. 'Not the last, nor by far the most precious. Sell them, if they will buy us this man – they are only jewels.'

'Your hand looks so naked without your ring,' he said.

'Do you think so?' She extended her fingers gracefully. 'It doesn't look it to me. But of course I still see his ring there. A diamond, you know, is only a rock. Men dig them from the ground. But a ring – a wedding ring – is far more than that.'

He felt a sudden stinging in his eyes and found that he had to look away. 'I'll see if I can find a jeweler,' he said. 'Will you come with me?'

'If you like,' she said quite nonchalantly.

There was not a great deal of trade in precious gems in the city, but they found one jeweler in a little shop behind the bank who was interested in seeing the pieces that were offered for sale.

'Umm,' he said, and again, 'umm,' staring at the emerald through his glass. He was not quite able to keep a greedy smile from curling his lips.

'Of course,' he said, removing the glass from his eye, although the gleam remained, 'there is not a great demand here in San Antonio for stones of this – this sort.'

'There are people here with money, are there not?' Anne asked haughtily. 'Surely one or two of them must have taste?'

'Yes, of course,' the jeweler said. He turned the brooch over in his fingers, then the ring. 'Shall we say – umm – a thousand?'

'Very well,' Anne said. 'And how much for the brooch?'

He gave her an indignant look and put the jewels down heavily upon the counter. 'I had in mind a thousand for both pieces,' he said.

'Two thousand,' she said. 'And even at that it's pure thievery.'

'Fourteen hundred. Not a cent more.'

'Sixteen hundred – and you can throw in that ring there,' she tapped the case. 'No, the gold one, the plain band.'

The jeweler hesitated a moment. Anne reached as if to gather up the jewels on the counter.

'Done,' he said, all but snatching them from her grasp. 'It's a pleasure to do business with you, Madame de Brussac.' Already he was beaming with delight at the baubles he had gained from the transaction.

'Mister . . . ' She hesitated.

'Johnson,' he supplied.

'Ah yes, Mister Johnson,' she said. 'You are living proof that even in this uncivilized country, gunshots are not necessary to commit a robbery.'

He had given her the money and the gold band before he quite grasped the nature of her insult.

Outside, Claude said, 'At least you won't have to be without a ring.'

'This is not for me,' she said, thrusting the ring at him with an angry gesture. He stared at it for a moment uncomprehendingly.

'Even prostitutes are rewarded for their services,' she said acidly. She did not wait for his reply but strode by him with a disdainful toss of her head and started back to their rooms.

It was annoying, really. Of course, she knew men could be dreadfully stupid at times, but somehow she had thought her son an exception.

Danielle had remained alone in the rooms. Night was falling and the room was getting dark, but she had not bothered lighting a lantern.

She was actually sick with her own feelings of inadequacy. It had broken her heart when she had watched Madame wrench her wedding ring from her finger, parting with the last of her treasures. And Claude, how tirelessly he had worked to get them this far.

But she, what had she contributed? Delays, problems, the loss of most of their belongings and provisions – if only she had something to give! But she had nothing, nothing but the clothes on her back.

Except . . . it came to her out of the darkness, like a serpent wriggling its way from the shadows into her consciousness. The sound of blaring music drifted up faintly from below, and from time to time the hoarse laughter of drunken men. Last night the ruckus had continued almost until dawn, and through her open window she had smelled the cigar smoke, the smell of stale liquor and unwashed bodies.

She had herself.

'The ladies had best use the outside stairs,' the clerk had warned them when they arrived. 'These men here, they only know one kind of woman – the kind they give money to.'

The mere thought frightened and disgusted her. And yet – and yet, Claude had explained, with sadness in his eyes, they hadn't enough money to continue the journey.

But they must continue the journey! They must start for California before he learned of her condition. Already, beneath the loose-fitting dress, her belly was beginning to swell. If he learned she was pregnant before they left, he would never take her with him; she was sure of it. She would be left behind, parted from the one who was her whole life.

She would rather die than face that possibility!

She went to the door and stepped into the corridor. The maid had not yet lighted the lamps and the hall was in darkness. To the left was the door to the outside steps; to the right, carpeted stairs led to the saloon below. There was a faint glow from the landing, and the music and laughter were much louder here.

She hesitated, wondering if she had the courage to do what she had been contemplating, weighing the alternatives.

Someone came up the stairs from the saloon, melting into the shadows as he left the landing. A man. His boots thudded dully on the worn carpeting. She stood frozen, unable to go forward or back. Would he approach her, try to embrace her? Would he thrust money into her hand and lead her to another room?

He nearly collided with her, swearing aloud, and putting his hand on her arm.

'Danielle,' Claude said, lighting a match, 'what are you doing out here? You know what the clerk said – what's the matter, are you crying?'

'I – I'm so ashamed,' she sobbed, unable to stop the tears that had begun to flow.

'Ashamed? But why, for God's sake, you don't mean . . . ' He paused, the match burning out in his fingers. 'You don't . . . you weren't going downstairs?'

'You said we – we need money. I wanted to help . . . '

'Jesus,' he swore softly. 'You shame me, both of you, mother selling her jewels, and you . . . it's I who should be ashamed.'

'Don't say that,' she said fiercely. 'Why, you, you've done everything, you've been so brave and so strong, and all I've been is a burden and a hindrance – you should have left me to the Indians.'

To her surprise, he reached and drew her tenderly to him, cradling her against his chest. It was the first time he had held her in weeks.

'Ah, no, my little peasant girl,' he whispered, kissing her cheeks that were wet with tears. 'Not a burden, nor a hindrance.' He found her lips then.

It was a long moment before he could add, 'Besides how could you be my wife if you were already some Indian's squaw?'

At first she did not seem to hear. Then, suddenly, she gave a squeal of disbelief and flung her arms about his neck.

He kissed her again and was glad that he had made his decision. He had realized for the first time love's power – the power to wound unconsciously.

He would make her happy, as she deserved; and if, in the secret places of his own heart, another face lingered, he was sure that in time that memory would fade.

This was a new world; in the weeks since they had begun

their journey overland to California, he had come to realize, in a way that he never had before, that it was a new life they were beginning. What had been, had been; but now they were here, in this time and place; Danielle belonged to the present, and to him.

And Antoinette? She was like the taste of a rare wine in his memory, rich and thrilling on the tongue, gone too soon, existing no more, only to be recalled on quiet nights before the fire, alone, when the past comes flickering through the flames.

41

Claude went early the next day to see the travel agent, to inform him that they now had the fifteen hundred dollars that was Gus Barnett's asking price to act as their guide to California. When he went back later in the day to get Barnett's answer, however, the news was yet another disappointment.

'He won't take us,' he told his mother and Danielle shortly afterward.

'But why not?' Danielle asked.

Claude shrugged. 'The only answer I could get is that he's just not interested in making the journey.'

'Then we must talk to him ourselves,' Anne said. 'Where is this man, anyway?'

'The agent says he's usually in the saloon downstairs, but I don't see what good it can do to see him. We can't offer him any more money. And they say he's as stubborn as a mule.'

'I did not choose to begin this journey,' Anne said. 'But having begun it, I refuse to end it here. We can at least talk to this man; surely he can't be as stubborn as all that. Danielle, you wait here. Claude, you will take me to this Mister Barnett.'

They found him, as predicted, in the saloon below. Gus Barnett was a bearded and wizened old man who looked hardly fit to travel across town, let alone overland to California. Seeing him, Claude could understand the man's reluctance to begin once more a journey that he must know from experience was long and rigorous.

If Anne had any such reservations about him, though, she

did not reveal them. She went directly to the table where Gus Barnett sat alone, drinking a beer and playing solitaire. He ignored her and continued playing out his cards.

'Mister Barnett?' she said.

'That's me,' was the answer. Another row of cards went down on the table, each card delivered with an impatient slap.

'May we sit down? We'd like to talk to you,' she said.

'I'm busy,' he said, still without glancing at her.

She sat down opposite him. Claude, somewhat reluctantly, seated himself beside his mother.

'Give me the money,' she said, holding her hand toward Claude. He took out the packet of money that he had counted for the agent earlier: fifteen hundred dollars in bills. She took it from him, thrust it across the table at Gus Barnett, disarranging his cards in the process. He shot her an angry glance.

'We want you to guide us to California,' she said. 'This is fifteen hundred dollars; it's virtually every cent we have.'

'Lucky for you, then, I won't take it,' he said, shoving the money aside and rearranging his cards.

'You won't take us to California?'

'Nope.' Another row of cards went down, slap, slap, slap.

'We were told that was your price.'

'It would be if I fancied to go to California, which I don't.'

'But we do,' Anne said.

'Then get somebody else to take you.'

Anne suddenly swept her hand across the table, flinging cards helter-skelter.

'Mister Barnett,' she said, standing so abruptly she nearly knocked down a man passing behind her, 'if there were anyone else, would we be sitting in this filthy saloon offering our last cent to an ill-mannered old fool who hasn't bathed since his baptism?'

She did not wait for his reply but swept haughtily from the room, leaving Claude and Barnett to stare after her in astonishment.

'Who's she, anyway?' Barnett asked finally, glancing about at his scattered cards.

'I'm afraid that's my mother,' Claude said, a bit sheepishly.

Barnett shook his head in what might have been awe. 'She's got spunk,' he said. He took a noisy drink of beer and wiped the foam from his beard with the back of his hand.

'Always did admire a woman with spunk,' he said.

To everyone's surprise, including Anne's, Barnett agreed to guide them to California, pocketing the full fifteen hundred in advance. Claude wired their banker in London, instructing him that the money they had left on deposit there should be forwarded to them at Los Angeles.

There was another bit of luck for the de Brussacs: They heard of a couple who had been unable to move out with the earlier wagon train because the wife had been taken ill shortly before the train departed.

Claude found them in the hotel, a Reverend and Mrs Willows, on their way to California to set up their own church there. They were not able to pay more than a token portion of Barnett's fee, but the hundred dollars they came up with was welcome. Far more important, there would be two wagons now instead of just one making the journey.

Reverend Willows was a man with a straight spine and a surprisingly melodious voice; one could easily imagine it calling some future congregation to a resonant repentance. He had eyes that gave the impression of always being on the verge of tears, and lips shaped into a contradictory and permanent smile; the two features combined to give an impression of tireless patience, even in the face of dire adversity. They said sweetly, I have suffered, but my innocence remains intact.

His wife was short and thick, kindly but in a stiff, standoffish manner. She rarely smiled, as if she thought her husband smiled quite enough for both of them, yet she did not seem unfriendly, only unexpressive. It was as if she had, over the years, damped a rather voluble nature in deference to her husband's prominence. They did not promise an easy familiarity as traveling companions, but they were the sort who could be depended upon to carry their own weight, and Claude was glad to have them along.

Reverend Willows was pressed into service to perform the ceremony wedding Claude to Danielle. It was of necessity brief and simple, yet for Danielle it could not have been more thrilling had it been performed in Notre Dame. This was for her a dream come true, and she knew that henceforth nothing that happened to them could mar her happiness.

They set out two days later, eager to be on their way as quickly as possible in the hope of catching up with the wagon train that had left just before them. The larger train, as Barnett had explained, would be forced to travel more slowly.

'Do you really think we'll catch them?' Claude asked Barnett when they were setting out.

'Maybe. Maybe not,' was the answer. 'We'll be crossing Apache land alone if we don't.' He spit violently to indicate what he thought of that state of affairs.

There were, at the time, no established trails across this stretch of land, like the Cimarron and the Santa Fe further north. Those traveling west from San Antonio followed the setting sun, or if they were lucky found someone like Gus Barnett who had traveled through before.

It soon became evident that the rigors of the first half of their journey were nothing compared to what lay before them. Nearly all of their travel from Saint Louis to San Antonio had been across flat plains and rolling hills, but the terrain they were crossing now grew more mountainous with each day. With their wagons heavily laden, it was soon necessary for the passengers to dismount for steep inclines and walk the horses up.

Danielle thought she had never known such weariness. Even the burgeoning life within her seemed to complain. She felt occasional spasms of pain that, fortunately, lasted no more than a second or two. At first she was frightened and wondered if perhaps the time hadn't come to tell Claude of her condition; but after a week or so the pains stopped; and she could once again put off what she saw as a frightening prospect. She was now into what she reckoned as her fifth month, but her slim boyishness and the loose clothing combined to conceal her condition. She hadn't, in fact, swelled very much at all, and Claude, preoccupied as he was and weary as they all were, made love to her too infrequently and too hastily to notice.

They made good time, considering the increasingly difficult terrain, but at the end of a month's travel they still had not caught up with the wagon train they were chasing.

'Maybe two days ahead of us,' Barnett declared finally. They had camped at the foot of a range of mountains. 'Them's their tracks right there, heading south, around the mountains. That's the easiest way.'

'Think we'll catch them?' Claude asked.

Barnett paused to stuff a plug of tobacco into his mouth and stare over his shoulder at the mountains towering close behind them.

'Them's the San Andres mountains,' he said. 'There's a pass through there could save us three, four days of travel. We'd be waitin' for them when they got around to the other side.'

'That's it, then,' Claude said enthusiastically. 'We'll take the pass.'

'I dunno.' Barnett shook his head and gave the women, who were busy preparing the evening meal, a doubtful look. 'It ain't an easy pass. Never took any wagons through there. Especially not with any women.'

It was Claude he spoke to, but Anne whose face he searched. She gave her head a toss and met his gaze evenly.

'Mister Barnett,' she said, 'we have been wafted across an ocean on the stink of rotting potatoes, jounced and bounced and bumped our way across two-thirds of a continent, been kidnapped and all but wedded by savages – you needn't fear that a mere mountain will daunt us.'

He nodded and spat noisily into the fire, just missing the skillet in which Mrs Willows was cooking and earning a frosty look from her.

'I figured not,' he said laconically.

By noon of the following day Danielle had concluded that Gus Barnett's description of their route as 'not an easy pass' was a profound understatement.

There was no trail as such, only the cleft of the rocks to follow. Almost from the time they set out, it had been necessary for everyone to walk to relieve the burden on the animals, and even then it was only through mighty exertion that the beasts were able to drag their burdens up the treacherous slopes.

Danielle's entire body ached from the effort of clambering over the rocky heights, and her limbs felt leaden. Once or twice when she paused for breath, it seemed as if the entire scene blurred before her eyes.

'It's the height,' Barnett explained. 'The air gets thin up here, makes it hard to get your breath.' He, in fact, seemed to have no difficulty at all; old and wizened as he was, he found his footing with the ease and sureness of a creature born to the terrain.

'Like a goat,' Anne remarked.

They had paused in the shelter of a rocky cliff to rest both humans and animals. They were on a mere shelf of rock that hung dizzyingly over a gorge. It was a spectacular view, but not one that any of them was much inclined to appreciate just then.

Even Claude, healthy and young as he was, could feel the

muscles in his legs knotting up from the unaccustomed exertion. He was beginning to wonder already if the decision to brave this pass were a wise one. His mother and Mrs Willows were obviously exhausted, and Danielle looked half-dead; she lay huddled against a boulder, her eyes closed, her face ashen. She did not even stir when the beef jerky and water that were to be their noonday meal were passed around.

'Let her rest,' Claude said. 'She can eat something later.'

Soon – far too soon, it seemed to the weary travelers – it was time to go on. They began to stir; only Danielle remained where she was, unmoving.

Anne knelt, shaking her shoulder gently. 'Danielle, it's time to start again,' she said.

Danielle stirred as if she would rise; then, with a deep groan, she sank to the ground again.

'I can't,' she said in a voice little more than a whisper.

'What's wrong?' Anne asked, but Mrs Willows, who had joined them, touched Anne's arm lightly and nodded toward the ground. There was a pool of blood where Danielle had been lying a moment before.

Claude was checking the horses' rigging when Mrs Willows approached him. 'Mister de Brussac,' she said, 'your wife is ill.'

'Poor little thing,' he said, smiling wanly. 'I thought she looked peaked. I guess we'd better put her in the wagon; the horses will just have to manage the extra weight.'

'I don't think she can be moved at all,' Mrs Willows said.

Her somber expression startled him. 'Why, what's wrong?' he asked.

'I'm afraid she's losing her baby,' was the matter-of-fact reply.

42

They were forced to remain there through the afternoon and night, clinging to their precarious aerie, while Danielle's shrieks and screams echoed from cliff to cliff and along the deep ravine.

Claude, Barnett and the Reverend Willows crouched about

a tiny campfire while the women remained with Danielle. There was nothing to give her for the pain but some whisky that Barnett produced from his saddlebags, watching sharp-eyed while Mrs Willows poured it into a cup. They boiled water and tore up a dress for rags.

It was nearly dawn when Anne approached the campfire. Barnett and the reverend had wrapped up in blankets and gone to sleep in the shelter of the cliff, but Claude had remained where he was, staring into the embers.

He heard the rattle of a stone and looked up to see his mother approaching. She looked wrung out with fatigue, and for a moment he could not help thinking of her as he had known her in the past, entertaining at their chateau, all bright smiles and gracious manners; or riding across the fields with his father, her hair blowing, her cloak billowing after her. He had brought her to this, with his hotheaded impetuosity; and Danielle . . . if only he had known of her condition; if she had told him . . . or ought he to have realized?

'Is she . . . ?'

'She'll live,' Anne said. 'But we couldn't save the boy.' She was feeling the same guilt as he; she blamed herself for not realizing the truth; she ought to have known – but the girl was so small. Even full term, the baby would have been tiny; perhaps under the best of circumstances he wouldn't have survived. Still, if they had been anywhere but here, clinging to a mountainside in the middle of this God-forsaken wilderness . . .

'I hate this country!' she said suddenly, with a vehemence that startled him. She turned suddenly from him, looking out over the gorge at their feet, staring down into its inky depths and then slowly upward until she was staring at the star-strewn sky above.

'I hate it,' she shrieked, shaking her fist as if in the very face of the god that had carved this dizzying perch upon which she stood. 'With every fiber of my being I despise this land. I shall always despise it.'

Nearby, Barnett and the reverend had wakened at her cries. They stared wordlessly at her as if at a madwoman. Claude could think of nothing to say.

After a moment her hands dropped to her sides. Her head down, she plodded wearily back to the wagon. He could tell from the heaving of her shoulders that she was crying, but no sounds issued from her lips. This weeping was a private thing.

He rose and went to where Danielle was lying. He longed to comfort her and share her pain, but he remained silent. He had no comfort to give.

Barnett insisted that they must start out again in the morning. 'If they's Indians within a hundred miles of here, they know we're up here now,' he said, making his disapproval of this turn of events quite plain. 'If they was to catch us up here, we'd be done for, sure as God made horny toads.'

Reverend Willows helped Claude scratch out a tiny grave in the rocky soil, despite Barnett's insistence on haste.

'I can't leave my son for the animals to feed on,' Claude said grimly. Barnett stumped off, muttering under his breath.

The sun was already well into the sky by the time they set off again. Danielle had been made as comfortable as possible inside the wagon.

'We'll go as slowly as possible,' Claude assured her.

She seemed to have aged overnight. Her wide, guileless eyes were ringed with dark circles, and her always-thin face had a pinched, colorless quality. 'I – I'm sorry about the child,' she said as he was leaving her.

'We'll have other children,' he said, squeezing her hand. 'In our new home, in California – we'll have a dozen children.'

She managed a feeble smile. He bent and kissed her forehead gently. 'Rest now,' he said, and left her.

His promise to go slowly had been unnecessary; it was impossible to travel at more than a snail's pace, particularly with the horses pulling the extra weight. Time and time again they were forced to stop so that both horses and people could rest.

Evening found them still within the pass. Before them lay the steepest slope of all, leading to an opening in the jagged ridge above them.

'That's the end of it,' Barnett said, pointing to the ridge. 'From there it's easy downhill going.'

Claude stared in dismay at what yet lay between them and the promised easy downhill; the slope up which Barnett proposed to lead them looked virtually impassable to him. A trail of sorts led up the steep incline, through patches of sandy soil that looked as if they would crumble under a wagon wheel and over barricades of rocks.

'Can we really get up that with the wagons?' he asked aloud.

'Dunno, I never tried it before,' was Barnett's answer.

They began at dawn to inch their way up the treacherous slope. They marked their progress in feet, even inches, and they kept losing ground as the horses' hooves slipped on the rocks and the wagons rolled backward before they could be stopped. Horses and humans alike paused every few minutes, gasping for breath, only to begin the tortuous exertions anew.

By midmorning they seemed hardly to have advanced at all, and now a new fear began to worry them: What if they did not reach the summit by nightfall? It would be impossible to climb this slope in the darkness, and impossible too to try to set up camp.

The men unloaded supplies from the wagons and strapped the supplies to their backs. At Mrs Willows's suggestion they reduced their provisions, discarding all but the barest essentials for the remainder of their journey.

And still the animals strained, their eyes rolling wildly in their heads, to haul the wagons up the incline. An inch . . . another . . . straining, heaving . . .

The lead horse on the de Brussac wagon lost his footing and suddenly the wagon was rolling backward, the horses unable to check its course.

'A rock,' Barnett called, while Claude strained at the leads and felt himself being dragged downward. 'Put a rock under the wheels.'

Willows and Anne between them managed to get a boulder under one of the wheels, and the backward rush of the wagon was stopped, but they had lost ground it had taken an hour to cover.

'You'll have to leave some of the plants,' Anne said, clinging wearily to the side of the wagon.

'They're our entire heritage,' Claude said. 'Everything we've got to build a new life for ourselves in California.'

'If we don't get some weight out of the wagon, we'll never reach the top of this pass, let alone California,' she snapped.

After a moment he said, 'You're right, of course.'

'No.'

It was Danielle. To their amazement, she began to climb down from the wagon. 'I'll walk,' she said. 'That will make the wagon lighter.'

'Danielle, you can't,' Claude protested.

'I can and I will,' she said stubbornly.

She was still pale, with a waxen look to her complexion, but neither her husband nor Anne could prevail upon her to return to the wagon.

'We're wasting a lot of time arguing,' Barnett complained.

At length Claude gave in reluctantly, and they set out again. It was heartbreaking to watch Danielle, so weak she should hardly have been standing, struggling up the rocky hillside. She slipped and fell, and clambered up and went on, only to slip again. But she neither complained nor asked to rest until Claude insisted upon it.

'You've got to rest,' he said, taking her comfortingly into his arms.

'They say that in China,' she said, trying to smile and not quite succeeding, 'women have their babies in the rice fields and go back to work immediately afterward.'

'Rice fields,' Anne said, 'are flat.'

It was like a nightmare in which one pursues an elusive goal without ever getting any closer to it; only they did advance; slowly, inexorably, the summit drew nearer.

Halfway up, the slope flattened slightly and they could make better progress, and at last they began to see that they would make it after all. Their spirits lifted, bringing new strength to their weary limbs. They pushed on.

Somehow, none of them afterward was quite sure how, they reached the top. The sun was already disappearing beneath the horizon when they pulled the wagon onto a flat table of rock at the summit of the pass and saw the vast desert valley spread beneath them.

Barnett, clambering onto a rock for a better view, gave a shout and a cackle of glee. Claude followed his pointing finger. In the distance he could see a flickering glimmer, like a faint star that had fallen to earth but still glowed dimly.

'Campfires,' Barnett said triumphantly. 'That'll be your wagon train, still half a day off. We'll catch 'em by sundown tomorrow.'

Claude stared at the distant glow. They had accomplished what they set out to do, yet at the moment he felt no sense of victory but rather a deep and abiding exhaustion, not only of the body, but of the spirit as well.

Anne woke early and, as Claude had done the night before, went to stand and look down into the valley before them. She had an awful feeling of discouragement. She had never before experienced the greatness of the vault of night, the vastness of the sky beneath which she stood. She realized, not for the first time, how much she had depended all her life on others, on Jean especially. The sense of isolation was like a knife in her side. She felt exiled, as if France and the Chateau Brussac and everything that was native to her, that made the air good and the language sweet, was gone from her, across this wild land and beyond the sea. It was a weighty thing to stand like this alone, in the dark of the night, beset by fears and anxieties. She would have given anything to have Jean with her, to comfort her and give her strength.

Would she ever see him again? This journey – she had not dreamed how great and difficult a thing it would be – and all this vastness now separated her from him.

She heard a sound and, turning, saw Reverend Willows approaching. He nodded and, like her, looked to the star-strewn skies and from there to the valley turning gray with the approach of dawn.

'Looks like we made it,' he said aloud. 'Barnett says after this the rest of it will be like taking candy from a baby.'

'Yes,' she said. 'But the price has been high.' She thought of Danielle, who had gotten the husband she wanted, but had paid dearly; and Claude – he would accomplish his goal, he would deliver them to his promised land, this California, but something of his youth, of his spirit, had been lost on this long trail they had followed.

'Everything has its price,' Reverend Willows said. 'The sunset costs us the moment in which we pause to look at it. We pay for a great love or a great dream in self-discipline, in self-sacrifice, in the giving of our love and our time and sometimes the sacrificing of our happiness.'

He grew silent. After a moment she realized that he was praying, his head bowed, his eyes closed. She was embarrassed, thinking that she was an intrusion upon his privacy, but when a moment later he opened his eyes, he smiled with surprising shyness and said, 'A very impressive cathedral, isn't it?'

He left her there. She looked and saw that the sky had turned pink and coral and gray, and as the light of dawn was born in the sky, a new light was born within her, too. There was a new day before them and with it new hope, new possibilities.

She had heard those clichés expressed a hundred times before and laughed at their glib sentimentality, but now she saw that she had heard them so often because to so many they had meaning; they gave relief. A thousand men before her, a thousand million people, had looked up at a reddening sky or had seen the fragile green budding of the trees in spring, had heard the sudden song of a bird winging skyward, and had felt hope rekindled in their breasts. The dark night was over, the long winter ended, God was still in his heaven. How plain, how often repeated those homilies, yet what succor they gave.

A bird cried somewhere in the rocks above her, and now in the distant valley she could see the glow of campfires and the smoke rising from the brown bosom of the land.

At last she turned and went down the path to the wagons.

43

OCTOBER 4, 1850
LOS ANGELES, CALIFORNIA
THE UNITED STATES OF AMERICA

My Beloved Jean,

It has been so many months since I have seen you, since I last heard your voice, and still there is no news. The attorneys in London tell us that Chateau Brussac is closed, but there is no word – at least they tell us there is no word – of your whereabouts. Are you alive? Are you well, free, or in prison? Will this letter reach you, or will my words remain unread? So many questions, all without answers. But I must write them and pray that they reach you and bring you comfort and perhaps someday soon guide you to us.

We have arrived, at last, at long last, in Claude's California, which is now a state in the American Union. I call it Claude's California because, having delivered us here, he acts quite as if he had invented the place – a fact that, were it true, would in my opinion be no great cause for pride.

Los Angeles is a mere village roughly the same size as Epernay, but there any resemblance between the two ceases to exist, for where Epernay was an old village, with charm and a certain degree of culture, however provincial, this is but a raw and dirty outpost in the wilderness. It sits in a valley that is little more than a desert, actually, surrounded by hills that are burned brown by the sun. They tell me that the rain only falls in winter, and that then the hills turn from brown to green, but I cannot imagine that it will increase the beauty of the place. The Indians call it the Valley of the Smokes because there are morning mists that often linger well into midday, so that one sees the sun through a haze, as if through smoke.

Our land – and it is finally our land, the grant having been confirmed by the local government and the surveyors that Claude hired having finally laid out its exact location – lies to the east a bit. Claude and Danielle have gone today to see it, but I declined to join them. I was not eager for another journey just yet, however short. I shall see it soon enough, I suppose.

They, Claude and Danielle, are married; she was not, of course, what I would have chosen for a daughter-in-law under other circumstances, but she is a sweet child and at least she is French. Anyway, those distinctions seem to blur somewhat when one is sharing hardships. They lost their first child, a son, and with Danielle's figure, I expect childbearing will remain a problem, but she is young and strong, and I have always understood that this was easier for peasant women than for women of station.

The cuttings have survived, even thrived, although I cannot begin to tell you how Claude managed that miracle. Soon, he says, they will be growing in our own soil.

They will not be alone. There is wine here, rather a brisk trade in it, in fact. It is made primarily from a local grape, something they call the mission grape – do you know of it? Claude calls the wine bile and says it is undrinkable, but that does not stop people from drinking it. It is produced chiefly by the padres at the local missions, I think. Claude says that when they begin to taste the wine from our vineyards, it will make us our fortune. And perhaps he will do what he has set out to do; establish a new Chateau Brussac where we can at last be together again, all of us.

I cannot tell you how I long for you, and were I to try, my tears would make it impossible for me to go on. You are with me always in my thoughts and dreams, and my constant prayer is that soon we can be together, you and I. You must write me, if you are able – it is very difficult not to know.

Trusting in God that this shall reach you and that I shall hear from you soon, I remain,

Your devoted wife,
Anne

Claude had rented a buggy and driven into the country to the site of their land grant. Claude had been out before, with the surveyors, but this was the first time that Danielle had seen it; he was sorry that his mother hadn't wanted to come, too, but he was sure that in time she would come to accept it.

For himself, there was something about this land – raw, lusty, harsh – that invigorated him. He was eager to begin the work of building their new home and had already ordered supplies and building materials. In the meantime he would live here out of the wagon and tend to the planting in the ground of the vines he had nurtured so carefully over so many thousands of miles.

He laughed when he thought of the Californians already growing rich on their inferior wines. Of the men he had talked to, only one had any French vines, and he was another French-man, Jean-Louis Vignes, but his El Aliso Vineyards, in Los Angeles itself, still relied primarily upon the inferior mission grape, brought a century or more before by the Spanish padres.

Already Claude had sampled countless bottlings of the local wines; some had had undeniable character, but none of them would stand up to the wines he would be able to produce. He had perceived one thing, though: Wine was already a booming industry in California; the soil and the climate seemed ideally suited to growing grapes.

He was convinced that California had a wine future, but the future would rest not upon the local grape but upon the classic European varieties.

The future would rest with him.

'Are we here?' Danielle asked. Claude had brought the horses to a halt and was climbing down.

'It's just over that hill,' he said, giving her his hand. 'I want you to see it properly.'

She smiled in anticipation as they strolled hand in hand up the hill. Despite all that they had gone through – the trip, the loss of her child, the dangers and hardships – she was happy.

And why not? Hadn't she married the one man in the whole world whom she loved? She, a mere peasant girl, married to Claude de Brussac. Oh, of course, here the name meant noth-ing – yet. But her belief in his dream was total and unchal-lenged. Someday his wines – her Claude's wines – would be the most famous in the country, in the whole world. All of their dreams would come true.

'I mean to call it the French Hills Winery,' Claude said. 'These hills will be half-French when we've finished planting them.'

They came to the top of the hill. He paused, letting her take in the view. 'This will be our home,' he said simply.

In the distance were the mountains – hills, really, in comparison to the mountains they had seen in crossing the country. They sloped gently downward, spilling into the valley at her feet, descending in undulating waves of brown and gold and dusty green. There were a few trees, low and stubborn-looking, but mostly it was scrub, and the earth itself, naked, unspoiled.

And she, child of the earth, felt a thrill of response within her. She was thousands of miles from France. Between here and there lay an entire continent and a vast ocean, and yet in her heart she suddenly felt that she had come home.

'Yes,' she murmured, clinging tightly to his arm, 'this will be our home.'

'And our land,' he added.

44

And the land was fertile.

No faulty plantings, no surfeit of crops, no careless hand had come before him to drain her richness. For a million years and more, she had lain in wait for him, like a virgin awaiting her lover's touch.

She had prepared herself. Her creams had been the dung of passing beasts, her lotion the silt of long-distant floods, her scent the grasses and flowers and shrubs that had grown and bloomed and died, and grown again. With upturned breasts, with aching loins, she had yearned for his coming.

And at last he was here, entering her, thrusting deep, planting his seed, and she had taken it and given birth. The grapes were their children, his and hers, the vintner's and the earth's. Together they brought them forth.

And they were good.

Claude planted his house in the middle of the little valley, building it of adobe in the style of the *ranchos* of the *californios*, the Spanish ranchers who had been here before

California became a state. He began modestly with a simple rectangle of a building with a verandah running its full length, both in front and in rear, and a roof of the red tile common to Los Angeles buildings. In time the house would become a quadrangle enclosing a patio – again, in the style of the *californios*.

Inside were plain walls of white plaster and open beams stained to an almost ebony darkness. One wall was occupied by the massive brick fireplace built for him by a local man who charged little but drank a generous salary in whisky. For now there was only this large room, which served a multitude of purposes; the kitchen; and two small bedrooms, one for himself and Danielle, the other for his mother. When Jean and the other children arrived, they would add other bedrooms.

Only, he had begun to phrase it, to himself at least, *if* they arrived. There was still no word from France, just an increasingly ominous silence. He knew that his mother had written regularly since their arrival in California, but there were no replies to her letters, nor were they returned.

He himself had written again to the London attorneys, asking them to make further inquiries. The results had been the same. Chateau Brussac stood empty; the vines that had once covered the land had withered and died for lack of care. Of his father, or Marie or René, or even Jeanette not a word. No one could say where they had gone. Most of those in the area who had been friendly with the de Brussacs were gone, too, many of them arrested as his father had been, others having fled the vengeance of Louis Napoleon for supporting his political enemies. Those who remained knew nothing or were too frightened to speak.

As for his mother, she seemed to have resigned herself to their new circumstances. She spoke very little of France, of the life they had left behind, or of her missing husband and children. Sometimes he came upon her unawares and found her staring wistfully into the distance, seeing not the scene before her, he knew, but some faraway place, hearing voices silent to him. He did what he could to make her comfortable and concealed from her whatever doubts he had about the safety of the others.

And Danielle – Danielle was happy, transparently happy. It amused him to see how easily he could bring the light of joy to her eyes, how grateful she was for the slightest sign of affection from him; but it troubled him, too, because he knew how much of his heart remained unopened to her. It was not that he didn't love her; it was that he could not love her as totally, as utterly as she loved him. It seemed unfair, and he felt guilty because of it, but that did not change things.

Though it was not entirely ready, they moved into their new home for Christmas. It had been intended to be a happy evening, but it went poorly. When they tried to sing carols together, his mother was unable to keep from crying, and when he gave her the present he had gotten for her, a simple wedding band to replace the one with which she had had to part, she went to her bed racked with sobs, and nothing they were able to do would comfort her.

For Danielle he had gotten a shawl, as the winter evenings had proven chilly even in this warm climate.

Danielle's present to him had been the news that she was again pregnant. It seemed to him a special blessing.

'Our son will be born an American,' he said proudly. 'And a Californian.'

'And a de Brussac,' she added, but the significance of that remark had been wasted on him.

Their ranch was nearly a day's carriage ride from the town of Los Angeles. At first Claude was worried about the stories he heard of bands of outlaws who roamed the not very distant hills. Although the Mexican-American war was two years over, these were said to be former Mexican nationals who refused to accept the status quo. They were known to sweep down upon isolated ranches to loot and kill before they disappeared, seemingly without a trace, into the hills and mountains again, and they wreaked their vengeance upon both whites and those Mexicans who had chosen to remain and accept citizenship in their new state and new homeland.

But there had been no reports of such activity in their particular area for a considerable time, and the local authorities felt that they had successfully stamped out the last of the outlaw bands.

The de Brussacs were not entirely isolated. There were other ranches and even other vineyards within a short ride from French Hills.

Their nearest neighbor was Don Diego de Torres. Don Diego was a *californio*, descendant of one of the original Spanish settlers. Despite his aristocratic heritage, however, Don Diego was enthusiastic about California's new statehood and an ardent believer in the democratic principles of the young American republic. He and Claude quickly became friends, and Don Diego's huge, rambling *casa* was the first American home to which the de Brussacs were invited as guests. It was a shock, after the long months of travel by ship, by carriage, by covered wagon, even on foot, to sit once again in a civilized home and enjoy an evening of good food and pleasant conversation.

When she listened to the intense discussion between Don Diego and Claude over political philosophies, Anne almost found herself thinking she was back in France, listening to Claude and his father debate much the same points – only here the discussion was in English, some of it French-accented and some of it Spanish-accented; it was like much of what she had seen in this new country, a potpourri of varying languages, customs and cultures that she was certain could never be melded into a homogenous whole. In France all things had been French, but here who could define what 'American' meant when it was so many things, often contradictory?

'This,' Don Diego would say with an expansive gesture of his hand that was clearly meant to take in not only the room in which they sat, 'this is the New World, truly, because here men are free. The freedom of the mind, of the spirit, of the human soul – if anything matters, these do.'

'There are men in France whose minds remain free,' Claude would say.

'That is not enough. In order for the human soul to flourish, it must grow in the very soil and air of freedom. But freedom, like heaven, is not a gift to be bestowed; it is a prize to be earned. This is the challenge we shall face here. The struggle for men's minds is never-ending; it is a battle to be faced every day. With each challenge we must choose anew where we shall stand.'

Sometimes while the men argued the women would sit quietly in their own corner of the large parlor and embroider or knit. Often Danielle found herself wishing she were with Claude and Don Diego; not that she minded Mother de Brussac's company; far from it; but she was never quite comfortable with Don Diego's wife.

Doña Elvira was a cripple, a chronic invalid who could not get around except in her wheelchair. As her world had shrunk to the size of their *casa*, so had her vision of the world; Doña

Elvira was a bitter, sharp-tongued woman who rarely spoke to anyone but her husband, and then only in the most shrewish manner.

'Freedom,' she would say in the most disdainful way, 'it is wasted upon the masses. Most men are fools. Maybe all of them,' she would add bitterly.

'Surely good men exist, too,' Anne would say.

'There is an old proverb,' Doña Elvira would reply, her knitting needles clicking arrogantly. 'It says there are only two things that really exist – one's death and one's conscience.'

'If that were true,' Anne said, 'then I have known a great many men who were only half-alive.'

That remark brought a hearty laugh from Don Diego, which rather pleased Anne; although she thought his wife a dried prune of a woman, she thought the don himself an admirable man, handsome and intelligent. She was pleased and relieved to discover that there were men of taste and elegance even here in California, and she was especially grateful for the friendship he had shown them since their arrival. Sitting at his well-laid table or before the fire in his sumptuous parlor, listening to intelligent conversation, she could, if only for a brief time, cease longing for France. They were the only really pleasant moments she had known since the day of Claude's arrest in France, which seemed so long ago.

'Madame de Brussac,' Don Diego said, coming to where she sat, 'you must try some of this wine. It's a California original. We call it angelica, after Los Angeles, of course.'

She took the proffered glass and sipped it tentatively, remembering when Jean used to bring her his new wines to taste.

'It's quite good,' she said.

'Too sweet for my taste,' Claude said, 'but it will age well. Still, I think the future of California wines will be in French grapes.'

'You may be right,' Don Diego agreed. 'Of course, it remains to be seen how they take to the soil and the climate here. But I'll tell you what – in the spring, when the plants have had a chance to put down proper roots, I will buy some cuttings from you if I may. We will both try with them and see what we can do. Perhaps one day we will give the mission brothers some competition, no?'

The two men lifted their glasses to one another to signal their agreement. Claude was pleased with himself; already the cuttings that he had brought here with such difficulty had produced a sale for him. It was a good sign.

This time as Danielle's condition advanced she had the benefit of proper attention. Not only did the doctor travel out from Los Angeles twice a month to see her, at Claude's insistence, but Don Diego sent her a midwife as well, an old Indian woman who had assisted his wife in her labors years before. Don Diego had lost both his sons; one to a childhood illness, the other when he had hotheadedly run off to Mexico to fight with the Mexican armies against the Americans.

'I will be godfather to your children,' he announced. 'It will be like having little ones of my own again, if you will not mind sharing them with me.'

'We should be proud,' Danielle said, flattered by the attention being showered upon her.

'Children are a nuisance,' was Doña Elvira's dour pronouncement.

After the fifth month Claude informed Danielle that they would have no further intimacy until after the child was born.

'I want this son born whole,' he said when she had argued that his caution was premature. 'This time we'll take no chances.'

He had no sooner begun his abstinence, however, than she began to worry if there might be other reasons. Perhaps his interest in her was waning. Had he only married her out of obligation after all?

Nor were her fears abated when he woke her one night tossing and turning on their bed, in the throes of some agitated dream. Exactly what he was dreaming she could not know, but he spoke one word in his sleep that sent a chill through her.

'Antoinette,' he said, as plainly as if he had been awake and holding a conversation.

She had been about to awaken him, but at the mention of that name, she let her hand slide from his shoulder and sank back unhappily against her pillow. His dream subsided soon afterward and he drifted into a more easy sleep, but she remained awake much of the night, staring into the darkness.

'This is an ill-advised pregnancy,' the doctor told her on his next visit. 'Your build, Madame, so narrow – I think I should speak to your husband about the future . . . '

'No,' Danielle said quickly. 'I – I will do it myself, at the right time.'

He shrugged. 'That is a private matter, of course; I can only advise,' he said.

'I appreciate your concern,' she said politely. She had no intention of repeating his warning to Claude; if he were to learn that he could not enjoy her as a wife in the future without endangering her, she knew that he would never again come to her arms; and how long would it be then before he went to other arms?

No, childbirth was a woman's business; they were about it all the time and they managed. And so would she, despite the doctor's headwagging.

The baby came in the spring. The first pains had begun at dawn, and Danielle had known at once that the doctor had been right – the birth would be an extremely difficult one. She contrived an excuse to send Claude to Rancho de Torres so that he would not be in the house to hear her screams.

The labor was a nightmare in which she began to think that not only the child but she as well had died, and that she had gone to hell to be punished for her sins. A peasant girl, presuming to marry an aristocrat – it was no wonder her punishment was so severe.

'But I loved him,' she cried aloud in her delirium, and Anne, bathing her face with a cold cloth, wondered what terrible visions etched such agony on her brow.

Claude did not return until after dark, to be greeted with the news that he was a father of another son, but this one alive and healthy.

'Wonderful,' he shouted, all but dancing in the middle of the room. 'When can I see him?'

'You may go in now,' Anne said. 'Claude,' she added as he rushed toward the bedroom, 'Danielle is all right, too.'

'Yes, I knew she'd be,' he said with a grin. 'There's something to be said for peasant blood, Mama, despite all the old prejudices.' He went in, almost colliding with the Indian midwife coming out.

Anne frowned after him, remembering her own promise to Danielle to say nothing of the difficulties of the birth. It was a promise she had not wanted to make, but the girl had been so desperate that Anne had finally consented. Now she rather wished she hadn't.

In the bedroom Claude cradled his infant son in his arms and offered up a silent prayer of thanks; although he had not confided his fears, he had been haunted for weeks by the memory of the child buried in the distant mountains.

'Shall we name him for your father?' Danielle asked.

'I was thinking – why don't we call him Adam, the firstborn in this new Eden of ours.' He beamed down at her and said impetuously, 'Let's have many more, darling; let's fill this place with his brothers and sisters.'

Danielle, basking in the radiance of his happiness, warmed by the glow of love with which he looked down upon her, forgot all the pain, all the difficulty of her ordeal.

'Yes,' she said, smiling wanly. 'We shall have many children.'

45

Doña Elvira was furious. Her husband had invited the de Brussacs to the birthday party she had planned for him without even consulting her.

'They are our nearest neighbors,' he had said when she objected vehemently. 'I merely assumed that you would want them to come.'

She had glowered angrily back at him. He knew quite well that she hadn't wanted the de Brussacs, she was certain of it; he was only mocking her with his innocent expression. And she knew well enough why he wanted the de Brussacs, too – it was so that he could spend the evening looking calf eyes at Madame de Brussac.

That woman! With her copper-colored hair! No woman her age could have hair like that without taking dye to it, whatever she said to the contrary. And a woman who dyed her hair, a Frenchwoman to boot – everyone knew what they were like to begin with.

She had accused her husband of being attracted to the de Brussac woman, but naturally he had laughed at the idea.

'Anne? Don't be foolish. She hardly knows I'm alive,' he had said.

'She knows.' It was not until much later that she realized he had not actually denied his interest in her, only hers in him.

Anyway, she had seen the looks he gave her, and she knew well enough what desires burned behind those looks: As well she might; once he had looked upon her in that fashion.

Theirs had been an arranged marriage, naturally. It was the way families such as theirs did things. She hadn't loved him; indeed, she had barely known him. But once she had married the handsome young *caballero* she had taken possession of him, regarding him as her property. After all, wasn't she the one who had to endure all that fumbling and poking in bed – favors she had granted with all the dignity of a queen conferring knighthood and that had produced with merciful swiftness two sons. 'Enough of a family for anybody,' she had assured him.

They had always had their separate bedrooms in the huge house, and after the birth of their second son, she had pleaded lingering effects from her labor as an excuse to postpone resumption of their marital relations.

Indeed, she would have been content to postpone them forever had events not taken the turn they did. By chance she came upon her husband one day with one of the servants, a pretty young girl of sixteen, in his arms.

He had insisted that the girl meant nothing to him; he had found her crying, he said, over a quarrel with her sweetheart, and had only been trying to comfort her.

Doña Elvira did not believe him, and even if she had it wouldn't have made any difference in her anger; he had committed a far more grievous sin: that of embarrassing her in front of the servants. Even if he were innocent, even if she had been willing to believe him, she was sure the servants would not. She was convinced they were laughing at her behind her back.

For a week she took to locking her bedroom door at night, to punish him. The first night her husband had knocked several times, softly calling her name and asking her to let him in, 'Just to talk.' She had ignored his efforts, not even deigning to answer him.

After a week something happened that made her even more furious – he stopped trying her door at night. She did not know which made her angrier, that he no longer tried to come to her, or that he accepted their new relationship with total equanimity. In every other respect he was the same to her as he had been before: courteous, deferential, gallant even. But there was something mechanical about it now, as if what he did was quite different from what he actually felt.

That was when she began the trouble with her legs. Originally it had been a deliberate decision. One evening when it was time for her to retire, she had risen from her chair and at once sank to the floor, crying that something was wrong with her legs, they would not support her. She had expected her husband to carry her to bed, as of course he did, and once there, past locked doors, she thought that the upper hand would again be hers.

To her surprise, however, he had left her maid to undress her and had sent for the doctor, not returning to the room until the doctor had completed his examination. By this time Doña Elvira had been nearly livid from the fury that she was forced to contain for the sake of her pretense.

'I can find nothing wrong with your wife's legs,' was the doctor's verdict. Doña Elvira had seen the quick, assessing look her husband had given her.

'Then you're a fool,' she had cried, flinging her fan at his head. When they had gone and left her alone, she sobbed with violent anger into her pillow; she felt that her husband and the doctor between them had managed to make her look a fool.

She stayed in her bed for three days. Finally, annoyed each day by her husband's polite condescension, she had insisted she wanted to spend the afternoon in the parlor.

'Do you want to walk or shall I carry you?' Don Diego had asked.

'I will have to be carried,' she had nearly screamed at him. 'No matter what that fool of a doctor says, my legs are useless to me.'

He had carried her gently, comfortably, into the parlor to her favorite chair. He had seen that she had everything she needed, he had left her maid to keep her company – and had ridden into Los Angeles, not returning until the following day. He brought with him a wheelchair for her.

She never walked again. After a time she forgot that her condition had begun as a lie. Her mind and her legs accepted their crippled condition and eventually she was as crippled in fact as she had been before in pretense.

'What a lovely gift.' Don Diego tore the paper from the package Anne had brought and lifted it up so the others present might see; there was the appropriate murmur of approval.

Anne had taken considerable pains with the gift. It had begun as a rather ordinary wooden box, the sort that a man might keep on his desk to keep letters in. She had spent several months, though, hand-painting a miniature scene upon its top surface. It was a painting of the main *casa* of the Rancho de Torres, and she had had to make several surreptitious visits to the hillside overlooking the house in order to sketch it first on paper. Jean had always admired her drawing talents, and she was not too displeased with the way the work had turned out.

She had gone to so much trouble because she was so grateful to Don Diego for all that he had done for them since their arrival. It was not only the money he had invested in French Hills Winery, although of course that was important; it would be two more years at least before their new vineyards began to produce grapes, even in small quantities, and another two years before the wine was drinkable.

Claude was ecstatic about this vote of confidence in his plans for the winery, but Anne herself was more grateful for other, less tangible things. Don Diego had been a friend – warm, kindly, cheerful – at a time when they knew no one else hereabouts and when she especially had needed friends. He had enthusiastically invited them to share some measure of his own very gracious living, and that had done much to soften for her the long and difficult transition from her former life to the one they had lived since leaving France.

'It must have taken you a great deal of time,' Don Diego said, coming to thank her on a more personal level.

'Time is what I have the most of,' she said.

'I would have said beauty,' he said, his gray eyes softening as they gazed down at her. 'Followed by charm, wit, elegance – time, I'm afraid, would be far down on my list of your greatest assets.'

He moved to take her hands, but she quickly snatched them away. She was quite sensitive over the way her hands had hardened and roughened on the overland journey; no amount of care and no lotions or creams had been able to restore them to their former loveliness.

If he noticed the gesture he did not show it. 'Have you tried the champagne?' he asked. 'We get very little of it here, you know; such a long trip from France.'

'One day,' Claude said, joining them, 'French Hills will produce champagne. Then there'll be no need to bring it all the way from France.'

Don Diego laughed in a kindly way. 'Champagne, from California? My young friend, you dream impossibilities.'

The two men drifted away, arguing the possibilities of Claude's vision. Anna smiled after them, thinking how odd it was that these two should be so much alike in their thinking when in other ways they were so different.

She turned her head and found Doña Elvira, whom she disliked, staring at her. The señora had wheeled her chair close, as if eager to hear the conversation that had taken place.

'That was a lovely present,' Doña Elvira said.

'No more than your husband deserves, señora,' Anne replied.

Doña Elvira gave a harsh bark of a laugh. 'Ah, I know better than anyone what my husband deserves, Madame,' she said.

'He is a very charming man.'

'He is charming to women when he is desirous of them.'

Anne gave her a frosty look. 'That was a scandalous remark, señora,' she said.

'My husband is attracted to you.' She made it a statement of fact.

'I am a married woman,' Anne said.

Doña Elvira lifted an eyebrow sardonically. 'There are married women, Madame, and there are married women.'

Anne said, coldly, 'That is true, señora. Just as there are ladies and there are – ' she paused, looking down her nose as she got up ' – ladies.'

Infuriated that she could not rise and confront her enemy on an equal level, Doña Elvira asked sharply, 'Are you so lonely, Madame, that you would steal another woman's husband? A cripple's husband? '

Anne's look was withering. 'You are to be pitied, Doña Elvira, but it is not for your legs; it is for the mind that could conceive such dishonor of a man as fine as your husband. As for my loneliness, that is no concern of yours; but rest assured, señora, that when I begin stealing husbands, I will not begin in California.'

She swept away, leaving Doña Elvira to glower after her.

Later, though, Anne found herself wondering for the first time if Don Diego really was attracted to her. Was that the reason for his kindness, his graciousness? Upon reflection, she was not entirely certain that Doña Elvira had been mistaken.

Of course, nothing could ever come of it; Don Diego was a perfect gentleman and she was Jean's wife, though it had been two years now since she had seen him or even heard from him, and she loved her husband no less than before.

Still, she was nearly forty; it was flattering to know that despite her years, despite all she had been through in recent times, a man of Don Diego's taste and sophistication might find her attractive.

'Why, Mother,' Claude remarked on their way home that night, 'you're singing – you must have had a splendid time.'

'It was an invigorating evening,' Anne remarked, smiling lightly to herself.

46

Four men stood on a mountain ridge, staring into the valley below. One of them, the one they called el Tigre, held a battered pair of binoculars through which he was watching the ranch in the valley below. The others alternately watched him and the distant ranch.

They had been watching the ranch – the Rancho de Torres – for nearly a week. Each day the *ranchero* and the Frenchman from the neighboring ranch had departed early in the day, taking most of the servants with them, leaving only the woman who couldn't walk and the Indian servant women. During the last two days the Frenchman's women had been there, too, coming with him in the morning and remaining until the men returned home late in the afternoon.

The *rancheros* were building a water channel to carry water to their vineyards from the stream in the hills. It was an ambitious project, one that el Tigre could admire, even, but he thought the *rancheros* were fools to leave their women unprotected. It was like an open invitation to renegades and bandidos such as he and his men.

El Tigre was their leader because they needed a leader, and because among vicious, savage men he was by far the most vicious, the most savage. He had traveled alone across most of the great southwest, a land peopled with hostile Indians. He had made and lost fortunes in the gold fields, and fled after killing a man in a robbery attempt. A posse at his heels, he had first been captured by and then become the leader of this wolf pack, a band of former Mexican citizens who, since the end of the Mexican-American war, had lived in the wilds. Once there had been nearly twenty of them. Now there were only these three and himself. They had grown more cautious now, of necessity. Now they must look before they rode down upon the ranches, looking for weaker prey.

Such as the little group of women below.

'Manuel,' he spoke to his second-in-command, 'the horses. It is time we paid a visit.'

'But why must we spend every day with Doña Elvira,' Anne complained.

Claude sighed and said, 'Because, as I have told you, there have been reports of bandit raids. I don't want you alone while I'm gone all day.'

'I'd rather face bandits than Doña Elvira,' Anne said.

Claude ignored that remark and said, 'It's only for a few more days.'

Danielle, busy with the baby, avoided taking part in the argument. She was no more fond of Doña Elvira than Mama was, but she had learned that it was primarily Mother de Brussac toward whom the señora's venom was directed these days, and she had a pretty good idea why. It was unfortunate, in her opinion, that Don Diego had a wife, and Mama – well, no one knew whether she had a husband or not. But it was obvious that she and Don Diego got along so well, and you had only to notice the way he looked at her to know that he had fallen quite in love with her. If the two of them were free . . . but there, they weren't, of course, and she had learned it was no use dwelling on what might be. It was the here and now you had to deal with if you were going to get along.

She was fortunate, at least. She had the man she wanted, and in the past year, since the baby had been born, Claude seemed to have settled into his marriage more. She had never gotten over her feelings of inadequacy; she supposed that he still dreamed of the aristocratic Antoinette. But for the sake of her love, she had decided that she could live with a man who only dreamed of other women; and he did love her, she was sure of that.

Don Diego pointed out to Anne and Danielle, as he had

before, where the guns were: the rifle case in his library, a loaded rifle on pegs near the kitchen door, and the shotgun just inside the door of the barn.

'Just in case,' he added. 'I don't really think there's any danger, but it's best to be prepared.'

'They say decent women have nothing to fear,' Doña Elvira grumbled.

'Oughtn't you to have a pistol?' Anne asked her sweetly.

'I never learned to shoot one,' Doña Elvira replied. 'Our class considered it unladylike.'

'Necessity has its own etiquette,' Anne said.

Once the men had gone, however, the señora settled into a sullen silence. She was working at a petit point in one corner of the parlor. Anne and Danielle were embroidering squares which they would make later into a quilt. The two Indian servants, who were maid and cook, were in the kitchen; occasionally a raucous laugh could be heard from that direction, but in time they grew silent as well. The silence seemed to Anne oppressive, like the ominous stillness that sometimes precedes a storm.

At length Doña Elvira grew restless. She put her work aside impatiently and called in the direction of the kitchen, 'Marie, coffee!'

There was no reply. With an angry snort Doña Elvira grabbed up the little silver bell with which she summoned the servants on more formal occasions and shook it vigorously. She cocked her head, listening for the maid's scurrying footsteps. After a moment she rang the bell again.

'I'll go find her,' Anne said, getting to her feet.

She was halfway across the room when the men came in from the kitchen, guns drawn, smiling. For a moment shock held Anne in place. Then, remembering the gun case in the library, she turned and tried to run, but one of the men, a swarthy half-breed with a drooping mustache, crossed the room in three long strides and seized her wrist violently.

'Oh, no you don't Madame Frenchie,' he said, twisting her around to face him.

'Who are you?' she demanded, struggling. 'How do you know . . . you!' She found herself looking into the face of Carl Betts, the man who had tried to molest her and Danielle on the banks of the Red River and had fled at the approach of the Indians.

'Flattered to see that you recognize me,' he said. 'To be

honest, I never thought we'd meet up again. I figured them Indians would make squaws of you two.'

'It's unfortunate you didn't get the same as Mister Rumford,' Anne said.

'Yeah, that was too bad about old Jim, but I'd a lot rather it was him than me. By the way, they call me el Tigre now; that's Spanish for the tiger. And these are my boys: that's Manuel, the fat one there, he used to be fatter but we haven't been eating so well the last few weeks; that's Pepe, and that's Tío, the old man there – he isn't actually anybody's uncle, we just call him that 'cause he's old.'

'What do you want?' Anne demanded.

'Where are the servants?' Doña Elvira asked.

'Them two Indian women? We locked them in the woodshed. They'll be all right, for now anyways. We may get around to them later. Then again, we may not.'

His eyes, dark and gleaming, had left Anne's face and were staring downward at the bodice of her dress. The other outlaws were just standing and grinning, apparently waiting for instructions from him.

'Doña Elvira,' Anne said, speaking calmly and evenly, 'get them all the money in the house.'

'You're mad,' Doña Elvira said sharply. 'Give away my good money, to these animals? They'll have to kill me first.'

Betts – el Tigre as he now called himself – shoved Anne aside against a wall and motioned for the others to watch her. He crossed the room to where Doña Elvira sat. As he came, he drew a knife from a sheath strapped to one leg. Its blade gleamed in the morning light.

'Well, now, that could be arranged, too,' he said, holding the knife just under her chin. 'So you've got some money in the house, have you? Where is it?'

'Go to the devil,' she replied. To Anne's horror, she spat directly into his face.

There was a moment of shocked silence. Even the other outlaws had stopped grinning, and it was obvious from their faces that no one had ever done such a thing to their leader before. Anne was dismayed, but at the same time she could not help feeling a rather begrudging admiration; you could not deny that the señora had spirit.

El Tigre thrust the point of his knife against her throat. Doña Elvira did not flinch but looked her own daggers at him.

Slowly the knife was lowered to her breasts. Then slowly,

deliberately, he began to cut the fastenings of her dress.

'What are you doing?' she cried, trying to slap the knife away; she succeeded only in cutting her fingers on the blade. He continued to cut away her dress, and she continued trying to slap his hands away.

When the fastenings had all been cut off and her dress was hanging open to the waist, he bent down and, gathering the silk fabric in his fingers, ripped it away from her body. She squealed and struggled against him, beating at his arms and his face with her fists, but he hardly seemed to notice her resistance. In a moment he had bared her to the waist. Her dried breasts hung pendulous and flabby, an obscene contrast to her fully clothed lower torso. Even her arms were still covered by sleeves; only her upper body, from shoulders to waist, was bared.

When he stepped back to survey his work, she flung her arms over her breasts, trying to cover herself.

'Swine,' she screamed, tears of anger and humiliation streaming down her face. 'Monster!'

Some of the explosive tension had fled the air, at least for the moment. When el Tigre began to laugh at the helpless woman in the wheelchair, trying futilely to cover her exposed bosom, his men chimed in obediently.

'You want to cover yourself, señora?' el Tigre asked, his obscene grin revealing yellowed and rotting teeth. 'Here.' He snatched Anne's shawl from about her shoulders and dangled it in the air before the humiliated woman in the wheelchair. Doña Elvira was in the position of having to cover herself with one hand and snatch for the shawl with the other; but when she reached for the garment, he held it away, out of her reach.

'You will have to walk for it, señora,' he said, teasing her with the shawl.

Forgetting her exposed condition, Doña Elvira actually braced herself on the arms of her chair and attempted to rise, but at once she sank weakly back down.

'I can't,' she sobbed in frustration.

Her anguish only increased the ribald laughter of the intruders.

Suddenly el Tigre's laughter stopped. His eyes, roving about the room, had spotted the cradle in which little Adam was sleeping.

'What's this?' he asked, moving toward the cradle.

'No,' Danielle screamed. She raced across the room and flung herself over the cradle. 'Don't harm him.'

The outlaw went to her and yanked her away from the cradle. Danielle lay where he had shoved her, staring wide-eyed. She remembered this man well from the wagon train; the unrelenting cruelty in his eyes had frightened her even then.

Something strange happened then, so briefly that she was uncertain afterward if she had actually seen it at all. As he gazed down at the sleeping infant, blessedly unaware of the danger about him, the bandit's expression seemed to soften. His eyes lost some of their savage gleam and his smile became a genuine smile, warm, almost tender.

As quickly as it had come, the mood disappeared. 'Take them outside,' he said gruffly to his men. 'Leave the baby here; he won't hurt anything.'

He walked to Doña Elvira. 'You want the shawl, Señora? Here.' He stepped behind the chair and brought the shawl down about her, twisting it into a rope with which he tied her to the wheelchair, bringing it up under her arms and leaving her breasts still exposed. When he had finished, he gave the chair a shove with his foot.

'Take her to the horses,' he ordered.

The wheelchair was pushed rudely outside, Doña Elvira clinging helplessly to its arms. Anne and Danielle were herded outside in her wake.

Outside, el Tigre ordered Doña Elvira's wheelchair pushed over to where their horses were waiting near the barn. He took a length of rope from his saddle and tied it to the back of the wheelchair.

'What are you doing?' Anne demanded.

'The señora refuses to walk,' el Tigre said, tying the other end of the rope to his saddle horn. 'So she gets a ride instead.'

With that he leaped into the saddle and spurred his horse. The animal began to gallop. The rope straightened, grew taut. The wheelchair was suddenly propelled along after the horse, the terrified Doña Elvira riding backward.

She began to shriek and scream as el Tigre rode his horse yet faster, circling the barnyard. Doña Elvira rode helplessly through a cloud of dust, flailing her arms and legs and shrieking ceaselessly at the top of her lungs.

'Oh, God,' Danielle murmured, but Anne could only watch in speechless horror as the wheelchair, unintended for such rugged use, began to break up beneath the terror-stricken woman.

A wheel fell off, the chair bouncing onto its side. Doña

Elvira's head was banged against the ground and she was obviously stunned, as her screams stopped suddenly.

'Stop it, you'll kill her,' Anne cried, but they ignored her. Around and around the man on horseback went and the battered chair followed after, righting itself now, the other wheel rolling free, spinning halfway across the barnyard before it came to rest. The unconscious Doña Elvira flopped about like a rag doll.

El Tigre's followers were absorbed in the gruesome spectacle, shouting and whooping with laughter. Danielle suddenly realized they were paying hardly any attention to her – and there, only a few feet away from where she stood, was the barn door, slightly ajar. Just behind it was the loaded shotgun Don Diego had pointed out to them earlier.

She began to inch toward the door. No one seemed to notice. The wheelchair was virtually destroyed by now, nothing more than a few boards to which Doña Elvira's limp body remained tied; she was being dragged over the hard ground, rolling and flopping over the stones and clumps of grass.

Danielle was almost to the door. Still no one had glanced at her; the men had seemingly forgotten her and Anne in their 'sport'. She took a deep breath and reached inside the barn. Her fingers touched cold metal.

There was no time to waste on threats or warnings. These men would respect nothing but action, and she took it.

She brought the shotgun out, hoisting it to her shoulder in one swift movement and simultaneously firing one of the two barrels. El Tigre saw her in the last few seconds, saw the gun being lifted – but it was too late. One moment his eyes widened in realization of what had happened, the next moment he was a headless rider, still rocking in the saddle as his horse circled the barnyard. The blast had blown away most of his head, leaving a bloody stump in its stead. The horse whinnied, tossing its head; then, as the reins went slack and its rider slowly slid from the saddle to the ground, it slowed and came to a puzzled halt.

It was several seconds before the others could quite grasp what had happened, and by then Danielle had the shotgun aimed in the general direction of the remaining three desperados. One of them, the one they called Uncle, still held his pistol in his hand, hanging down at his side. Pepe had a rifle, half-raised to fire. The other one, Manuel, had holstered his gun to push Doña Elvira's chair outside and had not redrawn it, thinking them in no danger from the women.

'You've only got one shot left in that thing,' Tío said, trying to duplicate el Tigre's cruel nonchalance and not quite succeeding.

'Enough to kill one more of you,' Danielle said evenly, though her heart was pounding. 'You, if you don't drop your gun – or you.' She inched the barrel slightly in the direction of Pepe. He took the hint. The rifle slipped from his fingers, fell to the ground.

At once Anne darted forward and grabbed the rifle from the ground, coming back to stand beside Danielle. The desperados found themselves facing two armed and determined-looking women.

Tío hesitated. The men were temporarily leaderless, cast into an unfamiliar confusion; and there was no doubt that the women had the nerve to kill – the one had already killed el Tigre, something a hundred lawmen around the state had been trying to do for four years.

Danielle cocked the hammer on the gun. It would take but the slightest pressure on the trigger to fire it again. She waited, beginning already to feel the unaccustomed weight of the heavy firearm.

'You're the fastest with a gun, Tío,' Manuel said. 'You take them.'

'I am going to count to three,' Anne said, staring directly at Tío and cocking the rifle as well. 'Then I'm going to kill you.'

'The boys'll finish you both off,' he said.

'Too late to give you any satisfaction . . . one . . . two . . . '

He dropped his pistol. Danielle gave a barely audible sigh of relief.

The others took their cue from him; all three of the bandits lifted their hands in the air.

After that it was a simple matter to disarm them. The Indian servants were freed from the woodshed and the bandits locked in the shed in their place.

Doña Elvira was dead, her poor body battered almost beyond recognition. Anne, who had disliked the woman in life, could not help but be moved by her brutal death. With the help of the maids, Doña Elvira's body was carried inside and covered with a blanket. Then Maria was sent to the neighboring ranch, run by the Carrs, to ask that one of the Carrs' sons be sent over to help guard the prisoners until Claude and Don Diego returned later in the day.

It was a singular homecoming that the two ranchers experienced. Don Diego went in alone to see his wife, and Anne did not want to guess what his feelings might be. She asked Claude to take them home.

'Our condolences can be paid tomorrow,' she said simply.

'That was a very brave thing you did today,' Claude told Danielle when they were alone later. It was from Don Diego's servants that he had learned most of the story of what had happened; both his mother and Danielle had been reluctant to discuss their experience.

He was already in bed; Danielle was at her dressing-table, braiding her long hair. He found himself watching his wife with a sense of impatience. The story of her daring in confronting the outlaw band had proven strangely stimulating, and he was eager for her to join him.

Danielle found her fingers moving more slowly than was usual. It was ironic, she thought, remembering the glimpse of wild excitement she had seen in Claude's eyes; normally it was she who was eager, impatient. Men found danger a stimulant, it seemed.

Tonight, though, she could not forget the man she had killed. She had been horrified once, seeing Claude kill a man, though the killing had been accidental. Today she had killed a man herself, and it had been far from an accident. It had been cold-blooded, brutal, and afterward she had been unable to feel remorse.

Yet she did feel remorse of a sort. She found herself recalling el Tigre, not as he had looked lying dead upon the ground but earlier, when he had gazed down at her son asleep in his cradle. She wondered what memories, what feelings had caused that quick softening of the light in his eyes. She would never know; the moment had died with him, would come to him no more. But the memory stayed with her.

At last her hair was finished. She extinguished the lamp and came to the bed, slipping beneath the covers Claude turned back for her. At once his arms caught her in a hungry embrace.

'You're not too tired, are you, darling?' he asked, sensing her reluctance but at the same time hardly pausing.

After only the briefest of hesitations, she said, 'No, I'm not tired.'

It was the first time her husband's embraces were not entirely thrilling to her.

47

'Mama, Mama, Papa's coming!'

Danielle, at work pruning the vines, stood up, arching her back to relieve the ache caused by the work that required much bending and stooping and by the additional weight she was carrying in front. Fortunately this child, although already six months along, promised to be smaller than the others.

'Are you sure? Adam, be careful Jean doesn't damage the vines.'

'He's coming, he's coming,' Adam insisted, grabbing his little brother's arm with such violence that he yanked him to his knees, causing Jean to put up a howl of protest.

Despite Adam's barely contained excitement, she had to stop to dry Jean's tears, so that by the time they finally reached the house, Claude was indeed riding up, grinning his pleasure at being home.

The boys ran out to greet him as he jumped down from his horse. Claude paused to lift each of them in turn over his head and swing him around before he strolled over to where Danielle waited in the shade of the porch.

'You've been working again,' he said. 'You're supposed to be taking it easy this time.' The year before, Danielle had lost another child in a miscarriage; the doctor had issued his usual stern warning to her, and as usual she had kept that fact from her husband.

'The doctor says there's no danger this time,' she lied. 'Anyway, you know I love working with the vines.'

She saw the quick, vaguely disapproving glance he cast at her dirty hands. 'You married a peasant girl, you know,' she added; her tone was intended to be bantering, but it came out instead a rather pathetic plea for reassurance.

'This is a democracy,' he said. 'Those things aren't supposed to matter here.'

'How did the legislators like your ideas?' she asked, to change the subject.

He shrugged. 'They liked them well enough, I guess, at least the ones that didn't cost any money. But we're winning friends. The figures on actual wine sales impressed them. I don't think most of them realized we were talking about that kind of volume.'

He had been a month in the new capital of Sacramento as head of a delegation from the newly formed Los Angeles Vinicultural Society, to urge the formation of a state wine commission and to press for laws to protect the state's wine industry. On his own he had also lobbied for his pet project – a state delegation to travel to Europe and bring back vast inventories of European vines, to be distributed by the state to local growers.

His own first wines had proved a mixed lot. The reds were disappointing, better generally than the wines produced from the local mission grape, but lacking some essential component in soil or climate that had given them their characteristic body in France. The first attempt at champagne had been even worse, a failure even by the kindest judgement.

Despite the failure of the champagne, however, the white wines in general were excellent. The cuttings from France had included the Sauvignon Blanc, the principal grape of the great French sauternes and Chenin Blanc, of the Vouvray region, and both had done well; but it was the Chardonnay, the grape from which the great white burgundies of France were produced, that gave the first solid hint of the success of Claude's vision of a truly fine California-produced wine. Ignoring the advice of the established California vintners, he put away the Chardonnay in oak casks he had built originally for the reds, to see how the wine aged.

The local growers called him a fool; they were in the habit of selling off their wines as quickly as they were produced, and they rarely bothered to keep wine from one variety of grape separate from another. California wines of the day were either white wine or red wine; the vintners did not trouble themselves much with the niceties of generic names.

Still, the fortunate ones came to taste the product of the winery and nodded their heads in begrudging admiration; they strolled the vineyards with the enthusiastic young Frenchman and attempted to learn the unfamiliar names of the grape varieties. Some even bought cuttings to add to their own vineyards for purposes of experimentation.

And throughout the state wine growers began to take notice of the vineyards slowly spreading across the hills to the east of

Los Angeles. The de Brussac name and the French Hills Winery were becoming known. The de Brussacs were far from wealthy, but they were at least established in their new home and their new land, with every reason to believe in Claude's promise to make the de Brussacs wine-kings of the new world.

'Where's Mother?' Claude asked, leading the way into the house, larger now by several rooms than it had been before.

'She's out riding.' Danielle hurried to pour her husband a glass of wine.

'Alone?'

'No, with Don Diego.'

Claude frowned. 'I think they're in love,' Danielle said, handing him the wine.

'I think Don Diego's been in love with her since he first met her,' Claude said. 'But Mother . . . it's hard to know what she thinks or feels; she keeps her thoughts to herself.'

'It's been a long time,' Danielle said. 'A woman gets lonely – all these years, and not a word . . . '

The fate of Jean, Marie and René remained as much a mystery as before. Claude had replaced the money taken from the London banks in the event that the others might somehow find their way to London, but there was no more word of them than there had been before.

The years following the flight from France had been increasingly turbulent ones for that nation. The February Revolution and the bloody June Days had cost as many as ten thousand lives, and at least that many others had been deported or arrested. Louis Napoleon was now the Emperor Napoleon III, ruler of the Second Empire, much as Jean had feared would happen. The emperor controlled France with an iron hand, and once inside his prisons, those who were arrested rarely ever again emerged into the sunlight of freedom.

Anne still wrote her letters, but privately even she had ceased to believe they would ever be answered.

Claude, too, thought his father dead; yet for all that, and for all that Don Diego was his closest friend in the New World, he could not quite rid himself of a nagging resentment of the relationship that had grown up between his mother and Don Diego.

It was inevitable, he supposed: two people of the same class, the same aristocratic background; lonely, isolated both by geography and their own natures from the crowds of man. Claude had often thought, although he had never shared the opinion with others, that Doña Elvira, had she lived, would have been doomed to suffer a hell of jealousy perhaps more torturous than the death she had suffered.

'A penny for your thoughts.'

Anne was lying in a tall stand of grass, staring at the cloudless sky. She thought she had never seen a sky as blue as this California sky, never known the sun to shine as golden. How beautiful it was, in its own unpolished way, its Creator's offhand masterpiece.

'I was thinking,' she said finally, 'that I hated it here when I first came.'

'And now you have learned to love it,' Diego said. 'As I do.'

'Perhaps not to love it, I don't think that's quite the emotion it inspires. To respect it, certainly, to admire it, appreciate it. One gets used to things.'

'As you have gotten used to me?' He propped himself on one elbow to smile down at her.

'You were rather easier to get used to,' she said, returning the smile. She suddenly laughed aloud. 'But me,' she added, 'how I must have looked in the beginning. I thought I would never be able to get clean again, after that journey.'

'I thought you were the most beautiful woman I had ever seen,' he said, growing serious. 'I still do.'

She did not reply at once. A hawk had winged into view overhead, circling lazily. She wanted suddenly to seize this moment, to hold it to her breast and prevent its passing. There had been a time, so long a time, when there had been no joy in aliveness, when living had meant struggling to survive each day, had meant nothing more than enduring.

To revel in the senses – the soft whinny of the horses as they grazed, the cool silkiness of the grass beneath her, the scent of earth and sage – was to suddenly be young again, to shed the years that had begun for a time to weigh so heavily upon her.

'Have you ever crossed the Great Plains?' she asked aloud.

'No, I was born in Monterey. We came here when I was a child. It's odd if you think of it – I've lived in New Spain, in Mexico and America – and I've never been out of California.'

'The country is so immense, so – ' she struggled for a word, finishing lamely ' – so open. You feel that man has never stood where you are standing, has never seen what you are seeing. It's foolish, I suppose; I'm sure people had followed the same route before, but they had left it unspoiled. And in our wake we left

an Indian village and all its inhabitants destroyed; we left what
had been a great herd of animals, they call them buffalo,
scattered lifeless across the plains. Wherever we went, we left
our mark, indelibly, destructively.'

'What are you trying to say?'

'I don't know exactly. All my life, you see, I never had to do
anything more than be a woman. I never had to think profound
thoughts, or take action – not real action, to cope with anything. My husband thought and did for me, and after that, for a
time, my son. But here, the land, the life, demanded more. For
the first time I had to think and do, I had to struggle and fight
and even kill. The woman I was before could never have survived here, and so she had to die, and I was born in her place;
but I am not she.

'All these years, I've longed to go back, but now – now I
don't know. The woman who lived there is gone, you see, and
how would a stranger like me live in that crowded place?'

'They write songs and stories about the men of the West,' he
said, 'but in time to come it is the pioneer women they will
praise.'

She laughed again. 'Claude called me that once, a long time
ago. At the time I was offended, but now I think it is rather a
compliment. It's satisfying to know that you have accomplished
something, however reluctantly or ineptly. To know that you
need never think of yourself as a "mere" woman. It makes you
more of a woman, actually.'

After a moment Diego said, 'And your husband? That
woman who died loved him very much, did she not? What of
her love, now that she is gone?'

'How can you ever stop loving – real love, I mean – isn't it
by definition something universal, something eternal? But it
has been ten years. Ten years without a word. If he is alive, he
will have changed as much as I. We would be two strangers
now, with only our undying love in common.'

'Anne,' Diego said after a long silence, 'will you marry me?'

She was not surprised by the question. She had long been
aware that it was in his mind and wondered what she would feel
when it was asked; strangely, though, she felt very little; perhaps later – but she knew, too, that what she had experienced
– her growth, her independence, her losses and her gains – had
reduced her capacity for passionate caring.

She was fond of this man; it would be pleasant to link her
life to his; but she knew, as the young Anne would not have

known, that if she did not the world would not end but would
go on turning.

'I am already married,' she said.

'As you said, it's been ten years. Your husband was not a
young man at the time of his arrest. How long do you think he
could survive, languishing in those French prisons?'

'Jean? It's hard to say. He was a man of iron will.'

'Anne, there are certain people I know – attorneys, government officials – not just here, but in Mexico, even in Spain. If I
launched an investigation – if they determined that your husband is dead – would you marry me?'

She was a long time in answering. The hawk who had been
flying above had disappeared, then returned; now he was
circling directly above them, as if she were the prey he was
seeking.

'I must have time to think,' she said, sitting up abruptly. She
saw the disappointment on his face and put her hand gently on
his. 'Not a great deal of time. Come to dinner tonight. I will
give you an answer then.'

She dressed with unusual care that evening.

'You look especially lovely,' Claude said, coming to her
room to greet her; he had been in the vineyards when she
returned to the house.

'Do I?' She had worn a new outfit that she had been saving,
a pearl gray silk that changed colors in its folds, taking on a
coppery sheen that matched her still-vivid hair. She wished
fleetingly for the old emeralds; they would have been perfect.
In their place she had the opals that Don Diego had given her
on her last birthday. Fire opals, he had called them, an appropriate name for the flames that seemed to burn within their
milky depths.

'What's the occasion?'

'Must there be an occasion? Oh, Don Diego is coming for
dinner.' She made the mention as casually as possible, but she
could not miss the fleeting look of disapproval on her son's
face before he went out.

It gave her a feeling of resentment. Hadn't she earned the
right to think for herself, to make her own decisions?

She glanced in the mirror; the answers that it gave her were
harsh, cruel. She saw not only the hair that had miraculously
kept its color, the splendid dress, the waistline that nature, with
the help of a few stays, had kept small; she saw as well the

little lines that fanned out from the corners of her eyes and formed little parentheses about her mouth.

She was forty-six. Jean, if he were alive, would be approaching seventy now. Even granting his iron will, could he have lived these past ten years in the prisons of France?

And her own life – suddenly it seemed to her that it was drawing rapidly, too rapidly, toward its own sunset. A few seasons more, and what was left of her beauty would no longer be fading but gone. She had lived so long without real happiness, without love, and now, surely for the last time, it was being offered to her. Dare she refuse it? Dare she accept the loneliness of the last ten years for another ten, twenty – for the rest of her life?

It was the looking glass that gave her her answer; if Diego learned that Jean was dead, she would marry him.

48

Diego met soon afterward with the attorneys he had hired, and again the following June. Their investigation by then had produced little more than was known in the beginning.

'There are some prisoners being kept here,' one of the attorneys said, pointing to an ink mark on a map of France. 'A small fortress, owned by a woman – the Marquise de Marcheval. They are kept in complete seclusion; it's possible they may be the family you are seeking, but no one knows that for certain.'

'There is no evidence that this Baron de Brussac is alive?' Don Diego asked.

'None.'

'What makes you think he might be here?' Don Diego tapped the map impatiently.

'It's only a guess. We've penetrated virtually everywhere else. People do not just vanish from the earth.'

'Unless they are dead.'

'We have no evidence of that.'

'We have the evidence of ten years of silence,' Don Diego said. 'It is preposterous to think that because someone – no one knows who – is being held in a fortress in the south of France, hundreds of miles from where this baron lived, that it is this man. Who is this Marquise de Marcheval, anyway?'

'A very important woman – related to the emperor, distantly, and to General LeFevre.'

'But of no connection to the Baron de Brussac?'

'None that we can discern.'

Don Diego turned his back on the attorneys and went to stand at his window, gazing out at his vineyards – vineyards planted by now largely with cuttings that he had purchased from the de Brussac plants, not because he had any serious ambitions as a wine maker, but because he had recognized from the first the validity of Claude de Brussac's claims – that these vines were superior to what had been here before. Don Diego de Torres had always instinctively recognized, and actively sought, that which was superior – the best, the finest. Only once in his life had he had to settle for less, and that had been in his marriage.

He had made the best of that unfortunate alliance, and as a reward for his patience, providence had seen fit to release him from it. He had seen it then as he saw it now: a blessing that freed him to marry the one woman he wanted more than any other in the world. Only one obstacle remained; and it was within their power now, his and the men in this room with him, men paid to do his bidding, to remove that obstacle.

'We shall conclude,' he said without turning, 'that this man is dead.'

'We have no evidence . . . ' one of the attorneys started to argue.

'We shall conclude,' Don Diego said in a firm voice, still without facing them, 'that this man is dead.'

The wedding was planned for the fall, but it had to be postponed when Danielle's baby came a few weeks early.

'My current baby,' she said jokingly. This one, following close on the heels of little David, born just the year before, was a girl. They called her Mary, for Claude's sister.

'Your last baby,' Claude corrected her. This birth had been the most difficult of all, and this time the doctor, ignoring Danielle's pleas, had spoken directly to Claude.

Claude had been surprised; despite the evidence of two miscarriages, he had clung to his old belief that giving birth was easier for women of Danielle's class, a delusion she had encouraged. Now, though, he was firm in insisting that there would be no more.

Danielle was pleased by his concern but frightened to think that Claude, for her sake, might avoid her altogether in the future. She could not bring herself to broach this subject with him directly, but it was much on her mind, particularly as the weeks passed after the baby's arrival and Claude made no move to resume their physical relationship.

There was talk of postponing the wedding until after the holidays, but Anne decided otherwise. She had a superstitious feeling that to postpone it from one year to the next might be bad luck.

'I'm sure old Henriette would have thought it ominous,' she said.

Consequently the wedding took place shortly before Christmas at French Hills. Only the family attended, but neighbors and friends from as far away as Sacramento flocked to the reception and fiesta afterward.

'Mostly for the wine,' Anne observed drily.

It had been an important year for French Hills; during the past spring Claude had expanded both the winery and the storage facilities, and this season's crop was being described as a vintage year. Claude had hoped to serve his own champagne for the occasion, but he and Don Diego had decided after tasting that it was still too short of the mark, and instead he had provided his best Chardonnay, bottled from their first vintage and aged since then. This news, as Anne had observed, had aroused a great deal of interest among the California wine makers and brought guests who might not otherwise have traveled so far for a mere wedding.

The house was complete now, too, the quadrangle that Claude had originally envisioned surrounding a lovely tiled patio with a tinkling fountain and a variety of ornamental plants. It was a gracious house, hardly smaller than Chateau Brussac had been, although of course of an entirely different style.

Danielle found that she tired rather quickly the last year or so; probably, she guessed, because of the close succession of the last two childbirths, both of which had been hard. She was glad that the attention was focused on Anne and that she was left free to sit with the baby in a shady corner of the patio and observe the festivities, rather than having to take an active part in them.

Luckily the party managed to run itself, for the most part. There was a great deal of talk of the election of the new president, Mister Lincoln, and of what was commonly referred to as 'the Southern problem'.

Claude was ardently antislavery and had ranted and carried on for days over the previous year's news of a raid on some place called Harper's Ferry by a man called John Brown. Danielle's sympathies were also with the slaves. In France she had been a peasant, and she supposed in general that was not too far removed from slavery, but the French serfs had been at least nominally free, and at any rate her own upbringing had been little different from that of Claude and his sister, whatever the differences in their station. Probably, she thought it was equally true that the lot of many slaves was not much worse than the lot of their masters, but creature comforts aside, there was something odious in growing up with the knowledge that you were inferior to others.

Why, if she had remained in France, if she had married in her own class, her children would be growing up part of an inferior caste; yet they would be no less wonderful than they were to her now. The only difference was that they had been born in California; and, of course, their father was Claude de Brussac.

Don Diego, seeing her sitting off by herself, brought her a glass of wine. 'The hostess should be able to enjoy her party, too,' he said. 'It is a lovely party, by the way – and a lovely wedding. Thank you.'

'I'm afraid it's Anne who deserves most of the credit, and Claude. I seem to have had my hands full with children.'

'French Hills' finest ornaments,' Don Diego said, toasting her.

'Don't let Claude hear you say that,' she said, sipping the wine. 'He thinks we're drinking French Hills' finest right now.'

Don Diego laughed, his eyes sparkling gaily. 'Ah, well, great wines are like children to the vintners, and your husband is a great vintner; even his severest critics are prepared to concede that now.'

'We've come rather a long way from that ragtag collection of refugees who arrived here ten years ago, haven't we?' she said, not without a faint trace of irony in her voice.

Don Diego noted the irony and his eyes took on a more speculative look. 'Your husband is a very ambitious man,' he said. 'And he works hard, for his family's sake as well as his own. Someday you'll have everything your heart desires.'

Someone stopped just then to congratulate Don Diego and the two men drifted off together, leaving Danielle to her own thoughts.

Everything her heart desired? What a meaningless phrase that was, really. Hadn't she already gotten everything she had wanted – Claude, a fine home, a new life in a new land, the children. Adam was almost ten and already the very image of his father, and just as engrossed in the grapes and the wine. And wherever the two of them went, six-year-old Jean was sure to follow, plodding along in their wake through the vineyards, listening as intently to every word that Claude spoke as if he actually understood it all. David and Mary, of course, were too young to have formed their personalities, although she had already observed that David was an unusually quiet child, bright enough, it seemed, but more content to watch and listen than his brothers had been. Mary, she was afraid, was already the family's spoiled darling and gave every indication of relishing the role.

Yet, with all that she had gained, she still suffered the old feelings of insecurity, of inadequacy. For all that she had, it sometimes seemed as if she didn't actually *have* anything, not anything that was really hers.

Not Claude, certainly. She had finally come to the realization that Claude would never truly be hers, despite his obvious affection for her, despite the children they had produced together. He was ambitious and restless; he seemed always to be searching, striving for something more, perhaps some goal that he himself did not recognize. She knew that she occupied but a small portion of his attention and his interest.

She had tried sharing his interest in the wines, partly because she, too, loved the vineyards as he did, and partly because it was something she could share with him, but in fact he shared this interest more with the boys than he did with her; he never quite seemed to approve of her interest in the work of the vineyards.

Even the children seemed more Claude's than hers; he was devoted to the boys in a way that he was not devoted to her, and sometimes when she saw him with the baby, Mary, she actually felt the pricklings of jealousy. He called the infant girl my princess, little darling, and my sweetheart, and in his manner with the baby was all the unbridled affection she had always yearned for herself from him.

'I'm being a fool,' she chastised herself. 'I am the most fortunate of women, and here I sit wishing for more.'

Still the nagging feeling of uncertainty refused to go away.

The party had just reached its full swing when it was interrupted by the arrival of a rider from town. He came in sweaty and covered with trail dust, but when they heard his news the others seemed not to notice his appearance but rather crowded around him, making him the center of all interest.

'The union's broken up,' he cried, bursting onto the patio.

Anne, standing with a cluster of women, had an odd sensation of dismay; for a moment she thought he was speaking of her new union with Diego. Even when she grasped, a moment later, that he was talking about the union of the United States from which South Carolina had just seceded, she could not quite rid herself of the feeling of uneasiness that his words had caused. They were like a portent of impending trouble.

49

It was the season of revolution. The de Brussacs had fled the political upheavals of France; now their new land was engaged in a civil war, a revolution whose far-reaching consequences would far outstrip those of the French turmoil. A nation was struggling to free herself from the bonds of slavery, a slavery not only of blacks but of whites as well; a slavery not only of chains and whips but of a nation's soul and spirit to the masters of fear and prejudice.

At the same time, to the south, the Mexican people were busily engaged in trying to unseat a French-imposed dictator.

Living in the isolation of their ranch, the de Brussacs saw and heard these struggles at a distance, like the thunder when a distant storm crept over the hills, giving warning growls but presenting no real and present danger.

Danielle, stirred by the eloquence of Mister Lincoln, was grateful that California was not a slave state.

They heard belatedly of places like Antietam, Gettysburg and Vicksburg. For a time it seemed as if the South might make good her bold threats.

Then a man called Sherman began an advance through the South. Reports began to reach California of plantations burned, cities laid waste. Refugees, white and black, began to trickle westward, homeless people weary with the bleeding and the dying. To many of these California seemed a golden state, but the treasure these men sought was peace. Some of them found it; others brought their nightmares with them.

The war ended, but not before the final tragedy had been played out in Ford's Theater in Washington. Like all the nation, the de Brussacs were shocked, and even Claude, who had found much disagreeable about the man while he had been alive, mourned him in the hour of his passing. Danielle grieved and wondered if the nation would ever heal its wounds.

Selfishly, she was grateful that the war had ended before her sons had grown old enough to take part in it. Adam, fourteen now, was adventurous, and in the last year of the war had begun to talk all too enthusiastically of going to help free the slaves.

'You've got quite enough to keep you busy here,' Danielle assured him when he expressed his disappointment that the war had ended without his participation. 'It's hard enough to get good help these days.'

Although the de Brussacs hired a great many of the refugees from both the American South and Mexico as seasonal workers, it always seemed as if there weren't enough hands at grape-picking time. Each year Claude reinvested most of the profits that he made, until their vineyards now spread across thousands of acres. From nearly a hundred thousand vines, French Hills now produced some thirty thousand gallons of wine annually. They had begun to ship their wines not only throughout the country but even to France, where they had earned, if not praise, at least a grudging acceptance.

The wine journals that had begun to appear referred to Claude as the nation's 'premier vintner', and wine makers from as far away as New York and Ohio traveled to California to study his methods and hear his lectures on the importance of importing French vines.

Adam and Jean were their father's ardent disciples, and despite their youth it sometimes seemed to Danielle that the two boys knew as much as Claude did about wine making. On the other hand, she was sure that David was a disappointment to his father; at six he was incurably shy and introspective, preferring the books that his grandmother was teaching him to read; he was a gentle boy, often the butt of his more mischievous brothers' jokes.

Mary had proved to be the spoiled pet Danielle had predicted, her father's princess and her brothers' imperious ruler. She followed no one's counsel but her own and ignored Danielle's every attempt at discipline – after all, there was always her father to appeal to, and he could be counted on to see that she got her way. She was a formidable tyrant who, once she had achieved whatever her goal, was as quick and determined in coaxing her way back into the good graces of the loser. She was, Danielle admitted with a sigh, as irresistible as she was irrepressible.

The year following the war was a boom period for the California wine industry. Import tariffs on foreign wines made the California product more attractive in price, and two large co-operative ventures, the Anaheim Community and the Buena Vista Vinicultural Society, had attracted the attention of big-business interests. Grapes were one of the state's three major crops, and wine had become a big manufacturing product. Investors and immigrants began to flock to the state, lured by promises of easy profits and ideal grape-growing land.

Claude's one complaint was the rise to prominence of the northern vineyards in such areas as Sonoma and Napa counties, closer to San Francisco.

'They'll never produce the kind of wines we can produce here,' he stated flatly whenever the subject came up, which was often among the vintners. 'Los Angeles will remain the grape-growing center of the state. It isn't just the soil and the weather – there's San Francisco up there, already growing into a large city, and Sacramento – in time they'll crowd the vineyards out of existence, and growers will be flocking back to the Los Angeles area to get away from the sprawl of cities.'

Los Angeles, however, was not entirely free from the effects of the population boom; the city had grown to some five thousand residents, and now boasted not only a social life but a social elite of sorts. Speculators were beginning to talk of a land boom in the area, although Claude frankly scoffed at the suggestion.

'This is agricultural country,' he insisted, 'grape country. Los Angeles will remain a small town, mark my words.'

Refugees continued to arrive from Mexico, too, where the Mexican people were still trying to throw off the yoke of French rule.

'Maximilian will have to go,' Don Diego assured everyone. 'The emperor in France has too many problems of his own; he can't afford to support a puppet government halfway around the world.'

His opinion was generally respected; Louis Napoleon's iron grip on France seemed to be weakening. There were refugees from France, as well, who brought stories of new opposition to the emperor and attempts to remove him from power.

Most of these French refugees were wine people – growers, pickers, vintners – attracted by the growing success of the California wine industry. Most of them arrived hopeful but penniless, with little more than what they could carry.

Some, however, arrived in lavish carriages, their wealth sent ahead to the banks springing up overnight in Los Angeles.

'Someone's coming,' Mary squealed, yanking the curtains aside to peer out the window.

'Mary, get down from the furniture,' Danielle said.

'It's a carriage, with white horses,' Mary added, ignoring the admonition and jumping up and down excitedly on her grandmother's sofa.

Claude strode to the window and lifted his daughter to the floor, but to no avail; she as quickly leaped back onto the sofa.

'Who is it?' Anne asked. It was her birthday and the family had come to spend the afternoon. She was not sorry for the interruption, as she no longer derived pleasure from these annual reminders of her advancing years. She was fifty-three; her tawny hair had softened to a muted gray-gold and her figure had gradually assumed a matronly roundness, although Don Diego had told her the night before that she had never looked more beautiful.

'That could be taken two ways,' she had pointed out, but she enjoyed his flattery. Indeed, in the six years since they had married, Diego had never ceased to lavish both gifts and praise upon her. She had no regrets at having married him. She rarely thought of the distant past now, and when she did, it was with tenderness but without longing.

'That's the sheriff riding alongside,' Claude said, lifting Mary to the floor. This time she stayed down, rushing out the open door in the wake of her two oldest brothers, who had run out to the porch for a better look.

'Adam, Jean, mind your manners,' Danielle called. 'Mary, do stay on the porch; the horses might be skittish.'

Visitors were still a novelty, and by the time the carriage had rolled to a stop in the drive, virtually the entire family was on the porch; only David, still shy and aloof, remained inside, vanishing quietly from sight into Grandfather Diego's study, where he was allowed to read the books on the shelves so long as he put them back in their proper place.

Don Diego strolled graciously out to greet the sheriff, who had dismounted by this time, but the curiosity of the others was directed at the elegant carriage. Anne had seen nothing of its like since leaving France – indeed, she would have ventured a guess that this coach was imported from France.

A woman's voice said something from inside the carriage. The sheriff, in the act of greeting Don Diego with an oddly embarrassed manner, hurried back to open the carriage door.

'Who do you suppose it is?' Danielle wondered aloud.

'Some dignitary, apparently,' Anne said, 'from the way the sheriff's bowing and scraping.'

Although Anne thought she saw both a man and a boy inside the carriage, it was a woman who emerged alone, holding her satin skirt aloft so that it would not drag in the dust. She wrinkled her nose distastefully and made a shooing motion as one of the dogs ventured close for an exploratory sniff. A stick, flung by Adam, sent the dog off with his tail down, and the visitor came to stand near, although slightly behind, the sheriff.

'Sheriff, what can we do for you?' Don Diego greeted the visitors. 'I hope this is a social visit.'

'Actually, I'm afraid it's business,' the sheriff said. 'We'd like to talk to your wife, if we might.'

Danielle had been staring at the woman who had alighted from the carriage. What was it that was so familiar about her – that yellow hair; those eyes, catlike, cunning, cruel? Those eyes had confronted her before, mocking her, making her feel little and unimportant. But who? Where?

'*Mon Dieu,*' she murmured, reverting unconsciously to French for the first time in years. Suddenly the scene seemed to swim before her eyes as she was transported back in time. She was no longer on a porch in California; she was in France, climbing a tree with Claude and Marie, three foolish, happy children, mischievously trying to get a glimpse of their new neighbors.

'Antoinette.'

For a moment she thought the name had come unbidden to her lips; then she realized that it was not she but Claude who had made almost a groan of that name.

Danielle turned in dismay to her husband, but he no longer seemed aware of her presence; his attention was riveted on the woman in the drive. His eyes were wide, his skin had taken on a ghastly, ashen color as if he had seen a ghost.

And in a sense he had. The woman who had gotten down from the carriage was none other than Antoinette de Trémorel.

Anne, who had never seen the woman before, knew the name; it was infamous in her memory; and she needed only to glance at her son or his wife to know that this was the same Antoinette, the woman who had brought ruin on them, who had driven them from their homeland and separated her from Jean. A wave of hatred, hatred and fear, swept over her so that she might have fallen if her grandson, Adam, had not seen her sway and put a steadying hand on her arm.

Don Diego was ignorant of the visitor's identity, but he could not be unaware of the flood of emotion that had engulfed his wife and her family.

'Perhaps we had better go inside,' he said; to Claude, he said, 'The children . . . ?'

The children were dispatched to play on the patio; Mary had to be dragged away, kicking and screaming her objections, and David was nowhere to be seen. Don Diego ushered the sheriff and Antoinette into the house. Claude, moving as though in a daze, followed, leaving Anne and Danielle alone for a moment.

Danielle could hardly bring herself to enter the same room as that woman. What could she be doing here? How had she found them, so many thousands of miles from Epernay?

Anne seemed to have recovered from her shock and now her eyes flashed angrily. She took Danielle's arm, her fingers threatening to tear the flesh.

'Come,' she said, fairly dragging Danielle inside. 'This is no time to hold back.'

Don Diego was just offering the visitors some sherry. 'We need not offer this woman our hospitality,' Anne said coldly. 'Or if we must, let us give her what she deserves – the blade of a knife.'

Don Diego, startled by his wife's vehemence, hesitated, but Claude crossed the room in three long strides and, taking the bottle from Don Diego's hand, poured the wine, offering it to the visitors. Antoinette accepted hers with a nod and an enigmatic smile. The sheriff declined, and Claude drained the glass instead.

'Maybe we should talk in private,' the sheriff said, obviously not relishing whatever errand had brought him here.

'These are my family,' Anne said with a toss of her hair. 'Say what you have to say and be done with it.'

'Yes,' Antoinette agreed coolly. 'Let's get on with it.' Far from looking disconcerted, she looked as if she were enjoying herself immensely.

'It's about your husband, ma'am,' the sheriff said.

'About me?' Don Diego asked, surprised.

'No, sir.' The sheriff paused and cleared his throat uncomfortably. 'It's about – about the lady's French husband.'

'My former husband is dead,' Anne said.

'Begging your pardon, ma'am, but this woman seems to think . . . ' He hesitated, again clearing his throat and shifting his weight from one foot to the other. 'She says she's got proof that he's still alive.'

The glass of wine slipped from Don Diego's fingers and fell to the floor with a crash.

50

'What is this proof?' Anne asked. She had not turned her head when the glass broke nor looked away from the woman facing her.

'I have letters,' Antoinette said. She put her hand into the bag she carried and produced a packet of letters, handing them to the sheriff. He held them out toward Anne, but she ignored him. After a moment Claude came and took the letters.

'They are my letters to Jean,' Anne said; she had known the moment she saw them; had known, she thought, even before then. She stared across the room at the woman called Antoinette, and her hatred was like a living thing that danced between then, making the very air shudder with its force. 'How did you get them?'

'I know people,' Antoinette said. 'When I heard that he was a prisoner, that the letters had been kept from him, I asked if I could have them. I was coming to California; I said that I could return them to you, but of course I didn't know . . . I thought from these letters that you had remained faithful to his memory.'

Anne started and Claude, half-fearing that his mother might actually attack Antoinette, put out a restraining hand.

'These don't prove that my father is alive,' he said, managing finally to regain his own equilibrium, at least in part.

'I have another letter,' Antoinette said. 'From him to – to his wife.'

She brought an envelope from her purse. She would have handed it, too, to the sheriff, but Anne, flinging off her son's hand, strode toward her and snatched the envelope from her fingers. It was from Jean.

'I should like to be alone,' Anne said, turning her back on the others.

'Ma'am, we've got to talk . . . '

'Sheriff, even if this is true,' Don Diego said, 'my wife has committed no crime. The circuit court in Los Angeles declared her husband legally dead before she married me.'

'Is this true?' the sheriff asked of Anne's back.

She ignored him, but Claude answered for her, 'It's true. My wife and I were present in court; we can verify it.'

'If that's the case, it looks like I've wasted a trip out here,' the sheriff said, giving Antoinette an angry look. She looked not at all perturbed by the news; if anything, her smile was triumphant, Danielle thought.

'Ma'am, I'm sorry to have disturbed you. I guess we'd better be going now.' Anne's back remained turned toward him. He looked unhappily about the room, nodding to each of the others. 'I'm sorry,' he repeated.

He was almost to the door when Anne, still without turning, said, 'I'm grateful for any news of my – ' she paused, then said, ' – my husband . . . from whatever source.'

When they had gone out, Anne walked quickly to her bedroom. There, alone, she tore open the envelope. There were two letters inside, one, a brief note actually, from Jean, and the other, equally brief, from Marie.

She read Jean's first, shocked by the spidery-frail writing:

Dearest Anne,

At long last they have given me one of your letters to read – I say one because I judge from its content that it is only one of many [oh, which one, dear God, let it be one in which I said the right things, the gentle, loving things!]. I cannot adequately express what it meant to me after these long years of darkness, that light of your love. To know that you are in California, alive and well, and that soon we shall be together again – the dream that has sustained me, to come true at last.

They have given me permission to write to you, and the jailor tells me I shall be returned soon to Chateau Brussac. I was surprised to know that it still stood, that both it and I have withstood the ravages of the difficult years.

I have been in a fortress in the south of France, it hardly matters where, any place was hell without you – but when I am once again with you, there shall be all the heaven I desire.

Please God, it shall be soon. I am weak now, but know that I shall mend quickly in the air of our home, and trust that by the new year I shall be able to come to you. Until then I am your devoted husband,

Jean.

She read it again, and yet again, the tears making it difficult to decipher the scrawl. Finally she turned to the note from Marie.

Dear Mother,

Since Papa wrote to you, we have returned to Chateau Brussac – Papa, René and I. It is greatly changed, as we are also, I'm afraid, and none for the better. Papa is optimistic in making his plans to come to California, but I suspect it will take far longer than he plans in order to regain his strength. That he is alive at all is a miracle, I suppose. I have suggested that you come to him instead, but he is opposed to this. He does not say it, but the fact is, they have stripped him of everything but his pride, and he is afraid that will be taken from him too if you must come to him while he is a broken invalid, when he wishes to come to you as your husband, as you remember him. I do not think, however, that will ever be possible. Forgive me for speaking frankly; we have had little occasion for social niceties in the past few years.

It was signed simply, *Marie.*

Anne reread this note, too. How cold and unfeeling it seemed. Marie, dear child, what had they done to her? Sixteen years a prisoner, all her youth gone, stolen from her; to leave the world a mere girl, and return to it a woman, changed, embittered. And René – poor, sensitive René, how could he

ever have endured without someone to care for him? Anne's
heart ached within her to think what they must have suffered.

Diego came into the bedroom. He looked, for the first time
since she had known him, unsure of himself, frightened even.

'Anne,' he said, 'I – I didn't know.'

'You told me he was dead.'

'I thought – there was no word of him . . . ' his voice trailed
off helplessly.

'Can you honestly say there was no doubt in your mind that
he was dead – that you were certain of that?' she asked.

For a moment his eyes met hers. Then, unable to say what
she asked, he looked away. 'At least there are no legal entangle-
ments,' he said. 'You broke no laws in marrying me.'

'Didn't I?' she asked coldly. 'There are more laws than are
written in books, Diego.'

'Anne,' he started to say, coming toward her, but she put up
a hand to stop him.

'No,' she said. 'I mean to return to French Hills with the
children. I think that's best till this is resolved.'

'You are my wife.'

She shook her head. 'No. No matter what your laws or your
lawyers say, I am still the wife of the man who wrote this
letter, and now I must go to him.'

'And what about us? What's to become of our – our
marriage?'

'I don't know,' he said, a note of hopelessness in her voice.
'I just don't know.'

Claude had followed the sheriff and Antoinette to the porch.
The sheriff continued to his horse, but Antoinette paused at
the steps. She smiled at Claude as genially as if the ugly scene
inside hadn't just taken place.

'It's been a long time,' she said.

'Yes,' was all he could think to say.

'I suppose you had forgotten all about me.'

'No, Antoinette, I hadn't forgotten you,' he said.

For a long moment they regarded one another silently.
Then, seeing Danielle in the doorway behind him, she smiled
again, the same haunting smile he remembered from the past.
It gave him a feeling of déjà vu, as if he had stepped backward
in time. They were in the courtyard of her house, she was
smiling as she came into his arms . . . a woman, teaching a
young man his first lessons in love . . .

'I'm at the Union Hotel,' she said. 'Room 211, if you want to see me – it would be pleasant to talk over the old days.'

She left him standing there and went down the steps and to her carriage. He caught a glimpse of a man's arm, as the door was opened for her from inside – her husband, he supposed, or perhaps a lover – he could not imagine Antoinette without a man. She was a woman of strong needs; even then they had frightened him a little, even as they had scorched his soul.

He watched until the carriage had all but disappeared down the long lane. Then, ignoring his wife, he went to where his horse was grazing, unconcerned with the problems of humans. He saddled the beast quickly, and in a few moments he was mounted.

Danielle came hurrying down to him as he rode out of the corral. 'Claude,' she said on a pleading note; he did not answer but began to ride in the direction of the hills.

'Claude,' she called, running after him with tears in her eyes, 'I love you – I love you!'

He seemed not to hear. He rode faster, leaving her behind, and still she ran after him, sobbing now and crying loudly, 'I love you,' over and over, until he had disappeared over a hill, and at last she stumbled and fell to the ground, still sobbing softly to the earth, 'I love you.'

51

It seemed the middle of the night when Danielle was awakened by the gentle tapping at her door. She made a light and dressed hurriedly. Claude was already up and dressed, prepared to leave.

The weeks since the arrival of the news from France had been strained for all of them. Anne had moved back to French Hills and refused to discuss the matter with anyone, saying only that if she were not welcome here, she would go elsewhere, which had effectively silenced all discussion.

She and Claude had quarreled at first over her plans to leave at once for France. Claude was opposed to her making such a trip alone, but at the same time he did not favor taking so long a time away from his business to accompany her.

'Nor can I afford the expense,' he argued.

It was Don Diego who suggested a compromise. He had been plagued with guilt over what had seemed to be an innocent deception. Anne had refused to forgive him. Indeed, since she had moved back to French Hills, he had seen little of her, and on those few occasions she had refused even to discuss their own relationship.

'I must go to Jean,' was all she would say. 'I belong to him. Afterward – but who can say what will be afterward; I don't know.'

One thing was clear to him: He would have no wife and no marriage until this other business had been resolved. Though in the end it might mean that he would lose her, he was as impatient as any of them to see it concluded. Anything, he assured himself, would be better than allowing the present situation to go on.

For some years Claude had been trying to interest the state legislature in sending a commission to Europe to collect cuttings of all the best grape varieties and bring them back to distribute among the state's growers. The financing of the expedition had remained a stumbling block, as the state's revenues were at present not only somewhat limited but erratic. In their last session the lawmakers had decided to postpone the commission for another year until there was more money on hand for such an experimental venture.

Don Diego suggested that Claude, with some backing from Don Diego himself, undertake the financing of the venture, traveling to Europe and collecting cuttings throughout the continent. True, it would take most of Claude's savings, but the legislature could reimburse him when he returned in a year.

It would be easy to include the Ile-de-France district and Chateau Brussac on the itinerary, and Anne could remain there until Claude was ready to return home; by then she would no doubt have made up her mind as to what she wanted to do. Whatever she decided, Don Diego had promised that he would present no obstacles.

At first only Claude and Anne had planned to make the trip, but it had seemed such a golden opportunity for Adam to observe the vineyards and wine-making techniques of Europe that in the end it had been decided he should accompany his father.

'Still, I'm not entirely sure about leaving you to take care of everything on your own,' Claude said.

'There's nothing to worry about,' Danielle assured him. 'We'll manage perfectly well. Jean's already very capable, and Don Diego will be available to call on for help if I need it. And it's such a perfect opportunity for Adam to learn firsthand.'

'I suppose you're right.'

Danielle had hoped that Claude might find some time to speak openly about their own problems before he left, but the time for departure had come and he had made no effort in that direction.

'Claude, about Antoinette,' she started to say, but he interrupted her curtly.

'I don't want to talk about it,' he said, his face taking on that closed look that it did whenever she had tried to broach the subject, though their relations had deteriorated badly since Antoinette had stepped into their lives again. She could only guess at the nature and the depth of the struggle going on within him.

'But I really think perhaps we ought to . . .'

'Danielle, I'm afraid it's time to go. I'll just go along to Mother's room and see if she's ready. You won't be long, will you?'

'No,' she sighed. 'No, I'm all ready.'

She followed him to Anne's room, where Anne was already dressed in a traveling suit and waiting for them. Anne and Danielle exchanged hardly a word, as if in her mind Anne had already dismissed those remaining behind and had fixed her gaze on what lay before her.

Though she would not have admitted as much to her husband, Danielle dreaded the thought of his being gone so long. Yet in a sense she felt that Claude had already left her; she could only hope that when he returned, it would be in spirit as well as in body.

Now, in the coolness before the dawn, they crept through the house by the flickering light of the single candle Danielle had brought. The house seemed to watch and listen and wonder. Here, where there had been happiness, was now anguish, fear and resentment, so that Danielle found herself wondering that the coming of one woman should have changed the entire nature of the house, as one bad odor will spoil an otherwise sweet room.

Once outside, they moved more briskly. The carriage was

ready. One of the servants would accompany them to Los Angeles, where they would board a coach later in the day. Although the railroad companies were hard at work on the finishing stretches of the transcontinental railroad, it was not yet possible to make the entire overland journey by rail.

Still, compared to the last journey they had made, this one would be simple indeed, even luxurious. They would travel by stagecoach as far as Kansas City, at the rate of some one hundred miles a day, in relative comfort and safety; from Kansas City trains would carry them to New York, where they would board a ship for France.

It hardly seemed possible that they had advanced so far from the wagon trains in so short a time.

The sky had begun to turn gray with the approaching dawn. In its pallid light Danielle could not help but observe the effects of the strain under which they had all been living. Their faces looked white and drawn as they approached the carriage.

One of the servants had set a lighted lantern on the ground and Claude took it up, so that they were able to walk more easily, but still with a guilty silence.

The horses stamped their feet a trifle petulantly at being called upon at such an odd hour, when they were accustomed to sleep.

Hardly a word was spoken among the group, except that Claude remembered some detail regarding the winery, which he passed on to Danielle. Danielle clasped her son to her for a moment, and she and Anne embraced briefly. Claude and Danielle exchanged a kiss, and it was done.

The travelers entered the carriage. The horses broke into a trot, and the light from the carriage sped over the broken ground like a will-o'-the-wisp. It dipped beyond a hillock and Danielle was left alone in the lane with the lantern in her hand.

After a moment the coach reappeared in the distance. It pulled up at the summit of the hill and, looking back, those in it must have seen her lantern and realized she had not yet returned to the house. The lamp was taken from the carriage and waved up and down three times as a farewell. Then they were truly gone.

Finally Danielle ceased to stare after them and, turning away, went along the lane toward home.

Claude had arranged their schedule so that there was time to spare in Los Angeles. He had made up his mind to visit

Antoinette. The decision filled him with guilt, and yet he had known, from the moment at French Hills when she had told him where she was staying, that the visit was inevitable. He had been able to think of nothing else since then. He knew that he had been unfair to his wife; he knew well enough the cause of the pain that was constantly in her eyes, despite her efforts to conceal it from him, but he could not help himself.

It did not occur to him that Antoinette might not wish to see him just then; if he were prepared to risk the loss of all he used to hold dear, surely she should not complain of a little inconvenience.

She seemed, however, neither disappointed nor surprised to find him at her door. Indeed, she looked as if she had been sitting waiting for him, although it had been several weeks since her offhand invitation.

She was not alone; a young man, who looked to be about Adam's age, was in the room with her. He was a handsome youth, with a promise already of that sort of devilish good looks that women so often find irresistible.

'Richard,' Antoinette said, 'why don't you go down to the lobby for a while. Mister de Brussac and I would like to talk.'

The boy went out, but not before he had given Claude a look that was surely too knowledgeable for a boy of his age. It embarrassed Claude and made him feel ill at ease when he was finally alone with Antoinette.

'Your son?' he asked.

'Yes,' she said and then, seeing from his suddenly startled expression the question that had occurred to him, she laughed and added, 'No, he isn't related to you.'

He was embarrassed again at having been so transparent. 'You're married, then, I take it,' he said.

'After a fashion.'

'Do I know the lucky fellow?'

'I'm sure you must – he was from the same part of France. François Homais – do you remember him?' The knowing smile was playing with the corners of her mouth, as it had in the past whenever she had been teasing him.

'François! You must be joking,' he said. His eyes swept the room as if he half-expected to find his old enemy hidden in a corner.

'I assure you, my marriage is hardly a joke. And you needn't look around like that; he isn't here, nor is he likely to be for a while.'

'How could you?' he demanded, angry out of all proportion. 'How could you marry that bully, that horse thief?'

Her eyes suddenly flashed angrily and the smile vanished from her lips. 'You've a lot of room to talk, haven't you, married to your peasant wife. At least I had plenty of reasons for what I did. My brother was . . . was dead, and you were gone. I was so alone, and so frightened. I'd always had someone to manage things for me. And then when you escaped, I was sure you would come to me, and I waited and waited, believing that you loved me, only to find that you had run off with . . . with that wench. You can't imagine how alone and abandoned I felt.'

She suddenly covered her face with her hands and began to cry noisily, her shoulders heaving. 'And then he came to me,' she said through her fingers. 'He – he forced himself on me. I didn't know what to do, I was so lost, so unhappy, and he was strong, he . . . I was afraid of him, if you want to know the truth, but there wasn't anyone else to turn to. And then when I found I was going to have his child, I . . . ' she choked and could not go on for crying.

'Antoinette,' he said helplessly. He struggled with himself, wanting to take her in his arms and comfort her, and knowing that if he did so he would be lost.

'Antoinette.' He moved toward her, but at once she put her hand out between them.

'No,' she said. 'I – I couldn't control myself if you – if you did that, not just now.' She found a handkerchief and dabbed at her eyes.

'Anyway,' she went on, calmer now, 'we had to leave France. The political situation there is unsettled, Louis Napoleon is losing favor with the people, and those we relied upon for protection were suddenly ineffectual. It seemed best to go, and François had heard there were fortunes to be made here in California. Of course I thought right away of you. I only wanted to see you again . . . '

'How did you get my father's letters?'

'Someone I knew – Louise, the Marquise de Marcheval – you remember, you met her once – I don't know how she got them, but she let it slip that she had, and I begged her, I insisted that she give them to me; I thought it would give me an excuse to see you. I never dreamed you had actually married that girl. And when I knew, oh, I got angry. I'm sorry, it was horrid of me, the way I handled it, but you can't think how long I had dreamed of seeing you again. I know what happened between us was nothing to you, just a young man's adventure, but it had been so much to me, it was my comfort through all these lonely years – can you forgive me?'

'It'll be far harder to forgive myself,' he said. He glanced at his watch. 'I must go. We're leaving for France.'

'So quickly?' she said. 'And will you come to see me when you return?'

'If you're here,' he said.

He went to the door and paused. She hadn't moved from where she had been, but her tears had ended as quickly as they had begun, and now she was smiling her haunting smile again. Incredibly, she was as beautiful as she had been before; the years seemed hardly to have touched her. And, just as incredibly, he felt himself to be the same gangly, inexperienced novice that he had been then. He wanted to kiss her and didn't know if he dared or even how she would welcome such a move.

'Well, goodbye,' he said, a bit awkwardly.

'*Au revoir*,' she said. She blew him a kiss from across the room, and after that it would have been clumsy indeed to have gone back to kiss her properly. He let himself out, and she heard his footsteps disappearing down the hall.

A moment later the connecting door to the next room opened and François joined her, coming to give her the kiss she had not gotten from Claude.

It was probable, she thought, that Claude might actually have passed François in the corridor and not known him; he had changed a great deal. François was still handsome, she thought, but leaner, harder-looking. He had acquired a brittle sort of sophistication that sat well on him and did not quite conceal the ruffian underneath. Women invariably found him attractive.

Only one thing had not changed about his appearance: His eyes were as hard and cruel as they had always been. Even when he made love, which he still did expertly, although not as often as she might have liked, his eyes never lost that vicious glint.

'I assume you were listening?' she asked.

'I nearly came through and put this in his back, just for the hell of it,' he said, taking a knife from his pocket and clicking the blade into view.

'You tried once before to deal with him your way,' she said, 'and it didn't work. Leave the de Brussacs to me; I'll deal with them. Anyway, it's my revenge, isn't it?'

François rubbed his jaw as if recalling the long-ago feel of Claude's fists. 'I've got a score or two to settle,' he said. He began to clean his fingernails with the tip of the knife blade. 'What do you plan on doing?'

'I don't know – oh, you needn't look so angry; I don't intend to sleep with him. But I will deal with him, never fear.'

He grinned, revealing his even, white teeth. 'You really hate him, don't you?'

Her eyes glinted as viciously as his. 'He killed the one person I loved more than anyone else in the world,' she said. 'If I have to follow him to the ends of the earth, I'll make him pay for that.'

François came to her suddenly and seized her in a rough embrace, pulling her hair and forcing her head back until she was staring up into his face.

'What about me?' he asked, grinning cruelly. 'Do you mean to say you don't love me?'

She laughed, a reckless, throaty sound. 'Love you?' she asked in her most teasing manner. 'But my sweet, I adore you passionately.'

Though she spoke in a joking manner, what she said was true. Despite the hatred and bitterness that drove her, despite the serpentine twists of character that made her the cruel and dangerous creature that she was, she had yet one redeeming feature: She was able to love, utterly and unreservedly, with a depth of feeling that went far beyond the worth of its object. Once she had loved her brother that way. In the years since she had loved this hard, brutal man who held her now in such a cruel embrace. Though in every other way she was utterly selfish, vain and grasping, for this man she would have made any sacrifice, even laid down her life.

It was lovely, this ability to love so completely, all the more lovely because it bloomed like a single, glorious rose in the dank garden of her perversity.

For a moment François looked as if he might use his knife on her. Then, suddenly, he laughed. She laughed with him and he lowered his mouth to kiss her bared throat, leaving little marks with his teeth.

Their son came in while they were making love, but it did not interrupt them. The boy was accustomed to the sight and rarely paid much attention anymore.

52

Although she had tried to prepare herself, the actual sight of Chateau Brussac was a shock to Anne. The gates stood open, one of them hanging askew from a rusted hinge, the stone gateposts crumbling and overgrown with vines. The drive itself was weed-choked and almost obliterated in places.

The house was a ruin of what it had been – crumbling walls, broken shutters, weeds run rampant everywhere. There had been a fire sometime in the past, and a great black hole still gaped like an open wound in one part of the roof. Except for a tendril of smoke that rose from a broken chimney, the place would have looked uninhabited.

They had written ahead from Paris to say that they were coming, lest the shock of their arrival prove too much for Jean. As the carriage that Claude had rented pulled up, a woman came out of the front door and down the broad steps. At first Anne did not recognize her; not until she had clambered down from the carriage and started toward the woman waiting by the steps did she realize that she was seeing her own daughter.

'Marie,' she said, and knew that she had not kept the shock from her voice.

'Hello, Mother,' Marie said in a voice that was flat and unenthusiastic. When she spoke, one saw that three of her teeth were missing in front, but it was not only this that made her look so old; her hair, once a lovely chestnut color, was gray and limp looking, and her face was haggard, her eyes the eyes of one who has looked too long on a world too unpleasant to bear watching. Her cheap, tattered dress and her peasant's shoes made Anne feel suddenly ashamed of her own elegant dress and the expensive carriage they had rented in Paris.

Anne had meant to embrace her daughter, but this austere stranger staring at her without affection or even interest did not invite such intimacy.

'Hello, Marie,' Claude said. He felt no less at a loss than his mother did; Marie gave him a long, measuring look before she finally answered.

'Hello,' she said. 'It's been a long time.' The way she said it sounded almost like an accusation.

'This is Adam,' Anne said, trying to smooth them over this first awkward moment, 'Claude's oldest son. Adam's going to be a vintner like his father, and his grandfather.'

She sounded even to her own ears as if she was babbling, but she couldn't help herself; Marie's unexpected appearance had only made the nervousness she had already been experiencing that much worse. She wished . . . but what was there to wish for? Nothing could be changed from the way it had been. And anyway, it wasn't her fault; that was what she longed to cry out – it wasn't her fault, what had happened those many years ago; she wasn't to blame.

'Come in,' Marie said abruptly. 'Things aren't particularly comfortable, but there's no shortage of room, as you'll recall. There's no help, of course, but I cleaned as best I could.'

'You shouldn't have troubled,' Anne said lamely. 'We could have made do.'

Marie gave her a peculiar look, that was impossible to read. 'This is a homecoming, isn't it?' she said. 'It isn't every day one is reunited with one's family. Especially after so many years.'

'I never – we never stopped thinking of you, or trying to find out what had happened,' Anne said. 'No one could tell us anything. You seemed to have just vanished . . . but we did try.'

'Yes, I know that you did,' Marie said, in an almost indifferent voice, as though none of this mattered very much. More briskly, she said, 'I've made up your old room, Claude; I thought you might like that. And there's the little room next to it, your son can sleep there.'

She turned her lifeless eyes on Anne again. 'Papa is in your room; it was where he wanted to be, but you can have his old room.'

Anne, who had wondered privately about those arrangements, was not entirely happy to learn that they had already been resolved for her, but she did not object.

'And René?' she asked, making her voice as bright as possible. 'Where is René? Isn't he here?'

Marie was a long time in answering. They were at the door to Claude's room before she said, as if it explained everything, 'René sleeps in the attic.'

'Let's go up and see him,' Claude said with an artificial

cheerfulness in his voice as well. 'I've missed –'

'No,' Marie said, in a suddenly stern manner; it was the first real emotion she had displayed since their arrival. 'René is – very frightened of people. You must wait until he decides to come to you. If he does,' she added.

Claude gave his mother a despairing look, but Marie had already started along the hall, and with a quick shrug and a shake of her head, Anne followed her.

Jean's old room seemed little changed, perhaps a little mustiness in the air, but that was to be expected, surely. She half-expected to see Jean standing before the mirror, shaving. His presence was so real in the room that for a moment it frightened her.

'I've fixed dinner,' Marie was saying. 'It won't be very good, I'm afraid, I'm not much of a cook, but it will do, I suppose.'

'Marie,' Anne said, impulsively seizing her daughter's hands in her own. But to her dismay, Marie looked down at their hands as if the contact made her uncomfortable. Embarrassed, Anne let her fingers slide away.

'I know it must have been horrible for you,' she said, wishing she knew how to get beyond the wall that was between them; she really had come for a reunion, to see not only her husband but her daughter and son as well, and instead here she was with a stranger – a rather frightening stranger. 'I'm sorry,' was all she could think of to say.

'It wasn't your fault,' Marie said. 'I don't blame you. None of us does.'

'But you – you've changed so,' Anne said before she could stop herself.

What was almost a smile passed over Marie's lips. 'That's to be expected, isn't it?' Anne did not reply, and after a pause, Marie said, as if answering her earlier question, 'It was awful at first. They took us to a fortress in the south, René and me. We didn't see Papa. It's funny, but he was in the same place, the whole time, and we never saw him until just before we were freed. Sometimes they let René and me go into the courtyard, but Papa was kept in a cellar. I don't think they ever let him out.'

'If it bothers you to speak of it –' Anne said helplessly.

'But it doesn't; not at all.' She paused. 'The soldiers used me for their whore,' she went on. 'I cried a lot at first, but after a while I began to learn which of them were the gentlest and which of them the others were afraid of, and who would do us favors in return or bring us gifts.'

She paused again; it was a long moment before she said, 'After that, it wasn't quite as bad.'

Anne bit her lip; she could think of nothing more horrible than the matter-of-fact way in which Marie had made her remarks; more than anything else, that sickened her, for more than anything else, it told of how the girl, little more than a child at the time, had been crushed by the weight of her imprisonment.

She knew that some remark was expected of her, and she was ashamed to be any less strong than her daughter had had to be.

'At least you are all alive,' she said.

'When you learn to do what must be done, you can generally survive,' Marie said. Then, with that abrupt change of manner that she had, she said, 'You'll want to see Papa. I'll tell him you're here, if you'll just give me a minute to prepare him.'

At the door she turned back. 'About René,' she said. 'He's never really recovered from the shock. I don't suppose he ever will. He may not know you.'

'Did they – did they treat him so badly?' Anne asked.

'He was so young,' Marie said. 'So young, and so pretty, like a little angel. The soldiers made him their whore, too. Soldiers aren't very particular.'

It was dark in the room that had once been her bedroom. The curtains were drawn so that Anne could hardly see the bed, let alone the figure in it. She crept across the room, thinking that he might be asleep, he was so quiet, half-hoping that he would be and that this meeting could be postponed for at least a little while. Her emotions had already suffered so many shocks, and she had wanted to be at ease when she saw Jean, not distraught and uncomfortable as she was.

'Anne?' It was a mere croak.

'Jean – it is I,' she replied. She came around the bed – how many nights had she lain in this bed, wrapped in the comfort of his arms – moving slowly. A hand stretched out, reaching for her, and she put hers into it, letting it guide her closer.

'You have come back to me,' he said, coughing slightly as if words were a novelty to him. 'I told them – a love to last the ages . . .'

She had tried to prepare herself for it, but not even her worst fears had prepared her for the shock of seeing him.

It was not Jean in the bed, smiling tremulously at her, his eyes straining to penetrate the gloom; it was a stranger, a shrunken shell of a man, old, older than she could have imagined. It was not the oldness of years alone, it was the look of a man who has come through hell and lived to remember.

'Lean down,' he whispered. 'Let me just see your face.'

She leaned obediently over him, trying not to let the shock, the dismay, show. Oh, Jean, Jean, she cried within herself, what did they do to you, to you all, my husband, my daughter, my son, all gone, gone in a way they could never have been in a mere grave.

He made a strange rattling sound in his throat that she realized with horror was meant to be a laugh of pleasure.

'Still beautiful,' he murmured, his hand dropping from hers to the bed, 'just as I dreamed. And still my own.'

The voice rose on the end, making a question of it. She stared, seeing not only the old man on the bed but another man as well; younger, splendid in his strength and his pride, passionate, bold, unbending.

She saw another figure too, cloaked in a shroud and with one bony hand upon her beloved's brow. She was glad at least that she had come; Jean would never have come to her. She had barely come in time.

'Yes, my darling,' she said, glad now for the dim light that would conceal her tears, 'I am still yours.'

53

The sound was familiar now. The first night, soon after they had come, it had terrified Anne, plagued as she was already by other ghosts, but now she knew it for what it was, and while it caused her profound anguish, there was no fear.

She got out of bed, hurrying on bare feet to the door, and opened it a crack. As she did so, she saw the door of Adam's room, across the hall, inch open.

She slipped from her room and across to Adam's. 'It's all right,' she whispered, coming in to stand beside him. 'Don't be frightened.'

'I thought it was a ghost,' Adam said.

'No, it's nothing ghostly.' She watched through the crack of the doorway, seeing the little circle of light from the single candle coming slowly closer.

At first she had not even recognized her wedding gown, it had been so long since she had worn it; and it was now tattered and yellow with age, hanging loosely on the thin figure; the veil, once sewn with jewels that had since been ripped loose, half-covered the face, leaving only the vague eyes exposed and adding to the ghostlike quality.

'My sons, my sons, where are my sons?' The voice seemed to come from nowhere, disembodied, haunting. The apparition glided noiselessly along the corridor, the candle held aloft, the eyes staring, unseeing.

Beside Anne, Adam's shivering increased; she would have to try to explain, but not here, not now.

They heard footsteps hurrying from below; in a moment Marie came into view. She intercepted the apparition.

'René,' she said, taking his arm firmly, 'it's Marie.'

'My sons, where are my sons?' René's eyes seemed to stare through her. For a moment his wandering gaze turned upon the door behind which Anne and Adam huddled. Anne had a horrible feeling that those eyes were seeing through the darkness, staring directly at her. She shuddered involuntarily.

'Come along,' Marie was saying, piloting him deftly back toward the stairs that led to the attic. 'You must go back to bed, it's cold here.'

He went with her without a protest, a child-wraith cloaked in tattered splendor. The light faded and was gone.

'It's over,' Anne breathed at last. 'And you must go back to bed, too. He won't come back now; not tonight.'

'That's my uncle, isn't it?' Adam asked. 'That's René.'

'Yes,' she said, and then to forestall any further questions she kissed his forehead quickly and gave him a shove toward the bed. 'Go to bed now, and don't be frightened; he won't harm you.'

She waited until he was in bed before she stole quickly and quietly back to her own room, where she lay awake staring at the ceiling.

Claude was out. It was the second time since their arrival four months before that he had stayed away, this time for two days. He had come back before disheveled and smelling of cheap perfume. She knew that he was being unfaithful to

Danielle, but she did not know what, if anything, she could or should do about it. It was better, she thought, to let him sort things out in his own way.

At any rate, she had problems enough of her own, and she hadn't fared particularly well at managing them. She felt as if she had returned to a household of phantoms. Nothing was quite familiar to her, nothing seemed quite real. She tried to grasp hold of things – Jean, the children, the past – but they all eluded her. Jean was dying; she could only hope that her coming had brought him some comfort. Marie remained distant, as unreachable as before. René did not know her at all; René lived in his attic and his fantasies, where he could no longer be reached or hurt.

She had roamed the house, the vineyards, she had even gone to the river to watch the water, yellow, violet and blue, where it ran beneath the bridge. She remembered that here Jean had killed a man for her sake, and they had flung his body into the river; but it was like something that had happened to another woman, a story she had read and been moved by, but that did not actually involve her.

And René – had Jean ever accepted his son without that faint look of doubt in his eyes? Or did he look at him at all now? Certainly he had not since they had been here.

She had gone too far, she supposed, to come back; or perhaps there was nothing for her to come back to. Her children were gone from her, gone with the past, gone with her youth.

It was nearly dawn. Restlessly she slipped from bed and went to the window. The trees were purple stains against the gray of the sky. She heard a horse's hooves, growing louder as they came nearer. It was Claude, returning at last.

Lest he think she was watching for him, she returned to bed, but still sleep, like the phantoms of her past, eluded her.

Claude had been to Paris. He was tired and felt soiled with more than mere sweat and dirt. He could still smell the acrid animal smell of the cheap whore he had lain with. She had unburdened his loins, but not his soul.

Seeing Antoinette again had precipitated a crisis in his life. He was thirty-five. Most of his adult life had been occupied with building a new life in America for himself, his mother, Danielle; with raising his family and building French Hills into a winery of which future generations of de Brussacs could be proud. He had been busy, and occupation had passed for happiness.

He loved Danielle – how could one not love her, so gentle, so loyal and devoted – and occupied as he had been, he had been satisfied.

But he had forgotten that love – and loving – were more than merely being satisfied. He had forgotten what it was to burn with passionate desire, to abandon oneself to sensual lust. It suddenly seemed to him now that he had missed something, he was not quite sure what: thrills, ardors, aches and pleasures – a young man's aches and pleasures. Behind the closed doors of his life, beyond the industry and efficiency he presented to the world, he sensed an emptiness – doors, and more doors, and somewhere locked deep inside was himself.

His love for Danielle had been no fit of passion. Their mutual dilemmas, mutual needs, their unique intimacy had brought them together in a way that could never have happened otherwise. Since fleeing France they had eaten the same meals, talked the same special language, breathed the same sometimes dangerous air. She had never known romance and had been ripe for it; he had been hot with the heat of adventure. It had been so natural to take her in his arms, to share that heat with her.

He had rarely thought of his age. He had been too active and too young, and somehow he had been vaguely sure that he would remain young.

Now he looked back upon those years that should have been golden and saw them as gray instead. They appeared to him now as a wasteland, barren from lack of a passion that might have made them glow, passion that was shared and joyous and free.

He had spent a third of his life stilling the clamoring voices of sensuality within himself, only to find the stillness suddenly frightening.

Alone in his room, in the grayness of the dawn, he tried to wash away the traces of the whore. He had not set out to find her. What he had set out to find, he supposed, was Antoinette.

But Antoinette was in California.

And so was Danielle.

54

Jean needed no doctors to tell him that he was dying. He did not especially mind. He had lived through the long, dark years of imprisonment on one wish, one dream, and that had been granted him with Anne's arrival. He had seen her again; that was enough. And if that couldn't cure his sickness, the doctors be damned.

Once he had looked across his life and searched for some meaning, and found nothing. But his life had changed since then, and he thought that after all he had found the one thing that did matter. He had found love.

He had not set out to find it, not consciously at least; it had seemed rather to find him. Nor did he know what it was exactly. Certainly not what he had once called by that name, and not the sexual wrestling of the past, although it was in that too; but somewhere in his experience with the woman who sat by the bed now, reading aloud to him (as she had once read aloud to her dying father, he recalled), there had come unawares an essence, a groping of souls toward one another in this darkness that was existence, a touching of two lives, briefly, faintly – and in that moment had come something eternal, something at one with the universe, with every man, with what was and had been and would be.

She paused in the reading, and he opened his eyes to find her looking down at him, in her eyes a sadness and a tenderness.

He was suddenly moved to say, 'This man, the one in California – is he a good man?'

She looked startled by the question. 'You knew?' she asked.

He chuckled, that rasping cough of a sound that more than anything else reminded her how near the end was for him.

'There was a woman who came, before I was released. She told me . . . all sorts of things.'

'I was – so alone,' she said falteringly. 'And he, Diego, he was kind, and gentle. They told me you were dead.'

'And so I was, to you,' he said. 'And so I shall be. Soon it won't matter, my love; I won't keep you long, I think. And it is enough that you came to me. It was all I could wish for, more than I dared hope for.'

'Oh, Jean,' she said, throwing herself across his weak, thin body, 'I wanted to be so much to you.'

'And you were,' he murmured, patting her consolingly. 'You were my life, the better part of it. What we have had, and what we have been – so much is mine, I will take it with me wherever I go. As for the rest, give it to him, with my blessing.'

She lay in his arms as she had so long ago and wept – for him, and for herself, and for all that they had known and would know no more.

She was hardly aware when the hand on her shoulder ceased its comforting pats, nor did she hear the last, halting intake of breath. She only knew, when she lifted her head once more to speak to him, that he was beyond hearing.

AUGUST 8, 1869
PARIS, FRANCE

My Dear Wife,

Is it really possible that sixteen months have passed since I left California? I tell you in all sincerity, I had not dreamed our mission would take so long. The lengthy delay of Father's illness, followed by his death, and the attendant settling of affairs there gave us rather a tardy start on the other purpose of our trip. I visited your mother's grave, by the by, and left some flowers there.

Since leaving the chateau Adam and I have been busy, traveling here and there, collecting samples of the best vines from each region. We have visited all the prominent wine countries except Hungary, and as the time has grown so long, I have resolved that we shall forgo that journey and start home instead as soon as all my purchases are assembled and have been shipped to California.

To be frank, I am weary with the traveling, although Adam seems inexhaustible. Your son, Madame, has acquired fresh knowledge at every stop to add to his already encyclopedic information. His knowledge at such a young age has been a source of amazement to many a vintner, and I have taken much pride in him, as I know you also would have done.

Mother has remained at the chateau with Marie and René, but I think she, too, will be glad to start for California. We extended the invitation to Marie and René (or rather, to Marie, for both of them, as René is frankly unable to grasp such a

*simple question as this) to return to California with us, but the
invitation was declined. Marie feels that she has no inclination
at this point in life to begin yet another life in a new world,
and would be more content to remain where she is. Accordingly, we have transferred the London monies to a bank here
so that she may have access; they should provide well enough,
as her expenses are not great.*

*I have another reason for wishing to return soon to Cali-
fornia, as I hear that the legislature will convene in January
and that it is expected to be a short session. It seems I have
spent us nearly bankrupt on the purchase of vines, the cost of
which somewhat exceeded my initial expectations, and I am
eager to present the results of my efforts to these august gentlemen and especially to obtain reimbursement.*

*And, of course, I am eager to see you, and the children.
I fear that my little princess will have grown quite beyond
recognition. Pray her not to forget her devoted father.*

> *Your fond husband,*
> *Claude*

Danielle finished reading the letter aloud. Her daughter, Mary,
sighed petulantly and said, 'Daddy's never coming home, I just
know it.'

'Hush,' Danielle said sharply, removing her spectacles from
her nose.

'Don't be silly,' Jean, quite the man of the house now at
fourteen, told his sister. 'He says right there in the letter he's
starting back soon.'

'He says January,' Mary argued, 'and that's months and
months away, after Christmas even. And that means we won't
have any Christmas presents probably.' Her pretty face suddenly took on a look of dismay as she contemplated this
particular tragedy.

'It will be enough of a Christmas present if your father is
home by then,' Danielle said.

To herself she wondered if that would be soon enough for
Claude to effect some miracle and save the drought-blistered
French Hills vineyards.

It was the second year of the drought that had hit the state,
particularly the southern regions, and nowhere had the
scorched earth taken a greater toll than in the area's vineyards.
The roots of the grape vines dug deep into the soil, but not
even they could reach the sinking water table. Danielle had

spent virtually all the money Claude had left them to hire workmen to carry water by hand to the vineyards, but as water supplies throughout the region had grown increasingly scarce, the cost of this operation had soared until the money had run as dry as the wells.

The channel that Don Diego and Claude had dug soon after their arrival here brought a trickle of water down from the hills. Each day Danielle and the children labored to carry this to the fields, but it was far too little, and each day she had watched their once-prosperous fields die a little more.

With an effort Danielle roused herself from her unpleasant reverie. 'Jean, David, hitch up the horses,' she said. 'Mary, do stop carrying on about Christmas in the middle of the summer.'

Don Diego had taken a spill from his horse a few weeks before and had been confined since with a broken foot; she had promised on her last visit to bring the children to see him. She knew how lonesome he was with Anne gone.

'There's nothing to do at Don Diego's,' Mary complained.

'It seems to me you find as much mischief to get into there as you do here,' Danielle said.

'All she does is boss everybody around anyway,' Jean grumbled, for which Mary stuck her tongue out at him when her mother wasn't looking.

'You'd better take the gun, Mama,' David said.

'I suppose you're right, although God knows I'd never hit the broad side of a barn.'

'I'll get it,' Jean cried, dashing for the house. 'If anyone tries to bother us, I'll shoot him.'

The prolonged drought had been a particularly severe hardship for the smaller farmers, and many of them, their crops burned up, their land turned into fields of dust, had taken to the road, as the expression went. It was not unusual to see entire families trudging along the dusty roads, their possessions strapped on wagons or carts. Sometimes they stopped at the farms and ranches along the way, begging food or water, or sometimes looking for work. Whenever they came to French Hills, Danielle tried to find something to give them, but her own supplies were already dangerously low, and there was no money to replace them or pay for work.

There were others on the road who did not beg for what they wanted or needed but took it, too often at the end of a gun. Although the outlaw bands that had once infested the mountains had been wiped out, these new highwaymen were hardly less dangerous for the unwary traveler.

Still, the road that ran between French Hills and the Rancho de Torres was not heavily traveled and Danielle had heard of no such attacks in this vicinity. With the gun on the seat beside her, she felt secure enough making the trip to Don Diego's.

For all her complaining, Mary outdid everyone in her delight at seeing Don Diego. In truth, he spoiled her as outrageously as her father did. The buggy had hardly stopped moving before she jumped to the ground and ran squealing to his arms, to be picked up and whirled about over his head.

'Don Diego, do be careful of your foot,' Danielle called. 'Jean, see to the horses, won't you?'

David had already hurried off to exchange his own more somber greetings with the older man, who was his favorite, too. Don Diego's library was always open to him, as David was a heavy reader, and Don Diego was always ready for a serious discussion of this or that idea gleaned from the pages of the books.

'Old sober-sides,' Jean called his brother, but David paid little if any attention to such criticisms; he was, Danielle thought, sometimes a bit anxiously, a particularly private person. It was impossible to know just what David was thinking; but he was a gentle and considerate boy, and if one discounted a personality particularly sober for a boy of his years, it was difficult to find anything to complain about in him.

Don Diego was glad to see them. He and Danielle had become rather good friends over the years; he was something of a father figure to her, just as she reminded him of the daughter he would have liked to have had. She shared Claude's letter with him; when she finished reading it aloud, she looked up to find Don Diego staring into the distance with a profound sadness.

'You still haven't heard from Anne?' she asked.

He sighed and shook his head. 'Not a word. I don't know if she will ever forgive me for what she considers my deception.'

'I'm sure she'll come back to you,' Danielle said, trying to boost his spirits; inwardly, though, she was not so sure. Claude's mother could be frightfully stubborn once she made up her mind to something. In her own way Anne was as private a person as little David; in the end she would do exactly what she wanted to do.

Danielle had hoped to ask Don Diego for help, but the sight of his vineyards, even more drought-wasted than her own, discouraged her, and she remained silent about their plight.

It was late when they started for home. Mary quickly fell asleep in Jean's protective embrace; David sat quietly beside his mother, occupied as usual with his own thoughts.

They were nearly home and had just rounded a curve in the road when Danielle saw something in the roadway before them. At first she could not make out what it was, but as they drew nearer, the bright moonlight revealed a body lying in the roadway and someone else kneeling over him. As the horses approached, the kneeling figure rose.

'It may be a robbery,' David said in a low voice.

Danielle hesitated; it was entirely possible that a robbery was taking place; or this might be nothing more than a ruse to trick unwary travelers into stopping so that they could then be robbed. But it was also possible that whoever was lying in the road might genuinely be ill and in need of assistance. She slowed the horses to a walk, watching the standing figure apprehensively.

'Why, it's only a boy,' she exclaimed when they were closer. She reined the horses to a stop and the boy came around to the driver's side.

'*Por favor, señora,*' he greeted her anxiously, '*mi padre* – my father – he is, how do you say, *enfermo.*'

'Sick,' Danielle said, handing the reins to David and clambering down from the buggy. 'What's wrong with him?'

The boy, who looked to be about David's age, burst into a string of Spanish, the gist of which, so far as she could determine, was that his father hadn't eaten in several days.

The man lying unconscious in the roadway was probably not much older than she herself, Danielle thought, but hardships and improper diet had made an aged skeleton of him. He roused himself slightly at her efforts, but he was too weak even to sit unaided and seemed unable to comprehend who she was or what had happened to him.

'We'll have to take him home with us,' Danielle said. '*Mi casa,*' she said to the boy, who had watched her with some trepidation while she bent over his father. He looked a little doubtful at first. There was a proud tilt to his chin, and she guessed that he was reluctant to have to accept charity, but in the end consideration for his father's condition outweighed pride. The boys helped her get the older man to the buggy and, crowded tightly together, they set out again for French Hills.

'How are we going to feed them?' David asked in a whisper. 'There isn't enough for us, is there?'

'We'll manage somehow,' Danielle assured him, although she wasn't certain just how.

55

For the next few days the boy and his father remained at French Hills; although Danielle offered them room in the house itself, they insisted on sleeping in the barn.

The boy was José Perreira, and his father was Manuel. They had worked for a rancher to the south who had finally had to abandon his drought-seared land. Since then José and his father had been wandering from ranch to ranch, refusing handouts and trying to find someone who would or could pay them for a few days' work. Two or three days before Danielle had found them – the boy wasn't sure now just how long it had been – they had worked for a farmer in exchange for some soup to eat, but the father had insisted that José eat most of his share, too.

They had nothing but the clothes on their backs; José's mother had died when he was an infant, and Manuel had cared for his son alone since then. Apparently they had fared well enough until recently.

It was apparent, too, that the father had instilled a strong sense of pride in the son. At first José was willing to accept food for his sick father, but nothing for himself. Danielle had to coax him to eat at all, and then only when she had agreed that he could work the following day to repay her.

He was up at dawn the following day, and despite his own wasted appearance insisted on putting in a full day's work in the vineyards. Long after she and the children were exhausted from the effort of carrying buckets of water to the field, José worked on, till she wondered that his scrawny arms could continue to carry the weight.

It was evening before he stopped, and then he would have returned to the fields after eating if she had not absolutely forbidden it.

By the third day Manuel managed to get up despite his still-weakened condition. He was able to care for the animals in the barns, in addition to carrying out some other simple chores.

Of course Danielle knew she couldn't afford two extra mouths to feed, but she was glad for the extra hands, and anyway, she hadn't the heart to turn them out and send them back to the hardships of the road. They stayed on, determinedly earning their keep, and within a few days the Perreiras had become an accepted part of the household.

Mary adored José, who was in absolute awe of her and sometimes paused to stare after her as if she were a goddess descended from above. Danielle had the impression that only a very deeply instilled pride prevented the boy from prostrating himself whenever Mary came by, which she managed to do with haughty regularity.

Jean, who considered the vineyards his personal responsibility, was quick to respect the younger boy's uncomplaining hard work in the fields.

But it was David who surprised Danielle; always something of a loner before, David promptly took the newcomer under his wing. They became the best of friends, and within a week they had made a project of learning one another's language.

Danielle prayed for something to replenish their food supplies and wondered how Claude would react to the news that their household had grown by two in his absence.

If only he would return soon.

The day came all too soon when the last of the flour was gone. They were left with little but some dried fruits and some nuts they had been hoarding. The last of the dried meats had gone the day before. Short of killing one of the horses, Danielle did not see how she was to feed them all.

'I'll go see Don Diego,' she decided. Although she knew he, too, was having difficulties, perhaps he would have some food to spare, even enough for a day or two, until she could decide what to do. There were wines stored in the winery, if only she knew which ones to sell; but Claude had always taken care of that part of the business and she didn't even know how to go about selling them. Perhaps Don Diego could advise her on that, too.

She left the children in the care of Manuel, who by this time had taken his place in the vineyards with the others. Because she was going alone she did not bother to hitch up the buggy; she would ride horseback instead.

She was in the barn, just finishing with saddling the horse, when she heard the rider approaching. At first she thought it might be one of the neighbors, and she had all but stepped into the glaring sunlight when she remembered the dangers of highwaymen and other scavengers.

Cautiously she stepped back into the barn, putting a gentling hand over the horse's muzzle, and peered through the crack in the door to see who the rider was.

It was a stranger. Instinctively Danielle shrank even further back into the barn's gloom, watching the man slow his horse to a walk as he glanced this way and that. His gaze passed without pause over the barely cracked barn door and went back to the house itself.

Danielle felt her pulse quicken; something about the man, or his manner, made her suspect that this was no harmless social call. He sat slouched in the saddle, a coarse-looking man with a straggly beard and close-set eyes that were squinty in the morning sunshine. He dismounted, flinging his reins over a fence post, and surveyed the grounds again. Apparently satisfied that no one was about, he sauntered up the steps to the front door. He knocked once; when there was no answer, he tried the knob. The door was unlocked. He opened it, and with a final glance around, stepped inside.

Merciful heavens, Danielle thought, a scavenger, and she was alone – the servants, the children, José and Manuel were all in the vineyards, but even if she screamed and they heard her, what could they do? The man was armed – she could be summoning the children to their deaths. There were guns in the house, of course, but she had not thought to bring one to the barn with her, and unlike Don Diego, she had never thought to keep a gun in the barn.

What could she do? Perhaps she could mount up and ride for Don Diego's. But if any of the children or the servants came down to the house while the intruder was there, they would still be in danger.

She was still trying to think what she should do when the man emerged from the house again. He was carrying a loaf of bread, tearing off great chunks and stuffing them into his mouth. It was the bread she had baked early this morning, with the last of their flour.

It was this that brought the sudden rage to her, so powerful that she completely forgot to be frightened. Their food, very nearly the last thing that she and her children and those who depended upon her had to eat, and this brute of a man was wolfing it down in great mouthfuls. She watched as he paused to take a swig of water from the tin cup he was carrying – their precious store of water!

Damn him, she thought, he couldn't just come riding up here and steal the food and water from their mouths as if it belonged to him. Forgetting that she was in danger, she swung the big barn door open and stepped into the light.

He heard the door creak and called, 'Who's there?' whirling toward her with his gun already in his hand. He saw her and his expression changed slowly from one of tension to a rather pleased smile.

'Well, I was beginning to think there wasn't nobody at home,' he said. 'What are you doin' hidin' out there anyways?'

'Who are you?' she demanded. 'And what are you doing eating our food?'

'Why, I was eatin' it because I was hungry,' he said. His eyes narrowed shrewdly. 'You all alone here, lady?'

'No,' she said, but her hesitation told him she was lying.

'Now, there's nothin' for you to be afraid of,' he said, setting the unfinished bread atop the porch railing and descending the steps toward her. 'Nobody's gonna harm you, providin' you act right.'

She took a step backward. She remembered the bandidos who had come down from the hills, and Carl, who called himself el Tigre, whom she had shot – but there had been a gun there, and this time she was unarmed while this dangerous-looking man strolled closer, looking altogether too sure of himself.

Frightened, she tried to run back into the barn. If she could lock the door, perhaps he would take what he wanted and leave.

He was quicker than she was, though; before she could get the heavy door quite closed, he was at it, pushing it open, and grabbing her wrist to drag her back into the sunlight.

'Why, that ain't very hospitable of you, to my way of thinking', he said, laughing coarsely. 'A man stops by for a visit, seems to me like you oughta try to make him feel welcome. How's about a little kiss, to show me you're sorry?'

He tried to kiss her lips. She turned her face violently away, struggling against him. She brought her foot up, kicking hard at his shins.

He swore aloud and for a moment his grip on her loosened. She pulled free and tried to run, but he tripped her and she went sprawling in the dust. With a whoop of glee, he fell upon her.

José, working closest to the house, had heard the sound of horse's hooves. At first he had thought it was the señora leaving, but then he had realized that the sound was coming to the house, not going from it.

He hesitated, wondering if he should mention this to the others. No one else seemed to have noticed. Finally, knowing from experience that there were a great many dangerous men on the roads these days, he began to make his way back toward the house. If everything were all right, he could make some excuse and come back. And it was better to be safe than sorry.

So it was that he came around the corner of the house to discover the two people rolling about in the dirt, the señora kicking and clawing at her attacker while he laughed as if he was enjoying the entire episode.

José did not stop to think that he was a mere ten-year-old, thin and weak with lack of proper food; he saw nothing but that the señora, the beautiful lady who had been so good to him and his father, was in danger.

José raced across the yard and, with a flying leap, landed square on the stranger's back, knocking the air out of him with the impact.

The stranger grunted, more startled than anything else by the unexpected attack. He twisted, peering over his shoulder, and saw that it was only a little boy pummeling his back so ferociously.

'Hey, you damn monkey,' he snarled, rearing up and shaking his shoulders to knock the boy loose. To his surprise the boy hung on, flinging his arms about the man's neck and all but strangling him.

'Let go,' he roared, flinging himself over on his back. He landed on José, all but crushing the frail body.

Danielle, gasping for breath, had a moment of freedom from the arms that had tried to embrace her, but she saw at a glance that the man meant to kill José. She must stop him . . . Her eyes darted about, seeking a weapon.

There, on the ground, a yard away, was a big rock. She scrambled to her knees, grabbing for the rock. The man had shaken José free at last, and now he was strangling him, while the boy's thin arms and legs flapped and kicked futilely.

Without taking time to think, Danielle lifted the rock and

brought it down on the back of the man's skull. There was a horrible crunching sound, like the breaking of eggshells, only louder. The stranger seemed to stiffen, his body jerking convulsively. Then he collapsed heavily over José's prone body.

For a moment Danielle could do nothing but gasp for breath as she stared down at the inert figure beneath her. Then she saw José struggling to free himself from the man's weight. She was sure the man was dead; the rock had caved in the entire back of his head.

Finally she screwed up her courage enough to touch the man's lifeless body and help José roll it aside. 'Are you all right?' she asked as he got somewhat shakily to his feet.

'*Sí,*' he said, his voice still a little tremulous. 'And you?'

'Yes, yes, I'm fine now; thank God you came.' She stood, brushing the dust from her skirt, but her eyes came back to the man lying in the dust.

'He will not bother us now, I think,' José said, stooping to pry open one of the man's eyes. 'He is dead.'

Danielle shuddered; now that it was over, she didn't know what she should do.

'I – I suppose you should go for the sheriff,' she said without much conviction.

'For him?' José spat disdainfully into the dust by the dead man's feet; now that the fight was over he seemed far more in control than she did. 'He is not worth the trouble; he is only a –how do you say . . . ?'

'A scavenger,' Danielle supplied.

'*Sí*, a scavenger. If he had been caught, he would be hanged – so, no matter, he is dead just the same.'

Danielle forced herself to look at the man; she thought José's remarks a bit cynical, but not without their logic.

'What shall we do with him?' she asked, finding it not at all odd that she should be asking a ten-year-old boy for advice. 'We can't just leave him here for the others to see when they come in.'

'We will bury him,' José said, smiling at his own cleverness. 'We will drag him behind the barn and dig a hole. No one will know.'

In the end, she agreed to the boy's suggestion. They managed together to drag the body behind the barn, where they took turns digging until they had dug a hole big enough to contain the body.

'Wait,' José said when she was about to roll the body into the grave. He knelt and went quickly through the man's pockets. He found some paper money and a leather pouch containing gold coins and some jewelry.

'I don't know if we should take that,' Danielle said when José would have handed it to her.

'Look – stolen things,' José said, indicating a woman's brooch and a ring among the jewelry. 'They are not his.'

'Nor ours, either,' she said, but she took them nonetheless. Perhaps she could advertise regarding the jewelry; as for the money – the paper and the gold coins – it would be impossible to find out whom they had been stolen from, and the boy was right: It was surely foolish to bury them with the man when they were in such dire need.

She buried the last of her qualms with the dead man.

She kept his horse, too; the animal was branded, so perhaps it was stolen. She would leave for Claude the problem of what to do with it.

'Señora,' José said, leading the dead man's horse into the barn. 'Your horse, it is still saddled.'

She had forgotten the mare, waiting patiently inside the barn. 'Unsaddle her,' she said, exhausted from the morning's experiences. 'I won't be riding to Don Diego's today.'

56

After a time Danielle's dreams ceased to be haunted by the memory of the man she had killed. This was still a savage land; sometimes one had to be savage to survive.

The money they had taken from the man's pockets was enough to replenish their supplies of food and water, although it was futile to think of saving the burnt vineyards.

Jean discovered the strange horse in the barn; Danielle and José had agreed between them to say that the horse had simply wandered in riderless from the hills. The explanation seemed to satisfy Jean and Mary, although Danielle saw that David looked speculative, and for several days he regarded her and José in a rather unnerving way. Whatever his personal thoughts on the matter, however, he kept them to himself.

It was just a month later that the letter came for which Danielle had been waiting – Claude was on his way home.

The transcontinental railroad had just been completed, linking Omaha with Sacramento. From there the travelers would journey to Los Angeles by stagecoach. Danielle was astonished to think with what ease and comfort they would make the journey that had been so difficult and hazardous only a short time before.

The entire family, and Don Diego, made the trip into Los Angeles to meet the returning travelers. 'And damn the expense,' Don Diego said, although Danielle thought there was anxiety underlying his show of gaiety.

José and Manuel, already important fixtures in the vineyards, stayed behind to tend the ranch.

'The señor,' José said when Danielle was preparing to leave, 'when he returns, will he want Papacito and me to leave?'

'Claude? Of course not; he'll be glad to have the extra help,' she said. Privately she could only hope Claude would see things that way.

Since the murder of Doña Elvira years before, Claude had grown increasingly prejudiced against California's large number of Mexican-Americans.

'They ought to all be herded up and driven back across the border,' he had said on more than one occasion, and no amount of reasoning, not even pointing out to him that this had been their home before it was his, had changed his mind.

She could not guess how he would react to the news that French Hills was now home to two Mexican-Americans.

The coach arrived late. The leaden gray skies had only served to add to Danielle's uneasiness. What should she expect? There had been a strain between them when Claude left, and his letters – polite, affectionate, and devoid of any real intimacy – had given her no clues as to what his thinking had been since.

She saw Don Diego, still somewhat stiff on his foot, pacing back and forth, and realized that his uncertainty was equal to her own.

Jean, who had wandered to the corner, saw the coach coming first and came yelling back to alert the others. In a few minutes it had swung into view, and then it was stopped in the street, and there they were, clambering down, Adam looking torn between his boyish desire to run excitedly to meet them and the new mannishness that demanded he match his father's dignified arrival; Claude, all business and efficiency, seeing to the baggage, seeing to his mother; Anne, seeming to have aged a great deal in the nearly two years they had been gone – or had Danielle simply not noticed the accumulation of years before she left?

Don Diego hurried forward, offering Anne his hand; she took it and then with a shy, almost girlish smile, she came into his arms, murmuring his name affectionately, and Don Diego knew that their estrangement was over.

Claude gave Danielle a quick peck on the cheek. She saw the way his eyes slid from hers and recognized his guilt for what it was. It brought her a fresh stab of pain, which she at once thrust aside. She gave him the brightest smile she could manage.

'Welcome back,' she said.

'It's good to be back,' was his answer.

Then they were caught up in the activity of getting everyone installed in the carriage, the baggage carefully strapped on top, the children all asking questions at once. Taking her seat inside, Danielle saw that she would have to wait until they were home before she explained to Claude about José and his father or had an opportunity to ask about France.

As the carriage rolled out of town, headed east toward French Hills, it began to rain. People could be seen running out of their houses, dancing around in the streets, and the children insisted on hanging their arms outside until Claude reprimanded them and had the curtains pulled shut.

'It's good to be home,' Anne said unexpectedly.

Claude said nothing but only sat and stared out the window with what Danielle thought was a wistful expression.

The rain did not by any means solve the problems at French Hills. For one thing, there was the question of José Perreira and his father. Claude was less than enthusiastic about these additions to the household, and on his own inclination would probably have sent them packing, but Danielle was adamant on that score.

'They work hard,' she insisted. 'They've been a real blessing since they've been here.'

'Just so they earn their keep,' Claude gave in reluctantly.

'I know you won't be sorry you let them stay,' she said, words that she would regret in time.

Claude might have made more of an issue of it, but he had

more important matters on his mind, and by the time they had been resolved, he had had time to see for himself that the two Mexican workers did indeed earn their keep.

Almost immediately after his return Claude left again, this time for Sacramento, to ask the legislature for reimbursement for the money he had spent on cuttings, which were already beginning to arrive.

He returned with the gloomy news that the legislature had voted not to reimburse him for his expenditures.

'They say they haven't got it,' he said.

'But Claude, what will we do?' Danielle asked. 'There's no money left.'

He shook his head unhappily. 'I don't know. Maybe sell off everything. Maybe we can borrow something.'

He was in his study. He went to his desk, riffling absent-mindedly through the papers stacked there.

'What are these?' he asked.

'They've been coming since you left. Letters from growers, wanting to know how they can get some of the European cuttings they heard the state was going to be obtaining. I was going to send them to Sacramento.'

Claude began to leaf through the letters, slowly at first, then more hurriedly. As he did so, his face broke into a smile.

'Adam,' he yelled, going to the door. In a minute Adam appeared.

'Get the bills for the cuttings we bought,' Claude said. 'Figure a cost for each and every cutting, and how much we'd have to charge to make a profit on them. Not a killing, just a decent profit. And you, Danielle, see if you can compose a letter to these growers. Tell them the state is out of the grape business but that *we* have cuttings for sale direct, every kind of grape they could want – Boseo, Vermentino, Malvoisea, Zinfandel – I'll make up a catalog of the varieties. We may be out of money but we've got something worth far more. As long as the state doesn't want to pay for them, the cuttings are ours to do with what we want. They're like green gold.'

It soon became evident how valuable Claude's green gold was. Within a month they had orders for a thousand cuttings, and more were pouring in regularly. The cuttings that Claude had shipped from Europe would be enough not only to restock their own vineyards but to replenish their fortune as well. The entire family worked day and night to replant the vineyards and at the same time to fill the orders for cuttings.

It was during this time that Claude began to appreciate the Perreiras' worth as employees; notwithstanding his prejudices, he was too dedicated a vintner not to recognize a good worker when he saw one, and the boy especially gave evidence of the sort of feeling for the vines that could produce a first-rate grower.

While the de Brussac household was thus gaining two new members, it lost one during the same time. Adam came to his father with a letter from a grower in San José, to the north. Unlike the others, this one did not want to buy cuttings, and in fact almost the first thing he explained in his letter was that he had no money to buy anything.

'He wants to trade for them,' Adam explained. 'Land for cuttings. He says it's good growing land.'

'We've got plenty of land right here,' Claude said. 'The best wine land in the state.'

'The best white-wine land,' Adam corrected him. 'We haven't had much luck with the reds. But they say the northern growers are beginning to make reds as good as in Europe.'

'Maybe so, but I can't be in two places at once. This place is enough for a man to run.'

'I could go to San José,' Adam said, standing and squaring his shoulders.

'Claude,' Danielle protested, 'he's only a boy.'

'I'm eighteen,' Adam said indignantly. 'The same age Pa was when he came to this country. And I know as much about growing and wine making as most of the men in the business.'

Claude stood and went to the window, staring out at the vineyards spreading over the hills. What Adam said was true; he was already a skilled vintner, far more knowledgeable than Claude himself had been when he had started French Hills. And although he hated admitting it, the northern growers were doing better with red wines than the growers in the southern part of the state; the soil, the climate, something in the north seemed to favor those varieties.

He knew Danielle still thought of Adam as a boy, but Adam had grown up a great deal in the course of their lengthy journey. Perhaps it was time he began his own adventures.

He had dreamed of the de Brussacs as California's wine kings – but why settle for a kingdom if they could have an empire?

'Very well,' he said, turning back to face his son. 'The land is yours if you want it. Take the man the cuttings he wants, and enough to start your own vineyards. There's just one thing I want from you.'

'What's that, Pa?' Adam asked, his eyes wide with excitement.

'Make me wine, son. Make me some damned good wine, the kind we can build an empire on.'

Adam beamed with pride at the confidence placed in him, but his younger sister observed with envy all the attention being paid to her brother.

'When I get older,' Mary said, 'I'll make wine, too. I'll have my own vineyards and my wine will be the best of all.'

Claude laughed and, seizing her about the waist, picked her up and swung her around, ignoring her petulant expression.

'That may well be,' Claude said, hugging his daughter to him. 'That may be.'

PART III

The
WINE

57

'Papa, can I have any dress I want?'

'That was our bargain, wasn't it?' Claude gave his daughter an indulgent smile. He tied up the horses, then came around to hand Mary down from the buggy, pleased with the admiring glance she got from a passing cowboy. As a little girl, Mary had shown a promise of great beauty; now, at fourteen, she was already on her way to fulfilling that promise.

At the moment Mary was having a difficult time smothering her girlish high spirits in an attempt to act like a proper young lady. This was her first trip alone with her father. The year before, when she entered his champagne in a wine-tasting competition, she confidently predicted that it would win, whereupon he promised that if her prediction proved correct, he would take her on a trip to Los Angeles and buy her a new outfit.

She mentioned the wine in her prayers every night for two weeks, and for added insurance hardly uncrossed her fingers the entire time except when necessity demanded. Although in point of fact she had no great interest in her father's wines and none of her brothers' natural aptitude for knowing what was bad and what was good, she had learned long ago that the way to her father's heart was through his wines, and like a clever parrot, she had learned all the right things to say. Her professed confidence in the champagne had been a bold gamble, but she knew that the wine was one Papa was particularly pleased with, pronouncing it within her hearing as the crowning achievement of his wine-making career.

So of course she had made up her mind to adore it, no matter what was the outcome of the competition. She would have gone to the guillotine (an expression which, she had learned, particularly irritated her grandmother) before admitting that she hadn't cared for the taste at all.

With the exception of the wine, though, and her grandmother, who sometimes frightened her, there was not a great deal that Mary didn't like. At times, indeed, she had a difficult time deciding just what in her young, crowded life she liked the most.

She adored Los Angeles with all its hustle and bustle, and she adored their new house that was being built on a hill just a short distance from here – Bunker Hill, they called it – and theirs would be one of a row of fine mansions topping the hill overlooking the city.

She also adored being rich; it meant you could never run out of lovely things to ask for; and she was wildly fond of her father, who never – or almost never – failed to give her whatever she asked for.

Of course, she loved her mother, too, although she was something of a stick, and her brothers, but they could be nuisances, too, especially when they refused to do what she wanted them to do – though that was, of course, a rare occurrence.

Most of all, though, she loved herself. She loved being almost grown-up, and knowing that she was beautiful. She was drunk on the sheer delight of being alive; she hated going to bed at night, resenting the time wasted in unconsciousness, and woke each morning with an almost agonizing sense of pleasure. Someday when she was old enough, she promised herself, she would never sleep at all but spend her nights dancing at the sort of grand balls popular among the Los Angeles society set. She only wished she could go to one of the lavish parties now. It was dreadful to have to wait to grow up – why couldn't one do it all at once, just by wanting to?

The proprietress of the dress shop came forward to greet them as they came in. She seemed to know Papa, as nearly everyone did, which gave Mary a sense of pleasure.

'Mister de Brussac, how delightful to see you again. And who have you brought me today?' Her small, greedy eyes gave Mary an appraising glance.

'This is my daughter, Mary, Madame Forsythe,' he introduced them off-handedly. 'Mary wants a new frock.'

'Ah, yes, the little dear,' Madame Forsythe purred, stepping back to give Mary's figure a critical scrutiny. 'Well, we won't have any trouble fitting her, with such a perfect young figure. What kind of dress did you have in mind?'

'Something red,' Mary said quickly. 'Something like that one.'

She indicated a dress on a mannequin in the front window; it was of scarlet velvet with white ruffles at the throat and the cuffs, and the loose-flowing skirt that was currently in vogue.

'Yes, well, it is a very popular number,' Madame Forsythe said in a doubtful tone of voice. 'Still, perhaps something a little more, shall we say, youthful?'

She looked to Claude for support but he merely grinned and shrugged. 'It's her dress,' he said. 'Give her whatever she likes.'

Madame Forsythe decided that it was not, after all, her problem if the girl wanted to dress in a fashion far too sophisticated for her years. She escorted her into the fitting room where, after Mary had stripped to her petticoats, Madame Forsythe began to take her measurements.

Claude seated himself in one of the hard wooden chairs near the front window and watched the passersby. He was not alone for long. He saw a familiar figure alighting from a carriage, and in a moment Antoinette de Trémorel had entered the shop, accompanied by a tall, very pretty young woman.

'Claude,' Antoinette greeted him with her usual sultry smile. 'How nice to see you. We were just talking about you.'

Since her untimely arrival some years before, Antoinette had become something of a fixture among the somewhat freer elements of the Los Angeles social scene. Despite her marriage to François, she affected to use her brother's name, and her son Richard had claimed the title of Count de Trémorel.

They were regarded as a bit 'fast' by the more conservative locals, but the title and their aristocratic background gave them a stature that they might otherwise not have been able to attain.

Their parties were said to border on the notorious and were frequented by all manner of artists, actresses and, it was said, a gambler or two. If any of the local citizens found themselves embroiled in a scandal of some sort, they could almost count on being invited to Antoinette's for a ball or a supper party. She seemed to thrive on the scandals of others, but for all that, no one could say with any conviction that her own behavior was not aboveboard. Of course, it was generally agreed that she flirted with anything in pants, but it was equally well known that she had a jealous husband, and so far as anyone could determine (and one or two of the local women had gone to great lengths to investigate the matter), her little adventures never went beyond flirtation. Whatever faults she had, it was generally conceded that she was a devoted wife.

Claude, when he found himself alone in Los Angeles, had gone to one or two of her dinners. He did not fancy that Antoinette had any personal interest in him, since she had rebuffed his every attempt at intimacy, but she remained friendly, and he had found that there were always a few unattached females at her little gatherings. Since his return from Europe, unattached females had become something of a habit with him.

'I suppose she's been telling you to avoid me at all costs,' he said, addressing Antoinette's companion. This was a particularly striking young woman with regular, even, aristocratic features: a long, thin nose, pale lips that were almost lost in the lightness of her complexion, and gently hooded eyes from which she seemed always to be looking up at whomever she was talking to, despite her own tallness.

She laughed at his remark, a surprisingly sensual laugh. 'Not in the least,' she said.

'This is Julia Benson, from Philadelphia,' Antoinette introduced her. 'Mister de Brussac is one of our wealthier citizens. He's a wine merchant.'

The tone of her voice at the last bordered on derision, but her expression was so admiring that one could not but think he had misread her meaning.

'A vintner,' he corrected, bowing slightly. 'And not too rich, I'm afraid.'

'Is there such a thing as too rich?' Julia Benson asked, smiling.

Mary, who had heard the voices from the next room, had hurriedly redonned her clothes, with a peevish Madame Forsythe trying her best to collect the rest of her measurements at the same time. They came into the shop now, Madame Forsythe trailing, her mouth filled with pins.

'Oh, hello,' Mary said, pretending surprise at finding anyone with her father.

Claude introduced her to the two women. Julia Benson gave her no more than a passing glance, but Antoinette gave Mary a searching look that bordered on rudeness.

'Since you're in town, you shall have to come to dinner tomorrow night,' Antoinette said. 'Everyone's coming, including that actress, Mademoiselle Darcy – at least she says she's an actress.'

'Do say you'll come,' Julia Benson added, giving him a languorous look from under her lashes.

'I'd like to very much, of course,' Claude said. 'But I'm traveling with my daughter, as you can see, and I'm afraid we came without any sort of companion for her. I hadn't planned on any social engagements.'

Mary felt a stab of disappointment, but her spirits immediately soared at Antoinette's next remarks.

'But your daughter looks quite old enough to come with you. You needn't stay awfully late if you don't wish. And my son has just come back from the Continent. I'm sure you'll enjoy talking to him.' This last was addressed directly to Mary herself.

Claude hesitated slightly; he knew well enough what Danielle would say to such an invitation. Still, it would be pleasant to get a little better acquainted with Miss Benson; what a ravishing creature she was – Antoinette had said *Miss* Benson, hadn't she? And surely Mary was mature enough to conduct herself properly at a dinner party.

'Oh, Papa, do let's go,' Mary said, forgetting herself in her eagerness.

'Well I guess it can't hurt anything, as long as we don't stay too late,' Claude said.

'Good,' Antoinette said, pleased with herself. 'Tomorrow night then, shall we say eight?'

The two women had come to pick up a package. They collected it from Madame Forsythe and left. Watching them go, Mary could barely contain her sense of anticipation.

She was so engrossed in her own emotions that she did not notice her father, with an expression nearly as eager as her own, watching the two women leave.

58

'Aren't you ready yet? It's almost seven-thirty?'

'Almost – oh, Papa, your tie, it's crooked. Let me retie it for you.' Mary herself was not even dressed; she was still wrapped in a peignoir, even though her entire energies since rising had been directed to getting herself ready for this, her first grown-up dinner party.

Nevertheless, she jumped up and stood on the sofa to be able to reach her father's tie, untying it and deftly retying it so that it suited her better.

'Are you all ready?' she asked her father.

'Almost; I've just got to put my stickpin in,' he said.

'Oh, don't do it yourself. Let me put it in; I know just where it looks best.'

'You'd better think about getting yourself dressed,' her father said, but with an indulgent chuckle he went obediently to fetch his diamond pin.

When he came back, she was just struggling into her dress. 'In a moment,' she cried, pushing the door to. 'Don't come in yet, Papa.'

When he was admitted some minutes later, Mary was wearing the new gown that Madame Forsythe had hastily altered for her. It revealed rather too much of her bare neck and her undefined bosom. She was thin, with the lingering angularity of early adolescence.

Still, he was struck by her loveliness; it was the first glimpse he had had of what she would be as a woman, and not even her father could be entirely immune to the effect she presented, half-child, half-woman. She had inherited her grandmother's coppery hair and much of her sensuous beauty, but her eyes were her mother's wide and luminous ones. The singular juxtaposition of features was arresting more than pretty; but it was the changing kaleidoscope of emotions and feelings forever flashing across her face that made a beauty of her face.

She turned to the mirror, adjusting a fold of her skirt, pushing an imagined stray hair into place.

'Don't I look pretty,' she exclaimed ingenuously. She pirouetted back to him. 'There, I'm ready, Papa,' she said.

He escorted her proudly through the lobby to the carriage waiting in front of the hotel. Antoinette's mansion was not on 'the hill', but almost two miles to the west, on the very outskirts of the city. Soon after their arrival some years before, François had purchased a considerable expanse of land in that area and since then had been promoting it as an ideal location for the homes of the rich, away from the crush of the city.

For a time they had enjoyed success with their venture, but since then other speculators had sprung up, promoting their own locales such as Pasadena, formerly Indiana City, to the north; and the national depression that had begun the year before, while thus far having little effect on the wine industry, had slowed the building boom considerably.

Sitting beside her father in the carriage, Mary was torn between her compulsion to fidget and her desire not to muss her dress. She restrained herself only by the sheerest of efforts.

It seemed as if she had not had a free moment the entire day to think of what lay before her; now, in the darkness of the swaying carriage, she was assailed by a sort of stagefright as she imagined what was awaiting her.

For some time now she had teetered tantalizingly on the verge of growing up. Just the year before she had kissed José on the lips, just so. She had been thinking of doing it for some time, if only to find out what it was like.

'You, you're so silly,' José had said, blushing hotly as he fled the room. She had been left behind to ponder what it was that grown-ups found so exciting about *that*.

It had been only play-acting, though; this was her actual entrée into the adult world, and she was deliciously terrified at the prospect. Even now she was hardly able to believe that it was actually coming to pass.

Then they were finally there, and in a daze she mounted the stairs on her father's arm, barely able to see through the blur of tears in her eyes. The lights were dazzling, and everywhere were elegantly gowned women and handsome men. She wished that she had had some jewels to wear. She saw that all the other women had them, and she thought the lack made her look naked and plain, without realizing that it made her stand out even more from all the overly dressed women, just as her stagefright made her forget the regal and majestic gestures she had rehearsed before her mirror that morning, with the result that she was all girlish tremulousness, which was far more enchanting.

Madame de Trémorel came to greet her and tell her how lovely she looked, and indeed, seeing Mary – her virginal innocence, her barely repressed excitement – Antoinette felt a stab of nostalgia. For a moment she remembered when she had been young and innocent, and the first party she had attended.

François came to stand near his wife after Claude and Mary passed inside. 'Is that the daughter?' he asked, watching her disappear into the crowd.

'Yes, she's stunning, isn't she?'

'Very. I think Richard will not mind so much after all having to entertain her.'

Their eyes met. Antoinette's expression was speculative. Since she had seen the girl yesterday at Madame Forsythe's, she had been trying to think how best to make use of the girl's loveliness. It was obvious that Claude was devoted to the child; what better way to strike at the father than through the daughter? Richard had inherited François's way with women; surely it would not be too difficult to seduce this trembling virgin. And afterward . . . but first things first. She must talk to Richard.

At the first opportunity she slipped away to look for him. She found him in his rooms, running even more behind time than usual, partly because he was sulking. Richard had made other plans for the evening and he had not relished giving them up merely so that he could help his mother entertain the 'visiting wine makers', particularly a mere child.

At the moment he was seated before a mirrored dressing-table, carefully trimming his already immaculate mustache.

'Richard, dear,' Antoinette said, running a fond hand over his sleek black hair, 'I want you to take this de Brussac girl in to dinner.'

'Will she need a sugar tit or is she old enough to be fed with a spoon?' he asked drily.

'I think you'll find her a bit of a surprise,' she said. Seeing his petulant expression, she lowered herself into his lap and pinched his cheek playfully.

'You will do this for me, won't you?' she asked. When he did not immediately answer, she brought her face close to his and kissed him hotly on the lips.

'You know I always do what you want,' he said huskily when she had finished. 'If it makes you happy I'll deflower this little wench under the table while the soup course is being passed.'

'Oh, not the soup course, it's your favorite – Lady Curzon,' she said, smiling. She brushed his lips again, this time lightly, and stood, smoothing her skirt. 'Perhaps during the dessert would be better.'

Mother and son laughed together, and Antoinette saw that his surly mood was passing. No one could be more charming than Richard when he put his mind to it, and she was confident the de Brussac girl would be as susceptible to his charm as every other female seemed to be.

59

Mary was certain she was making a good impression. She was aware that a number of people were looking at her and asking who she was, and the knowledge gave her a bit more confidence.

At first her father stayed close to her side; he seemed to know everybody, although she found herself wondering how that was possible. He introduced her to numerous people and invariably they told him in asides that were easily overheard what a charming creature she was. If she had not already been vain, she would certainly have been so after this evening.

When it was time to go in to dinner, however, it was not her father who escorted her but a breathtakingly handsome young man who turned out to be the Count de Trémorel, the hostess's son.

Mary had never met anyone as suave or sophisticated as this young nobleman. He hardly took his eyes off her throughout the entire meal, and he kept up a steady flow of polite, flattering conversation as if he did not notice how tongue-tied she was.

'I regret that I've been away so long,' the count said at one point. 'I suppose by now you've already selected a suitor from among your many admirers?'

'Oh, no,' she said breathlessly, forgetting to be coy. 'I hardly ever come to town. But we'll be moving to the city soon, when our new house is finished.'

'Los Angeles will be a far lovelier place then,' he said, gazing deep into her eyes.

Blushing, Mary lowered her eyes demurely and nearly emptied her glass of wine to hide her embarrassment. Hadn't he just all but offered to be her suitor? And to think he actually thought there were others; there was no doubt of it – she must look far older than her years. The count must be all of twenty-two or twenty-three, the same age as her brother Adam, whom she rarely saw now that he lived in San Jose; but Adam with his work-calloused hands and his hearty, down-to-earth manner was like a child himself compared to Richard de Trémorel.

Indeed, except for her papa, she had never known any men of the world; Jean was as common as Adam was, and David, well, it was impossible really to know what David was like, he stayed so much to himself.

Of course, there was José; she remembered with the tiniest pricking of guilt that she had sworn once, and made José swear with her, that they would be married when they were grown. But that, like the kiss she had given him, had been a child's game; this, she knew instinctively, was something far different.

When dinner was over, the women retired to the withdrawing room while the men lingered over their port and passed around cigars. Mary had thought this might be an awkward interval for her, but to her surprise and pleasure, the hostess made a particular point of taking her in tow, insisting that Mary sit by her side on a little divan.

'And you must tell me everything about yourself,' Antoinette insisted.

Encouraged by her friendly manner, Mary did find herself telling a great deal about herself. Antoinette was a good listener and knew how to put one at one's ease, so that by the time the men joined them, Mary felt as if she had given Antoinette her entire life's story.

It had seemed to Claude that that tiresome interval with the other gentlemen would never end. He had been able to think of nothing but the delightful Julia Benson.

He was at least honest with himself; he knew that he wanted her, plain and simple. Since his trip abroad a few years before, he had found himself less and less able, or willing, to resist the lure of a pretty young woman. Even the guilt that he had sometimes experienced in the beginning had faded and gone; he thought of himself as a man with strong desires and an appreciative eye for women. As for Danielle, he made every effort to be what he thought of as a good husband. After all, there was that difficulty of hers about having children, and in the last few years she had been noticeably run-down; it was purely for her sake that he had given up their former relations and was even planning separate bedrooms for them in the new house.

But a man couldn't be expected to be altogether celibate; certainly not when there were Julia Bensons just waiting to catch a man's eye.

Since he had first seen her at Madame Forsythe's, he had been obsessed with thoughts of her. He had responded to her sexuality at once, recognizing it for what it was despite her youth; and he was sure she was equally drawn to him.

At last the host rose from his chair and suggested that the gentlemen join the ladies. Claude fairly bolted from the room. He was relieved to see that Antoinette had taken Mary in tow; there was no danger of her being bored in Antoinette's company. He glanced around the room, spying Julia Benson sitting by herself against one wall, and started toward her.

Julia Benson had been waiting as impatiently as he had. She was bored by gatherings of women; bored, in fact, by most of the ways in which women entertained themselves. What she craved was excitement, challenge, the lure of the forbidden – such as another woman's husband.

She knew that her relationship with Claude de Brussac was going to be one of the exciting ones. Those dark eyes of his, so hungry-looking; that sensuous mouth, eager to devour her – how attractive older men could be, their familiarity with the ways of the flesh all too evident, the rough edges honed to a silken finish.

She had told him a great deal about herself during dinner: the old Philadelphia family, the moneyed background, the proper this and the proper that. She had not told him all; certainly not about that abortive elopement that had ended her virginity but left her unmarried status intact. Of course at the time she had blamed her family loudly and long, but in her own heart she had known that, having obtained what he wanted, Donald hadn't really had any intentions of going through with the rest of it. The truth was, her father's 'rescue' had come at a most timely moment, sparing both Donald and her a far worse embarrassment.

In fact, things had worked out rather well for them both. Donald had gotten a great deal of money in exchange for keeping his mouth shut, and she had been sent west to escape any gossip. More important, though, she had escaped the family as well. Oh, there was Aunt Gertrude, with whom she was living at the present; if she truly intended to be independent, Julia would have to find her own means of support, but it looked as if the answer to that problem had been handed her on a silver tray – or in a wine basket, so to speak. And Claude de Brussac had other attractions as well.

Sometimes she wondered why she thought so much about sex. Other women didn't, she was sure; they were invariably shocked when she brought up the subject – except for Antoinette. They were two of a kind, she suspected, she and Antoinette, although Antoinette could be a little frightening. There was something so . . . Julia groped for the right word . . . so hard about her, as if she would stop at nothing to obtain whatever goal she had set her sights on. Perhaps *relentless* was the word.

'And am I so much different from Antoinette?' Julia asked herself. 'Haven't I made up my mind to have Claude de Brussac, whatever the cost?'

As if on cue, she saw him emerging from the dining room. It gave her a little thrill of anticipation to see with what eagerness his eyes sought her. He started at once toward her.

Antoinette, seeing this, frowned involuntarily. She had not anticipated, when she introduced them, that Claude and Julia would hit it off quite so well. Though she herself had no intention of permitting any sort of liaison between herself and Claude, she had gotten rather used to his attentions – and tonight he hardly seemed to have noticed her.

'Excuse me,' she said, interrupting Mary in the middle of some story she hadn't been listening to anyway, 'I must see to my other guests – ah, here's Richard. I'm sure he wants a chance to get better acquainted.'

Claude and Julia were already engrossed in conversation by the time she joined them. 'Well, I see you two are getting along famously,' she said, with just the slightest edge to her voice.

'Miss Benson's a most engaging companion,' Claude said, 'but she's just confided in me that she has a problem, and she hasn't yet told me what it is.'

'It's quite simple, really,' Julia said. 'I need a job.'

'Really?' Claude looked puzzled. 'We do a great deal of hiring, of course, but it's awfully menial labor, hardly the sort of thing I'd want to offer a young lady.'

'Particularly one with your qualifications,' Antoinette said.

Ignoring that barb, Julia said, 'I was looking for work as a governess. Your daughter is lovely, by the way; you must be very proud.'

'Very. But you can see for yourself, Mary's practically grown. To be honest, I hadn't realized that myself until tonight. And the youngest of the boys is a year older – a little late for a governess, don't you think?'

'A tutor, then, if you prefer. It doesn't matter what I'm called. The point is your children's education.'

'It has been rather hit-or-miss,' Claude admitted. 'Their mother and grandmother have conspired to teach them the rudiments . . .'

'Exactly,' Julia said, smiling. 'But are the rudiments enough in today's world? Antoinette tells me that yours is one of California's important families. Your children need a proper education, particularly in the social graces, if they're to take their place in the world, and it's never too late to begin.'

Claude had to agree that her arguments made sense; of course the children, especially David and Mary, needed a bit of polish, particularly the sort of polish that came from Julia Benson's aristocratic background. His mother had spent less time with them than with Adam and Jean, and anyway, Adam and Jean were rough-and-ready types who would make their way by virtue of their eagerness and their willingness to work harder than anyone else.

But David – David lived in a world all his own, and Mary was so spoiled that it was impossible to teach her anything except what she wanted to learn. Danielle had done her best, of course, but Danielle could hardly impart the sort of aristocratic finesse that Claude wanted his children, particularly his daughter, to have.

He wasn't a fool, however, nor dishonest with himself. If he was excited by the prospect of Julia Benson coming to live with them as a governess, it wasn't solely because of the benefits to the children. The thought of that beautiful creature living under the same roof with him, sleeping perhaps in the next room from him . . .

'I'll have to talk to my wife, of course,' he said aloud.

'I'm sure you can persuade her,' Julia said.

'Yes,' Antoinette added drily, 'you have such a winning way.'

Neither Claude nor Julia seemed to notice her, however; at the moment they were engrossed in one another.

'Don't you want to show me the garden?'

Richard de Trémorel looked a little surprised by Mary's suggestion, as indeed she knew he had every reason to be, but he only smiled faintly and said, 'If you like.'

Mary felt giddy with her own audacity. This was the most thrilling evening of her life, and she did not intend to let it end without draining the maximum pleasure and excitement from it.

At the same time she could not help feeling a little frightened. She had never been alone like this with a man before, certainly not when there had been this sort of physical tension between them. She knew that Richard de Trémorel was bored – she thought he looked upon her as a mere child – yet she was sure nevertheless that he was attracted to her. There was an intimacy in the way he slipped his arm about her waist as he led her down the marble steps into the dark garden that made her legs feel all wobbly beneath her, so that she half-feared she might stagger and fall if he took his arm away.

Why had she never felt this delicious weakness before? And why did her heart pound so fiercely, so that she was sure she would cry, or run in fright, or do something equally foolish if he actually kissed her, though she knew that she wanted that as much as he – more, probably; she wanted to prove to him that she was not a child, she wanted this handsome man to recognize her as a woman.

'You're shivering,' he said, guiding her toward one of the stone benches under the trees. 'Are you cool?'

'Not really. I was thinking, I hope Papa did not see us come out.'

'I wouldn't worry about that if I were you,' Richard said. 'I'm afraid he's rather occupied himself just now, with the admirable Miss Benson.'

For reasons she did not understand, the innuendo irritated her. 'Do you mean that girl from Philadelphia? I'm sure he's just being polite to her.'

Richard de Trémorel laughed sardonically. 'I forget that you are a child,' he said.

'I'm not a child,' she said hotly.

'Indeed?' His amused expression seemed to be a challenge. He had seated himself close to her on the bench so that now his face was only inches from hers, and he was watching her intently.

Suddenly she wanted to kiss him, not in that childish way she had kissed José but in a man-woman kiss that would erase that amused tolerance from his face.

'Is this a child's kiss?' she asked, lifting her face to his.

His lips seemed to sear hers. To her a kiss had always been that gentle touching of closed lips, but this was something far more intimate, more electric. His mouth bruised hers and his tongue thrust obscenely into her, prying her lips apart, invading, raping, until it seemed as if it were her entire body, her entire being that was being assaulted by his kiss. She shuddered with a kind of horror and yet she could not control the violent thrill that shot through her like bursts of lightning.

She felt his hands upon her body, fumbling with her clothes. She knew that she should protest, should offer some resistance, but at the same moment another part of her burned with a desire that would not be quelled.

Is it as quick as this? she thought. She had always assumed there would be romance, courtship, advances and retreats – was it all to be done in a twinkling, in the shadow of a bougainvillea?

'Mary?'

Her father's voice was like a dash of cold water – for them both, apparently, for Richard released her so suddenly that she nearly toppled backward off the bench. By the time her father came down the steps and along the walk, Richard was standing and looking quite nonchalant, almost bored.

'Here you are,' Claude said, coming up to them. 'Miss Benson said she thought she'd seen you come this way.'

Mary avoided his penetrating gaze. 'We wanted some air. It

was close inside,' she said, resenting the untimely intrusion, though she knew it had prevented her from making a fool of herself.

Claude looked from one to the other of them. He was thinking it was a good thing he'd come along when he had; he'd been so engrossed in his own flirtation with Julia that he had been only vaguely aware of the attention Richard was paying Mary.

It made him angry, although he made an effort to conceal that fact. It was not only the difference in Mary's and Richard's ages; there had been twenty years' difference, after all, between his mother and father. And Richard was a count; Claude's chief ambition for his daughter was that she should marry well.

But Richard de Trémorel was François's son; try though he might, Claude could never forget that. And father and son were alike in more than appearance. Richard had a bad reputation, not only as a seducer but as a bully as well. He had taken his first mistress at seventeen and treated the poor girl so cruelly that she had killed herself six months later.

'I think it's time we were going,' Claude said aloud. Fortunately, nothing had happened between these two, and nothing would; he would see to that. Tomorrow, before he left for French Hills, he would speak to Antoinette; he'd heard that her son had a habit of accumulating gambling debts. A few thousand should be enough to interest the young man in traveling north to San Francisco for a year or two.

It was not until they were almost home, having ridden the entire distance in silence, that he said to his daughter, 'I think it might be wiser if we didn't mention tonight to your mother.'

'Yes, Papa,' she said. She did not add that the suggestion was unnecessary. She would never have shared with anyone the turmoil of emotions she was experiencing.

60

Danielle reacted first with disbelief, then with anger to the news that Claude had hired a governess.

'But the children are grown,' she said.

'They're never too old to learn,' Claude said, parroting Julia Benson.

'Anyway, they've already been taught. They read and write and do arithmetic. Mary can cook and sew, after a fashion, and the boys know everything there is to know about making wine. What more do they need?'

'None of them reads or writes all that well,' Claude insisted. 'And more important, they need some polish, some social graces. The de Brussacs are an important family in California now, you know. Being wealthy and famous has its responsibilities.'

'It seems to me we've managed well enough so far.'

'That's quite true,' Claude agreed. 'But it didn't matter so much with us; we were pioneers here and except for Don Diego we didn't mingle much with people of our own – with the upper classes, but it's different for the children; they'll have to take their proper place in the scheme of things. You wouldn't want them to be disadvantaged because they lacked the proper training.'

'No,' she admitted doubtfully.

Seeing that he had found her Achilles' heel, Claude smiled his most persuasive smile and added gently, 'And you know there are things that you can't teach them. Mother could, I suppose, but it seems unfair to ask her to take on that responsibility when we can certainly afford to hire a proper instructor . . .'

'Very well,' she said, knowing from the moment that he had touched upon the matter of class that she had lost the argument. He was quite right; she was hardly the one to tutor her children in the social graces that she herself had never quite mastered. 'Let us have this governess for a period of time and see what she can accomplish. But if the children fail to learn from her – and you know how difficult Mary can be – then she must be dismissed.'

Looking very pleased with himself, Claude said, 'Give her three months. She can begin when we've moved into town. If at the end of that time I don't see any discernible improvement, we'll give her the boot.'

Danielle, who had not even been permitted to meet this Miss Benson, let alone interview her for the job, had no sooner given in to her husband than she started having misgivings. She had wanted to ask if Miss Benson was pretty but had not done so for fear that she would sound like a jealous wife. At any rate she did not imagine that Claude, with his exquisite taste, would have hired an ugly hag of a woman, however well versed she was in social graces.

Or was she being unfair? She longed to trust her husband, to believe him faithful, even though her judgment told her otherwise. At times she could almost ignore the little signs – the guilty look when he came back from his trips to the city and found it difficult to meet her eyes; the rouge stain on his shirt front; the lace handkerchief thrust into his pocket and forgotten. She told herself that there were logical explanations for all of these if she only asked, but fear that she might learn otherwise kept her from asking.

Her husband was forty-three, still in the prime of life and more handsome, in her eyes at least, than ever. She could hardly suppose that he had lost all his former ardor merely because he had ended that aspect of their relationship out of deference for her health.

She wished that it were otherwise; she missed the physical part of their marriage and had tried in every discreet way she could think of to let him know that she did, but Claude was adamant on that score.

She sighed; she supposed she should be grateful. It was for her sake, after all, and yet it seemed only to have increased the distance that had somehow sprung up between them over the last few years. If only they were closer, if they could talk to one another more openly; a husband and wife ought to be as one, oughtn't they? Yet there were times when it seemed to her that they knew one another not at all for all the years they had been together.

Nor was the move to their new home in the city likely to improve matters. Their new home – how she hated it! Not that it wasn't quite grand, even beautiful, in a cold, awesome way, and she knew that Claude was quite proud of the ornate structure. But she also knew that she could never be comfortable or happy there, and not only because of the separate bedrooms Claude had insisted on. It was simply too grand, for one thing; and she didn't really care for living in Los Angeles, either. They would be expected to hobnob with the local society, and she had never fit in very well with those people. She could never get over the feeling that they were looking down on her because of her background.

Yet here, too, Claude's arguments had been reasonable. 'It's high time we had some kind of life besides just working in those vineyards,' he had insisted. 'We aren't either of us getting any younger. As for the ranch, the boys have been running it on their own these last few years anyway.'

By 'the boys' he meant Jean and José. José, whose father had died a few years before, had grown into a skilled vintner. There was little love lost between him and Claude – 'That greaser's getting mighty uppity,' Claude would say with an almost comic regularity – but Claude respected the young man's capabilities.

'Besides,' he added now, 'I intend keeping an eye on things. With that new road open, it takes no time at all to make the drive.'

Within the month they had made the move to Los Angeles, staying first at a hotel while the finishing touches were put on the house. Anne came, too, for a few days, to help Danielle select the furnishings, and Don Diego came with her, so that they ended up occupying an entire floor in the hotel. Miss Benson, who turned out to be even more ravishing than Danielle had feared, had a room on the floor below.

Fortunately there was a great deal to do, so that Danielle's mind was kept occupied. She and Anne spent most of their days shopping for the myriad items needed to complete the furnishings of the new house. Claude had insisted that the house and its furnishings be the grandest in the city. From Germany had come an ornate, square grand piano, carved of rosewood, and from the east, rugs for every room. The parlor and the dining-room both were to have chandeliers lit entirely by gas. The list seemed endless and kept the two women scouring the local shops as well as the offices of the importers.

The discovery of great veins of silver in Nevada – the Great Bonanza, the newspapers labeled it – had caused another wave of westward migration, some of which had spilled over into California, bringing yet another influx of ruffians and ne'er-do-wells to Los Angeles. Claude had made light of the problems, but Anne, who rarely left the ranch these days, had taken a certain malicious pleasure in warning them of the dangers of being killed on the streets, if not actually in their beds, within a fortnight of moving to the city.

Danielle supposed it was for this reason that Don Diego had insisted on accompanying his wife, and he was their unvarying companion on each of their shopping expeditions. With his fearless demeanor and ramrod posture, he looked, despite his years, a sufficient challenge for any rowdies.

'Besides, if any of those young city toughs try to give us a hard time,' Anne declared, 'I'll show them how pioneer women deal with trouble.' She brought her parasol crashing down across the back of a divan, raising a cloud of dust.

She was getting old. That flaming hair had turned the gray of ashes, with but a faint glow of its former brilliance. Her figure was still good – matronly, of course, but well proportioned, and although it was an effort, she walked with the same upright carriage. At home she was forced to use a cane, but vanity would not let her use one when she was in public. She carried a parasol instead, bent into a bow-shape from frequently having to support her weight.

But she was a Californian and took pride in saying so. Sometimes younger persons, especially her grandson David, tried to get her to talk about those early days as an émigrée, but she would only smile and say, 'Ah, that was an adventure'; she was rarely coaxed to say more. Her smile seemed to say, 'It was enough to have lived it once.'

'I suppose if we're going to shop for curtain material, we'd better get started,' Danielle said, collecting her things.

Claude kissed her absent-mindedly. 'You're not worried about going out, are you?' he asked.

'You mean Mother de Brussac's dire warnings about young toughs?' Danielle gave him a reassuring smile. 'You saw how she wields that parasol. But of course if you'd like to come with us . . . ?' Her voice rose hopefully.

'I've really got a lot I want to get done at the house,' he said quickly, feeling a twinge of guilt. What he actually hoped was that he might have a little time alone with Julia Benson. Of course, if Danielle had acted as if she were really afraid, he just might have changed his plans.

Maybe; or again, maybe not. He had not been able to get Julia Benson out of his mind since meeting her several weeks before. In the interval he had seen her a few times, but always in the company of Danielle and the children. Of course, she would be moving into the new house with them in a few days.

'Don't worry about us,' Don Diego insisted, thumping his walking stick loudly on the floor. 'We still know how to deal with troublemakers.'

'Claude – ' Danielle paused on her way out. 'I do love you, you know,' she said.

She left without waiting for a reply, leaving him to ponder what hidden meanings, if any, were in that simple statement of affection.

He wondered how much she actually knew, or suspected, about his interest in Miss Benson, or for that matter about the other women he had seen from time to time since his return from Europe.

It seemed to him that Danielle was embarrassed these days by the love she still held for him. She rarely expressed it openly unless he prompted her; perversely, as she had grown less open about her feelings, he had felt more of a need to be reassured about them. That did not, however, diminish his need for the other – for the Julia Bensons.

· Perhaps he was some sort of cad; still, he could not honestly see that he was being unfair to his wife. He gave Danielle as much as he had to give; what he gave to other women would not have been hers anyway; it came from some wellspring within him that she had been unable to tap, through no fault of hers or his own. If he could have poured out all his love on her he would have done so. She had been a good and loyal wife, and he was convinced that the very peasant qualities that he could not help despising in her had been vital in achieving what they had in California.

She was a woman of the earth who loved the vineyards as deeply as he did, loved them without quite realizing how much she loved them. Passions need proving, but the greatest loves, perhaps, are those one can afford to take for granted.

His reverie was interrupted by Miss Benson's bold knock at the door.

'I was wondering,' she said when he had let her in, 'if you were going to the new house. I had one or two questions about my room and I thought perhaps you'd let me come along with you.'

Her face was glowing with a barely contained excitement it was impossible not to respond to. 'It may be rather boring for you,' he said. 'I've got to take a lot of measurements.'

'I won't be bored,' she said, smiling slyly. After a slight pause she added, 'You've been rather standoffish with me, Mister de Brussac.'

'Have I? I thought it was the proper sort of attitude to take toward my children's governess.'

'Goodness, you make me sound such a spinster,' she said.

'I'd certainly never think of you as that.'

'Wouldn't you? Then take me with you. I'm not such terrible company, am I?'

After that he could hardly argue, even had he been so

inclined. Only Mary and David were in the hotel, and he considered David old enough and responsible enough to look after his sister. Adam was in San José, running his own increasingly successful vineyard, and Jean had been sent to France to study the latest methods of viniculture.

The house was receiving the finishing touches. Because it was Saturday, the workmen were not about, but their tools and worktables were everywhere. Upstairs, the walls needed to be papered and the woodwork stained, and the bare tubing where the gaslights would be installed thrust nakedly from the walls, but the downstairs rooms were nearly finished. Claude strolled from room to room, taking immense pleasure from the grandeur that was taking shape. The house was a symbol to him of all that he had accomplished since those desolate days after fleeing France. Here, in this elaborate architecture, in this leaded glass and sweeping stairs, was the de Brussac fortune, the de Brussac solidity, for all to see.

Following him through the rooms, Julia seemed to share his inner pleasure, as if an electrical current flowed back and forth between them.

'It's a lovely home,' she said aloud.

'As lovely as your home in Philadelphia?' Oddly, it bothered him that she might think he was one of the *nouveaux riches*; he had made a great point of telling her his background.

She shrugged. 'Philadelphia is rather a dull city. I'm the sort of woman who requires a certain amount of excitement.'

'And you've found it in Los Angeles?'

She gave him one of her veiled looks, her lips curving in a sultry smile. 'I think that the prospects are very good,' she said. 'Especially just now.'

It was an obvious invitation, and he did the obvious thing. He reached out and drew her to him.

'I still don't think this is a good idea,' David was saying. 'Papa didn't say we could come here.'

'He didn't say we couldn't,' Mary answered. 'Besides, I want to pick out my room before they're already all claimed.'

They had walked to Bunker Hill from the hotel. Actually, Mary knew that if they had asked, their father would have forbidden the walk. Though it had been three years since the Chinese race riots, many whites were still uneasy over the presence of so many Chinese in the city.

She had learned, though, that the best way to avoid being

forbidden what she wanted was to do it without asking. Anyway, far from being frightened by the city's teeming activity, she loved it. She found the Chinese, with their funny wizened faces, immensely fascinating. There were the Mexicans, too, despised by her father though she didn't quite understand why, and the cowboys, sun-dried and hardened by their life on the range. From the stores, homes and saloons along the way came an ever-varying mélange of sounds, smells and sights.

They were hot and flushed from the climb by the time they reached the house. They both paused in the street to stare up at its fanciful front, complete with gingerbread cutouts and even twin turrets.

'It's probably locked up,' David said.

'The back door's open; I heard Papa say that the locks hadn't been installed yet,' Mary said. 'Come on.' She tugged at his sleeve and David, accustomed to her rule, trudged uncertainly along with her.

'See,' she said triumphantly when they saw the open back door. Instinctively they had both lowered their voices to whispers, and as they stole along the hall that ran from front to back, dividing the downstairs into two neat halves, they walked on tiptoe. There was an odd air of listening about the house, as if it had not yet made up its mind whether to welcome them or not.

'Listen, I hear something,' David said, hesitating.

'Don't be silly, there's no one here but us. Mama is shopping, and Papa said he had business to attend to.'

Nonetheless, she paused, too, cocking her head to listen. It did sound as if there was someone else in the house – there, in the parlor, where the door stood ajar.

They crept closer, ears straining. There was something, not voices exactly, but sounds, like the rustle of clothing and breathing – harsh, raspy breaths.

Mary went first, peering through the open door – and froze, unable to move or speak. David pressed against her from behind, staring over her shoulder. She felt the shock ripple through his body as he too saw into the parlor.

It was Papa and Miss Benson, both of them naked, lying on the new carpet on the floor. Mary's face flushed hotly, and when David seized her arm and dragged her away from the door, for once she accepted his command without protest. They all but ran from the house, not slowing their pace or speaking until they were outside and well away from the site.

'What were they doing?' Mary asked finally.

'Nothing,' David replied curtly.

She blushed again at the memory. She hadn't really meant *what* were they doing – you couldn't grow up on a ranch around animals and not know something of the facts of life; she had actually meant why was Papa doing it with Miss Benson. With a sick feeling in her stomach, she remembered Antoinette's party and Richard de Trémorel's snide insinuations and knew that she would never again be able to feel the same untainted love and respect for her father that she had always felt, any more than she could derive the same pleasure from the crowds through which they now pushed their way.

Beside her, David was filled with conflicting feelings and thoughts; he was shocked by what he had seen and disgusted with his father. But there was another part of him that ignored his father altogether and thought only of Julia Benson. For a second or two, before his father had lowered himself over her, he had seen Miss Benson complete and unadorned. His eyes had been seared by the sight of those thighs, as white and smooth as fresh cream, parted in welcome; her breasts, naked and full, heaving with the force of her breath.

He had never seen a naked woman before; sometimes in his more shameful thoughts he had imagined such a sight, but the reality had been far from his imaginings.

Despite his shock and disgust, he was stirred; he felt hot, as if he had a fever, and he was only vaguely aware of things going on about him.

Of one thing he was certain; he would never again be able to look at Miss Benson without seeing superimposed over her image that other vision of trembling breasts and yearning loins.

61

Living in Los Angeles was even worse than Danielle had expected.

'Give it time,' had been Claude's advice when she had tried to discuss her unhappiness with him.

It was now a year since they had moved into the Victorian

mansion on the hill, and things had not gotten any better.

'If anything, they're worse,' she confessed on a visit to Anne and Don Diego. 'I just don't seem to fit into anything. There's that free society out on the West End, they think I'm too stuffy for them, and there's the old guard, downtown, the Dodsons and the like, they look down their noses because my parents were working people.'

'My first husband was a working man,' Anne said, 'and proud of it; he had no truck with idlers.'

'It's a lot of rubbish anyway,' Don Diego said angrily. 'I know most of those people. They're descended from fur trappers and panhandlers, but they think just because they made a killing on the railroads or in real estate that they've moved that much closer to God.'

'Claude thinks so,' Danielle said.

'My son is a snob,' Anne said. 'I thought that he might outgrow it, but the disease seems to be worse. And I don't know where it will end.'

'If only he would move back to the ranch,' Danielle said wistfully. 'At least here I'd have something to do. There, the time just seems to crawl by.'

Anne paused in her embroidery. 'Why don't you move back, bring the children – Claude would soon miss you; he'd follow in a few weeks' time.'

'I don't know. There's the children's education, for one thing. I doubt that Miss Benson would consider living in the country.'

Anne gave her a piercing look. 'There are other governesses, women who are not quite so particular – if the children actually need any more tutoring.'

Danielle avoided her gaze. She knew she was only parroting Claude's arguments in defending Miss Benson's position. She supposed in all fairness that the children had learned from Miss Benson; at least they had improved in the social graces that were so important in the new society in Los Angeles.

The truth was she doubted that she had the authority within her own family to exercise the kind of decision-making that Anne described. She could well imagine the kind of furor that would be raised if she announced that she was taking the children and returning to the ranch. The children, who were quite happy with the city, would sulk and rant and appeal to their father, and in the end she would return to the ranch alone, leaving Claude on his own with the admirable Miss Benson, which was not what she wanted either.

She had suspected from the first that Claude and Miss Benson were lovers, but she was at a loss to know what to do about it. To question Claude directly would be to stage a showdown, and she hadn't enough confidence in her own ability to emerge a winner to risk that sort of confrontation.

At the moment Claude was in Sacramento. Danielle had come to the ranch alone, leaving David and Mary in Miss Benson's care because she wanted the opportunity to confront her thoughts, but now she found that prospect none too pleasing. On an impulse she decided to return to the city. Claude would be back the following day; somehow when he was there, at her side, the rest seemed to matter less.

It was late when she arrived back in the city. She was surprised to see that a light was still burning in David's room. When she went up, she found him reading.

'I'm sorry, Mama; I didn't know it was so late,' he said.

'You should have been in bed hours ago. Does Miss Benson know you're still up?' Danielle had seen no sign of light from Miss Benson's room.

'Miss Benson went out,' David said.

Danielle was both surprised and annoyed by the news. She supposed David and Mary were old enough to look after themselves for an evening; still, she had left them in Miss Benson's care. If Miss Benson had planned on going out for the evening, oughtn't she to have mentioned the fact before?

Danielle went along to Miss Benson's room and, having knocked without getting an answer, went in. Miss Benson was still out, apparently, although it was well after midnight. Should she mention it to Claude when he came home, or not?

She was still trying to decide that question as she undressed in her own bedroom. Danielle removed her gown, shaking it out, and carried it into the dressing room to hang it. As she did so, something caught her eye. She paused, staring at the rows of dresses on hangers.

What was it that was wrong? Something . . . surely the dresses hadn't been hanging so haphazardly; and that topaz dress – had it been hanging just there earlier?

No, she was sure of it; someone had been going through her clothes. She thought of the maids and dismissed the idea. They would not have left things quite so out of order. The dresses looked as if someone had been rummaging rather carelessly through them; several of the gowns had apparently been removed from their hangers and then replaced none too neatly, and she was certain that they were not hanging where they had been before.

She studied the rows carefully, trying to determine if anything was missing.

Yes, the emerald-green gown that she'd worn to the governor's ball – it was gone from its customary place. She looked again, still more carefully, but there was no doubt of it; the emerald gown was missing.

Would Miss Benson have borrowed the dress? But that was too presumptuous, even for the free and easy Miss Benson. Surely she would not have been so brazen.

And yet Miss Benson had known that she was away, presumably until the following day. It would have been reasonable to assume that no one would ever know.

Danielle's face flushed angrily. No longer at all sleepy, she donned a peignoir and settled herself into the chaise-longue in her bedroom to await Miss Benson's return. She left the door to the hall open so that she would be certain to hear her come in.

At the moment Julia Benson, looking ravishing in Danielle's emerald gown, was at a party at Antoinette's, giving her friends a rather frank appraisal of Claude de Brussac's merits as a lover.

'Such a splendid build,' she concluded. 'And the stamina of a young colt. He's quite amazing, really.'

'Yes, so I recall,' Antoinette said, forcing herself to look pleasant, though in fact she was furious.

Julia, who was too pleased with herself to pay much attention to anyone else's feelings, remained unaware of her companion's resentment. 'Oh, but I'd forgotten, he was your lover once, too, wasn't he?'

'It's been so long,' Antoinette murmured evasively. For reasons that she herself did not fully comprehend, she had no desire to share her memories of Claude de Brussac with Julia.

'Well, I can assure you age has only made him better. I can't imagine why his wife would ever agree to separate bedrooms – but then, some women aren't interested in that sort of thing. Or they pretend not to be. It's a wonder men don't suffer frost-bite from them.'

'That at least is something a man needn't fear from you,' Antoinette said, but Julia did not seem to notice. She continued prattling on while Antoinette made a pretense of listening.

Antoinette could not really think why she was so angry with

the relationship that had developed between Claude and Julia. It was not as if she wanted Claude for herself. Heaven knew she had had plenty of opportunities in that direction since she had arrived in California, but in actual truth she loved her own husband very much. For all of her shortcomings, constancy was not a virtue that she lacked.

Yet at the same time she could not help resenting the thought of Claude de Brussac with another woman, whether it was his wife or Julia. She had had to force herself to listen with apparent interest to Julia's recitation of his merits.

She remembered only too well what he had been like long ago. He had been gauche and inexperienced, largely disappointing; and he had killed the one person in her life who had mattered greatly to her. She had no reason to desire anything but his destruction; she was constantly dreaming of that end.

Why, then, should she mind whom he had for a lover? If only Julia didn't look so pleased with herself.

Thinking to distract Julia, Antoinette interrupted her monologue to point out a distinguished-looking gentleman making his way through the crowds in their direction.

'There's Senator Wallace,' she said, nodding her head in the gentleman's direction. 'He's got his eye on you. I do believe he's quite smitten – or have you closed your eyes to other men?'

Julia laughed frankly. 'Oh, I've always said variety is the spice of life,' she admitted. 'As a matter of fact, there is someone else – do you know the de Brussac boy?'

Antoinette frowned, remembering. 'There's the one who lives up north – Adam, I think his name is – but I've only seen him once or twice, and another one who lives in the country . . . '

'I was thinking of David.'

'The quiet one? He's so young.'

'That's true. But quiet men are often such splendid lovers . . . ' Julia let her voice trail off, Senator Wallace having reached her side.

Constancy, Antoinette was thinking, was not one of Julia's virtues.

It was nearly two o'clock in the morning when Danielle heard the front door open and close softly and the sound of stealthy footsteps in the downstairs hall. Danielle laid aside her book and went into the corridor.

Julia Benson was creeping up the stairs, taking pains to make as little noise as possible. Her shining hair lay in untidy ringlets about her face and she was carrying her shoes. She was indeed wearing Danielle's emerald gown.

She did not see Danielle until she had reached the top of the stairs and was level with her.

'Oh,' she said, starting guiltily. 'You startled me.'

'Yes, I imagine I did,' Danielle said. 'Obviously you weren't expecting me back quite so early.'

Miss Benson's eyes darted for a second in the direction of the children's bedrooms. 'There's nothing wrong, is there?'

'Not with the children.'

'Oh, you mean the dress.' Julia fingered the silk fabric. 'I was invited to a party. I didn't think you'd mind.'

'Then we were both mistaken, you in borrowing my dress and I in trusting you in my home,' Danielle said icily.

For a moment Julia looked abashed; then, unexpectedly, she gave a haughty toss of her head. 'There's no harm done, is there? I haven't soiled it or anything. If you like I'll ask Mister de Brussac to take the cost of the dress out of my salary . . .' She hesitated her eyes narrowing slyly. 'Though to be honest, I'm sure he'll refuse.'

'Then we shan't trouble him with it,' Danielle said. 'You may consider yourself discharged, Miss Benson.'

'You mean now? This minute?'

'You may stay until morning. I'm sure tomorrow you can find someplace to stay. You must have many admirers who would be willing to – take you in.'

For a moment the two women stared coldly at one another. Danielle was nonplussed by the younger woman's effrontery. Julia seemed not at all embarrassed by what she had done, nor intimidated at being fired.

'We'll discuss this in the morning,' Julia said, starting toward her own room.

'There's nothing further to discuss,' Danielle said angrily.

'Isn't there?' Julia paused to look over her shoulder at her. 'Don't be naïve, Mrs de Brussac. I don't think your husband would appreciate your firing me in his absence. I'll be doing you a favor if I pretend we didn't have this conversation.'

She went into her room, shutting the door quietly but firmly. Danielle was left with burning cheeks.

'How dare she?' she fumed. She was furious, yet at the same time she could not entirely ignore her fear that there might be truth in Miss Benson's words. Claude would not be happy to return and find Miss Benson fired in his absence.

Miss Benson went about her business the following day quite as if nothing had happened. The green dress reappeared, tossed disdainfully over a chair, in Danielle's room.

Danielle seethed with angry frustration, but short of having Miss Benson physically removed from the property, it seemed there was nothing she could do until Claude returned that evening from Sacramento.

As the day wore on, Danielle began to feel more and more unsure of herself in the face of Julia's serene confidence, so that by the time Claude had actually returned, Danielle felt almost as if she were the guilty party and Julia the wronged one.

At least Julia had the tact not to join them for dinner as usual, but asked for a tray in her room.

Or was she, Danielle wondered unhappily, only saving her own arguments till she could talk to Claude in private?

Claude listened impassively to Danielle's narration. Danielle found herself stammering like a schoolgirl – if only Claude would give her some encouragement – but he regarded her as if he found the entire discussion distasteful.

'I see,' was Claude's remark when she was finished.

'I – I'm not sure that you do,' Danielle said. 'I fired Miss Benson. It seemed to me the only thing that I could do under the circumstances. But she – that is, I thought it better if you actually took care of discharging her.'

'It sounds to me like a tempest in a teapot. This dress – it was returned, you say?'

'Yes, but – that's hardly the point, is it?'

'Had it been damaged?'

'Why, it was wrinkled, of course, as any dress would be from being worn, but no, I can't actually say that it was damaged.'

'Well then . . . ' Claude shrugged. 'It sounds to me like that's all there is to it.'

Danielle was humiliated; she said without thinking. 'But that's outrageous. You can't expect me to have a woman living here who helps herself to what is mine. This time it was a gown – an expensive gown, I might add – and what will it be next? My jewelry, my – ' She caught herself just in time; she had been about to add, 'My husband?'

There was an awkward silence between them. After a moment Claude said wearily, 'I'll speak to her.'

Danielle pushed her chair back angrily from the table and rose. 'Please do,' she said, striding from the room.

Claude came to her bedroom later. 'I've spoken to Miss Benson,' he said without preamble. 'She's deeply sorry for what she did and apologizes for her lapse of judgment. In addition, she promises this sort of thing won't happen again.'

'I'm sure that it can't, if she is no longer in our employ,' Danielle said. 'Have you discharged her?'

Claude gave a sigh. 'No. I think you're making too much of this, to be honest.'

'Oh?' Danielle lifted one eyebrow. 'Are you being honest?'

'What do you mean by that?'

'You say you won't fire her – don't you mean that you can't?'

'Danielle, I –'

'It's true, isn't it, what everyone is saying. She is your lover?'

He had turned away from her as she spoke, but now he turned back to face her and there was a look of such agony on his face that for a brief period she was moved with pity for him and all but forgot her own pain and anger.

'Yes.'

Although part of her had known all along that this was the case, hearing it from his own lips was unexpectedly painful. For a moment she was unable to speak.

'I can't help myself,' he said. 'I've tried, but it's no use.'

'You mean that you love her?'

'Yes,' he said, adding quickly, 'but you've got to understand, that doesn't mean that I love you any less.'

'How can you say that?' she cried, wringing her hands together.

He brought his hands up and pressed them against his temples as if he would squeeze his thoughts from his head.

'It's insane. I don't understand it myself,' he said. 'How can I hope to make you understand it? It's like there's a great hollow space, a void, inside me. You're my wife, the mother of my children, and I love you, truly I do, but there's still been that void. I've tried in all kinds of ways to fill it – with my work, with the wines, with money and power, with other women, to be perfectly frank. And nothing helped – until Julia. Perhaps I despise her as much as I love her. I know she's not worth anything compared to you, and yet she satisfies some need in me. I must have her, even though I know she doesn't love me. Can you understand that?'

'I – oh, I don't know! What are you trying to say, that you mean to leave me?'

'I hope not. Only if you tell me I must. You've been such a comfort to me, so loyal, so loving, I can't imagine my life without you beside me. I'm only saying that I can't give her up.'

'You're asking me to share my husband with another woman.'

'No, I . . . yes, I guess that is what I'm asking.' He sighed. 'How is it possible for a man to love two different women at the same time? If anyone had asked me before, I'd have said it was impossible, but now I know that it isn't. I love you both. I want you both.'

Danielle went to the window, from which she could see the city of Los Angeles spread at her feet. She supposed there were hundreds, perhaps thousands, of women there in those teeming streets who, glancing up at her mansion on the hill, envied her. She had everything a woman could desire: a fine home, wealth, jewelry, lovely children, the husband she adored.

Yet she felt in her heart that she was the poorest of women. She longed to demand that he choose between them, but she was afraid; what if he didn't choose her? She could not imagine a life without him. Where could she go? What could she do? She could almost understand his agony; she, too, was enslaved by love.

'I seem to have no choice,' she said. 'I cannot be free of her without ridding myself of you as well, and I do not wish that.'

'Danielle – ' He came to her, clasping her shoulders, but she shrugged off his hands.'

'No,' she said. 'Go to her arms, if you must, or come to mine, if you will, but not from one to the other. I am your wife. Let her take what she will, I will remain that.'

She remained at the window until she heard the bedroom door open and close softly as he went out. She went to the door and bolted it after him. Only then did she fling herself across the bed and give herself up to the terrible sobs that she had been holding back.

62

For a time it seemed as if French Hills Winery could do no wrong. Although the national depression that had begun four years earlier in '73, with the failure of Jay Cook and Company, had finally had a disastrous effect on the California wine industry in general, it had no more than a minimal effect on the French Hills output.

It was the manufacturers of *vin ordinaire*, mostly from the still widespread mission grape, who suffered the most, and the makers of premium wines, from European-imported vines, who suffered the least. While other vintners throughout the state were selling wine at ten and fifteen cents a gallon and letting their pigs and other barnyard animals harvest grape crops, the de Brussacs continued to produce what were generally regarded as America's finest wines.

Adam's holdings in San José produced some fifty thousand gallons of wine a year, nearly half of what the southern vineyards produced. The northern counties now dominated the California wine industry, despite Claude's predictions to the contrary.

So far the opening of the transcontinental railroad had proved of little benefit to California's wine growers. Freight rates were so high that a case of wine worth $2.50 could cost twice that amount to transport to Chicago by train, with the result that most wines still went by ship. Claude was optimistic, however, and just the year before he had conducted a promising experiment: He had sent several packages of grapes by rail in an ordinary freight car that also contained several cakes of ice in the center; the grapes had arrived at their destination in Iowa in uncommonly good condition. If freight rates could be reduced, there was money to be made in grape crops as well as in wine production.

While others sold their wine for vinegar and dug up their vines to replace them with fruit and walnut trees, Claude continued to expand production and at the same time improve their wines.

For Danielle, however, it seemed as if life had come to a standstill. An uneasy truce, more of a stalemate really, reigned in the gingerbread mansion on the hill. Julia remained in residence even though David was now eighteen and Mary, just a year younger, disdained any further education.

Claude took pride in the lessons the two youngest children had learned from Julia. 'They could take their place anywhere in society,' he was fond of saying, but Danielle was not so sure.

Mary was more headstrong and willful than ever. Her enthusiasm for living contributed as much to her popularity as her outstanding good looks did, but Danielle could not help observing that her daughter was self-centered and often thoughtlessly cruel.

As for David, it seemed to Danielle that he had become more withdrawn than ever since the arrival of Julia Benson in the house. Indeed, in the past few months David had become so habitually melancholy that Danielle had begun to worry about him. She thought she could guess the source of his unhappiness, and once or twice she had even tried tentatively to broach the subject to him, but the result had only been that he had withdrawn still further.

She had come to the rather sorry conclusion that an unbridgeable gap lay between her and her children. When he came home for visits, Adam remained closeted with his father or spent his time in the vineyards, and Jean, home now from France, could talk of nothing but wines and the latest agricultural methods of Europe – she thought him a pleasant enough young man but a bit of a bore. David and Mary were virtual strangers to her; she knew them intimately, but not well.

No doubt the fault was hers; she had been so involved in Claude that she had excluded everything else from her life, even her own children. She had lived with but one goal – to make her husband her own – and in the end she had found that nothing was hers to own. She was like a man who, while others about him were building their houses upon well-placed supports, had settled instead for one massive column, only to stand now and watch it erode. She knew that when it went, the entire structure would topple.

On the surface, however, things went along peacefully enough, and when the peace was shattered, it was by the most unlikely member of the household.

'I want to become a priest.'

24

David's announcement was delivered while the family was at dinner. He glanced quickly around the table, but after a moment of surprise, the others – Jean, Mary, his mother and Julia – turned toward Claude, who was carving the roast.

Claude set his utensils aside and instinctively reached for his wine glass. 'And what do you think that will get you?' he asked.

David, plainly embarrassed at having disrupted dinner, tapped his fork nervously on the table.

'Knowledge,' he said. 'Understanding.'

'You don't have to become a priest for that,' Claude said. 'You've already got plenty of knowledge. Miss Benson's seen to that. And look at Adam and Jean, they've both got knowledge, too, of a practical sort. What you need to do is involve yourself more in the business instead of letting your brothers carry you the way they have to. Frankly, you aren't earning your keep.'

'That's just what I mean. I don't care a hill of beans about the business, and all this talk about vines and grapes and wineries bores me. I'll never make a decent vintner.'

Claude took up his carving knife again. 'Well, there are plenty of other lines to get into. This is a growing country, and you're still young enough to start an apprenticeship. There must be some line of work you fancy?'

'I wasn't thinking of any line of work exactly. I just want to learn.'

Mary started to say something but her father stopped her with a glance. 'To what purpose?' he asked David.

David hesitated. 'I suppose just for the sake of learning. I don't know if I can explain it very well, but sometimes I feel like I want to reach up and touch the stars. When I read the great philosophers, it goes to my head, the way the wine does for you. It's like standing high on a great mountain, someplace where the crowds of men never go, alone, breathing an air that's rare and unspoiled.'

'That doesn't sound very practical,' Julia said.

'Exactly,' Claude said, sounding miffed; he did not relish the idea of a priest for a son. Of course he had always known that David was a bit different, thoughtful and introspective, and he had taken pride in the patience that he had shown his youngest son, but he had been patient because he had always assumed that one day David would grow out of it and take his rightful place in the de Brussac empire.

'There must be something you expect to get out of this,' he

said. 'You can't blame us for insisting that you give us a little better answer.'

'I guess I want to find the answers to my questions,' David said. He turned almost hopefully to his mother.

'What questions?' she asked, not without sympathy.

'They're not very original, I'm afraid,' he said almost apologetically. 'They're mostly the same questions men have been asking for centuries. Who am I, what am I doing here? What and where is God? Is there a soul and what happens to it when I die? Why is there evil?' He shrugged as if he knew how futile those questions sounded when expressed in such banal terms.

'That's just the kind of rubbish you'd expect from someone who doesn't do any work,' Jean said.

'All young men wonder about those things at some time in their lives,' Claude said, ignoring Jean's remark. 'I thought about them myself when I was your age. But there's more to life than that. A man has to think about a family, and making a living.'

'I've got a family,' David said, smiling around the table.

'That's not what I mean,' Claude snapped.

'And as for money, I don't really care about making money.'

'That's easy enough to say; you've never had to worry about it,' Claude said. 'But when you don't have any, you appreciate its value. Anyway, you've got an obligation, a duty to the family. This family's looked out for you for eighteen years. Now it's time you were making some kind of contribution in return. What do you think I built up French Hills for, if not to pass it on to my sons – that's been my one ambition, to create something grand and precious for future generations of de Brussacs so that my sons, and their sons, would be something in this world. A man doesn't look at his newborn son, you know, and pray that he'll grow up to be an accomplished dreamer, or the world's greatest priest. He wants him to matter.'

'You've got Adam and Jean; they're the ones to carry on the winery,' David said. He grinned shyly and added, 'Besides, the world's got to have dreamers, too, to offset all you wide-awake ones.'

Claude banged his knife down on the table loudly, making the wine glasses rattle. 'The world may need dreamers and priests, but it isn't going to get them from this family. You aren't going into the priesthood and that's final.'

'I think you're entirely right,' Julia said.

'I don't agree,' Danielle said. 'It seems to me if he has his heart set on it . . .'

'I said my decision is final,' Claude said angrily.

Danielle was silent in the face of her husband's anger, but she could not help sharing the disappointment that she saw on her son's face, nor did she fail to notice Julia's look of satisfaction.

63

David was humiliated. It would have been bad enough if he and Papa had been alone, but to be treated like a child in front of the others – in front of Julia, especially. The worst of it was he could never have explained to Papa the real reason for his unhappiness, the real reason he wanted to join the priesthood. He could never share that with anyone.

Mary came into his room, as usual without knocking. 'Now you've done it,' she said, flouncing across the room to stand in front of him. 'You really know how to put the fat in the fire, don't you?'

'Now what?' he asked. 'Don't tell me everyone's still up in arms just because I want to become a priest?'

'Just because? According to Papa you've violated everything but the Constitution. And that isn't the half of it, either – he's so mad he refuses to take me to the Sheridans' party tonight.'

'So? What do you want me to do about it? I can't exactly renounce my vows, seeing as I haven't even taken them yet.'

'So Mama says I can't go to the party unless you escort me; she's afraid some tall, dark stranger will carry me off in the moonlight.'

'You're crazy – and so is Mama. There isn't an eligible bachelor in town who's still a stranger to you. Anyway, I'm in no mood for a party, I'm afraid.'

Mary threw herself into a chair. 'Don't you understand what I'm saying? If you won't go with me, I can't go, either.'

'That's no great tragedy. You've been to three parties already this week. It won't hurt you to stay home for a change. Isn't that what Papa's lecture was all about, keeping the family intact regardless of how the individual members feel about it?'

'Listen, don't take it out on me just because you're mad at Papa. And this isn't just any old party, this is the Sheridans' once-a-year party – everyone who is anyone will be there.'

'Well, you're not going to be, not if you're expecting me to take you; so you might as well go back to your room and take off that fancy dress.'

'You're horrible,' Mary cried, jumping to her feet. 'I hate you; you're just like everyone else, never thinking of anyone but yourself.'

She ran to the door. 'And don't think you fooled me with all that talk about finding the answers to your questions. I know why you want to become a priest – it's because you're in love with Miss Benson.'

David sprang from his chair, his fists clenched at his side. 'Shut up,' he said.

'It's true, you can't take your eyes off her. You're like a moon-struck calf, and you want to be a priest because you know that you can never do anything about how you feel, because she's years older than you, and besides, you wouldn't dare say anything or do anything because everyone knows she's Papa's – ' she caught herself before she said it.

David's face burned crimson. He almost shouted, 'Get out!'

The door slammed after her. He had a sudden urge to throw something, smash something, anything to release the pent-up emotions he was feeling.

After a moment, though, his anger gave way to a profound gloom. Mary was right; he was in love with Miss Benson – or perhaps not quite that, either. He was old enough and wise enough to know that a great deal of what he felt was sheer physical lust. Since the day he and Mary had accidentally stumbled upon their father and Miss Benson together, here in this very house, David's erotic longings had centered upon that one object, their governess.

There were times when he almost thought she was aware of his desire, though he had done everything in his power to conceal it.

'Obviously not enough,' he thought ruefully, since Mary had penetrated his secret. He wondered if the others knew, too. The thought that he might be an object of ridicule because of his longings only added to his sense of shame and frustration.

Mary was back in a matter of minutes, slipping meekly into the room. 'David, I'm sorry,' she said in a little-girl voice.

He managed a wry smile and opened his arms to her; she came running into them, burying her head against his shoulder.

'I'm such a harpy,' she said, sniffling.

'It's all right, puss, you were right; I was thinking of nobody but myself. I guess I've got a way to go before I make a priest.'

'You'll make a good one; I just know you will.'

He patted her shoulder. 'Not if Papa has his way,' he said.

She stepped back from him, smiling once more now that they had made their peace. David was by far her favorite brother. For all that she railed at him, she couldn't bear to think that she had actually made him unhappy.

'I guess I'd better go get out of this dress,' she said, fingering the amber silk.

'No, don't do that. Give me a little time to change, and we'll go to your party.'

'Will you?' Her face brightened, then fell again. 'Oh, you don't have to, just to please me.'

'It's all right, I don't mind. Maybe it will cheer me up a little anyway.'

She flung her arms about him again. 'You are the most wonderful brother – but what shall I do if you become a priest?'

'Maybe you should become a nun,' he teased.

'I'd do it, if it made you happy. Only I'd have to find an order that permitted parties – I couldn't live without parties.'

She dashed out, leaving him to smile fondly after her. After a moment he sighed and, shaking his head, began to change his clothes.

It was going to be a thrilling evening; Mary could feel it already as she stepped from the carriage. There was something that happened to her after the patching up of a quarrel; it seemed to leave her charged with a special luminance. She had that marvelous feeling she hadn't had in a while: that everyone was looking at and admiring her.

The Sheridans were maverick members of local society. She had been an actress before she married her husband, who had been a member of President Grant's cabinet. It was said that their entertainments had been among the most brilliant in Washington.

Randolph Sheridan had become involved in the Credit Mobilier scandal that had exposed the corruption rampant in the Grant administration. Though no formal charges had been leveled against him, Sheridan had resigned his post and the couple had left Washington.

It was not quite true, as Mary had argued, that everyone would be at their annual party; a great many of the members of established society shunned the Sheridans' company, Claude among them. But with the younger members, and particularly with the somewhat looser set that gathered around Antoinette de Trémorel and her husband, the Sheridans' parties were enormously popular. A stream of ladies and gentlemen, and others to whom those appellations did not quite apply, was pouring into the lavish West Side mansion.

'Isn't it grand?' Mary whispered as they went in; she remembered to cling to her brother's arm, though in truth she would have liked to run up the stairs ahead of him.

'It's crowded, I'll say that much,' David answered.

They had hardly entered the main salon, in which an energetic waltz was being performed by a sea of couples, when Mary spied Richard de Trémorel standing in one of the archways leading to the buffet tables.

It gave her an odd sensation to see him, as if she were somehow doing something improper by running into him like this. She had not seen him since that night at Antoinette's, when his kiss had left her so shaken.

No sooner was the waltz over than Antoinette came up to greet them. 'I'm so glad to see you again,' she said. 'Have you just arrived?'

'Yes, it's awfully crowded, isn't it?' Mary said.

'Too crowded, if you ask me,' David said.

'Exactly what I've been saying,' Antoinette answered. 'As a matter of fact, some of our friends are going to leave in a little while and come for an impromptu supper at our house. Do say you'll join us.'

Mary would have loved to accept, but before she could answer, David had said, 'We'll see.'

Richard chose that particular moment to join them. Mary saw him making his way through the crowd toward them. He walked without haste and with a deliberate arrogance; those in his path seemed instinctively to step back to make way for him, and in a moment he was standing at his mother's side.

'You remember my son, Richard,' Antoinette was saying, going on to introduce him to David.

Richard looked directly into Mary's eyes, almost smiling, and with such frank desire that it seemed almost ridiculous to

Mary to be so close to him, to gaze at one another like this, and not be in his arms.

'It has been a long time since I had the pleasure of meeting you,' Richard said. 'Too long, I'm afraid. But I assure you I haven't forgotten a moment of our last meeting.'

'Nor have I,' Mary admitted breathlessly, unable to remember the little flirtatious gestures and witty phrases that she used with such success on her other admirers. Richard's eyes seemed to be devouring her, moving like a lover's hand over her face, her bare neck, her bare arms, the cleft of her bodice. His gaze pleased her and at the same time frightened her; she sensed that between them there was not that protective veil of propriety that she was used to having between herself and men. She had a sense of some instinctive bond between them, as though they shared some guilty secret. But as yet they had done nothing more than kiss, once.

'Has my mother told you we're going on to our house in a while? Good. Do say you'll join us.'

Mary tried to look away from him, but in an instant her eyes were drawn back to his. He smiled, and his smile was so warm, so straightforward and confident, that she could not help smiling in return.

'We'd be delighted,' she heard herself saying, almost as if it were a stranger replying in her stead.

Mary felt as if she were moving in a dream. She watched Richard stroll away again, looking serene and quite sure of himself, and she was frightened by what lay before her. She seemed to have been possessed, to have lost her head completely. Was this falling in love? She had heard the phrase so many times, had even used it herself – but to refer to something quite different from this. She did not know whether the experience was more exciting or terrifying. If this was love, why was her conscience gnawing at her the way it was; and why did she feel as if she were no longer pure, when nothing at all had happened?

Richard had returned to Los Angeles because his behavior had been a scandal in San Francisco. He had accumulated a fortune in gambling debts, which he was unable to pay, and had recently seduced the daughter of one of the city's more prominent families. He had a penchant, too, for cavorting in the bars along the waterfront, and it was rumored that he sometimes formed unhealthy attachments with the sailors that he befriended there.

He had hardly thought of the young de Brussac girl since he

had left Los Angeles; the sight of her tonight was something
of a shock. She had been quite pretty before, but she was now
almost literally stunning, easily the most ravishing creature he
had seen in years.

'And I do enjoy little girls,' he confided to one of his cronies
a bit later, while they were admiring Mary's dancing. 'One gets
tired of the well-traveled roads.'

Tonight, almost as soon as he saw her, he had made up his
mind that he must have Mary de Brussac. Of course, marriage
was out of the question; even if he wanted to marry her, which
he did not, her father would certainly never agree to it. But what
a man promised and what he had to deliver were two different
things. It would trouble his conscience not at all to promise her
marriage in order to get her into his bed. As for what happened
to her afterward, when she learned he had no intention of
marrying her, why, that did not concern him; the problem, if
any, was hers.

Mary was surprised that Richard had not asked her to dance,
although she did not suffer from any lack of partners. She was so
busy she hardly had time for her brother at all, though she made
a point of dancing a quadrille with him a bit later in the evening.

Antoinette spoke to her again. 'Richard tells me you've
decided to join us after all. I'm so pleased,' she said. 'I'm afraid
he'd have given me no peace if you hadn't agreed. He's spoken
of nothing since you arrived but you, you little minx – he's fallen
hopelessly in love with you, it seems.'

Mary found herself blushing. 'I can't think why,' she said,
feeling pleased.

Antoinette laughed good-naturedly. 'Oh, indeed not; simply
that you are the most ravishing girl in the place tonight – that's
not enough, I suppose? Of course, if it annoys you . . . ? I could
ask him to leave you alone.'

'Oh, no, please,' Mary exclaimed without thinking, at once
blushing again at her temerity.

Antoinette's eyes sparkled mischievously. 'Tell me frankly, do
you like him, even just a little?'

Mary lowered her lashes, trying to conceal her eagerness. 'I
like him a great deal.'

'Well then – ' Antoinette shrugged. 'What could be more
natural?'

And hearing it put so neatly, Mary found herself agreeing; it
was indeed quite simple and natural, and anyway, why shouldn't
she do exactly as she wanted – she wasn't a child anymore.

David was not keen on lingering at Antoinette's once they had arrived there; although he had little experience, he could see at a glance that this was rather a notorious crowd. He felt inclined to take Mary home, especially since it was growing late, but she persuaded him to stay, 'Just for a while.'

Richard was standing near the door when they came in, obviously watching for them. He asked Mary to waltz with him, and during the dance he held her uncomfortably close and whispered in her ear that he loved her.

They danced a second dance, in which he said nothing, which confused her, and then a third, in which he told her that she was the most bewitching woman he had ever met.

'You mustn't say such things,' she whispered coyly, though his words thrilled her.

'You can't ask that of me,' he said. 'I can't help expressing what I feel. I want to marry you.'

The suggestion startled her; even her wildly circling thoughts had not jumped that far.

'It's impossible,' she blurted out. 'My father would never permit – '

'Oh, don't say that. I tell you if you don't agree to marry me, I shall run a sword through myself – here, tonight, in front of all these people. My blood will be on your hands.'

'Don't talk like that. You must be mad.'

'I am – mad with love for you. Is that my fault, or yours because you're so bewitching?'

She was glad and sorry all at once when the dance ended. Her head was spinning; she had had many admirers in the past, but no one had ever spoken to her as he had: with such frankness, such ardor. And it must be true that he was hopelessly in love with her – hadn't his own mother said so? Anyway, you could see it just by looking at him; you didn't have to be experienced in love to know it when you saw it in a man's eyes.

But to marry him? It was fantastic, it was impossible – she wouldn't have dared even mentioning it to Papa.

Still, for all that it was impossible, it was as desirable to her as it obviously was to Richard. If only there were a way!

In one part of her mind she had already guessed what Richard was going to say to her next, so that when his suggestion actually came, it hardly shocked her at all.

Antoinette had accompanied her to the powder room, teasing her about Richard's hopeless passion. They had gone to Antoinette's personal suite on the floor above, and when they came out into the little sitting room, Richard was there waiting for them. In a twinkling Antoinette had disappeared, and Mary found herself alone with her passionate admirer.

He came to her at once and took one of her trembling hands in his two strong ones. 'Mary,' he whispered her name in a voice hoarse with longing, 'tell me that all is not hopeless. I know it's impossible for me to come to you openly; your family would never permit that. But please don't tell me that my life is over because of that.'

She knew that she should leave, that it was scandalous for them to be in such an intimate setting alone, but he had barred her way, and his intense eyes were so close to her own.

'Come away with me,' he begged.

'I can't,' she pleaded, but in a moment he had kissed her and she felt the last of her resistance melting in the heat of his kiss.

'Not tonight, then, but soon,' she heard his words in her ear. 'We'll run away and get married. Once you're my wife, there'll be nothing anyone can do about it. Your family will accept me then, you'll see. Only say that you'll do it.'

As if in a dream, she heard her own voice answering. 'Yes, yes, I will.'

64

Once every year or so Claude liked to travel northward to look over Adam's vineyard at San José. Since Don Diego had purchased his own small property to the north, he was in the habit of making the trip along with Claude.

This year the man suggested that their wives accompany them. Anne, who found travel a hardship with her increasing lack of mobility, declined, but Danielle, glad for a chance to escape her uncomfortable life in the city, decided to go on the condition that Anne remain in the city with the children. Since the unfortunate occasion when Julia had 'borrowed' her clothes, Danielle was uneasy about leaving Julia in undisputed charge of things.

'You're sure you can manage?' Danielle asked Anne when they were preparing to leave.

'My dear daughter,' Anne said, 'one false move from that woman and I shall deal with her as you did with el Tigre.'

'You shouldn't talk that way, you know,' Danielle chided her.

'If you say so. But I do wish you'd consider it; it would be such a fitting end for her.'

Julia, who was no more fond of Anne than Anne was of her, made a point of avoiding the older woman, so that things went quietly for the first few days.

'Too quietly,' Anne found herself reflecting. David, of course, was always quiet, but there was something downright morbid about his behavior at present. That he was wrestling with some intense personal problem was evident; she supposed that he was in love, boys his age usually were, but they did not ordinarily look so unhappy about it, unless the object of their love was a married woman.

But it was Mary that worried her most. The girl's behavior was odd to the point of eccentricity. Her mood seemed to change suddenly from elation to gloom, and back again. She was confused to the point of distraction, and so preoccupied with her own thoughts, whatever they were, that she quite forgot to keep everyone else in an uproar as she usually did.

More than once she seemed on the point of confiding some great secret to her grandmother, and once Anne even went so far as to ask what was on her mind.

'Absolutely nothing,' Mary assured her.

'For the first time in your life I don't think that's true,' Anne said, but she was unable to elicit anything further from the girl.

She concluded that Mary, too, was in love, and from the secretive nature of her passion, Anne deduced that the object of Mary's affections was someone of whom her parents would disapprove. But who? And what, if anything, should Anne do about it?

She got the answer to the first question by chance one morning when she came into the kitchen to discuss the day's menu with the cook and she saw one of the maids accepting a note from a strange manservant at the back door. Seeing Anne, the maid looked alarmed and quickly pocketed the note, closing the door in the face of the stranger.

'What is that?' Anne asked, her suspicions aroused.

'Nothing,' the maid answered.

'Please do not insult me by telling me something is nothing,' Anne snapped, banging her cane on the floor. 'Give me the letter.'

The maid handed it to her; Anne saw that it was unaddressed.
'Who is this for?' she asked.

'The young miss.'

'Who sent it?'

'A servant brought it, ma'am,' the maid replied.

'Yes, yes, I saw that, but whose servant?'

'I wouldn't be knowing that, ma'am.'

Anne snorted her disbelief and turned the letter about in her
hand. Of course, it was rude to read another's mail; on the
other hand, the letter wasn't addressed, so its sender could
hardly complain if the wrong person read it, could he? Anyway,
it was her opinion that mysterious notes from unknown senders
usually led to no good. She unfolded the letter and read it
quickly.

Even without the florid signature at the bottom, she would
have guessed whom the letter was from. The stationery bore the
silly crest that awful de Trémorel woman and her consort had
affected since they'd been in California.

Nor was there any mistaking the purport of the letter; it was
a love letter, and the gist of it, couched in the most torrid terms
imaginable, was that the young couple were planning to run
away together.

Her first impulse was to march directly to Mary's room and
thrash the girl soundly with her cane, but on more sober
reflection she realized that might drive the girl away even more
quickly.

No, what was needed here was a bit more subtlety than that.
It was obvious from this letter that Richard de Trémorel had
done a good job of turning the foolish girl's head, and Mary
would not be easily dissuaded from her planned course of
action.

Anne folded the note up again and handed it to the maid.
'Have there been many of these letters? And don't lie to me –
I'm in no temper for any nonsense,' she warned.

'A few, ma'am,' was the frightened reply.

'I'll wager a few,' Anne said. 'Very well, you deliver this one
as usual, under her napkin or however it's done, and not a word
to her about my seeing it or so help me, I'll have your tongue
cut out and sliced into the soup, do you hear me?'

The girl's head bobbed up and down frantically. 'Yes, ma'am,'
she said emphatically.

Anne was satisfied that she'd put the fear of God into the
maid; but what was she to do about Mary? There wasn't time

to write to Claude and Danielle, even if she felt inclined to deal with the matter in that way, which she did not.

She decided to bide her time, hoping that some inspiration would come to her, but a few days later, when Mary began to act in a particularly nervous manner, Anne suspected that the time for the planned elopement was close at hand. She took the opportunity to look into Mary's room while the girl was at breakfast downstairs, and found in her closet a portmanteau that Mary had managed to spirit down from the attic. When she saw this, she was certain that Mary planned to run away the very same night.

In her own room Anne paced the floor, trying to reach a decision. It was obvious that she would need help; she was, after all, an old woman, however much she liked to fancy that she had kept her figure. There was her grandson, of course, but David was such a dreamer, and anyway, he was so under Mary's thumb that it was not out of the question that he was an accomplice to the scheme.

No, she would need someone young and strong, someone who she was certain would have Mary's best interests at heart and, moreover, someone who could be trusted absolutely to keep silent about this matter. If Claude were ever to learn what his dearest child had planned, it would surely break his heart.

At length, Anne came to a conclusion. She seated herself at her writing desk and penned a quick note, which she sent off at once, via a stableboy, to French Hills.

It seemed to Mary that the day would never end. As the afternoon wore slowly on toward evening and the actual hour of departure loomed ever closer, she seesawed violently back and forth between giddy exultation and stark horror at what she was doing. She could not bear to think how Papa would react to her eloping with Richard, nor was it any good pretending to herself that he would accept a *fait accompli*, as Richard insisted. Perhaps in time he would get used to it, but he would never forgive her.

Yet as much as she hated hurting Papa, she knew that she would do what she had made up her mind to do, as in a thousand little ways she had always done. It was almost as if all her headstrong young life had been but a preparation for this, the moment when she first took independent flight. She had always had her way, and she would have her way in this, too.

There were moments during the day when she thought that she must be mad, that Richard could not mean the things he had said; yet there were his letters, the words in his own handwriting; and didn't his own mother attest to the fire of his ardor, she who must know him better than anyone else?

Like a dog shedding water, she would shake herself free of her forebodings and would once again ascend to that exhilarating pinnacle of expectation.

Once or twice she thought her grandmother was behaving strangely toward her – could she suspect anything? But surely not; since the night of Antoinette's supper party, Mary and Richard had met only once, briefly, in person; everything else had been arranged by letter. No one could know.

Nevertheless, when her grandmother said, at dinner, 'You've hardly touched your food,' Mary set herself diligently to cleaning her plate in order to quiet any suspicions.

In her room Mary readied herself for bed as if this were an ordinary evening. Richard was to come for her at eleven. He would drive to the rear of the house, where she would emerge from the back gate, which she had contrived to leave unlocked.

At nine o'clock she went to bed, to satisfy the maid. At a quarter to ten she was up again, dressing carefully by the light of a single candle. No one was likely to hear her; her grandmother was on this floor, but she was a heavy sleeper. David's room was on the floor above, and Jean was staying at the ranch.

She was ready before time, the few clothes she was taking crammed rather haphazardly into the portmanteau. They were traveling only so far as a cabin in the mountains, owned by a friend of Richard's, where they would spend the night. The following day they would journey on to Santa Barbara, where they would be married. That she would be spending the night with a man who was not yet her husband had bothered her a little at first, but Richard's sensible outlook had prevailed – what difference could one night make?

She grew restless. The hands on her clock seemed hardly to move at all. At length, though, when there were still some twenty minutes until the appointed time, she decided to let herself into the garden and wait there. Taking up her bag, she went to the door.

At first she thought the door was stuck. She twisted the knob and tugged and jerked. It remained fast, and finally she realized the truth.

The door was locked.

Her initial horror gave way to rage. She began to pound upon the locked door with her fists. How dare anyone do this to her?

'Let me out!' she shouted, pounding. 'Open this door!'

At first there was no response. Then, unexpectedly, a key grated in the lock. Mary stepped back, still breathing heavily. Her grandmother entered the room, carefully closing and locking the door behind her.

'What is this? Why is my door locked?' Mary demanded.

'Let us not play games, child,' Anne said wearily. 'I know of your assignation.'

For a moment Mary was at a loss; then, with a toss of her head, she made a brave but somewhat tremulous show of defiance.

'Then you know that it's time I was going,' she said. She moved as if to go out the door, but her grandmother barred the way.

'You will not be meeting your would-be seducer,' Anne said with finality. 'Never fear, though, he will be met – and properly dealt with.'

Mary's eyes widened. 'What have you done?' she cried. 'What have you planned for him?'

Anne did not reply. Mary ran to the window, but it overlooked the street front. It was a long drop to the ground.

'This is horrible,' she cried. 'How dare you interfere in my life this way – you're hateful, I despise you, let me go!'

'You will not go,' Anne said stubbornly, not moving from before the door. 'Have you no shame? Do you not know what this man is whom you planned to run away with?'

'He's a wonderful man,' Mary said, beginning to sob. 'Oh, you don't know what you're doing to me.'

'You don't know what you were doing to yourself. A wonderful man indeed; do you think for a moment this cad had any intention of marrying you?'

'He would have! How can you say such a thing?'

'I can say it because it is true. He would never have married you. If that had been his intention, why could he not come to court you openly – why all this sneaking around at back gates? No, he meant only to ruin you.'

Mary ran and flung herself across the bed, sobbing hysterically. 'Then let me be ruined. It's my life,' she cried. 'And I love him.'

'Your life, bah. And what of your father, what of your mother – don't you care about them? Do you think your father would let such an insult go unavenged? Don't be mad, child.'

Mary's body was racked with sobs. After a time she said, in a broken voice, 'Leave me alone. I shall die. You hate me, you've always hated me . . .'

It was painful to Anne to hear her own granddaughter saying these things to her, and for a moment she nearly wavered; to spare the child this anguish . . . but she steeled herself and remained before the door.

Richard left the carriage at the end of the alley and stole through the darkness to the back gate of the de Brussac's house. The gate swung open at his approach – the little maid, he supposed, who had been enlisted to deliver his letters.

It was very nearly accomplished. In two hours' time they would be at the cabin he had borrowed for the night. The trembling virgin was as much as his; by morning she would greet the dawn as a woman. Perhaps they would stay for an extra day; there was no hurry. When he was finished with her, he intended to travel east – without benefit of her company. He supposed she would return to her family, but either way it was of no interest to him what happened to her afterward.

The gate swung to behind him. He found himself in the garden, not with the maid as he had supposed, but with a stranger, a dark-skinned, dark-haired young man somewhat younger than himself, who had the muscular, finely toned look of a man used to physical labor.

'Who are you?' Richard demanded, not without a certain note of fear in his voice. 'What are you doing here?'

'My name is José,' the stranger said, smiling an oddly unnerving smile as he stepped closer. 'I've come to give you what you came for.'

Richard, realizing that he had stepped into a trap, made a move for the gate. 'Get out of my way,' he demanded, but his command was ignored.

José seized him by the collar and whirled him about; a fist like steel collided with Richard's gaping jaw.

It was no match. Richard made one or two halfhearted attempts at defense before he descended to groveling and begging for mercy. He threw his hands over his head, trying to ward off the blows raining on him.

At last, bleeding and beaten, he was dragged into the alley and sent on his way with a hard kick to his rear. For a long time Richard lay on the hard ground, sobbing and trying to regain his breath. When at last he dragged himself to his feet, it was to discover that his carriage was gone, his driver having been frightened away by the sounds of the fight.

Not only was the intended prize not his, but he would have to walk in his bruised condition half-way across the city.

It was humiliating.

65

Anne waited until the following evening to pay a visit upon Antoinette de Trémorel. José, looking inordinately pleased with himself, had returned at dawn to French Hills.

Mary had not left her room throughout the day and had scarcely spoken to Anne, but she seemed sufficiently calmed from her initial hysteria that Anne no longer feared that she would run away. In any case, Richard de Trémorel was not likely to risk a second expedition if Anne knew anything about that young man's character.

Anne's visit to his parents was intended to insure that he did not make any further plans at some future date, when she was not on hand to discourage him.

She drove herself there in the little one-horse buggy. At the de Trémorel mansion she was shown into the flamboyantly decorated parlor; both Antoinette and François came in to join her a few minutes later.

'I will not mince words,' Anne informed them coolly. 'You have no doubt seen what your son's schemes brought him.'

'So, you're the one to blame for our son's condition,' François said angrily.

'No, he himself is to blame,' Anne said. 'And perhaps you two as well. You ought really to have warned him that it was dangerous to cross swords with a de Brussac – as I believe your infamous brother learned some years ago, Antoinette.'

Antoinette started angrily, but her husband restrained her with a hand on her arm. 'So, now you have come to give commands?'

'I have come to warn you, if your son does not stay away from my granddaughter, the consequences the next time will be far worse – for yourselves as well as for him.'

'Well, we don't take to warnings or threats,' François said, giving her the benefit of his cruel smile. 'Perhaps you have forgotten that we can be dangerous, too?'

'I have forgotten nothing,' Anne said. 'I have not forgotten, for one thing, that you are a murderer. Perhaps the authorities would be interested in that information.'

'Oh, I think not. It was long ago, in another country – so difficult to prove. I doubt if anyone would be terribly interested.' François paused to pour himself a brandy.

'If that is your worst threat, there's no need to continue this interview,' Antoinette said.

'But it is not,' Anne replied. 'You are right, that was long ago, in France – but this is here and now, in California. Here it is we who have influence, and money – a great deal of money – which means a great deal of power. I am told that you have invested heavily in land in this part of the city, and that as a result you are deeply in debt.'

'That is no concern of yours,' Antoinette said.

'I have made it my concern. I want you to leave the Los Angeles area. Go north, go back to France, I don't care where you go, so long as you leave here.'

'And if we do not?' François asked, looking more amused than worried.

'I shall buy up every available inch of land in this end of town. I shall sell it at a fraction of its value. Your investment will be made worthless overnight.'

'François,' Antoinette said, a note of anxiety creeping into her voice.

'You don't have that much money,' François said.

'I have enough. My husband's fortune is at my disposal. My son would not refuse me. There are at least a dozen of the wealthiest men in the state who would be willing to make me a loan on the strength of my word. I will buy the entire city if that's what it takes.'

'You're mad,' François said, less amused now. 'You'd go down in ruin.'

'Perhaps. But I would not go alone.'

Anne watched with satisfaction as the anxiety on their faces quickly deepened. She was bluffing, but they could not know that. Neither Claude nor Diego would ever agree to such a ridiculous scheme, and she hadn't enough money at her own disposal to make more than a slight impact on the local real-estate market; but she had lived long enough to know that the trappings of wealth and power were often enough to pass for the real thing.

François set aside his brandy. 'You would do that?' he asked.

'I would. I will, unless you are gone from here within a month.'

'Or unless you are gone,' he said.

For the first time Anne felt a twinge of fear. She had counted on their cowardice to win her argument for her, but she had made a dangerous miscalculation, she realized now for the first time. She had forgotten that even the most cowardly animal may become vicious when cornered.

She stood, trying to conceal her fear. 'I think we have said everything that needs to be said. We do understand one another now, do we not?'

She moved toward the door; to her alarm, François moved also, barring her way.

'It is you who do not understand,' he said. He advanced toward her.

'I warn you . . . ' Anne lifted her walking stick threateningly.

He brushed it aside, knocking it from her hand. It fell to the floor with a clatter.

'You silly old witch,' he said, his eyes gleaming viciously. 'You have forgotten how I deal with those who get in my way.'

Anne tried to flee but her limbs were far from agile, and she had gone no more than a single step when he seized her, hands going to her throat. She tried to scream, but the breath was cut off at once. He was smiling as if it gave him physical pleasure to be squeezing the life from her.

She struggled against him, but to no avail; she was weak and rapidly growing weaker. The room swayed; the hovering darkness began to close in upon her.

She knew a moment of stark terror and then, as sudden as the rush of wings, she felt peace and an eerie, tranquil acceptance. She seemed to sense a presence there, in the darkness, waiting . . .

'Jean.' She spoke his name, but the sound that escaped her lips was only a final gasp of breath rattling in her throat.

Her body was found the following morning in an alleyway. It was assumed that she had been the victim of a cutthroat derelict and, indeed, by that evening it appeared that the murderer had been found. Her horse and buggy were found in the possession of a migrant farmworker, Jesus Garcia.

Furthermore, Anne's little silver coin purse, containing

several gold coins and a ruby ring she was fond of wearing, were found in Garcia's possession, along with a handkerchief embroidered with her initials that had been pushed into the pocket of his trousers.

Garcia, who spoke little English, had a reputation for beating his wife when he got drunk, which was as often as he was able. It did not weigh in his favor; nor did the long lapses of memory that punctuated his narration of the events of the night in question, owing to the tequila he admitted consuming in a variety of saloons throughout the evening.

According to his story, he had been approached by a stranger who, after buying him several drinks in a friendly fashion, had explained that he had an engagement with 'a fair señorita', and had hired Garcia to drive his buggy home for him, saying that the señorita would bring him home later. He had given Garcia the change purse and the coins in payment for the errand. As to why the ring was in the purse with the coins, Garcia had no idea; he could not explain why the gentleman would pay him a ring worth a fortune for such a simple errand.

Worse, he could not say where he was supposed to have delivered the buggy. He had apparently confused the address, for when he had tried to find it, he had found there was no such house. He had then, it seemed, spent the night alternately trying to find the correct house, with the result that the address he had memorized had become muddled in his memory, and trying to find the stranger who had hired him. This latter entailed going from one to another of the city's many saloons, where a number of the purse's gold coins went to quench his thirst.

At length, drunk and hopelessly confused, he had taken the horse and buggy home with him, sure that in due time someone would come to claim them.

By morning he was not even able to supply a reasonable description of his alleged employer, or to say with certainty in which tavern they had met.

'A Mexican,' Claude said with bitter scorn when the story was related to him. 'They ought to pack them up and send them back where they came from – the ones they can't shoot for thieving and killing.'

That the story was a fabrication, and a ridiculous one at that, seemed evident to everyone. It would not bring Anne back, but at least Jesus Garcia would be brought to a speedy trial and hanged for his crime.

In fact, there was no trial. The would-be defendant was shot trying to escape. There was some mystery for a few days as to who had been his accomplice in the escape attempt; someone had contrived to drug the jailor and had provided Garcia with tequila, presumably to bolster his courage. Two empty bottles were found in his cell. And when Garcia had been shot by the sheriff after ignoring a command to stop, he had been riding a horse stolen some miles distant; no one could say by whom or how it had been brought to the jailhouse.

After a few days, though, the press tired of speculation, particularly as no answers seemed forthcoming. Stories regarding Anne's murder and the subsequent events were relegated to the inside pages of the papers and, in a few more days, had ceased to be printed at all.

66

José debated for several days whether he should go to anyone with his story, and in the end he waited too long. Jesus Garcia was already dead by the time José rode into town to talk to Claude.

There was not a great deal that he could tell, however; the señora had sent him a note urging him to come to town on an important matter. She had told him that a scoundrel was attempting to abduct the young señorita and must be taught a lesson; José had waited in the garden for the person to show up and had, he thought, taught him a particularly strong lesson.

As to who this person was, however, he had no name, and his description was limited because the clash had taken place in the dark and, for most of the time that they had been together, the stranger's features had been covered with blood.

Nor could José say with real certainty that there was a connection between this event and the señora's tragic death the following day. 'I do not think this one that I met in the garden would be the sort to come back again. He looked much too frightened when he left. Still . . . ' José shrugged expressively.

Listening to the account, Claude felt his grief over his mother's death turning into anger. He had been betrayed; even if the incident José had narrated had no bearing on his mother's death, and the evidence against Jesus Garcia had been persuasive, the fact remained that his daughter, whom he had idolized, had gone behind his back. She had been on the verge of running away with an unnamed suitor, and that discovery enraged him almost more than his mother's death.

He thanked José for coming to him and sent him back to the ranch. Then he went to his daughter's room. He found her seated in a chair by the window, staring out as if expecting someone to arrive. It occurred to him now that there had been something unnatural in the grief that she had displayed the past few days; now he saw that her grief had been as much for herself as for the loss of her grandmother. When she turned toward him as he came into the room, he saw that her eyes were red-rimmed from crying. Before he had been moved to think that she mourned the death so deeply, but now the knowledge that her tears were for some shabby, thwarted romance only fueled his anger.

'I've spoken to José,' he said coldly.

She stared at him without moving from her chair by the window. 'And?' she said.

'Perhaps you would like to tell me about this – ' he hesitated on the word, ' – this elopement you had planned while we were gone.'

For a long moment she regarded him evenly. Then, to his surprise, she looked back to the window and simply said, 'No.'

'No? No what?' Claude demanded, his voice rising angrily.

'No, I won't tell you anything,' she said. 'I didn't go – I wasn't *allowed* to go. That's enough, isn't it?'

'No, by God, it isn't,' he said, striding across the room to stand before her. Her defiance was totally unexpected – he had been prepared for tears, contrition, humility. It had not occurred to him that she might not regret what he had assumed to be an impulsive and childish action.

'I want the name of this – this scoundrel you had thought to run away with.'

She tossed her head defiantly and said, 'I won't give it to you.'

'You'll tell me or so help me, I'll – '

'You'll what?' he asked, a faint, bitter smile curling her lips. 'You'll punish me? That's hardly necessary. Grandmother saw to that for you.'

'Has it occurred to you,' he demanded, clenching and unclenching his fists at his side, 'that your actions might have caused your grandmother's death?'

'I don't care,' she cried with a vehemence that startled him. 'I hate her for what she did! I'm glad she's dead – now at least she can't ever interfere in my life again.'

Claude reacted so suddenly and so violently that he was surprised by his own action. His hand came up as if of its own accord, slapping his daughter's face soundly.

He was at once horrified at what he had done. If she had looked hurt or had burst into tears, he would have fallen to his knees at once and begged her forgiveness; indeed he was half-moved to do so, but the cold hostility with which she gazed up at him only infuriated him all the more.

'You can beat me all you wish,' she said in an icy voice. 'I won't tell you who he was.'

'You'll tell me,' he swore. He strode toward the door; suddenly he wanted to be away from her, because he could not bear the way she looked at him and because he knew that he could not trust his anger not to get out of control again. 'You'll tell me or you'll wish you had. You won't leave this house until you've told me his name – and apologized for what you said about your grandmother.'

To his frustration, she only smiled the same crooked smile again. 'I don't care,' she said, 'I haven't got anyplace to go, anyway. Making me a prisoner won't change anything.'

For a moment he looked as if he would like to strike her again. Then, with a muttered oath, he went out, slamming the door hard.

She sat for a long time staring at the closed door. This was the first time her father had ever struck her; the first time, in fact, that his anger had ever been directed at her.

She knew, with a sudden, startling certainty, that she would never forgive him.

For Danielle, Anne's death was a deep and personal tragedy. Over the years an unspoken closeness had grown up between them that had done much to soften Danielle's increasing isolation from her husband and children. Now it seemed to her that she had lost her best, perhaps only real friend, at a time when she was increasingly beset by confusion and uncertainty, plagued by questions to which there seemed to be no answers.

Something had happened to Mary while she and Claude were away; Danielle was sure of it, although neither Mary nor

Claude would discuss it with her. Mary's depression – hostility, even – went beyond grief over the death of her grandmother, but Danielle's efforts to try to talk with her were met with a coldness that discouraged any further attempts at intimacy.

'There's nothing wrong with me,' was all Mary would say, in a voice that expressed resentment at being questioned.

Danielle knew that Claude and Mary had quarreled, but Claude seemed to regard that quarrel as a private matter; he seemed almost to be ashamed of it.

David, too, seemed to have grown increasingly unhappy. Danielle listened during the night to the opening and closing of doors, the stealthy footsteps in the hall; as surely as Adam and Eve fell from paradise, another great tragedy was threatening them. But what could she do?

Her children did not trust or confide in her. Her husband took her for granted; she was an integral but no longer a major part of his life.

What could she do?

She chose, finally, the one alternative that seemed to offer hope of success. She announced at breakfast a month after Anne's funeral that she wanted to return to the ranch.

'Alone?' Claude asked.

'I thought we might all go.'

'I'm afraid that's out of the question,' Claude said. 'Those importers from France are due this week, and the vinicultural association meeting is next week. I don't fancy a lot of riding back and forth when it's not called for.'

She was not surprised; she had known of both upcoming meetings and realized, in any case, that Claude would be reluctant to leave Los Angeles. She turned to her daughter, managing her brightest smile.

'Mary, won't you come with me?' she asked. 'The leaves in the vineyards should just be turning colors. It's always a lovely season at the ranch.'

'Mary has been restricted to the house,' Claude answered for her.

'Why is that?' Danielle asked. Neither Claude nor Mary answered her. Danielle saw Mary give her father a defiant look, but she could not begin to understand the currents of tension between them.

'I see,' she said, and then added, 'Well, at any rate, there's no reason why she can't be restricted to the ranch as well as this house; she's not likely to see much of anyone there. And it might do everyone good to have some time to sort out their feelings.'

Mary said, 'I'll come with you.' She again threw her father a defiant look. For a moment Danielle thought he was on the verge of forbidding the trip, but he finally seemed to think better of it. She took his silence for assent and turned her attention to David instead.

'David,' she said, 'won't you join us? I know Don Diego must be very lonely just now. I'm sure he'd enjoy your company especially. And the ranch is a good place to get away from one's burdens.'

David glanced up from the food he had been toying with and stared down the table at his mother. For a moment he had an uneasy feeling that she actually understood the problem that was burning within him; her eyes seemed filled with sympathy.

But no, she could never guess his secret. Or if she did, she would be filled with disgust, even horror. His mother was too gentle, too passionless a woman to comprehend the forces that drove him so relentlessly.

And yet there was a tempting ring to her words. Perhaps the distance would help; perhaps there he could find some peace . . .

'Yes, I think I will come along,' he said.

Claude, reflecting on Danielle's remarks, which seemed to imply more than they actually said, took his annoyance with Mary out on David.

'You're not still mooning about that business of becoming a priest, I hope,' he said sharply.

'Claude,' Danielle said, but David silenced her.

'It's all right, Mother,' he said. He looked up the table toward his father. 'I still have every hope that you'll reconsider and give me your blessing. If you call that mooning about, the answer is yes.'

'Don't get fresh with me, young man,' Claude said.

David's reply was to crumple up his napkin and push his chair back from the table, leaving the room without a word.

Claude glowered briefly at his daughter; his anger was really for her.

Mary returned his look coolly, as if challenging him to forbid her to go. After a moment Claude followed his son's example and, with a muttered oath, hurled his napkin at his plate and left the table.

Danielle would have gone after him, but as she moved to push herself back from the table she experienced a sudden, peculiar shortness of breath, not quite a pain in her chest but rather a feeling of constriction, as if a band had been tightened over her breasts.

She realized that she must have given a frightened gasp; Mary was staring at her oddly.

'Mama, is anything wrong?' she asked.

'No. I – ' She found that she could breathe again and a great sense of relief overwhelmed her fear. 'I'm all right,' she said.

Alone in his study Claude drank and seethed. His anger was partly guilt and frustration that he had not been able to bring himself to patch up his quarrel with Mary, but as the drink took effect, he began to cast about for an excuse for his anger; he found one in Danielle's plan to take the children with her to the ranch.

How could he make up with Mary if she was not even here? As for David, the last thing Claude wanted was the boy off somewhere by himself mooning over his ambition to be a priest – in which, no doubt, his mother encouraged him.

Damn Danielle! Why had she picked now of all times to interfere?

Danielle was surprised when he appeared in her room, swaying a trifle unsteadily. He ignored her hesitant smile and, banging his fist on a writing-table for emphasis, greeted her with the statement he had been rehearsing on his way up the stairs.

'I've decided you're not going to the ranch.'

'I can't think why not,' she said, her smile vanishing. 'There's nothing requiring my presence here. The servants can manage the house quite well, and of course there's always the estimable Miss Benson on hand.'

'Leave her out of this. She's got nothing to do with it. I'll be damned if I'll have you taking my children from me.'

'They aren't children anymore, if you hadn't noticed. Anyway, it's more a case of you driving them away.'

He took a step toward her and nearly lost his balance. He was far more drunk than she had first realized, and his anger glinted dangerously in his eyes. She knew that she was being foolish to argue with him in his present condition, but his manner had been so rude, so demanding, that for once she could not help showing a little of her own anger.

'And what about me?' Claude demanded, putting a hand on the back of a chair to steady himself. 'What about your husband? Your place is supposed to be at his side. I suppose you've got no qualms about leaving me alone?'

'Hardly alone,' she said. 'And hasn't my husband left my side long ago?'

'What the hell do you mean? I'm here, day and night, under the same roof, in the mansion I built for you.'

'In this monument to your own success, you mean? Yes, you're here, devoting your days to your work, your nights to Miss Benson. Do you know this is the first time you've even set foot in this room since we moved into the house? And a fine – a fine . . .' Despite her efforts not to, she began to cry.

'So that's it, is it?' He gave a coarse laugh and, abandoning the security of the chair's back, made his way somewhat indirectly toward her. 'I should have known. That's what you've always wanted from me, from the very first. That's your peasant blood again, my dear. An aristocratic lady would never stoop to asking her husband –'

She had never slapped her husband before, and when she did so now, she was nearly as surprised as he. He brought his hand up to cover the reddened print of her hand.

'Perhaps with a real husband a woman wouldn't be reduced to such humiliation,' she said coldly.

For a moment Claude could do nothing but stare at her as if he had never seen her before.

'All right,' he muttered angrily. 'All right. If that's what you want . . .'

He seized her arm roughly and tried to drag her toward the bed. She struggled against him, but in his unstable condition he stumbled, and in a moment they had fallen together across the bed. He tore at her clothes, ripping the bodice of her dress.

'Claude, no, please,' she cried. 'Not like this, oh, God, you're hurting me . . .'

She kicked out, knocking over the bedside table. The sudden crash startled Claude into awareness. For a moment they lay frozen as they were; then, with a muttered oath, Claude got to his feet.

'Claude,' Danielle said, but he stumbled from the room, angrily knocking a chair out of his path. Not until he had left, closing the door softly, did she get up. She pushed her hair back from her face and, still breathing hard, sat down at her dressing-table to try to pull herself back together. She found, though, that her hands were too unsteady to manage her hairpins. After a moment she gave up the effort and, loosening her hair, shook it free.

How dare he, she thought, still trembling with frustration. She met her own eyes in the mirror and the two, woman and image, stared angrily back at one another.

She was packing when Claude came to her in the morning, cloaked in contrition.

'I hope you'll forgive me for yesterday,' he said.

She said, without looking at him, 'It was reassuring to know that I'm still desirable.'

'Danielle, you do understand . . . ?'

'Yes, of course I do,' she said, relenting in the face of his obvious unhappiness. 'And it would be very nice if we could kiss and make up before I leave, but I do hope it can be a little less energetic.'

He kissed her, altogether too gingerly, she thought ruefully.

'I wish you'd change your mind about going,' he said.

'I think not. It will be good for us, for all of us. But it isn't the end of the earth, after all; it's only to the ranch. It's a short trip now, as you've pointed out so often.'

'If you're sure . . . ' His voice trailed off lamely. 'And you have forgiven me for – all that other business?'

Her hesitation was so slight that he apparently did not notice it at all. 'Yes,' she said, patting his cheek as she used to pat the boys when they needed comforting. 'I forgive you for yesterday.'

67

'Manuel? Jorge? Where is everyone?' Mary squinted in the unaccustomed dimness of the stables.

'Depends on who you mean by everyone,' José said behind her. She turned to find him just inside the door. She was suddenly struck, as she had been a number of times since the return to the ranch, with how much José had changed. Somehow in her mind he had always remained the funny little Mexican boy that Mama had taken in a long time ago, one of her loyal subjects when she had been a childhood monarch.

But now, quite to her surprise, he was a man, and a very handsome one at that, with his dark eyes gleaming like onyx in his olive-hued face, and the haphazard curls that spilled over his forehead. Of course, he was not at all like the young men who'd been courting her so arduously in Los Angeles; she didn't suppose he owned a decent suit of clothes, and he hadn't a trace of polish or elegance – he was all sinew and muscle and a certain long-limbed grace that she found vaguely disquieting to observe.

At the moment, though, it wasn't his grace that she found disturbing but his odor. She wrinkled her nose. 'Ugh, what have you been doing?' she asked.

'It's called manure,' he said, grinning without embarrassment. 'The plants love it.'

'I'm so happy for them. But in case no one's ever told you, you aren't supposed to smell that way around a young lady. As a matter of fact, you aren't even supposed to mention that sort of thing.'

He shrugged. 'Seems to me like a young lady who grew up on a ranch ought to take a little smell in her stride. It's a way of feeding the vines so they'll produce better grapes, so we get good wine from them. In a way, you could say all your fancy living comes right back down to a heap of – '

'I don't want to hear about it,' she interrupted him sharply. 'Where's all the help?'

'Working in the fields. What is it you wanted?'

'Someone was supposed to saddle a horse for me.' She glanced around and then back at him, looking down her nose. 'It looks like you'll have to do it.'

'Why, it'd be a pleasure, little princess,' he said, still grinning. He put aside the pitchfork he'd been holding and went to fetch a saddle.

She watched him with a petulant expression, annoyed still further by the tuneless song he was whistling softly. She wasn't at all sure she liked him now that he had grown up. It seemed as if he was making fun of her all the time in an offhand way. She supposed he was jealous because she was a de Brussac and he was nothing but hired help, no matter how much they'd played together as children. She would be glad for an opportunity to put him in his place.

He saddled the pinto she liked to ride and led it out into the corral. Mary followed him into the sunlight and let him help her into the saddle.

'That's a pretty outfit you're wearing,' he remarked as she

was adjusting her hat; she had donned a riding habit made especially for her by Madame Forsythe in soft beige cowhide with a neatly fitted jacket and a skirt that would have been shockingly short if her leather boots hadn't covered the concealed ankles.

She was about to thank him sweetly for the compliment when he added, 'Course, out here we'd call that just a little bit fancy for riding. Looks more like something you'd wear to one of those teas I hear you're fond of.'

She tossed her head angrily and jerked the reins out of his hands. 'Oh, what would you know about pretty clothes or teas, you're nothing but a – a dumb greaser,' she said, using her father's expression.

If he was angered by the remark, he concealed it behind another broad grin. 'I may be dumb,' he said, 'and I may be a greaser, but at least I know enough to keep my feet in the stirrups when I'm sitting on a horse.'

He gave the horse's rump a slap, sending it galloping and almost unseating Mary, whose feet had not been properly in the stirrups.

She managed to regain her balance without falling out of the saddle or losing control of the reins, but she imagined that her exit from the corral had been less than dignified, and she was furious as she rode up into the hills without a backward glance.

'I don't know why you let her get away with talking like that,' Jean said; he had walked up in time to hear Mary's last remarks. He scowled his disapproval at his sister's rapidly vanishing back.

'Ah, she's just a kid,' José said. 'She'll grow out of her silliness.' He strolled back to his work, once again whistling happily to himself.

Watching him, Jean wondered, not for the first time, if José weren't in love with Mary.

'That would sure be a sticky one,' he thought.

To him, José's Mexican parentage was of little consequence. José had lived with them for so long, and the two of them had worked together so much in the vineyards, that Jean thought of him as a brother; indeed, he felt much closer to José than to his real brother, David, who was too much of a dreamer to suit his tastes.

But Pa, now, that was a different matter; there was no telling what he might do if he caught José making eyes at his precious daughter. Much as Pa valued everything José had done here at French Hills – and God knows it had been José more than anyone else who'd kept the place running like clockwork over these past few years when Pa himself had seemed to lose interest in it – there wasn't much doubt that he'd send José packing rather than risk tainting the aristocratic de Brussac blood. It would have been bad enough if José had merely been hired help; but to be Mexican on top of it was an unforgivable sin.

Jean's thoughts circled back to his brother David. Now there, if he was any judge of such things, was a fellow with a problem, and Jean had a pretty good idea what the problem was too. If José was asking for trouble getting ideas in his head about Mary, David had a twister by the tail and didn't know when to let go. That was the problem with dreamers like David; as fast as they piled up good arguments on one side of a question, they came up with just as many arguments on the other side.

That, in Jean's opinion, was what came of living with your nose in a book instead of getting out and getting your hands dirty in some good-growing soil. Living off the land, spending your time with nature's hard rules, made one a realist.

'Like me,' he thought contentedly. Though he was not exactly conceited, he had a good opinion of himself. He knew his worth as a vintner, and it gave him a confidence he might otherwise never have achieved. He was not as good looking as his brothers, and he knew it; where Adam had inherited his father's handsome good looks and David had that quality of soft innocence that he had gotten from their mother, Jean was plain at best and bordered on being downright homely. Fortunately he had inherited his grandmother's dazzling hair, though it was more muted than Mary's; that, and his warm, open personality saved him from being unattractive. He had an aggressive, unhesitant way of dealing with things and, particularly, with people that made him stand out in almost any group.

'He looks like his grandfather de Brussac,' his grandmother had been fond of saying, and with a sly smile she would add, 'He wasn't handsome either, but the ladies always found him appealing.'

And experience had taught Jean that this was another trait he shared with his grandfather.

His reveries were interrupted by the appearance of his father on the porch. 'Jean, get someone to hitch up the carriage for us,' he called. 'It's time Miss Benson and I started back to town.'

It would have been a whole lot better if Miss Benson had

stayed in town, Jean was thinking; he wondered that his father couldn't see what was going on under his nose – but then it looked as if Mother couldn't see what was going on under her nose, either; maybe that was one of the characteristics of getting older.

Well, all these machinations weren't his problem. There was one thing to be said for the vines: They couldn't go stepping out on you.

Unconsciously picking up the tune José had been whistling earlier, Jean went to hitch up the carriage himself.

Mary was furious. How could her father have brought Miss Benson here?

Oddly enough, it was not for her mother's sake that she was angry; sometimes she wondered if Mama even knew what was going on with Papa and Miss Benson. Anyway, Mary and her mother had always been distant toward one another. It was David whom she was upset about. David was the only one of her family to whom she felt close.

At first, when they had come down to the ranch, David's spirits had seemed to improve. For a few days he had even ceased moping about and looking as if he'd lost his best friend.

Then, out of the blue, Papa had showed up with Miss Benson.

'I've always wanted to see these vineyards I've heard so much about,' Miss Benson had said, making it obvious that the trip had been her idea. 'David, won't you show me where the wine is made?'

'It isn't made in the vineyards,' Mary had remarked drily. 'That's where the grapes are grown.'

Nonetheless, David had gone obediently to show her the vineyards and everyone – Mama, Papa, Mary herself, even David – had looked unhappy about it; everyone except Miss Benson, who seemed to be enjoying herself no end.

Mary slowed her horse's mad gallop. She supposed she was sympathetic to David's plight not only because he was her favorite but also because of her own recent experience with the agonies of love. When she was being perfectly frank with herself, she was not altogether certain that her grandmother had been wrong in her assessment of Richard de Trémorel; if Richard had really loved her as much as he said, he would never have fled as he did, would never have quit the field as quickly and as totally as he had. She was beginning to despise him for a coward and a fool.

That did nothing, however, to offset the anger and resentment she felt toward her family, particularly toward her father. Fanned by an unconscious but nagging guilt over her grandmother's death, her bitterness had festered until she could hardly bear to look at her father. She ached for some way to get back at him. Her thoughts were filled with escaping from the family that now seemed only to stifle and imprison her. She had even considered just riding away, leaving on her own.

But this was 1878, and even an independent and headstrong girl could not just strike out on her own with neither money nor masculine protection. She thought of asking David to come with her but realized that he would never sever his family ties in such a manner. As much as he wanted to leave to join the priesthood, he would never do so without Papa's consent.

Consent? She scorned the word. She would never again wait for anyone's consent but her own. The episode with Richard, futile though its outcome had been, had given her a taste of independent action, and she had found it heady.

She reined the horse to a stop and dismounted, strolling through the tall grass. The summer had been hot and dry; the brush crackled and groaned in the breeze. It seemed to her as if the tension within the family had been building and building throughout the long, hot summer, and she looked forward to the rains that would come in a month or so; perhaps the air, like the dry earth, would be less charged then. José said the hills were like a giant tinderbox, waiting to explode.

José; she frowned as she thought of him. She wished she hadn't said what she had to him, but he could be so exasperating.

José was a fool, too. Despite the way he teased her, she knew that he was in love with her; he had been since their childhood, notwithstanding the obvious futility of that passion. She knew that there were other girls who flirted with him and tried to capture his interest, but he seemed totally unaware of them.

'As if waiting will do him any good,' Mary thought disdainfully.

Still, he was a good-looking man in his Latin way. And so in love with her. If only he were someone else – if he were rich, or not Mexican. José would take her away, she knew that he would. It would be so easy. And it would hurt her father, as she had been hurt.

If only . . .

68

Claude and Julia had been gone two days when David, more restless than Danielle had ever seen him, announced that he was returning to the city.

'Are you sure that's wise?' Danielle asked. 'You seemed to be feeling so much better when we first came out here.'

'We can't always do what's wise,' he answered gloomily. 'If we could, I'd be a priest by now and not . . . ' he hesitated. ' . . . And not feeling so frustrated,' he finished lamely.

Danielle watched him ride off toward the city; she could not think where this nasty triangle would end; no doubt it would mean unhappiness for everyone concerned, but it seemed that the drama must be played out to its own conclusion, and nothing she could do was likely to have much effect.

Her idea of coming down to the ranch had not been a complete failure, however. For one thing, she herself was feeling so much better; she no longer seemed to be suffering that periodic shortness of breath that had been bothering her lately.

More important, Mary seemed to be recovering some of her former good spirits. She was not quite the old Mary; whatever had happened to her in Los Angeles had stripped her of some of her youthful ebullience and left her more wary, more thoughtful. She seemed at times to be engrossed in some scheme of her own, the design of which Danielle could not begin to guess.

If there was anything in her daughter's 'recovery' that made Danielle uneasy, it was the increasing amount of time that Mary and José were spending together. It was obvious that that young man was smitten by the girl, but Mary's attitude was a little harder to fathom. She seemed almost at times to be flirting with him, leading him on, although she must know as well as anyone the foolishness of such behavior.

That any sort of romance might develop between the two was unthinkable. Fond as Danielle was of the young man – and she knew that Claude respected him, although there was no great affection between the two men – she knew that Claude would never tolerate such a situation. Despite José's abilities as a vintner, Claude had never quite gotten over his own prejudices toward what he regarded as 'the servant class'.

That in itself would have been an obstacle to any relationship between the two young people, but José's Mexican parentage was an insurmountable barrier. Since that ugly incident years before in which Don Diego's first wife had lost her life at the hands of Mexican bandidos, Claude had had a distaste for people of that heritage, and over the years it had grown into a deep-rooted prejudice. In the last year or so, he had even taken to using such derogatory terms as *greaser* and *wetback*. Not even pointing out Don Diego's Latin heritage to him had made a difference.

'It's not the same thing,' Claude argued. 'In the first place, Don Diego is an aristocrat. In the second place, he is of Spanish descent, not Mexican.'

'So are most Mexicans,' David had once pointed out. But the remark had only angered his father while doing nothing to offset his prejudice.

If Danielle did not quite know what to make of the developing relationship between Mary and José, neither did Mary herself. She had found herself spending more and more time in José's company, with no real goal in mind – except that she knew that he was in love with her. At the moment her ego needed a certain amount of gratification.

When he wasn't being impossible, José was rather pleasant company. Indeed, it almost seemed as if he had been making a real effort to please her.

Not that he couldn't still be exasperating, as when he called her princess in a way that sounded as if he was mocking her. José's problem, she decided, was that he didn't have the proper respect for the things that mattered in life – good clothes, good society, wealth – which was particularly puzzling when you considered that he had grown up in the very bosom of their family. Yet he gave every impression of being happy with simple buckskin and the beans and rice favored by the household servants, and he was never so contented as when at work in the vineyards.

'Sometimes I think the vines are the only things you really love,' she told him.

His eyes twinkled as if he had some great secret he was keeping from her. 'Not the only thing,' he said.

Today was one of those days when José was being his nicest. She had expressed a desire the day before to ride up into the hills, and he had invited himself along. He needed a day off, he said, though she suspected his real reason was to look after her. She didn't mind; though the hills were built up a great deal more than they had been even a few years ago, they were still not the safest place for a girl to be riding alone.

'Why, José,' she teased, 'you don't mean you've fallen in love?'

'Maybe,' was the laconic answer.

She giggled with delight and twisted in her saddle to see his face. 'But who? Tell me, tell me, aren't you going to tell me?'

'Not yet.'

'But why on earth not? When will you tell me if not now?'

'Maybe when you're old enough,' he said.

'Old enough? I like that,' she said indignantly. 'I'm old enough right now. I know all about love.'

'Enough to be talked into running off with the first slick-talking snake that wriggles up to you?' he asked in mock seriousness.

She gasped with shock and anger. 'Oh! How dare you,' she cried, striking out at him with her riding crop.

Laughing, he dodged the blow easily. 'Very grown-up of you,' he said.

She spurred her horse to a gallop and rode ahead of him, but after a moment he caught up with her. She knew her pony was no match for the stallion he was riding, and she slowed her pace somewhat although she refused now to look at him and kept her nose tilted upward.

For a few minutes they rode in silence. Finally she said, 'I don't know why I ever put up with you.'

'It's simple — because I know what a spoiled brat you are and love you anyway,' he said.

There, she was sure he was teasing her again. He really was the most insufferable man she'd ever met. The worst of it was that it was impossible just to dismiss him the way she usually did when a man displeased her. All the young men she'd known in Los Angeles — the ones who tried to court her favor — had been quick to take flight whenever she had waved her hand and told them she wanted to be left alone. She had gotten rather accustomed to their willingness to do her bidding in order to curry favor with her.

She had already learned, however, that José was not like that.

He was not at all intimidated by her imperiousness, and even her worst temper didn't seem to frighten him at all. Even when she got into a virtual rage and stamped her foot at him, calling him vile names, he just laughed at her and acted as if it were nothing at all to him.

Yet though this lack of servility or humility annoyed her, she could not help feeling a certain admiration for him. The young men she had known in Los Angeles, for all their elegance and sophistication, seemed a trifle foppish in contrast, just as their graceful style of good looks – the proper clothes, the right grooming, the polished manners – that had seemed so attractive to her before, paled a little in comparison to José's rugged naturalness.

It was odd that she hadn't actually realized how good-looking he had become until Miss Benson had commented on it.

'Wouldn't they just adore that young god in Los Angeles,' she had said, and though at first Mary had thought she was joking, since then she had found herself staring at José when he wasn't looking.

He was handsome; his dark-hued face was sculpted in classic planes and his eyes were disturbingly liquid-seeming, with their long lashes and their way of changing from stormy dark to gaily bright in a twinkling. But there was something more, too, than his handsome face – an almost animalistic vitality that seemed to radiate from him; it was in his powerful physique, his hard-muscled arms and burly chest that he bared so often when working in the fields; in the surprisingly graceful swagger with which he walked; in the deep rumble of his voice, punctuated as it was with coarse phrases and breaking at frequent intervals into a warm, easy laughter.

Of course she would have died a thousand deaths before telling him any of this. As it was, she rather thought he was conceited, altogether too cocksure. There were times when it almost seemed as if he considered himself her equal rather than a hired servant of the family.

Mama had packed a lunch for them, and when they came to a likely spot they stopped and dismounted. They were on a bluff overlooking a ravine, shaped in the distant past by a shifting of the restless earth's surface. Some hundred and fifty feet below, the valley leveled off again, spilling in gentle undulations into the hazy distance.

Despite their quarrel, she was glad they had come. It was strange, but when she had been in Los Angeles, she had not been conscious of missing the country; yet now that she was here, she felt revitalized, charged with new energy.

'It's beautiful, isn't it,' she said, sipping the wine that José had brought in a leather flask. 'Mama said that when you cross the country there are stretches where you travel for weeks and weeks on end without seeing a town or a person.'

'Those spaces are shrinking, though,' he said. 'By the time we're the same age as your mother and father, we'll be in a new century. Seems like the world's changing too fast even to keep up with it. It's changing right while we're sitting here. If you look away and then back at the valley, it's liable to be different.'

Smiling, she looked away and then back at the valley. 'Looks the same to me,' she said. 'Papa always says things will stay the same here. He says there's nothing to bring anyone to Los Angeles.'

'Your father's a fool.' He rolled over on his back to gaze up at the cloudless sky above.

Mary was fascinated because she had never heard anyone express anything but the most profound admiration for her father; she had supposed she was the only one who had ever entertained such treacherous thoughts.

'Why?' she asked. 'The gold's up north, if there's any left. San Francisco's got the sophistication, the real society, and Adam says even the best grape-growing land is up north. If you think about it, we haven't got anything but dust and cattle – and French Hills, of course.'

'There's all this.' He made a sweeping gesture with his hand that took in the whole of the sky, the bright sun blazing overhead, the distant view. 'There's the air and the sun and the weather, warm in the winter as well as the summer, and dry, and even when it's scorching hot the nights are cool. And there's land, plenty of it, and cheap.'

'Why, it's nothing but a desert. Who wants to live in a desert if they can help it?'

'There's water. The grapes find it. The wells at French Hills go down to it. The Los Angeles River floods the valley with it when it comes down from the hills there. Once somebody finds out how to harness the water and control it, there'll be fountains of water all over the place – water enough for everybody.'

She laughed aloud. 'Fountains of water, in Los Angeles? You know, you're as crazy as a bedbug.'

'That may be. But your brother's right, and your Pa is wrong;

the place for a good vintner is up north. That's where I aim to go.'

She sat up and stared down at him. 'I didn't know you were planning on going. When?'

'Someday. I've been saving my money all these years so I could start a place of my own. I don't mean to be somebody else's Mexican field hand all my life.'

'What's holding you back then?' she asked.

'You, maybe.' His eyes met hers boldly.

She laughed and threw herself across him, lying over his powerful chest, her hair spilling downward to brush against his cheek.

'You may kiss me,' she said in a husky whisper. She closed her eyes.

To her surprise he didn't kiss her. She opened her eyes and found him staring at her with an odd light in his eyes.

'Aren't you going to kiss me?' she asked.

'No.'

'Well why on earth not?' That he should refuse what she viewed as a great favor bestowed upon him was incomprehensible to her.

'Because you're only playing a game,' he said.

'But we've always played that game,' she cried.

'No, you played the game,' he said. 'Only it wasn't a game for me. Anyway, I don't want to play anymore.'

'You mean you don't want to kiss me.' She was hurt, more than she would have expected to be. She'd never had anyone refuse her before; and that it should be José, who's devotion she had always taken for granted, was doubly insulting.

'I didn't say that either.'

She sat up, her expression hurt and petulant. 'I swear, I don't understand you at all – you say you don't want to kiss me, then you say you do, only you won't. What am I supposed to think?'

'You're supposed to think that I don't want permission to kiss some imaginary queen, and that I'll no longer settle for some child's game; I want to kiss a woman, someone who'll kiss me back, who'll give as well as she gets. That's what you can think.'

She got up abruptly, dusting her pants. 'Well, I hope you aren't expecting that from me,' she said. 'And I'm sorry if you don't want to play games anymore, because that's all I had in mind.'

She started for the horses. For a few seconds he watched her go; then, with a sudden look of determination, he jumped up and started after her.

'That's because that's all you've ever done,' he said. 'You want to go on playing child's games because you've remained a child. But maybe you're right, maybe it is time you were a woman.'

She was so surprised when he took her in his arms that she did not even try to resist. She let him crush her to him, let her lips surrender to his.

She was stunned by the experience. She had been kissed before, of course; indeed, it had been only a few weeks since Richard de Trémorel's kisses had left her so shaken. But in those kisses, for all her excitement, there had been something yet frightening, even shameful, as if her heart had known that this was not the way it should be between a man and a woman.

How then had she not known this before, this sudden shock of oneness, this flame of union of one with another? She had closed her eyes as she always did when kissing, thinking it more properly romantic, but now she found her eyes opening, found herself staring into his with surprise. She seemed to lose herself in their inky depths; for the first time, as he had prophesied, she did indeed feel like a woman, and it was he, whom she had known nearly all her life, who had struck the heretofore unsounded chord within her.

She was aware, as if in a dream, that he was lowering her gently into the tall dry grass; she felt the weight of his body upon hers, and still she clung to him.

Later, much later, when she was lying contentedly in his arms, she asked the question that had been circling about in her mind for some minutes.

'José,' she asked, running the tips of her fingers lightly over his chest, 'exactly how much money did you say you had saved?'

69

It is one of the perversities of human nature that once it becomes clear that a sought-for goal can be easily achieved, it ceases to be desirable.

So it was with Mary during that hot, dry summer. From the moment she had jointly seduced and been seduced by José, from the time it became clear that he could – and delightedly would – take her away from her family as his bride, she began to perceive that this was not after all how she wanted her future to be shaped.

It was not that she was displeased with that young man as a lover. Indeed, she found the reality of their relationship not only quite different from anything she had imagined in her romantic fantasies, but infinitely more enjoyable than she had anticipated. In the dusty, sunbaked fields during the long afternoons, in the silver, moonlit vineyards of the cool California nights, these two explored the pleasures of their own and each other's bodies with all the wonder, all the savage exhilaration of those who had explored this land a century before. If this was not love – and she doubted that it was – it was no less thrilling for that shortcoming.

Love, so far as she yet knew it, was what she had felt for her father – still felt, though she was able to despise him at the same time and with equal ardor. But, as if a wound had been lanced, allowing the accumulated poison to drain off, her anger had been drained, its energy rechanneled into a different passion so that, although she still chafed at the restrictions imposed upon her growing independence, although she still longed for a break from them, she no longer wanted to take such an irrevocable step as leaving with José.

And leave with him she must, if she were to marry him; her father would never forgive that, she knew beyond a doubt. She knew, too, that though she wanted to hurt her father and to demonstrate her independence from him, she did not want to lose him altogether as her swain. She wanted it both ways.

She might very well have had her way, too, had it not been for one tragic deficiency in her perception of the situation. For all that she had lived most of her life in the close company of the young man who was now her lover, she had never taken the trouble to know him. Even now, as she learned his body in intimate detail, she remained ignorant of what lay within.

Centuries before, the men who were to be the ancestors of that young man, little more than savages at the time, had set out on a long journey southward, a journey that continued for more than two centuries and traversed some of the wildest, most dangerous terrain to be found on the continent. Discovering a culture that was already old and infinitely advanced beyond their own, they had proceeded against all odds to conquer and assimilate it, building upon its ruins a civilization so grand, an empire so vast, that it would astound and dazzle the Spanish conquerors who came upon it two hundred years later.

The Spanish conquered the Aztec empire, leveling its splendid cities to the ground, toppling its idols, looting its treasures; but the Mexica, as these men called themselves, remained when their cities and their idols were gone. They assimilated their conquerors, just as they had generations before assimilated those they had conquered, and in time a new land emerged, peopled by men as old as their ancient tribes, as new as the blood of the *conquistadores*. Again, against all odds, the Mexica had survived.

Robbed of their wealth, stripped of their dignity, reduced to living as peasants on a harsh land in dirty, piteously poor villages, they had nonetheless risen in time to cast off the rule of the mighty French empire and, despite great losses, survived invasion by the ever more powerful United States Army, until at last they stood as the proud and independent nation they had always believed themselves to be.

They had survived, overcoming all obstacles, because of two curious idiosyncrasies that were virtually their only heritage from the once-savage tribe that had begun its southward migration some seven hundred years before. They had, first of all, a sense of pride that went far beyond what other proud men experienced, a pride that would not be beaten down through centuries of defeat and slavery; and they had the peculiar inability to perceive that they could not have what they wanted. When they set their eyes upon a goal, they saw it as already accomplished, and they were and traditionally had been unable to comprehend that anyone else might see it differently.

These were the men from whose loins José Perreira had

sprung, and these the characteristics he had inherited from them. Just as years before it had not occurred to him that he was too little or too weak to rescue the señora from a man who was assaulting her, so now it did not occur to him that he was too poor, or too Mexican, to marry the girl he wanted.

He had fallen in love with her as a boy. As children, they had sworn that they would marry when they grew up. He had waited with serene patience for her to become his woman, never doubting that it would come about, and indeed, hadn't his confidence been justified? In the absence of any frank statement from her to that effect, it simply did not cross his mind that they could not be married. He loved her; he took it for granted that beneath her childishness and her vanity, she loved him as well. He had proposed taking her north, where they could find land upon which to build their own vineyard, and she had seemed delighted by the prospect. Now he set about the task of accomplishing these goals, quite blind to any obstacles that might stand in his way, and Mary, foolishly perceiving him as her servant in love as well as in other ways, listened to him outlining his plans and assumed that he was only making pipe dreams, as she was.

Danielle, watching this growing relationship with anxiety, knew that Mary would never be willing to discuss the matter with her, but there was the possibility that José might be open to reason. He had always been a sensible young man. Accordingly, she watched for an opportunity, and when she found it, spoke to him alone.

'What would you have me do?' he asked when she had voiced her concern. 'We are in love.'

'But you must see that that love can come to nothing.'

'You married someone of a different class,' he said accusingly.

'I don't know that my experience is a good recommendation,' she said, not without a trace of bitterness. 'At any rate, you know Claude will never agree to such a marriage. In the end you can only force her to choose between you and her father. Either way, it will break her heart.'

José, who had been devoted to Danielle since his childhood, had no great respect or affection for the husband who he thought treated her shamefully, and he could not see that it would be so terrible if Mary were to be alienated from such a father. Nonetheless, he had already decided to do what he considered the right thing.

'I will talk to him,' he said. 'I have written to him, asking him for permission. I want to do the honorable thing.'

'Then go away now, before Claude receives your letter. Mary will be hurt, but she'll recover and in time she'll see that you did the right thing.'

'Never,' he said, his jaw set stubbornly. 'He will come. I will talk to him, man to man. I'll make him understand.'

He went back to his work in a way that indicated the conversation was over. Danielle, realizing that she could do nothing to sway his opinions, started sadly back toward the house.

She had long since come to the conclusion that there were really only two classes of people, the tolerable and the intolerable, and that the former were in the minority. But she was not such a fool as to be unaware of the heartache and loneliness these two young people were courting. For all the de Brussac fame and wealth, she knew that she herself had never been fully accepted into local society.

She did not mind especially. She knew that others, the women who ran the social scene in Los Angeles and Sacramento, looked upon her as a sort of freak.

'It's like having a wart on the end of your nose,' she had once told Anne. 'You can't grow up your whole life with it and not notice it's there. You see, they always say that people's talent or beauty is God-given, but where do you suppose warts come from?'

She had never dreamed that she would end with such an empty life. She had thought, when she married Claude, that he would fill it up, but as big a man as he was, he had not been that big.

In the long run, though, she had been more happy than not. There were worse things than to have reached beyond your limits, and after all, she had been reaching for a man she loved. And she supposed that if Mary and José truly loved one another, they would manage to find their own happiness.

The truth was, if she were to be honest with herself, it was neither Mary nor José she was thinking of, but Claude; as always, he was foremost in her thoughts.

His heart would be broken to learn that his precious daughter wanted to marry a common laborer, and a Mexican at that. Her husband had never shed his snobbishness. She knew that he was hurt by the way the Old World wine people still looked down at his California wines and on Americans in general. Despite all the wealth and prominence he had accumulated, despite his own aristocratic birth, here he was simply an American, and she knew that his one dream for Mary was to see her wedded to someone, if not of rank and title, at least of wealth and social position.

She dreaded to think of the result of José's letter.

70

José was right about one thing, at least. Claude did come, almost at once, riding up the lane in a cloud of dust and leaping from his horse almost before the beast had stopped.

'Claude . . . ' Danielle came out to greet him, but he went by her without a pause.

'Where is he?' he demanded.

'José? He's in the vineyard, but Claude, you mustn't . . . '

'The hell I mustn't,' he said, striding in the direction of the vineyards. Danielle hurried after him as best she could, having nearly to run to keep up.

José saw them coming and straightened from his work, waiting without apparent concern. When Claude was almost upon him, he said, nonchalantly, '*Buenos días*, señor.'

'*Buenos días* be damned,' Claude said, thrusting a crumpled letter under the young man's nose. 'What's the meaning of this letter?'

'I thought I made it plain,' José said. 'Your daughter and I wish to be married. I would like your permission.'

'Well, you damn well won't get it, not now and not ever.'

'Then we will be married without it,' José said with a shrug.

For a moment Danielle thought Claude would explode. He seemed to be unable to speak, managing to sputter instead, and his face turned an alarming purplish-red.

'So help me God,' he raged, finding his voice at last, 'if you've laid a hand on her, I'll kill you. Who the hell do you think you are, anyway, to be marrying my daughter?'

'I am a man who loves her, and whom she loves,' José said. 'That is all that matters.'

'Not to me it isn't, not by a long shot. You think I've raised that girl like royalty, broken my back to make a fortune for her given her the best of everything, clothes, education, so that she can marry some fool nobody. You – you're nothing but a field hand, a dirty . . . ' He paused, then spat out the word, 'A greaser.'

'And you, señor,' José said calmly, 'are a fool who doesn't even know that his son and his own mistress are sleeping together.'

For a few seconds a deadly silence reigned. Danielle put out a hand toward her husband, thinking to calm him down, but he brushed her hand aside. With a sudden roar like an enraged bull he charged forward, lowering his head. The two men crashed to the ground, locked in a violent embrace. They rolled this way and that, breaking down vines as they went, their fists rising and falling.

Mary, who had been upstairs dressing when her father arrived, came running through the vines.

'Stop them,' she cried, running up to her mother. 'Oh, can't you make them stop?'

It was an uneven struggle; Claude was no longer a young man and for the last few years he had not been accustomed to much physical work, whereas José was in his prime, conditioned from a daily routine of hard labor.

Yet for all of that the match was a violent one; Claude's weakness was partly made up for by the force of his anger, and though initially José seemed to be restraining himself out of a desire to avoid hurting the older man, he was soon engaged in a far more intense struggle than he had expected.

Both men were quickly bloodied, a crimson stream running down from a gash in Claude's forehead, and another equally lurid one from José's nose. Still they thrashed to and fro, but now Claude was plainly weakening. His arms rose and fell mechanically. He scarcely felt the pain of his cuts and bruises; it was a far worse pain he was suffering: the pain of humiliation. It had been years since he'd been in a physical fight; he had been a young man himself then, and there had never been a thought of losing, as he realized he was now going to lose. The knowledge was like a ragged strand of fire racing up into his stomach.

A fist crashed into his jaw and he felt his head bounce back from the impact. He put his hands down on the hard ground, trying to give himself the purchase he needed to rise, but his arms refused to support him. He slipped and swung out again, but his blows seemed to have no effect.

It was like a sickening form of drunkenness where he must keep at it, on and on, until it ended of itself, and throughout it all there was a horrible clarity of perception, each detail of his torture etched clearly in his consciousness. He continued to fight, but he never knew exactly when pride and instinct gave out and he surrendered to the burning humiliation. He lay gasping for breath and knew that the younger man had risen, was swaying unsteadily over him.

Finally he saw the booted feet walking unevenly away. He could not raise his head to see more.

'Claude.' Danielle was kneeling; he could feel her fingers on the back of his neck and smell the scent of the handkerchief she was using to wipe away the blood.

His eyes had drifted closed. He forced them open and saw his daughter, too, bending over him, her eyes filled with pain and with concern, but her concern was like another blow in the pit of his stomach.

'If he's still here tomorrow . . . ' he struggled to find the words, 'I – I'll kill him.'

'Papa,' Mary said.

He did not want to hear what she had to say. He knew, had known since the day it happened, that he had made a grave mistake when he had struck his daughter. He had been ashamed of himself for doing it, and in the weeks since he had longed to patch up their quarrel in some honorable way. But he was a proud man, at least as stubborn and headstrong as she was, and his pride and stubbornness had stood in the way.

Now he lay on the ground, shamed and beaten by the man she had taken as her lover in spite of his disapproval, and in his anger and humiliation he made a second mistake.

'You won't go with him,' he said. 'I forbid you to have anything more to do with him.'

Until that moment Mary had not seriously planned to go with José. She had not even known of his letter to Claude; had José told her of his intention to write it, she would have done everything in her power to dissuade him.

But this dictatorial command flew in the face of all her newly formed independence, and without a pause to consider, she repaid the blow that her father several weeks before had struck her.

'If José goes, I will go with him,' she said.

'Then go,' Claude swore, spitting onto the ground. 'You're no longer a daughter of mine; you can do as you damn well please.'

The ride to town seemed like an endless agony. There were

times when he had difficulty just remaining on the horse, and Claude was almost sorry he hadn't done as Danielle had begged and stayed at the ranch.

Almost, but not quite. He was like a man who will not rest until he has badgered his doctor into telling him he is dying; he had to push himself on to discover this final truth, to confirm this ultimate humiliation.

The house seemed still when he arrived. He had left his horse tied some distance away and come up the hill on foot. He let himself in, pausing in the downstairs hallway. The servants were gone for the day; the house lay still about him. Julia had told him she would be out shopping; David had still been in his room when Claude left.

He went to David's room first, moving stealthily and at the same time hating himself for his stealth. He prayed silently that he would be proved wrong, though the certainty within him had grown with each mile that he had ridden.

David's room was empty.

He hesitated outside the door to Julia's room. At first he heard nothing, and for a few seconds hope flared up within him.

Then he heard it: a soft, low ripple of laughter. He knew that sound; he'd heard it often; the mocking, sensual laugh with which Julia teased him when they were alone, when the air was charged with sexual tension.

He opened the door and stepped into the room. The naked pair on the bed stared wide-eyed at him. Julia reacted first, squealing and leaping from the bed, dragging along a blanket that she threw about herself.

David only gave a low groan and covered his face with his hands. Not even when Claude had stepped to the bed and begun to beat him about the head and shoulders did the young man make any attempt to avoid the blows or defend himself. He let himself be dragged from the bed, falling heavily to the floor, and lay there motionless while Claude continued to kick and beat him mercilessly, long after Julia had fled from the room, screaming.

71

During the night one of the infrequent Santa Ana winds, blowing in from the deserts to the east rather than from the western ocean, sprang up, making the night warm and the air seem to crackle with tension. Lying sleeplessly in her bed in the gray of dawn, Danielle heard a horse approaching. By the time she reached the front door, the rider was already dismounted and staggering up the steps.

It was not Claude, as she had hoped, but David. He was limping and leaned heavily on her for support as she guided him into the parlor. When she had lit a lamp, she saw the cuts and bruises that disfigured his boyish face. The blood had dried unwashed across his brow, and his nose looked broken.

'Oh, my God,' she breathed. 'Was it . . . ?'

'It's all right, Mama,' he said in a hoarse voice. 'He isn't hurt; I didn't try to fight him.'

She went to the bellpull and rang for the maid. 'Marguerita, bring water and some clean cloths,' she called out without waiting for her to appear.

David sat quietly while she bathed his wounds; she knew that there were deeper wounds that she could not touch and her heart ached for him, but all the while her thoughts kept turning back to her husband.

'I must go to him,' she said aloud when she had done what she could for her son.

'Mama, no,' David said. 'His pride . . . let him be for a while.'

She hesitated, half-in, half-out of the room. He was right, of course; at this of all times Claude would not welcome her. No matter how she ached to be with him, to comfort him, she must step back and wait.

'I'll send for Adam,' she said, fighting back her tears. 'He'll let Adam talk to him.'

Claude could not remember how long he had been drunk. The servants, he knew, had long since fled the house, leaving him to roam unhindered through the great, garish home he had built in the flush of success. Its inlaid floors and marble halls echoed to his footsteps, and when he shouted his agony aloud, it was his own voice that came back to him in echoing waves.

'My success, here's to my success,' he shouted, turning up a half-full bottle of wine and pouring it in a steady stream not only into his mouth but over his chin and down his stained shirtfront as well. The stream slowed and stopped. He held the bottle up to the light of a chandelier and, seeing it was empty, flung it against the stair rail, spilling a shower of broken glass across the stairs.

He had failed. He had failed on every count that mattered – with his wife, that dear, gentle creature whose only fault had been to love him.

He had failed with his children: a daughter who had defied him and gone off to marry a common peasant, a nobody whose skin wasn't even the same shade as hers; a son who had cuckolded him with his own mistress.

His father, dead in poverty; his mother, dead in an alley; his friends – but they weren't friends, those hordes of people who flocked to his house because of his money, his influence. They were leeches, parasites; he could hear them now, laughing behind his back because he had been made a fool of.

And Julia – that had been a failure, too; of course, she had never loved him; she was closer to his son's age than his own. A man was twice a fool to forget his own age and a woman's both.

Julia – had he loved her at all, or had she been only a last desperate bid for something that he had missed of life, or that had missed him? He could not say, and suddenly the question seemed important – who and what was she in his life? How had he come to this, to bring into the home of the wife he loved a woman he did not much care for? He had said he loved her, he had been intoxicated by her; yet now when he closed his eyes, her face would not even come – he could not think what she looked like. Her voice came back to him, the feel of her body, naked and warm against his, the smell of her, yet she was like a ghost: heard, felt – but invisible.

The great brass knocker at the door sounded. He staggered to answer it, calling, 'Julia, Julia.' But it wasn't Julia; it was a man, a stranger who turned out to be, when he squinted his eyes and looked again, his own son.

'Adam, what are you doing here?'

'Hello, Dad. Can I come in?' Adam, only not Adam, because

he was a little boy still, tagging along through the vineyards, and this was a man, tall, commanding in appearance.

'Come in, come in,' Claude said, flinging the door back against the wall with a resounding crash. 'We'll open some wine – the very best wine, French Hills, America's premium wine – they call me the wine king, you know that?'

'I don't think I want any wine just now, thanks,' Adam said, following him into the parlor.

'Well, that's too bad,' Claude said. He looked around and, finding no wine, staggered off to the kitchen, Adam trailing after him. There was wine there, bottles of it that he had carried from the wine cellar earlier because – why, because he wanted to drink the stuff, damn it, what other reason was there? He picked a bottle at random and struggled with the corkscrew.

'Let me help,' Adam said, reaching for the bottle.

'Go to hell!' Claude snatched the bottle away and, flinging the corkscrew to the floor, he broke off the top of the bottle against the kitchen table. He took a long swig from the jagged neck before setting the bottle aside with a bang and starting once more down the hall toward the front door.

'Where are you going?' Adam called, hurrying after him.

'I want to see Julia,' Claude said. 'No, you stay here, I've already shared her with one son.' He paused and then added, under his breath, 'The bitch!'

He took Adam's horse, but when he was on his way, swaying unsteadily in the saddle, Julia got mixed up in his thoughts with Antoinette, and it was to her house that he rode.

Antoinette was entertaining dinner guests. The butler who answered the door took one look at Claude's stubble of beard, his red-rimmed eyes and stained clothing, and tried to bar his way, but Claude shoved him violently aside and went in anyway.

'Julia?' He shouted, lumbering down the gilt-decorated hall-way. 'Julia?'

He crashed into the dining room. The people seated around the table barely had time to rise to their feet, staring wide-eyed at this wild-looking stranger who had burst suddenly into their midst.

'Why, Claude, this is a surprise,' Antoinette said; of all the people in the room, she alone looked unperturbed. François came to stand near her; their guests formed a semi-circle at the opposite end of the table.

'Where is she? Where's Julia?' Claude demanded.

'She's not here,' Antoinette said, smiling sweetly.

'You're lying.' His eyes swept the group at the end of the room, looking for Julia.

Antoinette gave a sigh. 'Very well, she is here,' she said. 'But she won't see you.'

He brought his gaze back to her, focusing his eyes with some difficulty. 'Did she tell you what she did?'

'Yes.'

'You don't look very shocked,' he said angrily.

'Why should I be? I encouraged it from the first.'

He stumbled toward her, stopping directly before her. 'Why, in the name of God? Am I completely mad? Why would you want to do such a thing?'

Her eyes glittered with an eerie gleam of triumph, of satisfaction. 'Because I hate you,' she said. 'Because I've always hated you, since you killed my brother. I've dreamed of nothing since but finding a way to humiliate you, to fling you down from the heights you'd built for yourself. It was why I came to California; it was why I tried to destroy your mother. And if that old fool of a woman hadn't intervened, I'd have ruined your daughter, too, through my son.'

He could hardly believe what he was hearing. Antoinette, the beautiful Antoinette, whom he had loved from afar for so long, who had been his dream of love through all his young manhood.

'You,' he breathed, seeing her for the first time as she really was, seeing the rot and the blackness behind the glamour and the glitter she had always shown to him. 'You're a witch. I ought to have killed you years ago, in France. I should kill you now . . .'

He made a movement toward her, but François and another man moved to block his way.

The table was spread for dinner. There, at her place, was the wine – his wine, the one triumph of his otherwise pointless life.

He suddenly seized a glass and flung its contents in her face. The red was like a stream of blood, coloring her hair, coursing down her face, disfiguring her.

She screamed. The men seized him, dragging him from the room. He was carried along the hall and thrown bodily from the front door, to topple down the steps.

In the dining-room the shocked women had gathered around Antoinette, all of them talking at once, but she fled from them and from the scene of her humiliation.

She was shaking with rage when François found her in her room. 'I want to destroy him,' was all she could think to say. 'I want to destroy him utterly.'

72

'I wish you weren't going,' Danielle watched José and Mary load the last of their things into the buggy. She had been willing to give them the buggy and horses, but José had saved out of his salary over the years and had insisted upon paying for them.

'I'm taking enough of the señor's,' he had said, indicating Mary. 'I won't take anything more without paying.'

'José says it's best,' Mary said. 'If we were still here when Papa came back, it would only mean another fight.'

They had been married the evening before by a *padre* from the mission. José had been willing to wait, to give Mary time to be certain of what she wanted, but it was she who had insisted upon having the ceremony performed as quickly as possible, as if she were afraid that she might weaken in her resolve if she delayed.

'Where will you be?' Danielle asked, seeing that they were nearly ready to go. 'How will I write to you?'

Mary shrugged. 'We'll be traveling,' she said curtly. Already she was regretting the impetuous actions that had brought her to this point, but to humble herself to try to patch things up seemed to her unthinkable.

'We'll write you when we've found a place,' José said. 'In a month, perhaps two. Don't worry about us.'

The last of their bags was loaded into the buggy; the horses, sensing a long journey, pawed the dusty ground impatiently.

'Well,' Mary said lamely when they were ready to go.

'God go with you,' Danielle said, embracing her. There were tears in Mary's eyes, and for a moment Danielle thought she might yet change her mind, but she gave David a quick embrace and clambered into the buggy as if impatient to be on their way.

José came to give Danielle a gentle hug, calling her *mamacita*, and to shake hands with David, and then they were gone, driving briskly down the lane, to what future no one could say. Jean, at work in the barns, came to the door to watch them leave, but he did not bid them farewell.

David put a comforting arm about his mother as they re-entered the house. 'I spoke to the *padres* yesterday,' he said. Since his break with his father, he had indicated his resolve to pursue the priesthood even without his father's blessing.

'What did they say?'

'Padre Moreno questioned whether my calling was a true one, or if I was only running away from my troubles. He thought I should come to live for a while at the mission and give myself time to decide if that is really the life I want for myself.'

'Will you be going soon?'

'Tomorrow,' he said simply.

Danielle was saddened beyond words by this splintering of the family. It had been nearly a week since Claude had ridden back into the city after his fight with José, and Danielle had not seen him nor heard from him since, although Adam had gone into Los Angeles to keep an eye on him. Both Adam and Jean had taken their father's part in his quarrel with Mary.

'If you marry against Father's wishes, you can forget about me as a brother,' Adam had told Mary sternly on his arrival from San Jose.

'I'm going to live my own life, without interference,' Mary had replied, adding, 'from anyone.'

Danielle had wept and tried to dissuade Adam and Jean from their stance, but both the boys and Mary had stubbornly refused to back down, and at the moment it looked as if the schism that had split the family in two was unbridgeable.

Nor did the weather help to ease the tensions. The Santa Ana wind that had begun blowing earlier had turned the weather unseasonably hot and dry. The sun had a hostile, glaring quality in the naked sky, and among the farmers there was talk of brush fires, to which the area was susceptible. Only a few years before an out-of-control fire had destroyed a trio of ranches.

Now one found oneself licking one's lips a great deal and waiting apprehensively for something to happen. It was said that if an Angeleno committed murder during a Santa Ana, he could plead the weather as extenuating circumstance.

Standing on the porch watching the buggy disappear in a distant cloud of dust, Danielle found herself wondering how a family that had seemed so prosperous, so happy, could have come to such a state as they had reached.

It seemed such a short time ago that they had been happy;

she remembered their arrival in California, the founding of French Hills, the births of her children. She had been married to the man she had always loved and wanted, and she had been young enough then to dream that in time he would love her back.

Now she was older and she knew that dreams didn't matter and 'in time' never came – it was only the cold realities of the moment that counted. Claude had never come to love her as she loved him; he never could have loved her that way; it was not his nature, nor her destiny.

Perhaps all that had happened was only her punishment for her arrogance in reaching so high.

Claude came at last, in the cool light of dawn, riding slowly up the lane as if afraid of the welcome he might receive. Danielle looked like a girl again as she ran to greet him in her night-gown, her hair hanging loose, her feet bare. His heart caught in his throat when he saw her.

'You've come back,' she said, hesitating on the verge of fling-ing herself into his arms.

'Forgive me,' he said.

'Forgive you? For being my husband, for letting me love you? No, I should thank you for that.'

They did embrace then, his arm enfolding her as she had longed to be enfolded for so many empty months.

'I love you,' he murmured.

'My darling –'

'I've been a fool. I've always loved you, always needed you. It was you that I got my strength from, you who made it all possible, you, you, you – always you.'

Later, when they were wrapped in the warmth of their bed, she tried to persuade him to forgive the children, but his contrition did not extend that far.

'They set their own course, let them pursue it,' he said, in a tone of such bitterness that she dared not challenge it.

73

The hot, dry wind blowing in from the desert made Antoinette's skin feel like parchment. It was more noticeable – and more perversely irritating – here in the country than it had been in town.

'This ought to be about right,' François said. He reined the horses to a stop and got down from the buggy, surveying the scene before him. They were in the hills overlooking the broad valley to the east of Los Angeles, not many miles away from the spot where a band of Mexican outlaws had stood some twenty years before. Spread below them were the vast vineyards of French Hills. Off to the right, if you shielded your eyes against the sun, you could just see the fringes of the Rancho de Torres through the haze.

'They look so far away,' Antoinette said, climbing down to stand beside him and gaze down at the vineyards. 'I don't see how starting a fire clear up here is going to do much harm to their vineyards.'

'I've heard men talk about the big fires in these hills,' François said. 'They say that once they start burning, there's no stopping them till they've burned themselves out.'

'There are so few trees,' Antoinette said, still with the tone of doubt in her voice. Here, in the hills, there were stands of some sort of pine, straggly and dull-looking after the hot, dry summer, but as they moved downhill towards the vineyards, the trees thinned out still more until in the valley there was nothing but scrub and grass, and the strange round bushes called tumbleweeds for their peculiar way of blowing before the wind.

François had spoken confidently of wiping out the de Brussac vineyards in a giant conflagration, but it hardly looked as if there were enough fuel here for more than a harmless grass fire of the sort that had sometimes burned in the fields in France.

'It isn't the trees, from what they tell me; it's the brush itself. It burns so fast it's impossible to contain it.'

He began to collect kindling – twigs, bits of brush, pine needles – which he placed in a little heap on the ground in the shelter of a scrub bush. When he judged that he had enough to start a blaze, he knelt and struck a match to the pile.

It flared up at once, evidence of the dryness of the plant life. The brush itself caught fire and the flames, all but invisible in the glare of the sun, shot upward, sending off an almost physical wave of intense heat.

It had soon consumed itself, however; the brush burned out, and though the fire could be seen racing through the ground cover and the fallen pine needles, it did not look particularly menacing, even to François.

'Damn,' he said, glowering. He looked around and saw a pair of tumbleweeds that had gotten wedged against a rock. Striding to them, he picked them up somewhat clumsily, trying to avoid soiling his lace-trimmed shirt, and carried them to where the grass was burning the hottest – hotter, indeed, than he would have expected at a distance.

The tumbleweeds ignited quickly. One of them, caught by the wind, lifted as if to sail into the air on a rising flame, then began to roll, still burning, down the hillside. It caught against the trunk of a spindly looking pine half-way down the slope. In a moment the lower branches of the tree had begun to burn.

'There, that's more like it,' François said. He gave the other tumbleweed a kick with his boot, sending it, too, tumbling down the hillside. The grass on the slope was now burning in two long strips, the paths down which the burning brush had rolled.

The wind shifted abruptly, a sharp gust bringing the smoke back toward them. The horses whinnied nervously at the scent, and Antoinette felt a stinging in her eyes.

'François,' she said, feeling the first nagging sense of apprehension. 'Perhaps we should go now.'

'In a minute. I want to be sure this is burning properly. Hey, look at that tree go.'

Another strong gust of wind had come swirling down the slope, bending the top of the tree with its force. The tree seemed to erupt suddenly, bursting into flame up its entire height. The wind caught bits of burning bark and sparks that had been pine needles and hurled them in a hundred different directions. They landed in the dry brush and as if by magic a new fire sprang up where each one landed.

Antoinette turned back toward the horses, and as she did gave a gasp of fright. The fire that had looked so harmless in the beginning seemed in a few scant seconds to have enveloped most of the area around them. As she stared, a clump of brush

a hundred yards or more away, and directly in the path by
which they had arrived, leaped into flame.

'François,' she said, 'the fire, it's cutting across the road.'

He turned then and his own eyes widened in alarm. 'My God,
how did it spread so fast?' he asked, almost unable to believe
what he saw.

'It – it's frightening,' she said, taking hold of his sleeve. 'Let's
go, please.'

He did not argue but hurried her along to the waiting buggy.
The horses were stamping and pawing nervously as the fire
suddenly changed direction again and began to race toward their
hooves. They snorted, tossing their manes in anxiety.

A sapling only a yard or so away from the horses suddenly
exploded with a hiss of boiling resin. The horses bolted, toppling
Antoinette, who had been climbing aboard, to the ground.
Before François could catch the reins, the frightened animals
were galloping off down the trail, trying to escape the threatening fire.

'Whoa, damn you, stop,' François shouted, running after
them, but in a moment the animals, with the buggy rocking and
careening after them, had disappeared around an outcropping
of rock. The thud of their hooves could be heard disappearing
into the distance.

Antoinette, stunned by her fall and the sudden flight of the
horses, lay where she had fallen on the ground, gingerly rubbing
a bruised elbow. The air was pungent now with smoke, and the
heat was fast becoming unbearable.

Suddenly she realized that the hem of her dress was afire. She
leapt up, slapping at it with her hands and getting a painful
burn on one wrist before she extinguished it.

'My dress is ruined,' she cried, holding the scorched hem aloft.

'Never mind your dress,' François said, grabbing her arm
roughly, 'we've got to get out of here.'

'But the horses – how can we . . . ?'

'We'll have to walk,' he said, propelling her along the trail.

It soon became evident that they would have to do more than
walk. By the time they had reached the outcropping of rock,
the fire that had been steadily circling about them, racing well
ahead, had burned across the trail. They found themselves confronted with a wall of fire where the thicker brush across this
section of the hill was now blazing.

Antoinette was genuinely frightened now. 'What are we going
to do?' she asked in a trembling voice.

François hesitated, glancing back over his shoulder to where the fire now raged in full splendor. They were cut off in front and behind.

'It's not possible,' he cried, as if to reason with the fire. 'It's only been burning a few minutes.'

Antoinette began to sniffle, as much from the smoke filling her nostrils and eyes as it was from anguish. She could still not quite comprehend the extent of their peril.

François glanced up. Above them the hill sloped steeply upward. The fire had been burning largely downhill; if they went up they should soon be able to get above the danger line.

'We'll have to climb,' he said, starting up the slope.

'But I can't – these shoes . . . '

In the moment or so that they had been standing there, the fire had already swept almost to the spot, and now they were engulfed in a cloud of thick, acrid smoke. Antoinette began to cough violently, so that she wasn't able to finish what she had been trying to say.

'Come on,' François shouted, scrambling furiously upward, dislodging sandy dirt and small rocks as he climbed.

Antoinette looked up and realized that she could barely see him through the smoke. She had a sudden horrible fear of being left alone in this smoke and fire, and she rushed to the slope and tried to clamber up it as he had done.

At once she tripped on her own skirt and came slithering and crashing back down. A sharp pain shot through her ankle, as if it had been broken.

'François,' she managed to cry, but the smoke rushed into her lungs and her shout ended in a choking cough.

'Come on,' she heard him shout, but he sounded as if he were far away already, and now she couldn't see him at all. She tried to shout again, but she could do nothing but cough.

She got to her feet, trying not to put any weight on her painful ankle, and started for the slope again, but she unexpectedly collided with a huge boulder that was not where she remembered it. She would have slumped against it for support, but its surface was scorching hot to the touch. For a moment she stood in dazed confusion as the skirt of her dress began to flame. Then her hair vanished in a halo of fire.

François had reasoned that the wind, blowing downhill, would push the fire in that direction, but his ignorance of the local conditions had led him into error. The gusty Santa Ana wind tended to swirl in giant eddies between the ridges and ravines, sometimes blowing this way and sometimes that, changing directions almost instantaneously; and the fire, now a major holocaust, created its own winds as its heat and smoke rose quickly upward, sucking fresh air in below and creating an upward-gusting breeze that carried the fire up as well as down-hill.

François came to a shallow ledge that seemed to run around the hill; above was an unusually thick growth of brush where the waters of the previous spring, choosing by some whim of their own this particular route for a runoff, had promoted a heavier vegetation than was usual for this sort of slope.

'Antoinette?' He paused on the shelf, calling her name, but there was no reply from below. He could see nothing through the smoke, and it would have been impossible to return the way he had come, even had he been a braver man than he was.

A wave of heat so intense that he smelled his own hair singeing suddenly swept across the ledge. He looked around. The ledge, which in fact would have led him to the shelter of the other side of the ridge, angled downward. Clinging to his idea that going up would lead him to safety, he chose the more difficult of the two routes, up the slope and through the thicket. In the distance he thought he could distinguish a cluster of pines. As the fire so far was confined largely to brush and saplings, which would be thinner where the pines were, he aimed in that direction, thinking that at any minute the thick brush which was slowing his progress would thin out and he could move faster.

It was like one of the nightmares he had had as a child. He struggled and struggled to move forward but his limbs felt unbelievably heavy. His ears seemed to ring and there was a tight band about his chest, making it hard to get his breath. The air, thick now with the rising smoke, seemed itself to hold him back, and the branches of the thicket were like eerie fingers catching at his clothes, scraping his skin, snaring him.

He broke through a patch of lighter growth and thought that he had made it to safety, but then it seemed to be thicker again. He tried to crawl through it and caught his jacket on a branch, tearing it. He could feel blood on his back, but he dared not stop to care for the wound.

He stood again, leaning against the slope, and crashed through some bushes, letting his weight and his terror carry him through, and then he was face to face with a pine, only the brush here was as thick as what he had come through, and he knew that to be caught in the fire here would mean death.

His heart was pounding so riotously that he had to pause for a moment, gasping for breath. He looked and saw that the fire had swept up the hillside faster than he had – a finger of it was reaching beyond him there to the right.

'I mustn't panic,' he thought. He looked and saw that the stand of pines he had been heading for was fairly close now. Surely there would be less growth there to feed the fire. He started off in that direction again, swinging wide to avoid the ever-advancing flames.

He came out of the thicket in smoke so dense that he could no longer be certain which way he meant to go. He found himself on a path, and for a few yards he ran pell-mell along it, but then he stopped short, seeing that the path was leading him back toward the fire. A thick billow of smoke swirled about him, making him cough until he thought his chest would burst, and the heat was now like an inferno.

'Antoinette.' He called her name for the first time since he had started through the thicket, but it was more a wail than a shout.

He turned back into the thicket, completely disoriented now. He flung himself upon the tops of the bushes, as if he meant to swim across them, and managed to scramble a few feet, but his clothes were now in shreds and a hundred rivulets of blood ran down from the many cuts and scratches on his bared flesh.

He was rapidly growing exhausted from the unaccustomed exertion and from breathing the smoke-thick air. He tried to make himself calm, to think of something that he could do. The dangling sleeve of his shirt suddenly caught fire from a spark and he ripped it off, flinging the scrap to the ground, where it immediately started the hot, dry growth to burning.

A white sheet of flame erupted not twenty feet away from him. It startled him into a new burst of effort. He crashed and crawled and struggled through the thicket, his eyes half-closed against the smoke, and suddenly he found himself almost directly in front of a pine tree, taller than most of the others he had seen. But, his expectations to the contrary, the undergrowth was still thick here, and the fire was burning ever closer.

Dizzy now with fatigue and lack of oxygen, he leaned against the tree trunk. Another smoke cloud swept about him, making him gag and retch. He felt light-headed and knew that he was close to blacking out.

A clump of bushes almost beside him began to burn. Suddenly he knew that he had no chance of outrunning the fire. Even when he had been rested and fresh, the fire had outdistanced him, and now he was numb with exhaustion and half-unconscious from smoke inhalation.

He began to climb the tree, more from panic than from any thought-out plan of safety. But he had climbed only to the lowest branches when the pine needles, their resins heated to boiling, hissed and erupted in flames. In a matter of seconds the entire tree was a column of fire.

74

It was the workers in the vineyards who first saw the blaze in the hills. In the beginning they found it a matter of some interest, without realizing that it posed an actual threat to them. As a result, the fire had reached the edges of the vineyard itself before the alarm was given.

Perversely enough, it was David who saw the smoke from the window of his room and, forgetting for the moment his estrangement from his father, burst into his father's office, where Claude and Adam were discussing business.

'The fields are on fire,' he said. At almost the same moment the big brass bell in the barnyard, used to summon the men to and from work, began to ring wildly; Jean, at work in the bottling shed, had discovered the fire too.

By the time Danielle, who was in the kitchen, ran to the outside, the men were beginning to gather in a crowd from all parts of the ranch. There was an atmosphere of confusion, even alarm, and mostly the men seemed at a loss to know just what they should do; they were waiting for someone to start giving them orders, to take charge, and they kept glancing from the distant fire to Claude. He, however, to their increasing confusion, seemed as lost as they.

'Claude, the vines, what are we going to do?' Danielle asked breathlessly, coming up to where he was standing surrounded by the workers.

He gave her a bleak look of despair. Unlike the pair who had begun this blaze, he had some idea of the power of a brush fire. Though French Hills had been lucky until now, he had seen other ranches and vineyards devastated by fires like this.

Now, watching the billowing clouds of smoke, the flames that leapt skyward as the approaching monster found some new source upon which to feed, he thought that he was seeing his final defeat, the destruction of all he had worked to build.

It was as if all that he had been through in recent days – Julia's perfidy, his disappointment in Mary, David's treachery, his sense of failure – had only been the painful approach to this, his personal Armageddon. This, then, was the punishment to be meted out to him for his hubris: to lose everything, to see it all swept away on a sea of fire.

'We'd better get what we can out of the house,' he said wearily. 'It's blowing this way.'

'No.' Jean had a look of steely determination as he faced his father.

'What else can we do?' Claude asked.

'We can fight it instead of just standing around watching it or running from it.'

'Fight that?' Claude indicated the holocaust that now seemed to stretch as far as they could see.

'Yes, damn it,' Jean said stubbornly. 'The same as you'd fight a drought with water, or a freeze with fires; the same as you'd fight any other act of nature, because we're men, not dumb animals, and because we can fight nature; because if man's ever going to tame this earth, he's going to have to learn to control the elements instead of being at their mercy.'

Claude looked around at the still-growing crowd of faces watching him. They looked expectant, frightened but hopeful, too.

To fight? It had been a long time since he had gone to battle; maybe – and it was not the first time he'd thought this – he was getting old. There had been a time when nothing exhilarated him like a challenge.

'All right,' he said, making his decision; suddenly the look of defeat left him and he looked, in Danielle's eyes, young again, rejuvenated, purposeful. 'We'll need rags to beat out the fire – bags, blankets, anything – and tools to build a firebreak. We'll have to clear a stretch of land between us and where the fire has already burnt. With luck, once the fire reaches there it will stop and burn itself out.'

He began issuing orders, assigning this group to loading

wagons with barrels of water, that to collecting all the shovels and rakes that could be found, still others to finding and distributing rags and other weapons to try to beat out the smaller spot fires that were the holocaust's advance army. With Claude now clearly in command, the spirits of the men rose to the challenge, and where before there had been only a dispirited confusion there was now an organized firefighting effort taking shape.

Almost before they took to the fields, help was beginning to arrive from the neighboring ranchers, who had spotted the fire too, some of them before anyone at French Hills knew about it, and had realized at once whose property was being threatened.

The first to arrive were workmen from Ranchos de Torres, and soon afterward Don Diego himself came galloping up the lane, pale and wizened but with his eyes glinting with eagerness for the fight.

Danielle had taken charge of the women, sending them scurrying in every direction for anything that could be used against the fire. Brooms were yanked from closets, towels and blankets from shelves, even the heavy brocade drapes from the parlor were tugged down from their rods.

While the maids piled the gear into the assembled carts and handed it out to the men, Danielle prepared to climb into a wagon just setting out for the fire area.

'No, you stay here, it's too dangerous out there,' Claude said, seeing her and taking a firm hold of her arm.

'I've got a right to fight for what I love, too,' she said, her chin set in a determined line.

He hesitated; then, in a way that made her forget for a moment the danger that threatened them, he grinned as he had used to grin years before, as that young man she had loved so hopelessly in France had grinned.

'It seems like you always have, and in the end it's your kind of fighting that usually wins, isn't it?'

She didn't answer, and with a quick movement that belied his advancing years, he lifted her up into the wagon as it began to roll toward the vineyards.

The smoke, as they drew nearer, was suffocating, and the heat unbelievably intense. At first Danielle thought the ground had suddenly begun to move. Then she realized it was the wild animals fleeing before the fire, too terrified of that even to be afraid of their natural enemies. Rabbits and field mice raced along between the vines; a frightened faun ran back and forth, bleating plaintively for its mother. A hawk wobbled through the air, stunned by the heat and smoke, and fell to the ground stupefied.

The wagon stopped and everyone jumped down. Danielle, her eyes watering, joined the others who were trying to beat out the advance rivulets of fire that swept across the ground. Beyond them, between herself and the fire, the men worked trying to clear the ground to provide a firebreak that they hoped would stop the main advance of the blaze. She caught sight of Jean. He seemed to have taken command of the forces in the field, shouting orders, directing men here and there according to some plan of his own that was quite beyond her grasp.

It was back-breaking work. She had come in a wagon loaded with wet sacks, with which they were beating the ground. Within a few minutes she was soaked with sweat and short of breath, and her arms and back ached with the effort.

Still she did not pause or falter. Everyone – Claude, the boys, their neighbors and friends as well as their employees – was working together now, driving themselves beyond their usual limits of endurance.

The wind had dropped down slightly, but the fire by now was making its own winds, whipping the heat and the smoke about them in relentless gusts. José had left a swath of land unplanted this year, 'to let the soil rest,' and it was here that Claude had decided to make his firebreak.

Already dry at the outset, the air was made drier by the intense heat that sucked the moisture from everything in its reach, and now entire vines seemed to explode of their own accord, far in advance of the main body of the fire. For a moment it would seem as if they had managed to extinguish the fire this side of the break, and then suddenly, like a great torch, another vine would erupt. Leaves wilted before their eyes, grapes popped their skins as their juices began to boil away.

Danielle had lost track of time; she might have been here in this heat and smoke for minutes or even hours; it was impossible to say. Someone appeared at her side, but at the same moment a new shower of sparks fell to the ground just in front of her and she concentrated on beating them out before a new fire flared up.

'Mama, you ought to be back at the house,' David said beside her.

'But this is where the fight is,' she replied, not pausing in her efforts.

He smiled proudly, although she did not even see. Then, more soberly, he said, 'The fire's in danger of swinging around our fire line. If it does, we could all be cut off here. I'm going to warn the others. If you hear me yelling, hightail it out of here.'

Danielle hardly heard, nor did she notice when he left. She ran her tongue over her scorched lips and tried to force more air into her aching lungs.

Jean, working at the fire line, thought for a few minutes that they might have won the battle. It looked as if their firebreak might hold, at least across the main part of the vineyards; the fight now was to create a second swath to surround the fire before it could sweep out and around the break. To accomplish this he had deliberately started backfires, controlled blazes intended to burn toward the main conflagration and meet it, leaving nothing behind for the holocaust to feed on.

It was a dangerous gamble; so long as the winds stayed minimal and the backfires were controlled, they were safe, but if the fire broke around them, he and the people working with him could swiftly be cut off from any retreat, caught between the main blaze and the backfires.

Suddenly the winds came up again in a violent sweep, hurling showers of sparks and fire through the air. A hundred spot fires sprang up everywhere. Those fighting the spot fires shouted for help in trying to control them, but there was no one to come to their aid – everyone had his own fire to try to put out. As fast as Danielle was able to put out one fire, another one sprang up around her.

She heard someone shouting, but not until David had actually run up and snatched the smoldering sack out of her hands did she realize what was happening.

'The fire's jumped the break,' he shouted. 'We've got to get the hell out of here.'

He grabbed her arm and started to run. It was hard to see more than a few feet in the thick smoke, and harder still to breathe. David kept yelling to the others, some of whom were standing in hopeless confusion, to run toward the area that had already been burned, that would be their safest route. One of the housemaids, dazed from lack of pure air, staggered into their path. David grabbed her with his free hand and, fairly dragging the two women with him, ran along the rows of vines.

They came upon one of the workers furiously battling a burning vine, so intent on what he was doing that he had not yet realized the danger. David shouted, and the man looked over his shoulder, blanching as he saw that he was virtually surrounded by new columns of flame that had sprung up in the last few minutes. The man froze in panic.

'Come on,' David shouted again. 'This way.'

After a horrified moment the man dropped the shovel he had been using and ran after them.

Danielle's sides were aching with their own fire, and she thought her limbs had turned to lead. She felt as if they were moving through something thick and viscous that held them back and made their movements slow and languorous. She gasped for breath, coughing, and filled her lungs with searing smoke. Blindly, weakly, she clung to David's arm, knowing that she could not go much further.

David was following a line between the two fires, angling off at a downhill slant, but suddenly there were more fires ahead of them. They were engulfed in smoke, and the air was hotter than a furnace. The little housemaid running with them began to sob.

'We will die,' she cried. 'We will die!'

'Shut up,' David shouted, shaking her violently while hardly slowing his pace. 'I don't want to die any more than you do. Do as I tell you.'

They could no longer see the sun, nor even familiar landmarks. David wondered anxiously if they were even running in the right direction. Suddenly they were out of the vineyards, in the open brush.

He'd come too far! Here in the brush the fire was sure to sweep over them in seconds. He paused, squinting his eyes, trying to guess where they were. Finally, praying that he was right, he began to follow the slope of the land downhill. They were stooping down now, trying to breathe the safer air closer to the ground, shuffling along in a funny, bent gait. Ash and soot rained down upon their bent heads. David knew from the heat and sparks that the fire was closer to them than ever; in a matter of minutes it might overtake them, and still he had no idea where they were or where to go.

Then there was a wall of fire before them. The maid shrieked in terror.

The fire was only another spot fire, blazing outward in an ever-expanding ring through the open brush. In its center it would be hotter than Hades, but there at least there would be no fire – everything flammable would have burned.

'We've got to go through it,' David shouted, indicating the wall of orange-yellow flame. Danielle licked her lips, her eyes wide with fright. She tore off a piece of her singed skirt and flung it over her head. Then, at a signal from David, she ran directly into the fire. David, fairly dragging the maid with him, came after her, and in a moment the worker had followed.

Beyond the wall of flame they were in a scorched-out island of earth. Their clothes were burning, even Danielle's shoes were smoking, and the heat was nightmarish, but for the moment they were safer than they had been.

Danielle's heart was pounding dangerously. She let herself be shoved to the ground, ignoring the burns that she got on her hands and arms. Here the air was a little better, and she swallowed it in great mouthfuls.

75

It was nightfall. The air had grown cooler, and though there was still a breeze, it was gentler now. The Santa Ana wind was dying, and as it died, the fire lost some of its intensity. Now a vine might burn without igniting the one next to it. The firebreak had checked the main advance of the blaze, and Jean's efforts at backfires had helped still more. The spot fires that had circled about the main break had met up with the backfires and were now burning themselves out on the scorched earth. Everywhere across the hillsides and the valley, the holocaust was dying. It grew gradually smaller and weaker, and now the exhausted men could begin to push it back, and could see that they were winning.

Claude, battling his own exhaustion, began to take stock. They had lost, as nearly as he could determine in the darkness, at least half the vineyards; and there was certain to be some damage throughout the rest. French Hills had suffered a major disaster, but it had not been total. There were still vines left, vines from which new wines would flow. Something he had built had endured.

At last, leaving others to manage the business of mopping up, he went in search of Danielle. He found Jean, who had last seen her in the fields, and Adam, but not David, and not his wife.

He began to ask more anxiously, hurrying up and down through the rows of people being fed at the makeshift facilities erected in the barnyard. Danielle and David were nowhere to be found.

He paused at the edge of the vineyard, staring in horror in the direction of the burned-out sector, where the smoke still rolled and columns of flame still suddenly flared upward.

They had remained on the hot ground, each of them praying in his own way. David listened to the sounds of the fire, trying to gauge which way it was blowing now; a critical change in wind would mean death.

Then, lying close to the ground, he felt a gust of fresh air. He sat up and tried to yell, but his throat was too dry and parched.

But the others had felt the wind too and realized its significance. They sat up, exchanging anxious looks. When they saw David's face, they began to grin with relief.

'We made it,' David said, realizing for the first time that the darkness was not from the smoke alone – night had fallen.

Danielle held a hand to her aching breast and labored for air in her lungs. 'Yes,' she said. 'We made it.'

Inwardly, she was wondering if she would be fortunate enough to see Claude again.

Claude was just in the process of organizing a search party when a shout went up, and a moment later the dirty and disheveled quartet came into view, making their way down from the burned-out sector of the vineyards. He went to meet them, walking hurriedly at first and finally breaking into a run.

Danielle came wearily into his arms. 'You're all right,' he said, holding her close. 'Thank God, you're all right.'

Danielle said nothing but only clung to him with a desperate fervor.

Though the fire smoldered through the night and occasional flareups had to be fought by little crews of volunteers, a victory celebration of sorts was held around midnight. The women from neighboring ranches had brought food throughout the afternoon and evening, and Claude rolled out casks of his best wines. Most of those present ate at long tables set up in the yard, under the light of lanterns that had been hastily strung.

Inside, in the dining room, Claude gathered his family and closest friends to give thanks that real disaster had been averted.

Prayers were offered, toasts were drunk, and the elegant de Brussacs set upon the food before them as ravenously as any field hands.

Later, when exhaustion combined with the food and the wine to make them all feel drowsy, Claude stood at the head of the table and lifted his glass in a salute.

'To French Hills,' he said, 'and to all those who helped save her today – but especially to those of you here.'

He let his eyes rove about the table. Some were missing: his mother was gone; and Mary, his beloved princess, was no less dead to him than his mother. He still felt a pang of grief when he thought of her, but he quickly thrust those thoughts aside. Don Diego was absent, too; he had been overcome earlier by smoke inhalation and had been taken home in a carriage, still arguing that he wanted to fight the fire.

But like the vineyards themselves, while some had been lost, others had been saved. 'To my son, David,' he went on, 'soon to become a priest – with his father's blessing.'

Danielle felt tears stinging her eyes and she saw the flush of pride that reddened David's smiling face.

'To all my sons,' Claude said, lifting his glass to each of them in turn. 'But most of all, let me say my thanks before God for my wife – for all that she has wrought.'

Danielle was suddenly in a confusion of embarrassment. Everyone was looking at her, grinning widely, and there were shouts around the table of, 'Hear, hear,' and 'That's right.' She tried to say something clever in return, but no words would shape themselves in her mind and she could do nothing but bury her face in her hands and cry, until at length Claude came to her and escorted her gently from the room.

Later she lay in her bed and thought of the things that had transpired, and of Claude's tribute to her.

What had she accomplished, after all? She had married and loved a man who had come to love her back, but only in his own way and in his own time. Perhaps it had been wrong of her to ask so much, like a greedy child.

She had raised a family, sons who would go their own ways, shape their own lives. She supposed she hadn't been a perfect mother; she had been so engrossed in pouring her love upon Claude that it had sometimes seemed as if there weren't enough to go around for her children, yet she had loved them as best she could.

Mary was a tragedy. She wished she could have the time to try to soften Claude's bitter stance toward his daughter; maybe they, too, had loved one another too much. She who had let her life be dictated by love was not too blind to see that love could sometimes get in the way of things.

What else? Oh, she had done her part, surely, in getting them here, in getting them established in their new world. And French Hills – Claude's vineyard, of course, but hers, too – it gave her a sense of pleasure to know that when future generations of Americans drank French Hills wines, they would be drinking something of hers.

When you added it up, it was hard to see that her accomplishments were many or very great; in the end all she could say was that she had done her best; she had made the most of what she was given, and the least of what was denied her.

She supposed, after all, that it was an accomplishment of sorts.

She smiled and turned over on the bed, her one hand outstretched toward the pillow that was Claude's.

That was how he found her when he came to join her later, leaving his sons still drinking in the parlor. He smiled tenderly down upon her, at her still-childlike loveliness, at the gentle smile that curved her lips.

He was reluctant to disturb her sleep, yet he longed to touch her, to express in some physical way the love for her that welled up from within him. He laid a gentle hand upon her brow – and found that it was cold.

José woke to find that the spot beside him, where Mary had been sleeping, was empty. Alarmed, he scrambled from under the wagon to find her seated on the ground a few feet away. She took no notice of him as he approached, and when he had come near, he saw that she was crying.

'*Querida*,' he murmured, dropping to the ground beside her and cradling her in his arms.

'It's nothing,' she sniffed, clinging gratefully to him. 'I just suddenly felt so – so sad. Oh, José, I want to go back. Take me back, please.'

'We can't go back,' he said, gently but firmly.

'Papa will forgive me; I know he will.'

'Probably. But then he'd never forgive you for that,' he said. 'Come on, now; as long as we're awake, let's have some breakfast and get an early start. It's almost dawn anyway.'

He took a very businesslike attitude toward her, and she let herself be directed, fetching water, cooking breakfast for them over the fire he had prepared.

By the time they set out again, in the first light of dawn, she knew that José was right. They could not go back.

76

Danielle was buried in the vineyards, among the first vines that had been planted nearly thirty years before. David, despite his father's orders to the contrary, had tried vainly to find Mary and José, but no trace of them had been found; they were apparently somewhere on the road.

Afterward Claude asked his sons to come to the office; there was something he wanted to say to them. Don Diego, who remained a stockholder in French Hills and who had come for the funeral, joined them.

'I'm quitting the business,' Claude announced when they were all assembled.

'Giving up French Hills?' Adam asked, surprised.

'Not exactly.' Claude smiled wanly and looked around the table at his sons. They were fine young men, each of them in his own way, and competent. He knew their worth as vintners and it was considerable – far more than his own had been when he had founded this place.

'I'm giving it to my sons,' he said, adding, 'To all three of my sons.'

'Mine may end up going to the order,' David said. 'It's too soon to say yet, of course.'

'That's as you wish. Perhaps the *padres* will want to make some wine of their own,' Claude said, grinning. 'That's how all this California wine business got started, after all. They're the ones who deserve the real credit.'

He paused, giving them time to ponder his announcement. 'Adam and Jean can run this place and the one up north,' he went on after a moment. 'They both know more about it now than I do, anyway. And to tell you the truth, though I take great pride in the French Hills wines, there's little joy left in any of it for me.'

There was an awkward moment of silence, each of the young men pleased by the vote of confidence they had been given and at the same time saddened by the circumstances that had prompted it.

'I for one applaud your decision,' Don Diego said, breaking the silence finally. 'I have only one request: that my small acreage be joined with that of French Hills. For me, too, there is little joy left in what I've built, and you see, there is no one for me to turn it over to. Perhaps in this way I can pass on some sort of legacy as well. And I feel that my time must soon come to an end.'

'A new era is beginning,' Claude said. 'Already men are beginning to talk about a different sort of life, a different sort of country. You,' he said, indicating his sons with a sweeping gesture, 'you will live to see it, to experience it, while we, Don Diego and I, will die with this century.

'And that is as it should be. This nation, California, her wine industry, they belong to the young, to the farsighted. I – we – are the European cuttings, brought to this alien soil, grafted to the land; but you are the new hybrids, stronger, richer, more infinitely varied, from which the new blood of this country, and the new wines, will flow.'

He paused, staring down at the table, and in that moment each of the young men at the table saw his father as he had been unable to see him before: as a man – beginning to bend under the weight of his years, but proud still, and strong, not afraid to be right nor ashamed to be wrong. He had traveled the road before him, no better and no wiser than other men, no more to be despised nor worshiped than any other, and yet a man to be respected for who and what he was.

77

Later, in the coolness of twilight, Claude went alone to the vineyards. He had brought a bottle of wine and a glass. The wine was the last that remained of the first wine he had made from their first crop of grapes. It was getting old, too old, he knew, to be at its best; yet it had acquired in those too swiftly passing years *something* – he could not name it – that years alone could not give a wine.

He seated himself on the ground as he used to do when he had been a young man and did not wear expensively tailored clothes, and he opened the wine. He drank, listening to the hum of a late-circling bee, smelling the still-scorched scent on the evening breeze, feeling the ground grow cool beneath him.

He had no thoughts; that is, he had no thoughts formed into words, into phrases. He felt, and felt, too, that something there shared his feelings, that he was not alone. Nor had he ever been, for always, even when he had not realized it, her presence, her love, had been with him, like a mantle against which the world's coldness was as nothing.

He had told her once, recently – too recently – that he owed everything to her, and that had been no tribute of passion. Without her love, her confidence in him, would he ever have had the confidence in himself, the daring to do what on the face of it would have been impossible to do? Even when he had strayed, it had been with the knowledge, however unconscious, that she was there to come back to, and that the coming back mattered more than the straying.

Once he had thought that her love was not enough for him. Now, too late, he realized that it was he who had not been enough for her love.

It was dark now, and from the house he heard one of the boys calling his name. The wine was nearly gone, though he could hardly remember drinking an entire bottle. He held it up toward the faint glow of the moon.

'You were finer than I knew,' he said, speaking aloud. He stood, a bit unsteadily – when had his legs grown weak, why hadn't he noticed? He paused for a moment over her grave and then with a slow movement he tilted his glass and poured the last of the wine upon her grave. It vanished at once into the soil, seeking downward, as if returning to its own.

He placed the glass, top down, over the spot, and began to walk slowly, resignedly, back to the house.

And still, for all his sadness, he did not feel that he walked alone.

THE HEART LISTENS
by Helen Van Slyke

THE HEART LISTENS is the story of Elizabeth Quigly, a woman of infinite compassion and courage who fails, if at all, only because she is ready to give too much.

In loving detail *THE HEART LISTENS* follows Elizabeth through her long and richly varied life, intimately describing her relationships, her joys, disappointments and her incredible capacity to survive misfortune – and not only to survive, but to retain optimism and go forward to new and wonderful achievements.

With rare skill the author has sensitively explored many facets of love – though this book is much more than a recital of love affairs. *THE HEART LISTENS* has at its centre a strong, memorable woman, Elizabeth Quigly will catch your imagination as you begin the book, and will have won your sympathy and affection long before you reach its end.

NEW ENGLISH LIBRARY

THE MIXED BLESSING
by Helen Van Slyke

THE MIXED BLESSING continues the story of Elizabeth Quigly's remarkable family – and particularly that of her beautiful granddaughter. Antoinette Jenkins. For 'Toni' is the adored daughter of a mixed marriage that divided Elizabeth's heart and her family. Toni herself is torn – between loyalty to her mother and grandmother, who urge her to proudly acknowledge her heritage, and to her remorseful black father who begs her to deny it.

NEW ENGLISH LIBRARY

NEL BESTSELLERS

T046 133	HOW GREEN WAS MY VALLEY	*Richard Llewellyn*	£1.00
T039 560	I BOUGHT A MOUNTAIN	*Thomas Firbank*	95p
T033 988	IN THE TEETH OF THE EVIDENCE	*Dorothy L. Sayers*	90p
T038 149	THE CARPET BAGGERS	*Harold Robbins*	£1.50
T040 917	TO SIR WITH LOVE	*E.R. Braithwaite*	75p
T041 719	HOW TO LIVE WITH A NEUROTIC DOG	*Stephen Baker*	75p
T040 925	THE PRIZE	*Irving Wallace*	£1.65
T034 755	THE CITADEL	*A.J. Cronin*	£1.10
T042 189	STRANGER IN A STRANGE LAND	*Robert Heinlein*	£1.25
T037 053	79 PARK AVENUE	*Harold Robbins*	£1.25
T042 308	DUNE	*Frank Herbert*	£1.50
T045 137	THE MOON IS A HARSH MISTRESS	*Robert Heinlein*	£1.25
T040 933	THE SEVEN MINUTES	*Irving Wallace*	£1.50
T038 130	THE INHERITORS	*Harold Robbins*	£1.25
T035 689	RICH MAN, POOR MAN	*Irwin Shaw*	£1.50
T037 134	EDGE 27: DEATH DRIVE	*George G. Gilman*	75p
T037 541	DEVIL'S GUARD	*Robert Elford*	£1.25
T042 774	THE RATS	*James Herbert*	80p
T042 340	CARRIE	*Stephen King*	80p
T042 782	THE FOG	*James Herbert*	90p
T033 740	THE MIXED BLESSING	*Helen Van Slyke*	£1.25
T037 061	BLOOD AND MONEY	*Thomas Thompson*	£1.50
T038 629	THIN AIR	*Simpson & Burger*	95p
T038 602	THE APOCALYPSE	*Jeffrey Konvitz*	95p

NEL P.O. BOX 11, FALMOUTH TR10 9EN, CORNWALL

Postage charge:

U.K. Customers. Please allow 25p for the first book plus 10p per copy for each additional book ordered to a maximum charge of £1.05 to cover the cost of postage and packing, in addition to cover price.

B.F.P.O. & Eire. Please allow 25p for the first book plus 10p per copy for the next 8 books, thereafter 5p per book, in addition to cover price.

Overseas Customers. Please allow 40p for the first book plus 12p per copy for each additional book, in addition to cover price.

Please send cheque or postal order (no currency).

Name ....

Address ....

....

Title ....

While every effort is made to keep prices steady, it is sometimes necessary to increase prices at short notice. New English Library reserve the right to show on covers and charge new retail prices which may differ from those advertised in the text or elsewhere.